MIRRORS

A.L. WOODS

REFLECTIONS BOOK 1

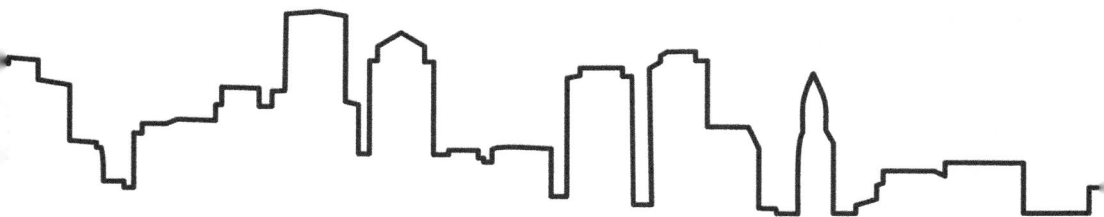

Photography: Boyko Viacheslav
Cover Design and Interior Formatting: Ana Beatriz Cabús Rangel,
instagram.com/_yumenohana_
Editor: Bettye-Lynn Underwood, Red Pen Edits
redpeneditsbyblu.com

ISBN-13: 979-8692073587

PLAYLIST

"Ashley" by Halsey
"Carry the Weight" by We Came As Romans
"Your Own Disaster" by Taking Back Sunday
"Deathbeds" by Bring Me The Horizon
"Disposable Fix" by The Plot In You
"Imaginary Enemy" by Circa Survive
"Everything I wanted" by Billie Eilish
"Sweet Caroline" by Neil Diamond
"Cherry" by Lana Del Rey
"Party Up" by DMX
"Ridin' (feat. Krayzie Bone)" by Chamillionaire
"Old Friend" by Sea Wolf
"Dark Paradise" by Lana Del Rey
"Aphasia" by Pinegrove
"Noise and Kisses" by The Used
"Your Clothes" by Can't Swim
"Seek & Destroy" by Metallica
"Catharsis" by Motionless In White
"Running With Scissors" by I See Stars
"Hard To Love" by Too Close To Touch

"Lose It" by SWMRS
"Knots" by Speak Low If You Speak Love
"Helena" by Abandoning Sunday
"Blue Blood" by LAUREL
"Fallingforyou" by The 1975
"Sweet Surrender" by Sarah McLachlan
"Torn" by Hands Like Houses
"You Are The Moon" by The Hush Sound
"Cry Little Sister" by Aiden
"Broken (feat. Amy Lee)" by Seether

Scan this code to access the playlist on Spotify

CHAPTER ONE

Raquel

ALL I NEEDED to do was open the car door.

My hand lingered on the handle, the metal as cold as my insides. My gaze flitted from the lever to the front door of the job that was beginning to wear down my patience. I had just sat in my car for an hour, doing the white-knuckle routine on the steering wheel while competing against traffic on the Mass Turnpike that made me feel like I was part of an annelid—and moving at the pace of one, too.

My stress hadn't let up when I reached my destination ten minutes ago and immediately launched into my daily pep talk: "It's just a job, it doesn't define you" and a bunch of other mumbo-jumbo new age mantra bullshit that wasn't in my DNA to buy into.

I relinquished my hold on the handle, slamming my back against the driver's seat of my weathered Camry, frustration seeping into my bloodstream. I thought I'd heard the car wheeze under my aggression, and my lids shut in a grimace. I couldn't afford to replace this thing right now if it shit the bed on me. It didn't matter how much the circumstances surrounding my career sucked—it was a job, the only one I had, and I needed to make the most of it.

It was all I had going for me, anyway.

Conceding defeat, I flung the car door open and ducked my head out, the blustery kiss of late fall's wind biting at my cheeks. Thanksgiving hadn't even arrived yet, but snow didn't wait for winter's official arrival on the calendar; it didn't wait for anyone. I could benefit from taking a page out of Mother Nature's book and learn to just get the fuck on with it.

Slinging my messenger bag over my shoulder, I closed the car door with my hip. The treads of my black lace-up Doc Martens crunched the previously untouched snow that had fallen in true Massachusetts fashion the night before, the sound soothing my nerves as I approached the door of the converted mid nineteenth century two-story redbrick building with sloped roof and decorative dormers where I worked.

The rush of heat from the thermostat nearly suffocated me as I stepped inside, closing the door behind me, the air stifling and stale. That was the problem with being the only one under thirty in this building. Everyone else was perpetually cold, while my veins were steeled from the elements. Then again, I suppose that was a by-product of what happened when you grew up with a furnace that was barely functional half the time because your parents couldn't be half-assed enough to ask the landlord to fix it.

You just learned to adapt to survive.

"Morning, Raquel!" chirped Sheryl, the receptionist with the tightest fucking curls since Shirley Temple. I didn't know why we even had a receptionist, or what Sheryl actually did—no offense. It just seemed like a luxury to have her around, especially when our numbers were shit and we were barely staying afloat.

Without uttering a word, I simply held up a hand in greeting. The worn hardwood floors groaned under my weight when I passed her desk, my legs carrying me farther and farther into the depths of my nightmare. The distinct scent of old newspapers, strong perfume, and body odor filled my nostrils, activating the part of my brain that screamed: *"This shit again?"*

Yes, brain. This shit again.

The breath I had been holding escaped me when I rounded the corner to my cubicle. The wraparound desk was bare because I wasn't into tchotchkes or anything that would have provided insight into my otherwise bleak existence. There was nothing on my desk save for my computer, which was one of the earlier model iMacs from a decade ago that we had only recently acquired via donation from our oh-so-generous mayor—gifted to keep my mouth shut, but more on that in a second—a desk phone that was just as old, and an archive of past papers that I had filed and stored.

There were no desk plants, no photos that depicted loved ones or of me doing anything remotely interesting or fun, no stuffed animals from boyfriends past or present, or even a damn compact to powder my nose at lunch or before meetings. I wasn't into that shit. I had a single black pen and one yellow highlighter. No one needed to know anything more about me than necessary. Even the highlighter already felt like an unnecessary indulgence that my boss had insisted on.

"Raquel!" Speak of the goddam devil, although my boss looked more like a cherub still nursing his mother's tit—he behaved with the naiveté of one, too. I dropped the messenger bag onto my seat, slid my leather jacket off my shoulders and dropped it over the back of my chair. I felt his presence before he even stepped into my space.

"It's so wonderful that you're here," he said.

I had to fight the urge to do an eye roll. It's important to note that I have arrived at work at a quarter to nine every single weekday for the past four-and-a-half years, and Earl, the editor-in-chief, always behaved as though my appearance was a pleasant surprise akin to a gift discovered under his tinsel-laden tree on Christmas morning.

"Hi, Earl," I mumbled, tossing the knock-off Wayfarers and beanie to the edge of my desk. I tucked the messy locks of my shoulder-length brown hair behind my ear.

Earl was a nice man, too nice at times, and had about as much spine as a jellyfish. He didn't argue when anyone told him no, inanimate objects included. He once apologized to the printer for a paper jam and asked us all to respect the machine's boundaries.

We waited until he left for the night to free the wayward 8½ x 11 page from the clutches of the copier, and when Earl came in the next morning he thought the printer had finally had a change of heart.

And who were we to ruin his moment?

"Are you ready for this week's meeting? I have dozens of ideas for the upcoming issue."

No, no, I wasn't ready. I wasn't sure I would ever be ready. I pegged him with a weak smile, willing the Dunks caffeine rush to hit me. Earl's ideas were about as original and inventive as a kid discovering the inside of their nose for the first time.

"Sure am!" I spoke in a saccharine tone, but Earl was such a space cadet, he didn't notice.

"Fantastic! I'll see you in there."

I exhaled loudly as he whistled his way back into his office, singing "Good morning" to every other person he passed.

I hated Mondays.

Dropping my ass into my chair, I took a couple of minutes to log into my computer and check my email from the weekend. There were —to my surprise—no new story leads to cover in town. When the clock hit 8:55AM, I got up and headed into the kitchen, where I was able to grab another cup of coffee undetected—I really hated small talk —before I trudged the short distance to the boardroom, which was really nothing more than a Formica-topped round table with a bunch of black plastic chairs around it in a bright room with frosted glass windows. I tucked myself into the chair closest to the door, already preparing for my escape, staring up at the stained ceiling tiles as people began entering the room.

The Eaton Advocate employed all of ten people: five columnists; three typesetters and graphic designers; Sheryl, whose position I was growing increasingly suspicious of; and Earl, the editor-in-chief. We were partially funded by a couple of subsidies issued to us by the town plus the revenue from a bit of advertising space.

People wanted news faster than we could provide it, and with the shift to online sources, our revenue was dwindling and our ship was sinking faster than we could move. To make matters worse, the recession was killing the economy. People were too worried about their bottom lines to buy ads—few were spending money anymore.

Earl started the meeting the same way he did every week, with a quick roll call (as if it would be impossible to account for all ten of us otherwise), a summary of last week's stories, our revenue to date, and finally, by launching into his story ideas for the week. Earl was receptive to other ideas but had a tendency to err on the side of caution… lest we ruffle any feathers.

We are a G-rated paper, after all.

"Raquel, could you cover the fire department's charity car wash? The mayor loved your piece last year." Earl's smile was earnest, honest, pure.

I caught the scoff that threatened to leave me, the sound lodging in my throat.

The mayor? Yeah, *okay*. Mayor Patrick Murphy had about as much love for me as he did for his wife (which wasn't saying a whole lot, given he had not one, but *two* side pieces, the licentious Lothario). I think the words he had used to describe me during our first meeting two years ago, when I tried to get a real story out him, were, *"You're not quite the right fit for our town."*

He could probably smell the townie on me, and shit, I didn't blame him for wanting to take an aerosol can to me. Southie was a stench that stuck to the fibers of your clothes more strongly than a prostitute's cheap perfume.

I would know; my mother had been a hooker.

Unfortunately for Mayor Murphy, he had made the mistake of getting caught quite literally with his pants around his ankles and his dick five inches deep in the pussy of a woman who wasn't his wife last December, backstage at the town theater. Yours truly had witnessed his last four thrusts before he came all over a certain lady in red. I had laughed out loud, startling both him and his familiar guest of honor. He had scrambled for his pants, valiantly trying to steel his face and reset his equilibrium, as if what he was doing was perfectly appropriate, but I hadn't missed the fear that had bloomed in his serial killer blue eyes. Two days later, the iMac G3s showed up, alongside a note from the mayor himself expressing his unending thanks and support for our tiny little paper.

I wasn't above remedial efforts in the form of computers that actually worked, or an unspoken agreement to stay out of each other's fucking way. I could go the rest of my life without seeing his little prick again, that was for damn sure.

Earl cleared his throat, tearing me out of my thoughts. I met his stare, struggling to keep my expression still. A hopeful glint lit up his eyes, which were flanked by horn-rimmed glasses too small for his pudgy face. His nose crinkled when he pushed the frames further up the bridge of his button nose with his index finger, his hazel eyes taking on the appearance of coffee saucers the closer the lenses got to his pupils.

The room became quiet, five sets of eyes waiting for me to reply, their stares jumping from me to Earl and back to me, as if we were engaged in some sort of stand-off in which I had shown up with a gun, while Earl came with a little guitar and an off-key rendition of *Imagine*.

At least John Lennon had sported glasses that fit his face.

"Sure," I heard myself say, a noncommittal sound leaving the back of my throat.

Exaltation painted his face, the corners of his eyes crinkling. "Splendid!"

His elation made me want to bang my forehead against the table until I either drew blood or knocked myself the fuck out.

It was a job, I reminded myself. A good job. A sensible job. My reality.

I was doing what my parents never could: surviving through honest means. I had a bachelorette apartment in the city that was the size of a shoebox and ate up forty percent of my income. I could afford to put gas in my car without siphoning it from some poor unsuspecting fool, and my only vices were Pall Malls and my one-sided love affair with pints of Samuel Adams. They both warmed the numbness that enveloped my body every night.

Nothing could change the fact that this wasn't *the* job I fantasized about when I was pouring my heart out into eloquent purple prose while in college, or scribbling out story ideas as a teenager against the background of my parent's belligerent screaming matches. Nor when I was binding paper together with my Crayola-inspired scrawl that depicted a story of a girl much like myself, who discovered that she was actually a princess from a faraway land, sent down to earth to redeem the souls of her malefactor human parents.

Look at me putting my creative writing degree to work.

I slouched in my seat, jealously flanking me when Karen, the office sycophantic, was assigned the story about the new gazebo that had been erected in the town square in memoriam of the town's mascot, a turkey named Jebediah, who had met an untimely demise from an overzealous leaf peeper armed with a hunting rifle last fall.

There was some meat to that story, pun intended, and he had given it to fucking Karen.

I couldn't believe I was getting pissed off over a turkey and gazebo. Twirling my black pen between my fingers, I looked out the frosted windows, even though I could see nothing.

The Eaton Advocate wasn't the *Boston Globe*, *The New York Times*, *The Wall Street Journal*, or the *Washington Post*.

It was a community paper, and it was a job, and I should have been grateful.

And I was in a lot of ways.

To people back in my neighborhood, I might as well have been Arianna fucking Huffington. I hadn't ended up another Southie statistic. I had it made. I wasn't working the produce aisle of the Stop & Shop, pumping gas, or working the night shift at the packaging plant for minimum wage. I wasn't bogged down by a child I had too young, or a good-for-nothing deadbeat husband who was snorting our rent payment up his deviated septum.

I had a job, a real job, one that paid me legally, an abysmal 401(k) I only contributed to at my best friend's behest, and was well on my way to becoming a spinster at twenty fucking eight.

My stability didn't snuff out the ache in my chest that pervaded me anytime I allowed myself to remember that this was not where I saw myself going when I fled my old neighborhood a decade ago to go to Boston University with nothing but my dreams of being a big-time writer coupled by my willpower to keep me going. While I worked my way toward my degree, I had dreamed of book signings, lavish launch parties, fat book advances, and a jaw-dropping house in the Cape—anything that was a far-cry from the derelict neighborhood in which I had grown up, where the exchange of gunfire and sounds of arguing had served as lullabies for my younger sister and me.

I had dreamed wildly, without inhibition, and my dreams were what had kept me going. My dreams were going to get my baby sister and me the hell outta there.

That was the very problem with dreams. Sometimes they were just that—dreams. I was desperate when I took a job in this bucolic town that looked like something straight out of a frigging Hallmark-movie, right down to the idyllic houses with meticulously kept lawns and residents who knew each other's first and last names, blood types, and whether or not you failed to recycle properly.

There was nothing wrong with writing for a wholesome little news-paper, all while waiting for Candace Cameron Bure to show up looking like a candy cane princess with her sugary, mawkish voice and shimmery blond tresses in brushed-out curls. Of course, she wouldn't, because Eaton was a suburb an hour away from Boston that didn't have much going for it. Unless you cared about errant cats stuck in trees, fire department charity car washes, and new gazebos.

There was some irony here, considering I had grown up slugging it out with some of the worst people—my anxiety probably needed the change of pace, especially after what I had gone through. There was no need to look over your shoulder here, because if someone was hot on your trail in the dead of the night, it was probably because they wanted to return the wallet you dropped or they wanted to remind you that aluminium was a recyclable.

People here saw my sarcasm and ambivalence as edgy and youth-ful, a true glimpse of what the "big city" mighta looked like—*The Eaton Advocate* loved what I had to say, and the interview had lasted all of five minutes before Earl had practically thrown himself at my feet and told me, *"You simply must join the team!"* as a columnist.

As Earl warbled on and doled out story assignments, I propped my chin up on the palm of my hand, my elbow leaning on the edge of the table just as my best friend's caller ID flashed on my phone that lay face up on the table. I excused myself from the meeting, taking on a serious, pointed expression as I dipped out of the boardroom, rushing toward the back exit and muttering something along the lines of "I need to take this; it's a story lead." No one questioned me, seemingly forgetting that there was no lead, and there was no story.

Penelope Louise Cullimore had been Connecticut born and raised, and as much as I had chastised her for being a debutante in those earlier years, she had become a real Masshole over time. When we first met a decade ago, she was about as WASPy as they came. On paper she was the cliché perfect, poised blonde, loaded, and on a surface level about as artificially sweet as could be. She had waltzed into our shared dorm room looking like Elle Woods in *Legally Blonde*, right down to the Mary Janes on her feet and blond curls in her hair.

That is, until her tight-ass parents finally left our dorm room with a peck on both her cheeks and their noses in the air. She had all but flung off those stuffy shoes with a deft kick of her legs and then undid the tight buttons of her cardigan, revealing an Iron Maiden T-shirt that she had tucked into her pleated kilt. The smile she shot me that day was sly and knowing, like she had decided right then and there that we were going to be best friends.

"I'm Penelope. I like Maiden, Marlboros, and muscular men—not necessarily in that order, but I would take all three at the same time. What's your name?"

We've been inseparable ever since.

"Hey," I breathed, a sigh of relief escaping me when I pushed open the exit door, fresh, cold air rushing at me. I fished a cigarette out from the pack tucked in the pocket of the oversized denim shirt I had picked up from a thrift shop, jamming it between my lips. The friction wheel of the lighter aroused my best friend's suspicions, a harrumphing sound greeting me from the other end of the phone.

"Kell, are you smoking right now?" Penelope asked suspiciously, not even bothering with a greeting.

I stopped myself from rolling my eyes, even though she couldn't see me. I braced myself for the impending lecture about wrinkles, lung cancer, and all the other nefarious things that my nicotine addiction was going to do to me. She had gone on a crazy health kick after graduation and given it up. Frankly, I smoked enough for the both of us, so it was probably for the best.

"Morning to you, too, doll face," I jested, pinching the cancer stick between my fingers and taking a drag, exhaling the smoke that settled in my lungs, a fog of calmness enveloping me.

"Raquel."

"Penelope." I rolled the vowels of her name, my accent thick as my inflection headed upward, the way everyone in Southie spoke.

"You're going to look fifty before your time."

"Good. Maybe it'll put me in a hole a little faster."

"That is morbid, even for you," she drolly remarked.

"You still wearing Iron Maiden T-shirts to bed?"

"Maiden is not morbid; Maiden is life," she declared, as if I had just told her that socks with sandals was acceptable attire to wear to church on Sunday.

"Yeah, yeah." I flicked the ash from my cigarette, watching a flock of Canadian geese overhead, flying south for the winter. "So, what's up?" Penelope had left BU with a degree in English literature and ended up getting caught up in the allure of interior design. She launched her own business against her parents' wishes—refusing to deign to them—soon after college. She had managed a steady stream of projects over the years. Her current one was located in Eaton, which was great for me, as it gave me an excuse to meet her for lunch.

Her cleared throat acted as her segue before she launched into the reason for her call. "I had the most brilliant idea."

My blood ran cold, I fought the urge to groan. Penelope had a penchant for "brilliant ideas," and often they required me to do things I didn't want to do. "Remember how I told you I was doing that design job for Dougie's boss?"

My mouth slid into a frown. Dougie was Penelope's new flavor of the month. Well, sort of. This one had managed to make it to the six-month mark, so we were in good shape. No tears, no complaints, and apparently he was endowed with a dick the size of Alaska that dipped slightly to the right.

Not that I had requested that detail, but Penelope had never been one to mince words. She was the literal embodiment of an open book.

"Yah-huh?" I purred, taking a drag on my cigarette.

"You think you could convince Earl to run a story on it?"

I coughed on the nicotine in my lungs. "Uh…" my voice carried as I toyed with the idea.

Earl had fallen in love with Penelope at the holiday party I had brought her to as my plus one last Christmas, not that I could fault him. Penelope had won the genetic lottery with her aristocratic face, lithe figure, and Atlantic Ocean blue-green eyes with specks of yellow in them that nearly stopped your heart in your chest if you stared at them too long.

"You mean you don't want to read another story about the fire department's charity drive?" I said.

"You can do so much better than that; c'mon."

I turned to put my weight flush against the wall. Penelope's statement had been loaded; it wasn't just a *"You can write something more interesting,"* it was a *"What the fuck are you still doing working there?"* She had been practically begging me to let her ask her father to pull some strings to get me a reporting gig with the *Boston Globe*—he was friends with the paper's publisher, John W. Henry. I had been tempted. The pay would be better, the commute would be virtually nonexistent, and it would be a million times better than the *Advocate.* But I didn't need anyone's handout, and I sure as shit didn't want to ask Daddy Cullimore for anything.

It was impossible to reconcile that Penelope's parents were actually her parents. Her mother looked at me as if being poor was a contagious disease, and her father tossed me glances that suggested he couldn't decide if he wanted to fuck me because I fulfilled his closeted rich man/poor woman fetish, or demand I stay away from his daughter lest she start speaking with a distinct South Boston lilt. (Mighta been too late on the latter; sorry, Pops.)

"So, is this favor for you or for your *boyfriend?"*

"Both," she replied quickly…too quickly.

"I'm starting to think things are getting serious with you and Dougie. Look at you, trying to call in favors for him," I teased, not really meaning anything by it. Penelope bored easily, and I imagined it would only be a matter of time before she swapped Dougie out for an upgrade.

Penelope cleared her throat with a freneticism that aroused a swirl of uncertainty in my gut that I didn't really like. Penelope dated regularly; I did not. Frankly, she dated enough for the both of us, so I never really felt like I was missing out. And that suited me just fine.

I suspected it was only a matter of time before her parents tried to marry her off to some blue-blooded prince toting an Ivy League degree and seven-figure income. She was "getting up there" in age by WASP standards, and her mother had already been attempting to henpeck her into submission for the last couple of years, slinging comments like: *"Haven't you gotten this middle-class lifestyle out of your system yet? Honestly, Penelope Louise."*

Still, I selfishly hoped that our plan to grow old and gray together came to fruition, and that I'd never run the risk of being alone again. She was the Thelma to my Louise. We had plans to ditch New England in pursuit of something climatically warmer and frankly, farther from both our problems.

"What's in it for me?" I asked, ditching the cigarette into the bucket that had been filled with sand with me in mind.

"Seriously?" Penelope snorted in a way I knew woulda earned her a scolding had her mother heard. "You really want to write about the car wash drive *again*?"

"Not really," I conceded, tucking the phone between my ear and shoulder so I could pick at the cuticle on my thumb, "but I already came up with a catchy headline already: 'Blazing Charity Initiative Sounds the Alarm on Children in Need'."

"First of all, that is a terrible headline."

I made a gasping sound, feigning insult.

"Second of all," she continued, "you don't give a shit about that. Trust me. You'll love this house. Dougie's boss does nothing but century-old home restorations."

I considered it for a moment, rolling the concept around my mind like a piece of modeling clay. "So, kinda like giving things a new lease on life?"

"Exactly!" she squealed, and I didn't have to see her face to know she was grinning from ear to ear, her dimples deeply set.

The idea felt kind of tired, but at least it would be a change of pace for me. I was a little curious about what was happening with all those century-old homes in Bristol County. Eaton, New Bedford, and Dartmouth, just to name a few towns, had thousands of 'em that were in desperate need of either restoration or a date with a wrecking ball. And this guy had taken it upon himself like a real-life Bob the Builder to fix 'em all. How noble. I could do something with that. My mind spun, the angle for the story lodging its way into the spot that had previously housed the car wash charity drive.

I felt around for the cigarettes in my pocket again, but decided against lighting up another one. Marinating on the idea for all of thirty seconds more, I cleared my throat, ready to strike a deal. "If Earl agrees—"

"*When* Earl agrees," she cut in, "head to five-eighteen Riverside Avenue. You gotta drive across the bridge on Main Street and swing a right past that Presbyterian church. It'll be on the left-hand side. You won't be able to miss all the crew. You do your interview, and then we can hit that sandwich place you like so much in town."

"You're buying," I grumbled, pushing off the wall to head back inside.

"Yeah, yeah. Just get your ass over here. And do not show up smelling like a pack of Pall Malls." Penelope hung up before I could argue.

Asshole.

I swung my stare at the door, my hand gingerly lingering on its handle for a few moments before I pulled it open. Penelope was gonna owe me big time for this.

CHAPTER TWO

Sean

I DIDN'T LIKE THIS.

I didn't like this one bit.

"Sean, why do you look like someone died?" Penelope crooned, fluffing another stupid fucking pillow for the umpteenth damn time. All that woman had brought me since I accepted my sister Maria's suggestion to hire her had been nothing but fucking throw pillows, brightly colored rugs, and a pounding headache.

"It's an interview," she stressed, flipping a lock of her layered golden hair out of her stormy blue eyes that had been made up with thick mascara. "It's good press."

I didn't need press; I needed a sale…and a Tylenol.

Penelope would have been fine, and I use that word loosely, if my best friend and foreman, Dougie, hadn't decided to make a move on her. I had wanted to scrub the stupid shit-eating grin off his face the first time his forest green eyes landed on her. It was as close to infatuation at first sight that would have contended with the plot line of any of the telenovelas my ma liked so much.

It wasn't that I was jealous. Penelope definitely wasn't my type, and she talked way too damn much to make the sex component worth it, even if she was aristocratic pretty with her high cheekbones and perfect posture.

Ever since her royal highness had waltzed into our lives six months ago at the design stages of this project, I couldn't seem to get rid of her —or this fucking house.

Her sigh ate up the silence of the room, her tongue tsk-tsking against the roof of her mouth.

"Can you please lose the constipated look?" she huffed, not even looking at me. Instead she shifted a vase on the fireplace mantel three inches to the right, paused, and then slid it back into its former position. She settled her hands on her hips, propping the tip of her right foot on the floor the way she always did when she wasn't satisfied. This woman's life's purpose was to stage homes into oblivion, to "build the space, set the mood, tell a story."

At least, that had been what she told me when I interviewed her. I had foolishly relinquished entire control to her and my younger sister, Trina. Everything from picking out a color palette in the preliminary stages right down to staging this place. This house was a showstopper, if you were into walls that were frankly too damn dark, accented by white teakwood furniture and a million different mirrors of various sizes that she called a gallery wall, imploring me to trust her judgement because the hipsters would love it.

My eyes had rolled back in my head at that sales and marketing spiel. I mean, hipsters, in Eaton? I think not. They weren't leaving the convenient confines of Boston to flock to this Podunk of a town.

She turned on her heel, a small smile tugging at the corners of her lips. Once those blue peepers of hers landed on me, though, the smile flipped and in came that tight frown she always wore when she was displeased.

"Now what?" I groaned.

"Your tie is all messed up." She moved toward me, her hands outstretched in that domineering way that left me feeling a little put out. I took a step back, my thigh hitting the arm of the suede couch. "Here, let me just—"

I held out a hand to her. "You can stage the house, Penelope, but you can't stage me."

At that, she stilled. Her lips pursed and her eyebrows pinched together, as if she'd just tasted tequila for the first time in her life and didn't have her lime wedge chaser ready.

"I'll have you know that I pulled a lot of strings to make this possible," she warned, that dour look still on her face.

I didn't care what strings she pulled, because it seemed like none of them were getting me what I wanted—a fucking "Sold" sign on the front lawn. I felt like an idiot, pacing around the house I had rebuilt alongside my crew, looking like a fucking pansy. My shoes didn't even have scuffs on 'em. They were so uncharacteristically shiny that I could practically see my reflection in the unmarred brown leather.

"I hired you. You work for me," I stressed, tucking my hands into the fucking ridiculous wool-blend tailored suit jacket she had insisted I wear. She had conspired with Trina (who failed to understand that blood was thicker than water) earlier to locate the closest thing I had to dress clothes this morning before she told me what was happening.

Penelope harrumphed, her expression growing smug. "As of..." she considered thoughtfully, tapping her bottom lip with a manicured finger in a way that made me feel as if I wasn't going to like what came out of her mouth next, "two weeks ago, when your checks started bouncing, I'm more of a volunteer." Her pout bloomed into a smarmy smile, looking positively beside herself that she had socked me where it hurt.

She may as well have actually just grabbed my balls and twisted them. Her words settled into my bones, blood rushing to my head. My brain squeezed in my cranium as the migraine attacked me with another untimely smack of the proverbial elastic band.

Two thousand eight was proving to be the worst year I'd had in awhile.

The recession had made banks reluctant to award anyone with less than an 860 credit rating a mortgage, which meant my bottom line had been in some serious jeopardy. In a last-ditch effort, I had accepted Maria's recommendation to hire an interior designer to compensate for the choppy waters in the market. The suggestion had had a double purpose; we both thought that Penelope's presence on the site might entice Trina to come work with me for a while since it wouldn't be such a sausage fest anymore and inspire her to...well, do something either than mourn her broken heart.

As Maria had predicted, Penelope and our kid sister got on swimmingly. It was the first time she had ever experienced being motivated by someone with whom she didn't share a blood connection. Penelope was good at what she did, I would give her that. She saw every room (and person) as a blank canvas, asking to have some life brought to it.

I had admittedly gotten more desperate the further the market tanked, fulfilling every single suggestion and request Penelope and Trina presented to me, no matter what the cost. They called their suggestions "must haves" for prospective buyers, assuring me this would make the difference between a lowball offer and a bidding war (a pipe dream in this economy), and like a fool who should have known better, I had obliged.

I was paying the consequences for my desperation now. All I'd gotten was radio-fucking-silence and the painful reminder that no one was buying houses right now—people were abandoning them for non-payment.

I ground my molars together, my jaw tightening. "I'll get my finances back in order," I said, my voice apologetic yet still gruff as I considered how the fuck I had ended up in this position.

Oh yeah, that's right. I hadn't had a choice.

Look, the job itself is fine, and when the economy didn't suck like a bad blow job that you wished would just end, it more than just paid the bills. When things were good, it had kept the cash flowing like a damn waterfall instead of the dried-up pond it was right now. It was just on days like today when my head was throbbing and Penelope was nagging that I craved the life I had given up to be here.

A decade ago, I had just been a dumb kid who couldn't tell you what the fuck a supporting wall was, the difference between a beam and a joist, or how to drill a hole into a brick wall without eating the bit. I had learned everything I knew out of desperation because time was not on my side. I absorbed every lesson, every injury, every failure, and every success entirely on my own. Over time, I had developed an eye for seeing potential in houses that others had long since given up on, and started snatching up foreclosures and condemned properties to restore them to their former glory.

This one, though, I should have known was going to be a dud as soon as I pulled into the overgrown driveway. The roof on the colonial had barely been intact when I put in an offer on it; the porch had been holding on by a thread, the door had been kicked in several times, and some clown had tried to hold a fucking seance or some weird-ass shit inside, because they had spray painted a pentagram in the middle of the hardwood living room floors, which had inevitably made them unsalvageable...and had added another cost to the lengthy list of needed repairs.

"Don't sweat it," Penelope said, breaking up the barrage of my thoughts. She crouched low to the floor in a squat, balancing her weight on her ankle boots while pulling the corner of the earth-toned area rug with geometric print toward her. She studied the effect, first tilting her head to the left and then to the right before standing upright again. "Dougie told me you're good for the money."

Not that she needed it, but it was the principle. It wasn't news that Penelope wasn't rubbing two pennies together trying to make a dollar, but it still pissed me off that she and Dougie were talking about me. My spine grew steely, my jaw granite as the thought bounced around in my mind some more.

Dougie was never crass when he spoke of Penelope, but he had been elusive when it came to her—offering nothing but noncommittal head nods when probed, shrugging his shoulders and making periodic remarks about how they were just having fun. From the sound of it, though, his version of "just having fun" was forming a budding relationship with this pedigreed Satan.

He wasn't fooling me with that shit, which was just fucking great.

Dread hit the depths of my stomach as I contemplated what the next two hours of my life would be like with someone who associated herself with Penelope. I didn't have the patience for this today. I hated indulging people. Now I was going to make nice-nice and act like I "had my shit together" as per Penelope the entire time.

"I hope to God she's not as annoying as you are," I muttered to myself, moving toward the full-length mirror in the adjacent foyer that opened up into the living room. Penelope had informed me that I could have afforded a shave, but she had sprung this shit on me at the last minute, demanding I get to the house ASAP. My beard was neat, not in a meet-the-parents kind of way, but presentable. Clean. I had conceded on the suit jacket, but I had refused to wear dress pants. Both Penelope and the kid had met me halfway and agreed to hole-free jeans—and the shiny shoes, as per her highnesses' royal decree.

There were just some battles not worth going to war over.

"I heard that," she sing-songed. I shuddered. Her supersonic hearing was on par with that of my mother, and that woman never missed anything. "But I wouldn't worry. Raquel's a fan of brevity."

I frowned. What the fuck did *that* mean? How could anyone who worked in a print-based industry be reliant on brevity? They talked all the time; they had to. Was that some kind of fancy term to suggest this Raquel person only spoke when spoken to?

How could you speak only when you had to when you're a writer?

Was it writer? No, Penelope had said she was a journalist. I paused, frowning. That didn't sound right, either. Or was she a columnist?

I gave my head a shake, suddenly realizing I was spending my last few precious minutes of freedom before I had to turn on my airs and pretend to be civil while I got read the riot act by someone cut from the same cloth as Penelope. I wondered if her friend was a social elitist, too. If she'd roll up in a Mercedes, with the same red-soled shoes that would make my kid sister gasp with delight, or if she would be a bottled blonde with good bone structure and the best rack money could buy.

Hell, a little piece of eye candy might be exactly what the doctor ordered to kill the pounding that lived between my eyebrows.

Then again, I couldn't imagine some silver-spooned reporter/writer/journalist/whatever-the-fuck-she-was working for some low-tiered borderline inconsequential product based in Eaton, of all places. That place was tiny next to the forty-nine square miles that made up Boston.

Eaton, Massachusetts was an unassuming and bucolic bedroom community nestled in Bristol County that lived up to its Old English name. The town ran parallel to an ambling creek that spilled into the Taunton River. It was as forgettable as it was boring, but the real estate was cheap, and the commute was short enough for me to drive in from Fall River, yet too far for my Ma to make the trek out to chastise me or my guys every day.

We reserved her lectures for Sundays. She was doing the Lord's work after all, and someone needed to remind me for the hundredth time that I was getting old, needed to settle down and give her a legitimate grandchild (I'll get to that one in a bit), since Maria, her firstborn, was married to her work and about as interested in settling down as sitting on the turnpike on a Friday night at 6PM. My two younger sisters had no business even so much as sharing the same oxygen as another guy.

The waiting game was making me antsy. I tugged on the ends of my dress shirt, feeling completely out of my element in the getup, the unsettled churning in my stomach gnawing at my insides. I was more of a Hanes white T-shirt and work jeans kind of guy...not whatever Penelope had called this while smacking her mint-flavored chewing gum.

Oh, yeah. *"Very Wall Street."*

"Also, before you ask, she doesn't have a boyfriend." Her tone was unusually businesslike as she rounded behind me, like it would have only been a matter of time before I asked that question. She frowned, her hands coming to my waist, adjusting the shirt that I had just modified to make myself feel less like the innards of a burrito. "But you're one hundred percent not her type, so let me spare you the trouble and tell you don't even think about it."

I let out a breathless laugh. "No problem, Princess." I had enough headaches as it was right now, and I didn't need to add fucking one of her friends onto the agenda. It would be enough if she was a nice piece of ass, but I wasn't looking to date anyone of her ilk. There were about a hundred other things that would have been a better investment of my time and emotional well-being, that was for damn sure.

The sound of a car in the driveway had Penelope's ankle boots thundering across the foyer, a whistle shriek that was barely perceptible to most but grating in my fucking ears leaving her throat. This was why she didn't have to worry about me showing even a morsel of interest in one of her friends. I imagined they would be an exact carbon copy of her, or at least trying to emulate her to some degree. The inhuman sound that had left her just now settled things for me like a gavel had been struck down—case closed.

As soon as I could get rid of Penelope and her convoy of "brilliant ideas", she was outta here. Then I was going to consider taking a very long break, maybe go somewhere warm for awhile: palm trees, stiff drinks, the ocean, sand between my toes, sleeping till noon, fucking a few broads with low expectations—the whole shebang.

The wooden front door we had stained a deep red on the exterior swung open, allowing a cold draft of air to circulate across the foyer and making goosebumps erupt across my skin underneath my shirt.

"Hi!" Penelope called, her voice suddenly several octaves higher than normal.

I was going to be sick.

A female voice with a thick South Boston accent barked out a hoarse laugh that sounded like she had smoked a pack a day for the last twenty years.

"Close the door, you're messing up my shot."

Penelope obliged, beaming at me like a child who had just been informed she could singlehandedly eat an entire chocolate cake. I scoffed, arousing her attention. She turned her head toward me, pegging me with a tight smile and eyes that screamed, *Behave, or I'll turn your balls into earrings!* all while beckoning me toward her with a jerk of her head, her beaded chandelier earrings singing as they swayed from her earlobes.

I hesitated, but that smile seemed to strain a little deeper on her face—her thin lips curling in a way that told me if she had to silently warn me again, it really wouldn't just be the beaded earrings she would be sporting anymore.

Okay, I got it.

Penelope swung the door open once the knock came from the other side, stopping only to wave me forward with her hand in a cupped motion, like she was scooping air, before she was out of my sight.

"Raquel," she began. I heard Penelope's heeled boots creaking along the porch as I rounded the open doorway. I took a fortifying breath, swallowing my underlying anxiety as my frame filled the threshold of the front door.

"This is Sean Tavares," Penelope concluded.

Cinnamon eyes shrouded by long, dark lashes flickered from the porch swing I had constructed myself, to meet my own. My balls tightened, my heart jerked, and my lids grew hooded as I gave her the once over, though her gaze never left my face.

Where flaxen golden strands grew out of Penelope's head, this woman's locks were a deep brown color that fell to her shoulders, the ends bluntly cut. The mid-morning sun cast soft shadows across the curvature of her heart-shaped face, her nose was cute and pert with a dusting of faint freckles against her alabaster complexion. Her lips looked almost too full for her face, her bottom lip noticeably fuller than the top.

Raquel was Penelope's opposite in every way, and I was fucked from here till next Tuesday.

Danger whipped through me, every alarm ringing violently in my brain. My synapses demanded I abort my mission, retreat away from enemy territory, but I was already too far gone, standing here in the doorway gaping at her like a total idiot.

This was the all-consuming and wild attraction my mother had warned me about when I first started dating as a teenager. The *bruxa* who left me spellbound, beguiled by her smoldering cinnamon stare and unimpressed pout as if it really was witchcraft at play.

Women like Raquel were dangerous; they were the kind that men incited wars over just to have a taste.

"Mr. Tavares." Her cadence dripped with a hybrid of luxury, but the vowels carried a sort of depth that only came when you had been raised deep in the heart of Boston's blue-collar community. Her inflection rolled upward, taking my breath with it.

I said nothing, my throat working frantically trying to free the words that were trapped in my larynx alongside all my other previous vitriolic sentiments from all of five minutes ago, when Penelope had warned me not to even consider pursuing her best friend.

What had I said again?

"No problem, Princess."

No. This *was* a problem. A huge problem.

"I'm Raquel Flannigan. I work for *The Eaton Advocate*."

I stared at her outstretched hand. Her nails were short, sensible, and free of any polish. The skin of her hands was smooth with no marks, a slight sheen to them, as if she had just moisturized. She smelled like freshly squeezed citrus and vanilla with just the faintest traces of musk from tobacco—a lethal combination that tangled into a tantalizing aroma that set off a warm buzz in the depths of my stomach.

I was suddenly afraid to touch her for some inexplicable reason, as if the connection alone would make me liable to do something crazy and out of character. I stared at her proffered hand like she was anything but ball-wrenchingly beautiful, like she didn't have said balls kicking to life demanding I do anything to touch her at all.

The tragedy would be that I would never know how soft her skin was against mine. I didn't need this kind of liability in my life. Not now, not when I barely had my shit figured out.

"I know who you are," I said, my voice clipped, keeping my hand at my side, my fingers twitching against the seam of my jeans. "Take off your shoes when you come inside."

Guilt jerked my insides, and I winced, the white pain shooting to my belly button. Her face was impossible to read. If my brisk greeting insulted her, she didn't show it. I watched as her cinnamon gaze swung from me to Penelope, an amused look blooming on her face as she drew in her bottom lip, stifling a laugh.

I thought I heard Penelope mutter a death threat, but it went otherwise unnoticed.

This approach was for the better.

Besides, I was sure Raquel was used to dealing with worse than me —she certainly looked like she could hold her own. I wouldn't do either of us any favors. She wasn't getting anything more out of me than necessary. Once this shit was over, I was going to go home and stroke one out and be done with this little influential Hemingway-wannabe before this story hit the presses.

"Sure," Raquel said with a shrug of her shoulders. She sidestepped me to enter the house, her back flush with the door, sliding forward. Traces of her perfume wafted off of her as she passed by me, the scent teasing the inside of my nostrils in the process, "Let's start the tour."

Get a fucking grip, Sean.

I stifled the groan that managed to claw its way through my throat —bypassing all the polite pleasantries I should have greeted her with. Penelope's stare bore into me like hot beams, the veiled threat obvious in her eyes as though she was going to crack the vase on the mantel over my head any minute now.

I probably deserved it, but it was hardly my fault, and Raquel wasn't doing me any fucking favors right now. She bent over at the waist in the foyer, unlacing her boots. I tried to keep my eyes fixated on the portrait above the fireplace, but they seemed to unwillingly drop to her ass and the denim straining against her peach-shaped cheeks.

Penelope cleared her throat, drawing my attention to her. She folded her arms across her chest, tilting her head at me, pegging me with the unspoken reminder that I could look at the menu, but I wasn't allowed to order from it.

This was gonna be a long fucking morning.

CHAPTER THREE

Sean

"SO, WHY CENTURY HOME RESTORATIONS?"

If Raquel's question was meant for me, it was hard to tell. She didn't bother to level her eyes on me as she paced around the living room in a sort of timed and choreographed dance, pausing to snap photos of the small details that had been put in place at Penelope's behest—the stained ornate mantel that encased the fireplace, the statement ceiling light fixture, and the herringbone floorboards. Penelope, who had seemed to forget about my existence, stared at her with the kind of reverence and adoration better suited for a mother watching her first-born during a ballet performance—hand to chest and all—and not her best friend, a grown-ass woman, whose mere presence was quickly doing one hell of a number on both my balls and my mental health.

At my silence, she quirked a brow from behind the camera that was at eye level. "Does he speak?" she asked, her tone sardonic, while lowering the camera to look at Penelope.

"Sometimes. We're still working on helping him form complete sentences."

The snort that left Raquel's throat was unflattering. My body bristled, heat creeping up my neck. I hadn't been the one to arouse the humorous response from her, I had merely been the cause—the butt of the joke.

"Money," I bit out, the single noun sucking the air out of the room, sobering everyone in it.

If Hemingway wanted a story, she would get one.

Raquel tilted her head toward me, a hostile look blossoming on her face, as if she wasn't impressed by my response any more than I had been—but it was the truth.

When cancer had ripped my father from my family prematurely, I had to act fast. In spite of the success of his Portuguese-American immigration story and how well he had appeared to be doing, things weren't as they had seemed. The whole thing had come down like a house of fucking cards when we realized that the life we had been leading was a massive fucking lie.

Humans are interesting creatures when we're forced to act out of desperation—we make sacrifices at the expense of our own undoing. I gave up everything to ensure my family's survival: to keep food on the table, the heat on in the house, to keep my older sister's career ambitions alive so she could get through law school, to ensure that my younger sisters never wanted for anything—money was the objective, the name of the game. Its procurement would be what would make things right. I sacrificed so they wouldn't have to, made hard choices quickly to avoid causing any more turmoil during a point in our lives where everything was as fragile as heated glass. That was who I was. That was who I had been raised to be.

Struggle. Fight. Survive.

Raquel's face was expressionless as she held the camera in my direction, her finger finding the shutter, setting off a flash of light in my direction that illuminated the room.

"I'm not part of the house," I snarled, ignoring my body's demands to preen under the assault of her lens.

"You're right," she offered flatly, adjusting the zoom ring before pegging me with another shot. "It's part of you."

Blinding white dots filtered over my vision as the flash went off again, her words etching themselves onto my brain. There was something profound in the statement, the astuteness of her observation, the lack of falter in her cadence, like she had never been more sure of anything in her life despite my having said no fewer than twenty words to her.

"Kitchen?" she asked, not waiting for me to reply. My heart thumped as my stare found the one room in the house that I loved to hate the most.

"This way," Penelope cooed. I could hear the smile in her voice even though I didn't see her face. She was loving every minute of this. Raquel's footsteps were nimble against the hardwood while she made her way into the kitchen. Despite my reticence to venture into the heart of the home, my body followed her like a child chased a star that shot across an inky night sky.

The countertops in the kitchen were black quartz with cream swirls weaved throughout. The oak cabinets were painted a macadamia white with sleek black knobs. Penelope had insisted that prospective buyers would lose their minds over the farmhouse sink, and when Raquel let out an audible purr of approval, I knew why.

I also knew I would give just about anything to hear that sound leave her mouth again, but under much different circumstances. She breezed by me, her fingers running along the lip of the stainless steel sink.

"I'll be back," Penelope said, giving her friend's shoulders a squeeze while simultaneously looking at me, as if she had every intention of ending me as soon as she could.

What else was new?

Raquel took careful steps around the kitchen, stopping only to look out the kitchen window into the yard.

"Penelope's got good taste," she murmured, a slight smile playing at her lips. I liked her smile, the thoughtfulness in its appearance, the slow and lazy sprawl, like a cat undulating after a nap. She smiled in a way most people didn't: with intention, not just for the sake of doing something with her face.

If I just concentrated on her smile, it would distract me from how fucking uncomfortable I felt being in here. I shoved my hands back into the pockets of my suit jacket, watching as she moved around the kitchen, her fingers grazing against every single surface as if she couldn't believe the opulence of the space, pausing here and there to take a photo.

"Are you ready to properly answer my question now?" She lowered her camera, her fingers now wrapped around the focus ring. She had the kind of luminous eyes that smoldered you like a flame the longer they appraised you.

I kicked my chin out at her in defiance, my gaze tapering. "What was your question?" I remembered her question just fine, but I would have given anything for her to continue to speak at that moment.

She drew her full bottom lip between her teeth, displaying her top row of teeth, which were surprisingly straight save for a canine that seemed to come slightly over the incisor next to it. They were imperfect, an innocuous flaw that meant nothing to me in terms of lessening the gravitational pull I felt beckoning me to her like the negative and positive ends of a magnet, an electrical charge demanding I break the distance between us. I stayed rooted, watching her cheeks grow ruddy when she realized I was staring. Raquel freed her lip from its hold and resumed snapping photos, the flush of her skin dissipating as she busied herself.

I wondered what she was thinking right now…if it was just me drowning in the throes of my attraction, or if she felt it, too. That inexplicable pull, the kind that consumed your every thought and controlled your every breath.

"Why did you decide you wanted to restore homes?" Her voice was stiff, like she decided I had pissed her off by staring her down moments ago. She turned on her heel in my direction, tilting her chin toward the ceiling, exposing the long length of her creamy neck while her eyes scanned the crown molding that trimmed the edges and the pot lights above us.

I hesitated, my mind percolating on the question.

"People are generally quick to give up on things when they can't see their beauty anymore…and beauty is sorta…"

"Skin deep?" she offered with a tight laugh at the cliché.

"Yeah, sorta," I finished.

Houses were a lot like humans. With time and the effects of different kinds of people living within its walls, its personality and history changed. Sometimes for the good, sometimes for the worse. But when it was the latter, I believed it took a certain kind of person to restore it to its former glory and show that there was still life left to be lived, love to be experienced, and memories to be made.

She lifted the strap of the camera over her head, placing its heavy weight onto the countertop. There was an uncertainty swirling in her eyes, waiting for me to continue.

I didn't.

No one was privy to the other parts of myself, that gentler side. Not even her.

"Did you always want to work in restorations?"

"No."

She rephrased her earlier question. "So, what drew you in? Your father pursued commercial contracting jobs previously, no?"

My throat moved, the lump from earlier re-forming. Raquel knew more than she let on, wielding it to her advantage. I would have to be careful.

Penelope burst into the kitchen, her chandelier earrings announcing her presence before she did.

I had never been more grateful to see her before in my life.

"Raquel, did he show you the soaker tub? It's divine." She sighed, clasped hands clutched against her chest.

I felt a sigh of relief leave me as the previous question disappeared from the room. I didn't like thinking about the real reason for my chosen field. It meant confronting the parts of myself I preferred to keep buried, because reminders hurt too much.

A cool breeze floated through the house as I heard the latch on the front door get squeezed.

"Sean!" my kid sister's squeaky voice called from the front of the house.

"In the kitchen, Trina." I heard her footsteps moving across the smooth hardwood. She shook the bottle of relief in her hands as she made her approach. "I have your Tylenol."

Her footsteps faltered when she entered the kitchen, her eyes bouncing from me to Penelope before they finally settled on Raquel, curiosity arching her brow.

My sister's mid-length hair—which had been green a few weeks ago—was now a brilliant shade of pink that made her honey-brown eyes seem nearly unearthly. If it weren't for her chameleon-like tendencies, she could have passed as my mother's doppelgänger. Instead, she had done everything in her power to rebel—or as she put it, be her "true self." Her septum piercing sparkled under the cool light of the pot lights—its glint the cause of another one of my mother's gray hairs.

If you had asked me ten years ago if I would have ever worked with this little shithead, my answer would have been no. Trina was, for all intents and purposes, a stereotypical shit disturber. With nearly a decade between us, I was the clichéd older brother who found her painfully taxing despite the fact that I would have taken a bullet for her if it required. I had stepped into my father's role after he died, forcing her to grow up in the process—sometimes she accepted my unsolicited attempts at parenting her, but more times than not, she told me to shove it up my ass.

She took six steps to the island, sliding the bottle of Tylenol in my direction before mouthing an apology in Penelope's direction for interrupting this clusterfuck of an interview.

Why did she deserve an apology? This was all her fault.

But sure, Penelope needed an apology.

Trina moved to leave the kitchen, her footsteps tapering off when she got to the archway. Tossing her head over her shoulder, contemplation filled her small features while she gave Raquel a once-over. Her eyes swept over the interloper with appraisal, as if piecing the puzzle together on her own accord.

Do not turn around.

In typical Trina fashion, almost as if she'd read my thoughts, she did the opposite. Spinning on her heel, she grinned in Raquel's direction.

"Hi," she started, taking hastened steps toward her like an incoming wave with a proffered hand.

Raquel moved forward to receive the outstretched hand, a genuine smile curling up the ends of her mouth.

"I'm Katrina Tavares, Sean's—"

I cleared my throat noisily, interrupting the union. My sister was not going to be the one to touch her first.

I would be.

"Out, Trina." I pointed to the living room, sending her a look of warning. This was already enough of a circus, and while my sister wasn't my competition by any means, I didn't need her leering at me in my most vulnerable state and repeating it at dinner on Sunday to my Ma and sisters when I inadvertently fucked it all up.

Hard fucking pass.

Trina feigned insult, placing a hand gingerly to her chest, harrumphed, and ducked out of the kitchen.

Thank God.

Raquel seemed unruffled by Trina's abrupt departure. "Why don't we finish the tour and then sit down to chat." Again, I couldn't tell if it was a question or a statement. Her gaze felt feathery light on my skin, a litany of shrill alarms going off in my head warning me not look at her so intently, even if her ass really was the shape of a peach.

She was off limits.

At least, that's what I kept telling myself the rest of the afternoon.

31

CHAPTER FOUR

Raquel

IF THERE WAS one thing I hated more than writing about charity drives or Mayor Murphy's philandering, it was being gawked at. Sean Tavares was a voracious gawker with about as much game and stealth as a third grader trying to line their coffers with stolen candy from a Cumby's—all while looking the clerk dead in the eye.

He wasn't fooling anyone with his apathetic airs, fitted suit jacket, and false bravado.

He hated me almost instantaneously, and that was fine. I didn't exactly fit into the setting of his perfect monolithic house, although neither did the cute little pink-haired woman he had dismissed.

I couldn't figure out how the woman fit into all of this. She didn't exactly look like your run-of-the-mill construction worker, and Penelope had never mentioned her when she recounted stories of her workday or the class acts she dealt with here.

Sean had looked at the woman with a lifetime of familiarity, had held her stare when he sent her out of the kitchen. He hadn't bothered with polite platitudes, which left me believing that their relationship wasn't just boss and employee. They certainly didn't share any physical similarities, either.

The woman had seemed too comfortable here, but the way she reacted to being dismissed gave me the impression that she was scorned in a way one might be if they were romantic partners.

I guess he liked his women just barely over legal.

Great.

During the rest of our tour, Sean had scowled anytime I pressed him for an answer, anytime I so much as breathed too deeply, or veered farther into a room than he would have liked. My patience hadn't lasted long. I wasn't enjoying this any more than he was, but that's life: We frequently have to endure difficult situations, and that includes having people we don't really like infiltrating our space. Sometimes those dislikes happened to be a twenty-eight-year old journalist who really only wanted to be here so her best friend could buy her lunch because she was currently living off of cheap instant noodles and coffee.

I had to admit, the house was truly a sight to behold. Creamy white clapboard made up the exterior of the well-fenestrated colonial that was tucked back on the sixty-by-hundred-foot lot. The long, gravel driveway was framed by newly planted maple trees bordered by cherry red mulch that had been laid carefully in a circle around its base.

In its reconstruction, an addition had been built at the rear, bringing the square footage from two thousand to north of four thousand and boasting five bedrooms and three-and-a-half bathrooms. Hardwood floors ran throughout, save for the bathrooms and kitchen, where white porcelain tiles had been laid. The house sported a fusion of styles that married a mid-twentieth-century twist with traditional nineteenth century New England, a love affair I would have never come up with.

Penelope, though? Penelope had a vision...an eye for what made things work. Between her creative eye and Sean's hands, they had created a fucking Picasso with this house that belonged on a postcard or a fridge magnet as a keepsake for a tourist passing through.

This house, with all its unwavering beauty, was the kind of place I had told my younger sister Holly Jane about as she struggled to fall asleep over the never-ending screaming coming from the living room back in our parents' triple-decker. Some nights, I didn't even think she slept at all. She just waited with bated breath for their violent fights to kick off...a wayward comment from our ma to set off our father into a rage that would bathe our bedroom in blue and red lights, and the melancholy of a siren to finally carry us off to sleep. Ma liked to fight—she was like a wasp at a picnic; no matter how often you swatted her away, she came back for more. She loved pissing Dad off more than she loved fucking our landlord behind his back every Thursday night while he was working at the packaging plant.

I had grown indifferent to my parents' standoffs... had learned to ignore the fist-sized holes in the drywall, or the tiny droplets of blood that stained the tired living room carpet like my very life depended on it—and in a way, it had. My sister, unfortunately, internalized that shit until it consumed her very being. I don't think she ever experienced a full night's rest in her short seventeen years of life. As a kid, she would scurry from her bed to mine, pulling the sheets back and pressing her thin, clammy body against mine. It would take ages to settle her; she rattled like a snake, her teeth chattering, though she wasn't cold to the touch. As the fear ripped through her, her head bent to her chest, her arms squeezed tightly around my waist. That all stopped when she realized it was no longer cool to crawl into bed with her older sister, and she turned to other things to help her fall asleep. Things I couldn't protect her from. My sister didn't know what safe was, and my only regret was that she never would. I hadn't been able to give it to her.

This house encapsulated safety with its open space, bordering woods on a street that epitomized the kind of shit that would play back in my memory for many nights after this. A place like this would have changed everything for us. It was everything I had promised her back then but had never been able to deliver to her.

I swallowed the thick lump of emotion that felt like razor blades lining the inside of my throat, blinking back tears that burned behind my lids but would never fall. My mother had a rule about crying: You didn't do it unless you wanted something to actually cry about. My sister's death hadn't been an exception to the rule.

After the tour of the house, Sean had led me into the study on the main floor for the rest of the interview. He shut the doors after I entered, before rounding the desk and settling on an office chair behind a fussy red cherry antique desk while I sat stiffly in a stationary chair on the other side of the desk. Floor-to-ceiling bookshelves that had been stocked with books, decorative vases, and nondescript trinkets lined the wall behind him. His frame looked too large for the chair he sat in. The tips of his fingers were steepled together in front of his face. His head tilted to the right, eyes trained on the scenery outside.

This morning had been frustrating. He had said nothing as he led me into various rooms around the house—apparently adopting some sort of vow of silence after his...what the hell was I supposed to refer to her as? Girlfriend? Wife? Jailbait?...had left the kitchen.

I'll admit, inappropriate jealousy had burned in me at her untimely appearance. I was a little ashamed to confess that the only thing that had abated the green-eyed monster was the lack of affection that bloomed in his face at her presence. It wasn't my concern to understand the dynamics of their relationship, but I wasn't a blind idiot: Sean was attractive, and if they were together, I was allowed to look at a minimum, even if I didn't touch. I wasn't my Ma; I had standards, boundaries...common fucking sense.

"Was it your dream to inherit your father's business?"

The sound that left Sean startled me. It was a growl, the timbre vibrating in his chest loud enough to be perceptible by ear, despite the width of the desk that kept us apart.

"No."

So far, I had successfully obtained one adverb, a noun, and one somewhat full sentence that I had to help him complete. Tavares was not much of a talker.

I wasn't entirely sure what I had been expecting when Penelope had called and pitched the idea to me. I had assumed at a minimum that he would have exuded a modicum of interest at a minimum or put in even a dash of effort to answer my questions. I got radio silence. Nothing but that scowl, pinched brows, and his tall frame hunched over with his hands stuffed in his pockets as he silently led me around the house. But I had a job to do, a column to write, a sandwich to eat— and the faster I got outta his hair, the sooner I could stop eye fucking a married man, write my columns, and get along on my way. It was time to get this show on the road.

"Look, if it's easier, I can just speak to your girlfriend," I offered uncomfortably, biting my lower lip and twisting my body around in the chair, my eyes searching for his tiny pink-haired partner through the glass-paneled doors that were currently shut behind me in the study.

Or whoever she was.

I didn't really want to talk to her, truthfully. I didn't want to put myself through that psychological warfare as I attempted to understand their attraction to one another (he didn't strike me as the type to be into septum piercings and bright pink hair) or what made her a better partner than me (which I'm sure was many things outside of her outward appearance, but not limited to: being emotionally available, having a personality, viewing life as something worth cherishing, and not having enough baggage to drown the entire Commonwealth in like it was the end of the damn world and not even Noah's Ark would save them.)

If he obliged me, I would dissect her, and then I would use the same scalpel sans a sanitization routine to anatomize myself. To find all the things that made her good and whole. Then I would almost without doubt, end up in bed with my ex-boyfriend because I wanted to remember what it was like to be wanted again, even just for five minutes, which would result in Penelope getting angry if I told her about it. Really, really, fucking angry. She might not talk to me for five business days before she would, with the reliability of a *TV Guide*, call me at ten to three on a Saturday afternoon and declare that she was still pissed at me, still hated my poor decision making…but to meet her at O'Malley's for happy hour. It was one of the things I loved about her—the consistency in our friendship, her dependability, the playful diatribe. I would grow old with my best friend, and nothing, no guy (no matter how big his cock), no job, and no other person, would ever come between that.

"My *girlfriend*?" he asked, interrupting my reverie, his eyes finding mine again. For some inexplicable reason, my heart chose that exact moment to squeeze in my chest in a way I hadn't experienced since high school. It fucking fluttered, like a freshman girl who had just been asked to the prom by a senior. My heart didn't flutter. I'm not the fluttering type. But when he watched me with too much interest, when his eyes tracked my lips with every word that left them, despite nothing worth mentioning leaving his lips, my heart did the same thing again.

"Yeah," I confirmed, wondering how the fuck someone forgot about someone like her, but based on the unbridled confusion filling his face, I suspected I had either befuddled him or made a gross error.

His thick left brow arched north. "I don't have a girlfriend."

An iota of hope struck me dead smack in the center of my chest. Hope I shouldn't have had. Hope that didn't belong to the likes of someone like me. Sean was an enigma, a Rubik's cube I struggled to solve. A handsome paradox with broad shoulders, a chiseled face and eyes so dark they appeared almost black.

My throat worked across the lodge that had re-formed in my throat, his darkened stare never leaving mine. "So, the girl from earlier..." I didn't miss that the noun had been punctuated as it left me, my curiosity undermining the modicum of professionalism I was supposed to have, "she isn't your wife, either?"

Sean sighed, his hands dropping to his lap. If he had been unimpressed before, it paled to the look he was rocking now. His features were granite, his eyes searched my face, looking for what, I would never know.

"She is not."

"Who is she?" I wanted to punch myself this time. No, seriously. I should have knocked myself out earlier in the boardroom. I had no business being here. I didn't know how to behave in front of a man who wasn't a lewd city worker spreading his seed from one Hallmark princess to the next, a group of firemen who should have long since retired, or a man who was in an abusive relationship with the photocopier. I could barely get a solid read on the men I'd grown up around. Why would Sean be any exception?

This was dangerous. This was foolish. This was really fucking bad.

The bemusement that took residence on his handsome face from out of nowhere was a crippling hybrid of both sexy and infuriating that set my skin on fucking fire.

"Why?" he said. "Are you jealous?"

My expression must have escaped me, because he barked out a laugh that sent an inexplicable current of electricity rushing through me.

Lust and rage swirled inside of me like the insides of a snow globe, my skin prickling with an awareness that felt like my body and mind were betraying me, demanding two different things. Heat licked up the slope of my neck, my face growing ruddy, while my heart thumped loud enough that I felt its steady rhythm in the soles of my feet.

And still he looked on at me, the impish calculation a glint in his dark eyes, as if he had me all figured out. I barely had time to celebrate his singleness before he antagonized me once more, laying down a trap laced with a hearty slice of expensive cheese I would never be able to resist.

"Over what?" I conceded, taking his bait like the idiotic mouse whose foibles would earn it a quick death.

"That there might be someone in your place."

I jerked my body out of the seat, my knees slamming into the front of that hideous desk that reminded me of that of Penelope's father. Ostentatious. Cocky. Arrogant. The supposition that Sean might have gotten along too well with Mr. Cullimore left me unsettled, my vision momentarily tossing my equilibrium out of whack, raking in breaths as if I couldn't draw air fast enough.

"Was it your dream to restore houses?" I repeated forcefully, in hopes he'd give me more than a one-word response. My spine steeled as I fought to regain control of the narrative. My blinks were rapid, the silhouette of his body blurring as I quarrelled with my sex drive and ego. I was breaking every fucking rule in the book today. You weren't supposed to think about the people you were interviewing being naked. You weren't supposed to be interested in their romantic status.

Or whether or not there was a double meaning when they stared you down.

That was Journalism 101. Basic common sense. Somewhere between being impartial and accurate, there must have been a lecture that stipulated that you weren't supposed to give the interviewee come-fuck-me eyes just because he gave them to you first. Maybe I had missed the class, had opted to sleep in that day.

His pheromones had done something to my brain in the last couple of hours and replaced my sensibilities with that of a teenage girl who was still dry humping her boyfriend in the back seat of his parents' Suburban every Friday night because she was too scared to go all the way. That was the only explainable answer.

Sean was tall, lean, had a V-shaped waistline and looked damn delectable in a suit jacket—a far cry from my aforementioned ex-boyfriend, whose jeans sagged in the ass and for whom the idea of wearing a belt would have been a slight against his personal aesthetic. This was what it felt like to appreciate a man whose clothes fit. The gray fibers of the jacket had played with the intensity of his dark eyes. Outside, sunlight broke through the clouds, allowing a small stream to pour in from the window in the study, softening the deep opulence of the rich brown closer to his pupils, leaving a ring of whiskey gold around them. He was different. That was what made him interesting. That was what made my thighs clench together, heat roll through me, and an unfamiliar wave of lust tighten below my belly button.

That was all.

"Relax, it's a joke." The casualness of his voice cooled my blood pressure, my heart rate slowing. He nodded toward the seat, subliminally demanding my body to acquiesce. Whether I wanted to or not, my body decided for me, my legs sinking downward until my ass hit the lip of the chair again.

"Katrina is my sister."

"You could have just said that."

"Where's the fun in that, Hemingway?"

Hemingway? I bristled, my hands balling into fists in my lap. He was openly making fun of me, humiliating me at every turn. Abusing my unintentional attraction with the breadth of his broad shoulders and intense dark eyes that were full of mockery.

"I don't think you're taking this very seriously," I groused. I was the *this* in this situation. I wasn't used to being made fun of. I was formidable at the paper. I commanded respect. Hell, even Karen generally stayed out of my way, even if she did get the better stories. I didn't like the smirk that Sean housed on his face, as if he had just discovered that I was capable of being anything but professional. Challenge lit up in his face like he had every intention of starting a war.

And winning it, too.

CHAPTER FIVE

Sean

WATCHING Raquel sputter was a high I never wanted to rid myself of. It was the kind of euphoria that was achieved when you rode a high velocity rollercoaster that shot you through the air, lurching your heart up and down with it. Her cheeks had turned ruddy with the ease of my jests at her expense. I had practically preened in my seat, watching the heat crawl up her slender, creamy neck like wild ivy infiltrating a building's outer walls. It hadn't been my initial intention to antagonize her, but she had almost made it too easy at the mention of a wife.

Me? With a girlfriend? A wife? Nothing would have made my Ma happier, but I was mulish about waiting for the right woman to appear before I even so much as entertained the idea. I knew when that moment presented itself, it would be a thought that commanded all of my attention, and I would stop at nothing until that lucky woman was mine.

During our interview, I had remained fastidious about evading questions I didn't want to answer. It had been endearing in the beginning, when she posed well-meaning questions about the origins of the family business; I had indulged her at best. Our exchange was controlled, my answers concise. That wasn't enough for her, though, and her next batch of questions were more thought out, more complex, in-depth.

"If money wasn't your motivator, what else would you do with your life?" The question had been neither pertinent nor salient to the interview, but it still nudged that deep-seated anxiety I kept carefully tucked away. I suppose when she wasn't getting anything else out of me that was remotely interesting enough to twist into a story, she had to start digging the same way a dog might to excavate a bone.

"Money is, and always will be, the thing that makes the world go round," I had replied. I didn't have to look at her to know that the response had annoyed her. I could feel the loss of her patience dripping from her in heavy, drunken waves that pooled at her feet. Surprise had sucker punched me when I finally looked at her, only to find her visage a blank canvas.

Raquel wasn't dense, not by a long shot. This was not her first time at the rodeo, and I was not the first asshole to try to play her at her own game. But I wanted something out of her, anything outside of what she was currently giving me. I needed to find something that would act as a guiding tool to ensure I steered myself clear from the chances of humiliating myself—even if it meant it was at this woman's expense.

Undeterred, she just found another roundabout way of asking the same question. Sometimes she got away with it, but for the most part, I took a vow of silence that was on par with that of Buddhist monk, opting for the reliability of heavy sighs and knitted eyebrows.

If I'm being honest, it wasn't that I didn't want to tell her. At least, it hadn't been my initial intention to not give her the answers that she was hounding me for. I just discovered that I enjoyed watching her feathers bristle under my rankled apathy more than I did giving her what she wanted. With every averted answer, those slender shoulders of hers rounded upward, her brows lifted, the nostrils of her pert nose flared, and a darkness flickered in her eyes that I desperately wanted to see erupt into flames so I could taste her chaos.

I wanted anything from Raquel other than the controlled professionalism. Somehow it felt unnatural coming from her with her distinct outlier tendencies.

She was the lit wick in the candle, and watching her burn had become a sick fixation fast. My breath hitched unceremoniously every time she pulled her bottom lip between her teeth, a petulant look flashing on her pretty face, until she schooled her features, subduing the muscles in her expression back into place like a piece of Plasticine that she had worked her thumbs over. A labored, tight breath would leave her in shallow exhales, her fingers finding the shutter on the camera again, illuminating each room as we went. I liked the way her features pinched with concentration every time she found something new to focus on, her mind loud with thoughts. Though I couldn't hear them, I could feel them in the wayward glances she shot me when she thought I wasn't looking.

I needed to know what lay beyond her schooled expressions, the even tone of her cadence, the pressing of her questions. I wanted to know what made her tick...what was her purpose...what made her grow hot.

I just hadn't anticipated it coming to a head so easily.

"I don't think you're taking this seriously," she spat in my direction, seething in her seat.

A divide had appeared in Raquel's facade when I suggested that perhaps she was jealous because she had detected a threat (although, if I'm being honest, there wasn't a threat within a two-state radius that could have contended with the likes of her). She hadn't liked that speculation much, the suggestion causing a bleeding chasm to appear in the otherwise still surface of her expression. Provoking her was the most fun I'd had in years, but I had my reasons: I was curious to know whether this attraction that thickened the air in the room was one-sided or not, and try as she may have to act otherwise, I practically smelled her arousal from the other side of the desk. It was heady, a scent I was almost too willing to get myself drunk off of.

"I am taking it seriously, Hemingway," I replied evenly, my face reflecting with boyish charm and all the other appeal I had used to woo countless women before her. The moniker hadn't been well thought, but it seemed fitting nevertheless. I didn't believe Raquel had gone to school to become a journalist; I didn't think any writer really did. Just like I hadn't gone to culinary school with the intention of inheriting my father's business before I ever got the chance to really work in my knives. I had been on an entirely different trajectory before tragedy had struck, and my family's untimely loss had equipped me with the foresight to see when other people also had to abdicate on their initial ambitions for the realities and confines of real life. She had dreamt of something much bigger, larger than her, something that was on scale with the real Hemingway's influence.

"Stop calling me that." She shot me a scowl.

"Why?"

"'Cause that's not my fucking name." Her facade parted like Moses and the damn Red Sea, her chest heaving with every inhalation she took.

I grinned, glad to see her personality bleeding out from behind her pretense. "You've got a wicked temper on you." My cadence emulated hers, my inflection rolling upward.

She didn't miss the mockery. "Fuck you."

I rolled my neck, felt the tight heat of her eyes tracking me like a lioness about to pounce on her prey. And I was ready to be hunted. I was ready to go to war.

"I think you'd like that," I murmured, my voice barely perceptible over the hum of the house's HVAC system kicking to life.

Her eyes popped up, her brows hitting her hairline, jawline growing as hard as a piece of fucking steel. "Don't kid yourself."

"I never kid around when it comes to fulfilling a woman's needs."

I expected her to flee, but instead, she leaned forward, her elbows biting the edge of the desk, a storm of curiosity brewing in her cinnamon-colored eyes that practically had me panting.

"I don't think you'd know what to do with me if I came with a

fucking instruction manual." Her face belied the force behind her statement, and this time I took the bait.

"Well, lucky for both of us," My hand shot out just as she moved to
withdraw her arm, the pad of my thumb working across the smooth
stretch of skin, an eruption of goosebumps lighting up her skin, "I'm a
quick learner. I've got the patience of a saint, and the prowess of a
god."

Raquel's lids dropped, and she made a little choking sound, as if an
unbidden thought had imbibed her senses and captured her mid-
exhale. When her lids flipped open, the intoxication had all but
vanished from her eyes, leaving behind a warpath of rage in its wake.

She ripped her arm away, my hand slamming onto the desk with
an unprepared thud.

"Two things," she snarled, collecting her things and shoving them
back into her bag. "From my experience, guys who have to talk a big
game like they know what they're doing, generally don't have a damn
clue about the female anatomy." Her fingers fought with the zipper of
the camera bag, the fastener getting caught the harder she pulled.

"And the second thing?" I blew out a breath, pissed at myself for
the folly that caused my own downfall.

"The closest you will ever get to fucking me is in your dreams. But
then again, I suspect that even your fantasy version of me would have
the good sense to tell you to *go fuck yourself*." She punctuated the last
three words, her accent raw. She rose to her feet again, her body trembling with anger that rolled off her in heady waves, her hands
snatching her things from the chair next to her.

"Raquel," I called after her. She swung the doors open with such
force that the handles bit into the drywall. It was a miracle that the
glass didn't shatter. I winced, making a mental note to check if the wall
needed to be patched. Rising to my full height, I rounded the stupid
desk and trailed after her. Her perfume lingered in the air.

"Pen," she called, her voice quaking, "I'll meet you at the cafe." She
shoved her feet back into the boots I had made her take off, not bothering with the laces. When she put her hand on the doorknob, I took
the opportunity to touch her again, my big palm wrapping around her
slender fingers. The kindling between us sparked another inferno, its

warmth running through every strand of hair on my head. She felt it, too. I knew she did from the way her eyes widened, confusion filtering through them, a lack of understanding in the unexplainable dynamism that was coursing between us.

I watched as the blaze was extinguished before my very eyes, her expression darkening, her hand stiffening in mine.

"Don't fucking touch me," she said, her voice a growl.

"I didn't mean to offend you." It wasn't a lie. Yeah, I had pushed her for my own gain, but I hadn't intended to make her so...rattled. I had gotten carried away. Cocky. Arrogant.

She wasn't buying it from me. Her lips tightened into a thin line and her eyes narrowed. "Cute attempt at an apology. Try that shit on someone who cares." She slapped my hand away.

My skin stung from the contact, but my desperation to feel her again stung more.

"Move," she ordered.

I had all of twelve seconds to contemplate her request when the unsettling sensation that came with being watched swept over me, sending a wave of chills down my spine.

A loud *harumph* from the top of the steps summoned my attention. Trina cleared her throat three times, an unimpressed look blooming on her face. It was hard to discern how long she had been standing there, how much she had seen, or how much she had heard. I dragged an open palm over my face, then shoved my hands back into my pocket and stepped aside. Raquel glanced at the stairwell, a pained expression taking residence on her visage that almost made me remorseful for how strongly I had come onto her.

Almost.

The cold fall air swept inside when she finally opened the door, the heavy oak slamming shut behind her, rattling the gallery wall of mirrors in the family room.

Silence filtered between us, my eyes burning a hole through the solid wood. A wheeze of an engine coughed to life, her tires skidded against the driveway, and then, without seeing her, I knew she was gone.

"You are," Trina started, shaking her head so hard a curl of her pink hair loosened from behind her ear, "a giant, fucking idiot." I didn't miss the smarmy smile that had birthed to life on her round pout. My sister didn't miss any opportunity to goad, especially at my expense.

"Who's an idiot?" Penelope warbled. She leaned over the bannister, her features warm and eager, obviously hoping to be let in on the interaction like the damn interloper she truly was.

Then a thought slammed into me.

She hadn't heard a damn thing.

I swung my glare at my sister, threatening her a hell of a whole lot of more pain if she so much as opened her mouth and revealed one detail.

I would give Raquel that honor.

Trina stiffened on her roost. She couldn't compromise with me.

I was all she had left right now.

Her nostrils flared, realization dawning on her.

"No one," she murmured, fleeing down the stairs, breezing by me, disappearing into the kitchen.

"Where's Raquel?" Penelope asked, seemingly ignoring my sister's premature departure, I guess playing it off as typical early-twentysomething histrionics. She stood akimbo, her long neck craning as if searching for her friend.

"She told me to tell you to meet her at the cafe." The cogs of my mind churned so loudly that I was certain Penelope would pick out the half lie.

Instead, she sighed, shaking her head. "Typical. She never waits for anyone."

The weight of that sentiment hung between us as she came gliding down the stairs like she was the lady of a grand *maison,* and not an interior designer who was also fucking the foreman, whose weekly take-home was less than the cost of the designer bag she picked up from the console table tucked against the stairwell.

"Want me to bring you something back?" she asked, sliding into her camel-colored car coat, freeing her trapped hair from the collar with a wave of her delicate hand. "I'm grabbing Dougie lunch, too."

I ignored the rumbling of my stomach. I suspected I'd be wearing

47

whatever she brought me back if I accepted the offer, and I had no intention of bringing this jacket to the dry cleaner.

"Nah, I'm good."

At that, she shrugged, opening the door, a chill rushing in. "Suit yourself."

I glanced at the clock on the wall, deciding that if I left now, I'd be back in Fall River before Penelope could arrange a cavalcade of people to show up at the house waving pitchforks and lit torches in my direction, demanding retribution for my disgrace.

Hell, maybe I'd have time to move and change my name, too.

CHAPTER SIX

Raquel

PENELOPE HADN'T BEEN EVEN MARGINALLY surprised when I told her about the stunt assclown had pulled. In fact, she laughed into her stupid blackened chicken salad, spearing a piece of avocado onto her fork and shoving it into her mouth to stifle her giggle.

"I did tell him you didn't have a boyfriend," she tittered.

I paled, my brows bending inward together–I was beginning to think she had been the catalyst to that ostentatious conversation.

"How the fuck is my dating life relevant to an interview?"

"Raquel, lighten up. You're attractive to a blind person."

I rolled my eyes in disdain. I'd always felt homely-looking at best, I didn't need her well-intended compliments. "I have no tits to speak of, one of my eyes is larger than the other, and my parents really could have saved me some ridicule if they had gotten me some braces. I am failing to see what you find marginally attractive about me."

"Stop being self-depreciating." Penelope dabbed at the corners of her mouth with a crumpled napkin, appraising me with her sea-blue stare. "It's natural to have one eye that's marginally larger than the other. I happen to think your teeth are endearing, and besides, Sean is an ass man."

"How on earth do you know *that?*" I pressed, becoming hyper-focused on the latter detail.

She shrugged noncommittally, giving me a tilted smile, batting her long lashes at me as if she was part of his inner circle. And for some painfully asinine reason, I wanted to be in it, too.

"I overheard him and the guys on the site talking about it."

"Gratuitous pig."

"He's a man, Raquel," she said, as if I had forgotten what was going on between his legs since we left the house, like that gave him some sort of license to objectify me with his arresting stare. And then she swung her sword of moral superiority directly at the soft spot at my neck, making contact, "And I'll have you know that I caught you eye fucking him in the kitchen. So save your holier-than-thou speech." Her eyes narrowed at me.

I slouched in my seat, the fingers on my left hand curled behind my neck, the heat of my embarrassment warming them.

Busted.

"I looked, so what." Still slumped, my hand retreated to help pick up the overflowing roast beef sandwich, taking a generous bite, my jaw working the sinew.

"So, you're no better than him. He just happens to be aware of his likes, that's all. There's nothing wrong with that...and frankly," she paused, frowning, "you could afford to develop some taste." Her nose crinkled, and for a moment, it was hard to discern whether it was at me, or the dried date she had just picked off her plate, disposing of the pruned fruit onto a side plate.

My brow arched north. "What the fuck is that supposed to mean?"

"Exactly what I said." She sipped her sparkling water, her visage demure in contrived delicacy. "Your taste in men is abysmal at best."

"I've been with one guy," I hissed.

"That's my point," she stressed impatiently, as if I was slow to catch up. "One guy. You don't even know what you like." She sipped her soda water again. "Broaden your horizons. You liked looking at Sean, and that is a massive upgrade from who you've been...doing." Her smile strained just before she popped a small piece of bread into her mouth—her fifth roll since we had gotten here.

Penelope wasn't into carbs, but I guess the conversation had made her work up an appetite.

"I don't think I entirely understand what you're getting at." I was playing coy, and we both knew it.

She tucked the fork under the side of her plate with perfect precision. Her freed fingers knit together, a cursory look tacking itself onto her suddenly severe face.

"Let me spell it out to you in a way you'll understand, then." Her lilt rolled upward, far away from her expensive Connecticut boarding school territory, heading toward the slums of South Boston. "Stop fucking a chucklehead whose nickname is a wicked misnomer."

I blinked at her before annoyance flanked me. "No one says 'chucklehead' anymore," I muttered, ignoring the truth in her words.

Tobias "Cash" Peake was about as chuckleheaded as they come— my dad had called him "that 'friggin 'igit kid," never bothering with his name. My dad wasn't wrong, and neither was Penelope. Cash's preferred moniker didn't exactly have any merit. That guy was perpetually broke, despite living rent-free with his Nan.

Still, he kept loneliness at bay when my thoughts threatened to consume me as Holly Jane's anniversary approached, and frankly, that was enough. But it wasn't enough to satisfy my best friend who looked at me like I had just told her Michael Kors was better than Prada. (She got kinda prickly about that shit.)

"Raquel." I heard the warning in her voice, like an Amber Alert over the radio. Penelope's temper was known to be on par with a Nor'easter if you pushed her hard enough—don't let the glossy hair and high cheekbones fool you.

"It's fine, Pen. Stop stressing; it's not good for you. Premature wrinkles and all that shit." I waved her off, giving her a chipmunk smile just before popping the last bite of my sandwich into my mouth.

"You just," she paused speaking into her salad, her chin bent downward, a hand framing her forehead as she contemplated loud enough that I was sure the entire shoebox-sized cafe was about to hear.

"I just...?"

"You need better coping mechanisms. Especially during this time of year."

My throat worked at the tiny granules of sand that had filled the stretch of my neck without warning. Gone was the jovial nature of our conversation, Penelope's eyes grew glossy with unshed tears. The ghosts of my past danced throughout the cafe, setting off an eruption of goosebumps along my arms for all the wrong reasons. The hairs on the back of my neck rose at half mast, and I blinked at her with the tenacity of a nervous tick.

I hadn't forgotten that the anniversary of my sister's death was coming up.

I had compartmentalized it. I didn't talk about it. I had stowed the painful memory into a box and shoved it into my storage unit in the basement of my apartment, seldom, if ever, looking at it. Instead, to Penelope's point, I buried it, or let someone else, help me bury it instead. Every year without fail, Cash found himself in my bed, whispering all kinds of pointless sweet nothings in my ear that were irrelevant to me because it didn't change my reality.

My little sister was dead.

And she was dead because of me.

No amount of talking about it was going to remedy that. There was only suppression and suffocation now. My best friend was raised by moneyed parents' who believed in therapy even when you weren't despondent. Maybe it was grooming their daughter for the inevitability of her life, or perhaps they genuinely cared about what was doing in her head—they had tossed around thousands of dollars to ensure her sylph-like shoulders were stress-free. Yoga retreats and mindfulness training had all been part of Penelope's youth. Even now, in her late twenties, she still had weekly visits to her therapist at his

Back Bay office. Penelope's parents had cared about ensuring she knew what to do about the ugly parts of life when they confronted her.

My parents were not frays on that proverbial rope. They communicated their thoughts and feelings through their fists, and any sentence that attempted to articulate how they were making you feel might have earned you endless ridicule and a slap that would have required Neo's Matrix-like reflexes to avoid.

I didn't bottle this shit up because I liked it; I contained it because I didn't know what else to do with it.

"You going to eat the rest of that?" I asked, jerking my chin at her salad.

She exhaled with defeat, the waves of her hair loosening as she shook her head—whether it was at me, or at the salad's looming future, I didn't bother to confirm. I stabbed the field greens and popped the end of the fork into my mouth, training my gaze outside.

Penelope said nothing else for the remainder of our lunch, but I felt her disappointment over my indifference all the same.

CHAPTER SEVEN

Raquel

IT HAD BEEN a week since the interview from hell.

I leaned back in my desk chair, my eyes skimming over the newspaper in my hand, the aroma of the printed ink on the cheap newsprint an intoxicating fragrance. Penelope's judgement call had been spot on —not only did that resplendent colonial look good on the cover, Sean did, too.

My insides flipped, the tip of my finger tracing over the photographic image of the sharp angles of his face, the stiff and hard outline of his body. His linebacker shoulders were wide, his hands tucked into his pockets. Hands that had made me feel things I had never felt before…things that left me feeling confused and strangely vulnerable.

I hadn't communicated that part to Penelope. She would have gotten ahead of herself, and ultimately, nothing would ever transpire between Sean and I, so why even bother planting the seed of an idea in her pretty little head. She would try to cultivate an entire overgrown field of wildflowers for Sean and I to fuck in; anything that would sever my physical ties to Cash. Hell, I was convinced that was why she had gotten me that ridiculous vibrator in the first place: to teach me that self-love was important, and it started with my nether regions. My vibrator wouldn't be there to mop up my tears, though, would it? It wouldn't understand my pain or the depths of my grief. It wouldn't swallow my sobs or stay with me until after the anxiety blew over.

Cash did.

And whether Penelope wanted to see it or not, I didn't have her grace, or her garden party-like beauty. I was a thorny weed, my stems prickly. The kind that people blindly picked at sans gardening gloves, only to recoil when they felt the stab of my predatory instincts.

Just like Sean had.

My lids dropped shut for the briefest of moments, an unbidden memory barreling toward me. I would never admit I had liked his attention once I learned that Trina was his sister, and not his wife. My body warmed with the heat in his awareness that literally sucked the air out of my lungs and made my brain turn into slush. I felt naked under his appraisal, despite being fully clothed, like he had seen all the things that I had masked. This man, who knew nothing about me beyond what he saw at a superficial level, only had to touch me, and a world that had always seemed dull and colorless suddenly seemed bright and promising.

The interaction had been cheap, and I felt feeble for the mental investment I had committed to repeatedly reliving the interaction. I would never see him again.

On an exhale, I forced my lids open again, my gaze fanning over the headline and my byline.

He photographed just as beautifully as the house. He was imposing and impressive, profile slightly turned to the left, his lips tight, but his eyes—his eyes were cavalier, with a wry, boyish charm that didn't fall in line with his initial greeting. It was only after I pressed him, only after I had naively taken the bait, that I learned what Sean was.

A womanizer.

Still, he looked good in print, and if this photo got more people to pick up the paper in spite of the vapid headline, I didn't care.

LIFE REBORN
FALL RIVER MAN GIVES EATON CENTURY HOMES A SECOND CHANCE
by RAQUEL FLANNIGAN

Earl hadn't given me a choice in the matter of titles; in fact, prior to the agreed-upon title, he put the kibosh on my three initial versions of the fleshed-out story. He flustered with my first iteration *(SEEMINGLY DECENT FALL RIVER MAN GIVES OLD HOUSES A SECOND CHANCE)*, nearly had an aneurysm over the second, *(MONEY HUNGRY JACKASS FROM FALL RIVER FIXES BROKEN HOUSES TO MAKE HIMSELF LOOK LIKE LESS OF A DICK)*—before we met halfway in the middle on the third.

"We are a community paper, Raquel."

Like I had needed the reminder.

Earl had his own ass to protect; I got it. In his mind, we had already taken enough risks by snubbing the fire department—we needed to err on the side of caution. The Eaton FD got their story too, just not the front page. They would get over it, and if they felt the need to hose someone down, I'd be the sacrificial lamb, pool floaties and all. Earl was still nervously tittering about it, cautiously looking over his shoulder everywhere he went, as though not running the story on the first page was a liability.

The charity car wash story was on page three, above the promo of the Old Maid Cafe's Thanksgiving special in the next four weeks.

Thanksgiving.

For most, the time of practiced gratitude was a welcome reprieve, nipping closely on the heels of silver bells and mistletoe. Thanksgiving was my version of hell. It meant enduring my mother's ridicule, picking curiously at a Thanksgiving TV dinner with cranberry sauce that tasted like paint thinner and turkey that had the texture of leather. My stomach cramped at the very idea of it, my lower abdomen twisting.

56

It was hard to say what would be worse—my mother reminding me that it should have been me in the car, not Holly Jane—or the bullshit she tried to tell me was all she could afford to feed me with.

My Ma had money, her money and my own.

See, on top of being a desperate and consistent lay for Cash once a year when I needed to just not think, I was also the spineless twit who forked over a large chunk of her paycheck to ensure my mother went without nothing her blackened heart so much as dreamt of.

Yeah, I know. Surprised? I am, too. When I left that house ten years ago, I swore to God I would never have anything to do with her again. I didn't answer her calls or Dad's. My sister made a point of using Cash's pager to get hold of me when she needed me, and that was our primary form of communication.

Then Dad died, and Holly Jane went a few months later.

Then Ma started crying about being hungry or her power bill, my guilt had settled in after I landed my first full time job, and I did what Flannigans always did.

I took care of my own, because that bitch didn't have anyone else.

Honestly, ten years later, I still couldn't believe Dad had gone and gotten himself killed over something so stupid, so ill-planned, so poorly contrived. For a man who had carried the weight of the world on his shoulders, had provided for his daughters, his good-for-nothing wife, and so many others, it was next to impossible for me to reconcile that he had died the way he did.

I'll be honest; my father hadn't been good man. He took care of his own with no remorse, just like everyone else did in our pocket of Southie. But, if you asked anyone who knew him, really knew him, he wasn't a bad one, either. He had been susceptible to the perils of love, just like any other man who got caught up in that novel idea of forever. He had spoiled my mother to a fault. And that woman was vile, ostentatious, and plain fucking evil. Her motivators were very easy to understand: sex and money. It didn't really matter where either came from or who she had to crush under the sole of her cheap high heel to obtain it. She had shown up on my grandparents' doorstep, pregnant with yours truly. Dad had done what his very Irish Catholic background demanded of him: 'til death do us part.

57

He had tried to give her the world, which in his eyes had meant stability, a roof over her head, children—tiny humans who would depend on her for the fulfillment of their every need. Someone else to love more than herself.

In my father's one-dimensional mind when it came to the feeble matters of the heart, Ma had just needed a purpose, needed someone to believe in her, something to believe in. He was a die-hard romantic, that one, and what had that gotten him? A broken heart, two kids, a couple of stints in prison, and a poorly hatched plan to fill my mother's acrylic-nailed, nicotine-stained fingers with Benjamins that led to an early grave.

What had I gotten out of my parents' disastrous union?

Survival instincts I wished I didn't possess. Reflexes that were always on high alert. More grief than I knew what to do with. An inability to form a real attachment with anyone outside of Penelope, and a brain that could have doubled as a dartboard for a psychologist who wanted to play target practice.

To make matters worse, there was the unspoken yearly obligation to spend Thanksgiving with my mother, even though I knew what awaited me beyond the beaten-in door of my parents' triple decker was going to leave me worse for wear for days. It was a whole lot of pain and unnecessary heartache I didn't need to subject myself to—but did out of respect for my late father...and perhaps, because in some twisted, sick way, I felt like I deserved it. The pain. The discomfort. The vitriolic ridicule. My selfishness had killed the one good thing in our family, so if for two days out of the year I had to endure even a sliver of what I had left *her* to deal with—then that would be my cross to bear until either the cigarettes got me or Ma finally drank herself to death.

Sliding my mouse next to the keyboard, the monitor sprung to life, casting offensive blue light at me that burned my retinas. I was surprised to find an email already in my inbox after checking it all of an hour ago before the paper's regular Monday morning meeting. Excitement ticked through me when I read the subject line from an email address I didn't immediately recognize.

STORY.

The noun had me buzzing at the prospect of being able to cover something else again. As incorrigible as Sean Tavares had been, writing something outside of what had been initially assigned to me had felt like a strange sort of homecoming, a reminder of a dream I had left behind.

Double clicking on the email, a separate box populated on the screen, and just as quickly as the excitement had lit up inside of me—it vanished.

CHAPTER EIGHT

Raquel

SEAN WAS the last person I wanted to hear from.

My body was practically vibrating in my chair as I reread the email that sat like an unpinned grenade in my inbox. I waited for the email to detonate and wipe itself from existence, but as my luck would have it, it sat there like a dud. The actual fucking audacity of that guy to contact me after the way we had parted. Unbridled rage suffused through me as I pulled on the edges of the window that housed the email, elongating the frame while my eyes worked at expunging the blithe email from existence and into my deleted folder through telekinesis.

My jaw rocked from side to side the longer I sat and reread the message that taunted me.

TO:RFLANNIGAN@THEADVOCATE.COM
FROM:COOK4U78@HOTMAIL.COM
SUBJ:STORY

Your story was cute.
Sean

A labored breath wheezed out of me as my eyes worked back and forth across the four-word sentence over and over again, the words embedding themselves into my brain. My eyes ran over every single letter that formed the email address, a blast of heated rage slamming into me as I found myself snagging on his adjective of choice.

The logical part of me knew better than to engage, but the anger only deepened as the jab marinated in my mind. Cute? My story was *cute*? My hand quaked when I punched the reply button with my mouse, fingertips battering the keyboard with the fury of my response, the loud clicking carrying through the office.

TO:COOK4U78@HOTMAIL.COM
FROM:RFLANNIGAN@THEADVOCATE.COM
SUBJ:RE: STORY

Fuck. Off.

I didn't even consider for one moment that our office Internet firewall features might catch the response upon my clicking of Send. In fact, I didn't think of much else, my ego having forced my pert nose into the air and turning my spine into a steeled piece of rod. I hope he found my response cute. Better yet, I hope he found it *endearing*.

I didn't have even two minutes to savor the joy of my juvenility because the icon on my inbox lit up, the preview of a new email dancing in the upper right corner.

My finger was on the trigger before I could process what I was doing, heart kicking in my chest, nostrils flaring.

```
TO:RFLANNIGAN@THEADVOCATE.COM
FROM:COOK4U78@HOTMAIL.COM
SUBJ:WRONG FOOT?

I'm an ass. Let's start over.
I want a rewrite.

Sean
```

Seething, I was seething. It felt as though someone had dropped a red-tinted piece of glass before my eyes. He wanted a rewrite? Well, wasn't that just fucking peachy. Again, I didn't pause to consider the ramifications of my hostility, my brain pushing my body into autopilot. I hit Reply, and began to type.

```
TO:COOK4U78@HOTMAIL.COM
FROM:RFLANNIGAN@THEADVOCATE.COM
SUBJ:RE: (CUT OFF) YOUR FOOT.

Go play in traffic. There's your rewrite and
conclusion.
```

Delayed hesitation swept through me after I hit Send. Admittedly, I had perhaps been needlessly caustic. Sean just seemed to arouse the worst parts of me, slivers of myself that I didn't like. He also brought on a host of emotions that felt familiar and new all at the same time: Anger and frustration were old acquaintances, feeling like an occasionally worn pair of jeans that pinch a bit at the waist. Attraction and vulnerability, on the other hand...those were new contenders in my repertoire of emotions, and I didn't know where they fit.

It was as though two sides of my brain were at war with each other.

Unsettled, I minimized the screen and got up for a cigarette break. I dug through my messenger bag on the end of my desk for the crinkled packet of Pall Malls. Would he reply? Did it matter? My central nervous system was out of control, my palms were sweating and my heart racing; it was the rational side of my schema that assured me that when you treated people this way, they backed off.

It would probably be best for both of us if he didn't reply.

Several minutes later, I returned from the blustery cold of outdoors, cheeks reddened with the dissipating sting of frigid temperatures, and knuckles that were splitting from the lack of gloves. A warm hum consoled my soul from the nicotine, a forced spring in my step for the oh-so-endearing "coming soon" story I would write about the Eaton Theatre Group's rendition of *A Christmas Carol* for next week's issue. When I sat in front of my computer, another email waited, the little red icon taunting me.

And like a crack addict, I jumped for the next hit.

TO:RFLANNIGAN@THEADVOCATE.COM
FROM:COOK4U78@HOTMAIL.COM
SUBJ:HEMINGWAY

Here's a quote for you.
"The best way to find out if you can trust somebody, is to trust them."
I know you're scared, but give me a chance, Hemingway.
Sean

63

My breaths were ragged as they raked out of me, the words entrenching themselves into a part of my brain that felt alien. Trust? How did you trust someone you didn't know? What was I to trust him with? The statement was too broad, too forward, to come from someone I barely knew. Trust was earned, not given. Especially for someone who had made a point of humiliating me, and then manipulating me when I made the mistake of showing him that he had my attention.

Held my attention…

My desk phone jangled, the ringtone intrusive in the otherwise quiet office, nothing but the photocopier and barely perceptible murmurs acting as background noise. Suspicion swept through me, my eyes narrowing at it, an awareness coursing through my veins as I moved to lift the phone from the receiver, pressing it against my ear.

"*Eaton Advocate*, Raquel speaking."

My thighs involuntarily clenched together at the dull thumping of hammers in the background and a bedlam of other sounds that belonged on a construction site filled my ears.

Silence seemed to stretch on between us for what felt like an eternity until I heard him draw in air through his lips, impatience forcing his hand.

"You were taking too long to reply, so I thought I'd take my shot."

Whether I wanted it or not, my ears were greedy for the sound of his voice, my lids dropping shut, absorbing the intoxicating baritone sound with his Bristol County pronunciation.

For some reason, at that exact moment I recalled my dad's words:

"Take your shot, kid, ya never know when you're gonna get another one."

"What do you want?" I said in a clipped tone, straightening my shoulders.

"Well, since we're cutting straight to the chase, I want you."

Time seemed to stop, his words bouncing in my mind in a room that suddenly went quiet, ricocheting off walls, bumping into stilled bodies, colliding into furniture, and landing at my feet. The proverbial ball in my court, demanding I take my shot, too.

My gaze dropped to the discarded newspaper, his arresting stare matching my own with a smug self-possession that pissed me off. I

64

flipped the paper over, getting his mug out of sight. I didn't need to feel the intensity of his imposing presence right now; let him grin at the surface of my desk.

"That's too bad." I countered, my voice unnaturally even despite the anxiety with a smattering of exhilaration that clawed at my insides.

His laugh was deeply masculine, a rich rumble in his chest. I felt the corners of my mouth lifting with an unconscious smile that upon realization of its appearance, I struggled to force it off, wanting to stow it away for someone who deserved it.

"I'm real busy, so if we're done here, I'm hanging up now."

"I'm sorry if I upset you last week, Hemingway. Penelope caught me off guard with the interview, and you weren't what I was expecting to come barreling through the door."

My heart galloped forward, the errant muscle having developed a mind of its own in the last eight days, to the point where I wasn't even sure I was myself anymore. "And what were you expecting?" Not that I cared, but for curiosity's sake, I wanted to know. I was a writer, after all.

"Someone a little more like Penelope."

I caught my features tightening in the reflection of my monitor—those iMac G3's are notorious for glare—that had darkened with its unemployment.

"Sorry to disappoint you."

"Disappoint?" He chuckled. "Hemingway, if I had known it was you coming through the door, I would have shaved."

Shave? But I liked his beard. I had found myself wondering what the scruff of it might feel like on the inside of my thighs after a long day at work, what the calluses of his hands that trailed alongside his mouth would do to me when they finally reached their destination.

"I really do have to go," I murmured, a dampness forming between my legs that was humiliating.

"Have dinner with me," he pressed, as if the inevitability of my departure was irrelevant.

"No." I winced as my mind unleashed another inward diatribe that was so vitriolic in nature, it was on par with that of my mother's tirades.

"Dinner," he repeated. "And if you still hate me afterward, I'll get outta your hair."

A challenge. "Somehow I don't think that's true," I mumbled, just clearly enough for him to make out my words.

He chuckled, the sound a drunken melody in my ears that made my head spin, "True. I would just find another way to keep you till dessert."

The natural ease of his jests spurred something inside of me, a pained longing that carried a kind of inexplicable sadness as it swam over me, soft waves kissing the surface, ebbing closer and closer to the shoreline.

"What do you know about me, Sean?"

My question was met with a pregnant pause. I heard a wisecrack that sounded muffled, yet somehow loud over the silence that filtered between us.

"Not much, but," he stalled, his contemplation deafening, "I know you felt that..." he was searching for the word. A word that I myself had struggled to come up with. "That shift in energy when I touched you."

My eyelids dropped.

Molten lava swept through my body, a heat so unbecoming that I felt myself oscillating between fear and exaltation of the newfound thrill that was on par with what it felt like when his skin had grazed mine. I knew what he was talking about, because I had relived it for hours. It had felt like fireworks going off...dozens of Roman candles eating up the darkness of the sky, robbing the stillness of the night with their crackle and flash. A sight so enthralling, you couldn't look away.

But then there were the sparklers, so innocuous, a child's delight, that wrote out a warning to me so brilliant and dazzling that it nearly robbed me of my vision.

Run.

My lids popped open, and I lengthened my spine for no one but my wounded confidence. "I didn't feel anything."

It wasn't a lie, because what I had felt wasn't anything–it was *everything*.

He chuckled, and for the briefest of moments, I thought he realized how pointless his efforts were with me. I was elusive, like a rogue butterfly who would never settle long enough to be strapped within the confines of his net.

"So, let me give you another demonstration."

My body swayed in my seat, my rib cage eating the edge of my desk. One hand tangled itself into my hair, my fingers pulling on the short strands, and another tightened breath dragged itself out of me.

"Sean, do me a favor." My hackles rose as I adjusted the sails on my boat, steering the helm toward another trajectory, one that was safe and familiar. "Stop wasting my time."

"I will when you stop wasting mine."

"What the fuck are you talking about? I'm not calling you, you're calling me." I hastily got to my feet, the phone clutched tightly in my fist, my knuckles straining, fingernails digging into the lacquered plastic.

Karen, like a gynecologist appointment you had been avoiding, chose that exact moment to stick her head into my cubicle, a smarmy smile teasing the edges of her mouth. Her hazel stare was reminiscent of that of a snake, searching for its next kill.

"Everything all right in here, Raquel?" Her saccharine tone told me everything I needed to know—she had the attention of the entire office.

Everyone always paid attention when they heard the sound of a rattlesnake approaching, you would be foolish to miss that vibration of warning.

"Everything's just peachy, Karen."

"You sure?" she asked, her paralyzing venom lacing the edges of her question, her gaze fixating on the phone like it was a new structure in my hand. "Did you want to forward that call to me? I do have a better head for the more difficult interviews than you do."

I shouldn't have taken the bait, but I did. I ran toward it headfirst, like a rogue soldier leading a charge into an open battlefield where I was outnumbered, out-weaponized, and fucked...royally, totally fucked. I was a mouse who thought she could outrun the snake because she was smaller and more nimble on her feet—forgetting that the snake had length and tactics to it.

"Get. Out," I snapped, my molars contacting, chest rising and falling. On the other end, Sean whistled, the sound absorbing into a laugh.

I was a joke. A running gag amongst everyone around me.

Karen touched her bottom lip with the tips of her fingers, her mouth popping open as she invoked her flare for drama. "Oh dear, I'm only trying to help."

"No, what you're trying to be is a—"

"It's not worth it, Raquel." Sean's voice was like a beacon in a darkened room, the easy-natured tone of his voice free of humor, a kind of safety net I hadn't realized I needed. My mouth clamped shut, lips rolling into a line so thin and painful, I thought they would bruise.

Karen's brow quirked. "I'm trying to be a...?"

I wanted to say, *A nosey, self-righteous pain in my ass.*

The office was generally quiet, but now I could hear the traffic of the town square two streets over...the hot dog vendor peddling to lunch seekers. Most importantly, I heard the sound of my heart pounding in my chest, demanding I trust Sean with it long enough for him to inevitably break it, etching another scar on it, to serve as a reminder of how close I danced on the edge of danger.

If Karen's brows crept any higher, they would be in her hairline. In a single exhale, the thoughts I had collected left me in a rush. "You're trying to be helpful, but I really do have it." The words wounded my ego as they left me. My smile felt weak on my lips, but it was there, and it was enough to melt Karen's frosty exterior.

Her jaw went slack and her hand dropped to her side, wrapping itself around her opposite wrist. My calm reaction surprised her as much as it did me.

Balance had been restored. The soundtrack of the office resumed, as if someone had hit the Play button again. Earl scolded the photocopier, Shirley started the coffeemaker, columnists brainstormed together.

Karen and I looked at each other in a provisional truce. She didn't give me the satisfaction of acknowledgement, instead turning on the wedge of her boot and slithering out of my cubicle in search of her next victim.

When I heard her voice several desks over, my knees gave out on me, body sinking into my seat. I could feel my pulse beat behind my eyelids, my insides swirling at the confrontation, at the words that no doubt would have left me had it not been for Sean.

The initial source of all my frustrations.

This had to end. I couldn't afford the burden of his presence in my life. It was a weakness, and I didn't need any more of that. I had that area of my life well covered.

"Don't call me again," I said, "Don't think of me, because I won't think of you."

"Somehow, I don't believe that," Sean drawled.

"What you felt was attraction, and it was one-sided," I loftily replied.

"I pegged you for a lot of things, Hemingway, but a liar wasn't one of them."

"Thank you for proving my point about not knowing me at all."

"What are you so afraid of?"

You. Everything about you. Aloud I said, "I'm not afraid of anything."

His laugh was bitter, a forced sound that didn't carry his warmth from earlier.

"Right, and what other bullshit do you like to fill that pretty little head of yours with?"

"I'm hanging up now." My hand shook as I clutched the receiver, but I didn't hang up.

"You actually can't handle the idea of someone wanting to get to know you."

"What you want, you can get from any other woman, but it won't be me."

"Do you honestly think I would put in this much effort for a lay, Raquel?"

My name on his mouth sent my insides tumbling, a stifled gasp escaping me. It sounded so beautiful and familiar on his tongue, like a languorous melody, that I wanted to hear him say it over and over again.

I swallowed before I mustered a reply. "I don't know what you would do to get laid," I said, the impending lie swirling around my palate as if it were an acerbic wine, "but I'm not interested in finding out. I meant what I said to you last week."

"What part?" His voice was tight.

"The closest you'll ever get to fucking me is in your dreams." The words were whispered so softly, I barely heard them.

But he did. A seductive chuckle reverberated from the other line of the phone.

"In that case, I'll see you in my dreams. Nighty-night, Hemingway." He hung up before I had the chance to do it first, taking my ego and dignity away with him.

CHAPTER NINE

Sean

THE REMAINDER of the workday dragged at a snail's pace. The job site was alive with last-minute fixes to the house, mulch being added to garden beds, additional trees being planted in the backyard. When I wasn't licking the wounds caused by Raquel's remarks, I spent my time puttying and sanding the hole she had left in the office drywall with the doorknob a week earlier. I was sure there was a metaphor somewhere in there—filling the void created by someone else.

When five o'clock came and the yard had emptied of workers, leaving nothing but the sound of Canadian geese flying south, Dougie stuck his ugly mug into the office, dirt up to his elbows, his fingernails stained by earth, toting an emptied lunchbox, and announced that he was coming over.

Behind him, Katrina sat on the bottom step of the stairs, resting her elbows on her knees, her hands cupped around her face. She sported a beguiling look, eyes fixed skyward, as if she hadn't mentioned something passively in Dougie's ear. Trina had the same deadly affliction the rest of my family did—they just couldn't mind their own business, even if their lives depended on it. She held her hands up in deference when my stare narrowed on hers before making herself scarce, feet beating it up the stairs. It didn't take a family session with Dr. Phil to know that the little shit had read my emails.

That was how four hours later, Dougie ended up sprawled out in the corner of my sectional, his feet up on the distressed coffee table next to a nearly empty box of pizza. While he concentrated on the video game in front of him, I recounted to him the interview a few weeks back, the article (which I was all too ready to hand over to him, but immediately regretted once his eyebrow hit his hairline and his smile grew slimy), the emails, and finally, the phone call.

When I had nothing else to add, I leaned back against the couch, resting my head against the leather upholstery in defeat.

"Well," he chuckled, pausing the game, stretching to reach for his beer on the coffee table, "You've got it bad for this broad."

I didn't miss the tinny smugness that laced his words as he tipped his beer bottle back, forest green eyes appraising me with mischief.

I scowled at him, my scathing stare making words unnecessary. *Thanks, Captain Obvious. I never would have drawn that astonishingly observant conclusion on my own.*

The statement hung between us. I managed to lift my shoulder in a shrug, peeling the damp and fraying label away from my own bottle. I had dated my fair share of women in thirty years. The last ten years alone had been a revolving door of problematic relationships, including one that had been a hell of a close call.

It wasn't that marriage wasn't on my radar so much as I hadn't really had the time to make that kind of emotional investment in anyone. I had spent the last ten years focused on keeping my family's financial needs met, and that didn't leave me with a whole lot of time to date seriously. I had my fun. I knew where to find a bed partner when I had a need for company that went beyond the grip of my own hand. The arrangement had worked for me, and it had worked for the women I slept with. There was never any confusion with what I was looking for, and they were amenable enough to agree to the terms. I wasn't big on the dinner and a movie thing, or walks along the Quequechan River Rail Trail, or spooning after the deed had been done.

Sex was transactional. We both came hungry, we both left satiated.

Raquel, though, she was like a tempest. She was the kind of phenomenon that meteorologists tracked for days; and just when you thought you had an understanding of its pattern, it changed course and uprooted every single tree across the state, turning everyone's lives upside down.

Thoughts of her invaded every spare orifice within my mind, like heavy rapids of water desperate to move and find a new home. A storm had brewed behind her eyes when I had touched her, and that had been all I needed to reassure myself that it hadn't been one-sided, that she felt it, too.

I was willing to do the dinner and move thing—hell, I *wanted* to do the dinner and movie thing. She wanted to walk along the Quequechan River Rail Trail? I'd fucking buy hiking shoes. I wanted to spoon this woman, imprint the scent of her in my sinus tract until I was drunk on vanilla, citrus, and tobacco.

But I had been out of the dating game for so long that I wasn't sure how to get from the bedding part to the heart-conquering component —and at the number of my missed hits with Raquel, I would be lucky if I managed to get the first three digits of her area code confirmed for me.

Dougie had always been better at the dating thing than me. Not because he was particularly better-looking than me—not with that busted nose, no offense—he just carried himself with a swaggering confidence, like he had a pair of brass balls between his legs. You couldn't replicate that shit. Women flocked to him, the normal kind— not the ones who appeared perfectly normal, only to...well, it doesn't matter now.

The point is, Dougie knew what he wanted and generally went after it. He never took no for an answer, and that was how he had wound up with Penelope, who was not only out of his league, but out of the orbit his galaxy revolved around.

Yet somehow, she had not only agreed, but was now seven months shy of birthing his child.

"Do *not* tell Penelope I told you," he had warned me through a mouthful of pizza an hour ago. "She'll kill me if she finds out I told you before she had a chance to tell Raquel."

"So, not just your fuck buddy, huh?" I had jested, slamming a closed fist into his bicep. He winced, but a bashful smile blossomed on his face. My best friend was happy, and there was no one else who deserved it more.

Twenty odd years ago, Dougie had taken me under his wing. When you leave one country for another, nothing can prepare you for what's about to unfold. At eight, I was still naive enough to believe my parents when they told me things would be easier in the great US of A. Dad had a job lined up already at a brickyard, Ma's sister got her an opportunity with the local Portuguese *padaria*—that's "bakery" in English—where her days would start at three in the morning, but she would be home by lunch toting loaves of freshly baked *pão* stuffed in clear bags for sandwiches.

My parents' optimism had me believing that I would be able to assimilate easily in our new home with zero struggle. Learning English would be a cakewalk, making friends even easier, and maybe if I was lucky, I would convince an American girl to grant me my first kiss before I headed into fourth grade.

And like most well laid plans, things did not go accordingly.

Dad's new boss jilted him pay that made it hard to keep the lights on. Mom never made it home for lunch, and when she did, she was sporting a deep wrinkle between her brows, her arms too stiff to move. My older sister Maria cried every single day over the homework she didn't understand, and I was failing to make any friends. People treated us like we were lepers; even the ones who had experienced our plight so many years before turned up their noses at us. They had struggled once, too, so in their minds, why should they help us? We weren't deserving of any kind of advantages that hadn't been offered to them.

Turns out, when you're an interloper starting life in a new place, people aren't always that hospitable—especially schoolyard kids from blue-collar neighborhoods. Those little assholes will find your biggest insecurity and run with it until you've got a therapy bill that's higher than the price of your first shit box car.

Inhibition is natural at some point in time for most people, but at that point in time, everyone at Oak Grove Elementary School had something that left them vulnerable to relentless teasing, or bullies that stalked them as they ambulated through tree-lined neighborhoods on their way home, only to wind up breathless once their worn sneakers hit their own property line, their heads cocked over their shoulders.

Every student had a weakness, only mine was not understanding them.

For weeks, I heard their voices, the mockery of their pitch filling my ears, but I was never the wiser. I masked the hurt that filtered within me from the acerbic venom of their tones and the cruelty in their sneers, all while convincing myself that they were trying to be friendly. It was when the school bully, Peter Filch—who was teetering that fine line between overweight and obesity—shoved me off the playground set that quick and lean eight-year-old Douglas Patterson had had enough.

He took the schoolyard bully out and was inaugurated as a hero to our classmates with one single, well-placed shove.

So it was only natural that we would grow up to be thick as thieves, getting into mischief, talking ourselves out of trouble. Dougie had been more like a brother to me than a friend over two decades. He knew me as well as my sisters and Ma did, maybe even more so.

And now I was going to take advantage of his almost one degree of separation to help me get what I wanted…

Raquel.

CHAPTER TEN

Sean

"SO," I said, making no real effort to be slick with Dougie. "What do you know about her?" I assessed him over my bottle of Harpoon IPA.

He didn't meet my stare, but I caught the quizzical quirk of his brow. "Raquel?" he asked, as though he needed any clarification.

I nodded, just to humor him.

In response, he cracked his neck, a bored expression settling on his face. "Not much, to be honest. We've met maybe three times over six months, and every time I see her, she looks like she's ready to claw my eyes out like a harpy."

"You think she's in love with Penelope?" Alarm pulled my brows together. If she did play for the other team, there was nothing I could do about it.

He scratched the space above his left brow, tilting his head in consideration. "Definitely not *in* love with her, but loves her in a sisterly kind of way." A ghost of something passed over his face, his lips thinning in a tight line while rubbing the sparse smattering of facial hair that littered his jaw line. "I think she's lonely, and I'm poaching the only thing she's got." His head lolled to the right, an attempt at a smile failing to lift the corners of his mouth. "Penelope told me she's had a pretty sad life. That might be the only redeeming part of her."

"What do you mean?" I ignored the sinking of my heart in an open body of water with no life raft in sight.

"Sorry, man." He held up both his hands in surrender, giving me a pointed look, as if I should have known better than to ask him to betray his future baby mama. "Not my story to share."

Translation: *If my baby-mama finds out I told you anything incriminating, she would have my balls wound tight around her little fist.*

God, that was weird to think about, Dougie having a kid. Dougie having a kid with *Penelope,* of all the damn people in the world. It dawned on me then that these moments between him and I were going to become rare commodities. My house would become a safe haven for him when they argued, or on Superbowl Sundays.

I didn't feel sad about it, like maybe I should have. If anything, the thought that kept slamming into me like a jackknifing semi was that for the first time in my life, I wanted it, too.

The girl. The kid.

"So, what are you going to do?" he pressed, pulling my attention back to the matter at hand.

My throat worked at the thought, my sarcasm coming out from within the metaphorical wooded forest where I'd left my brain and balls. "Eat some Papa John's, rub a few out, and fall asleep with my hand on my dick and *Die Hard* playing in the background once you decide to get out of my house."

"You invited me, asshole," he reminded me, throwing his head back with laughter. "Trust me, I would much rather be between Penelope's thighs right now than listening to you whine about a woman who won't give you the time of day."

"Correction, *Trina* invited you—but thanks for the reminder."

Dougie bent at the waist in a half bow while remaining seated, sweeping his arm across the space in front of him, "I aim to serve, sire."

"You practicing your bowing for when you break the news to Mommy and Daddy Dearest, Jeeves?"

It was clear that Penelope's parents weren't going to take too kindly to their prized trick pony being tainted by a blue-collared stallion with no pedigree, no college degree, and maybe five grand in accessible funds to his name.

"Don't remind me."

"Maybe they'll taxidermy your head and place it over their fire-place mantel."

"Hopefully next to their trophies and ribbons of achievement." Dougie beamed, as if that was better than winning the Powerball.

"Smug bastard." I said with a shake of my head, the laugh tight as it left me.

"Seriously, man," Dougie's said, his tone turning earnest, "What are you going to do about this Raquel thing?"

"Yeah, what are you going to do?" A familiar high-pitched voice chimed in from behind him.

Bemusement hit me as a startled Dougie propelled himself upward from his end of the sectional couch, eyes wide with unbridled alarm, as if the stories his mother had taunted us with about hostile Fomorians in our youth had finally come true.

"Jesus Christ," he bit out, scowling in my sister's direction. "Why are you slinking around?"

Trina blinked, something sly glinting in her eyes, a sideways smile tilting her mouth.

"I prefer Trina, but Jesus Christ has a nice ring to it."

Dougie fisted a hand through his hair, shooting her a look of daggers. His thick brows drew together, frustration etching into his rugged bone structure. After a few moments he let out a labored sigh, his face softening as the irritation ebbed away from him.

"Hey kid," he finally greeted, smoothing his clothes, as if he was looking to busy himself while he collected his bearings. In the end he simply settled back onto the couch, gaming controller in hand.

The youngest of my sisters beamed, skipping over to the couch. She launched herself next to Dougie with a dreamy sigh of youthful contentment that carried over The Used track coming from the game on the TV— clearly pleased with the reaction she had gotten out of him.

In the months since she moved in with me, Trina had been trying to scare me, but had been failing miserably. I was impervious to her cheap scare tactics, and she lacked the patience that was truly required to build up the intensity of a true attempt at freaking me out. Dougie didn't have any siblings, so mine spared him no mercy when he entered their territory.

He was a cheap kill.

"How's it going, big head? Long time no see." Trina placed a chaste kiss on his cheek that was pebbled with dark, unruly facial hair. All was forgiven in that moment, his concentration never breaking from the TV, the pads of this thumbs aggressively working an analog stick and an X button.

"Shit," Dougie huffed. I watched as he went for the touchdown, only to be intercepted. "Brady, you useless motherfucker." He tossed the controller to me with indifference, the handles damp with sweat, flopping against the back of the couch, "This game sucks."

I cringed inwardly, knowing we were both reliving the loss of the Pats. "You're just pissed that art is emulating real life." I knew it was a bad idea when he pulled out the copy of *Madden NFL '08* from his coat pocket.

"The Giants should have never fucking won. It was highway robbery, and you know it."

He wasn't wrong. It had been a painfully tight game, the three-point loss devastating.

"You're the one who rented this game." I reminded him, wiping the controller with the ends of my shirt, my lip lifting with revulsion. Amusement twisted his features, his anger gone as mischief glinted in his eyes. He settled his gaze on my shoddy attempt at cleaning the controller.

"I lubed it up for you," Dougie purred, shooting me a rogue smirk that elicited a groan of despair from Trina.

79

"Aw, baby," I jested, delighting in her embarrassment, tossing him a suggestive look, my teeth sinking into my lower lip, "you didn't have to do that."

"You're both actually disgusting," Trina whined from her spot on the opposite end of the sectional, her face set with discomfort.

Dougie howled with delight at his revenge, tossing a pillow in my sister's direction.

"No one invited you," he teased.

"Well, what else am I going to do with my night either than hang out with you two bozos?"

"Go out with your friends?" I suggested, hitting the Start button on the controller with one hand, downing my beer with the other.

"And miss out on this shitshow?" She laughed, with a swift shake of her head, "I don't think so."

"How do you deal with this one?" Dougie asked, his expression growing incredulous.

"Not like I got much of a choice," I muttered.

Six months ago, my unmarried kid sister found herself pregnant with a baby she didn't want. She might have considered keeping it, had the charming son of a bitch who knocked her up not gone ghost as soon as word was out about her predicament. So, she made a choice to terminate the pregnancy, and my other sisters and I supported her decision.

Except when your mother was still living under this naive pretense that she was going to be canonized, well, this was a mar on her life's greatest work that just simply wouldn't do, and Trina got the boot.

Let me preface by saying that my Ma isn't a bad woman—and I know the sentiment is wasted when you have to start with that, but she really isn't—she's just religious, as pious as a fucking nun, and that really skews her ability to see a situation clearly over the holy water and the stench of incense. It was one thing for Trina to wind up pregnant; it was an entirely different issue to terminate her pregnancy. It was too much for Ma, her moral complex, and her baby Jesus.

That's how Trina wound up living here, with me.

She pulled the box of pizza from the coffee table, settling it on her lap. When she lifted the lid, a strangled sigh left her throat.

"Why do you guys always put onions on your pizza? It gives you the worst breath." She flicked a rogue piece of onion to the corner of the pizza box, ripping its brethren off with the finesse of an eight-year-old.

"Awesome. Free birth control." I chuckled just as I made the touch-down Dougie had failed to achieve. The digital crowd erupted into cheers.

I shot a grin in Dougie's direction. He congratulated me with an unceremonious middle finger before returning his undivided attention to my sister. "I can confirm that onions only carry an eleven percent effectiveness rate when used with a consensual partner."

A laugh erupted out of me, a shit-eating grin taking up half of my best friend's face at his well-timed joke.

"'Gratulations, by the way," she said through a mouthful of pizza, nodding at him. "'Bout 'da baby."

The smile slid from his face, a small blaze igniting in his eyes as he glared at me. "I said don't say anything, asshole."

"I didn't, you clown," I replied. "She hears everything."

"It's true, I do," Trina agreed as she wiped her hands free of the grease that ran down her palm, balling the tissue in her hand. Her gaze sprang back over to me. "Which is why I want to hear about your incredible plan to pursue Raquel."

I let out a tight breath I hadn't been totally aware I was holding, falling against the headrest of the sectional. "I don't have one," I admitted.

Sometime between Dougie's arrival and Trina's appearance, I had decided it was a long shot to even bother pursuing Raquel, and there was probably a good likelihood that I was wasting my time. I had fuck buddies who required little maintenance; I saw no point in trying to acquire a new one who had about as much interest in fucking me as she did in contracting a venereal disease. It seemed hopeless, and it didn't matter to me that I felt a manic energy that I suspected would consume both of us if given the chance, or that my heart beat a little faster when the pitch of her unimpressed voice hit my ears, or that my balls literally kicked at the idea of touching her and having that touch reciprocated.

It was infatuation at best...the kind you needed to get out of your system by replacing the source of your discomfort with something else.

It wasn't exactly sexy living with your kid sister, and to Trina's point, she heard everything, so she didn't require the soundtrack of my steady rotation of women. What I was feeling right now toward Raquel was six months of pent-up energy that would be consoled when my current consistent partner was no longer my five right digits stroking my own dick.

If I knew my mother like I thought I did, she would invite Trina back home sometime after Christmas, when Livy would start classes at New England College and leave the house vacant. Then I would be free to take care of business properly.

"Ten years of being an on-and-off bachelor and you don't have a plan?" My sister tsk-tsked, her lips pinching together, nose crinkling.

"I've never *needed* a plan," I stressed, threading my fingers through my hair, still damp from my shower. "And I'm not having this conversation with you."

Trina waved her hand in front of her face, as if the small detail of her being my younger sibling carried about as much weight as a fly annoying her. "I am the closest thing you have to a woman's perspective, unless you want to ask Penelope."

"I think that would be a better idea," I grumbled.

"Should I call her?" Dougie chimed in, retrieving his discarded phone from the couch cushion.

"Yes," Trina said, giving him a perfunctory nod. "Maybe we should leave this diagnosis to the professionals."

"The only diagnosis required here is how you're going to cure yourself of your inability to not eavesdrop."

"I'm sorry, but the condition is terminal." She gave me a solemn look, her brows bending inward as if she had just delivered me bad news. Taking Dougie's lead, I threw a pillow in her direction that she evaded with a quick dodge of her head, humming at me with triumph, a wicked cackle leaving her that put me on edge.

Dougie chose that moment to clear his throat, drawing our attention to him. "So..." His voice was barely audible over the din of the TV

He took a long inhale through his nose that sounded like a struggle through his deviated septum.

Trina and I glanced at him, the laughter fading between us. Something serious tightened the fine lines of his features. I watched as he dug in his pockets, pulling out the contents. Loose coins rolled across the room, his car keys landed on the coffee table, followed by his wallet and a gas receipt from God knows when. Finally, a tiny, yellow Post-It note that had been folded twice fell to the floor. Exhaling another held breath, he bent at the waist, picking it up off the floor, his fingers pinched around it as if the thing would detonate any minute. "Penelope asked me to give you this."

For about twelve seconds, I felt like I was in high school again, receiving notes from a middleman. He held out his hand to me, a look of worry flashing across his face ever so briefly before he steadied himself. "She told me to tell you please don't make her regret this."

When I didn't make any immediate move to retrieve the Post-It, my heartbeat filling my ears, feeling my pulse in the soles of my feet—Trina lunged for it, snatching it in her hands before her feet beat across the other side of the room.

She unfolded the palm-sized piece of paper. "Is this *her* number?" she wheezed, her excitement palpable.

That launched me upward faster than a deploying rocket. Rounding the coffee table, I was at my sister's side in six seconds flat. "Have you not done enough snooping for one day?" I growled, towering over her, pulling the Post-It note free. "Give me that."

"Are you going to call her?" she pressed, standing on the tips of her toes to try to steal another glance at the writing on the Post-It, as if there was some subliminal message hidden within the ten digits.

"Go to bed," I barked, giving her a gentle shove out of the living room. She resisted, feigning insult—until I got her into a headlock, her head pressed beneath my pecs, the shadow of my fist curled above her head descending toward her. That was all she needed as incentive. Her hands pushed upward on my bicep to unhook herself. Her pink hair stood in several different directions. She blew a lock out of her face, holding her hands up in surrender, taking several steps backward.

"You guys are so boring," she warbled, fleeing the room, her footsteps fading as she disappeared down the hallway toward her room. When her bedroom door clicked shut, and the crooning of Patrick Stump resumed from her speaker, I spun on my heel to face Dougie, who now stood, collecting our empties and used plates.

"Why?" I breathed, holding up the piece of paper. Penelope had pretty handwriting, but it was clear she had contemplated the gravity of her decision with every stroke of her pen—each line practically broke through the thin paper.

Dougie rubbed the bridge of his nose, tossing me an equivocal look. "Guess Penelope doesn't dislike you as much as you dislike her."

I didn't miss the jab. It wasn't that I didn't like Penelope, she was just…okay, I hadn't exactly been nice to Marcia Brady's incarnate, who was I kidding? I had chastised her for months, and she just smiled and bore it. She never had rich girl airs about her, she never intentionally got on my bad side (even when she uttered words like "Caesarstone"), and she was the estrogen Trina had needed to level with her.

Sighing, I stuffed my hands into the pockets of my sweatpants, passing Dougie a feigned downtrodden look. "I don't not like her," I said, looking at him seriously.

He chortled, rounding the sectional with the plates in one hand and the empties tucked against his chest with his other arm.

"Yeah, all right."

I followed him into my kitchen, watching as he moved around my space like he had done a hundred other times before. After tossing the empties into a recycling bin and the dishes in the dishwasher, he breezed by me, heading toward the front door.

I followed after him. "I mean it," I pressed, watching as he stuffed his feet into his Nikes, then pulled his denim jacket off the hook of the coat tree, slinking it over his hoodie. "She's not bad."

"You're only saying that because she gave you an olive branch in the form of Raquel's phone number."

So? Semantics.

My mouth popped open, preparing to speak, but he cut me off, boredom filtering in his eyes. "O'Malley's tomorrow," he announced, changing the subject, no longer interested in hearing what other pretend make-good I would offer him or Penelope.

84

"In Boston?" I grimaced, knowing exactly what shithole he was referring to. That bar was a dingy local watering hole that drew in the Irish expats in droves.

"We're going to tell Raquel about the pregnancy. Better to do it on her and Penelope's turf. Do me a favor and play stupid," he said, adjusting his jacket in the floor-length mirror by my front door. "Hell, maybe you could do me a solid and prime her tonight. It'll make it easier if she doesn't hate you and me at the same time." The frigid night air swept through the house when he opened the door, the sentinel tree in the door yard rustling, a deep melancholic groan coursing from its branches. I told myself it was singing a prayer for mercy to whatever god was listening on my behalf.

"One more thing," Dougie added, looking at me over his shoulder, the caterpillars he called eyebrows furrowing together. "Do not fuck this up. I don't want to deal with the aftershock of the Harpy's rage, and Penelope is hormonal enough without needing to emotionally detach from her best friend, too."

Roger that.

I saluted him as his feet hit the porch stairs, watching as he stomped toward his black F-150 with tinted windows that was parked behind my Jeep.

Closing the door behind him, I turned off the porch lights when I saw his headlights bounce off the foyer walls from the sidelight windows. The Post-It note felt heavy in my fingers as I moved down the hallway of the single-story Cape Cod, yet in spite of its weight— which felt on par with a small brick— my insides were light as air, swirling with childlike glee at the unexpected opportunity.

Fall Out Boy caroled out another song at an offensive level as I passed my sister's bedroom, the wood floors creaking beneath my feet. As the cymbal of drum solos increased in tempo, I took my opportunity and made a run for the door. I had to take advantage of her distraction before she realized that Dougie was gone and her ears perked up like she was fucking Nancy Drew. It was a little asinine to feel compelled to sneak around my own house like a teenager trying to tiptoe back inside before his parents noticed he'd been gone—but I couldn't take any chances with Big Mouth in the room next door.

She wasn't above using news about me as a means of getting back in our Ma's good graces, and I didn't need Ma planning out our entire wedding before Raquel even agreed to a date.

All in good time, Maria Conceição.

The treble of the song died down just as my bedroom door clicked closed with a whisper. Using what little moonlight poured in from the slit of my blackout curtains, I shuffled my way over to the nightstand and switched the bedside lamp on, illuminating the room. My king-sized bed ate up a majority of the space, leaving enough room for only two custom nightstands I had personally crafted to be narrow enough to fit, and a dresser three feet away from the bed that held a thirty-two-inch flat screen TV with a mirror partially visible behind it. My bed was draped in a plush dark feather duvet with stark white bed sheets underneath that made the room feel fresh. Throwing myself on the mattress, I looked up at the popcorn ceiling above me, trying to collect my thoughts.

I couldn't afford to fuck this up—I'd heard the veiled threat in Dougie's warning at Penelope's behest. I'd have *one* shot.

Opening my flip phone, my finger hovered over the phone icon until a thought occurred to me. If I didn't want Raquel to perceive me as a threat, I needed to create the space she wanted, and give her the option to reply at her own pace, at her own volition.

Pressing the small envelope icon that indicated text messages, I opened a new draft, punched in her number, and then watched as the pads of my thumbs concocted different introductions. I invested ten minutes considering the right way to do this, which was ten minutes too long, quite frankly—but I was admittedly nervous about shitting the bed on this one.

Hey, how's it going? was too predictable.

Hi Raquel, it's Sean felt too ordinary.

And then it hit me like a freight train. A one-word message that would tell her everything and nothing at all.

It was enough, so I hit Send.

CHAPTER ELEVEN

Raquel

THE FIRST THOUGHT I had when I woke up that evening was that I was going to kill whoever was calling me right now.

The vibration coupled by the shrill ringing of my cellphone rocking against a solid surface sent my hackles on edge. My teeth ground together, a sharp pain shooting through my jaw muscles that momentarily squeezed in protest before releasing, my stress making its way to my temple.

I felt around blindly for the damn thing, refusing to open my eyes in fear that the small lamp on my nightstand would rob me of my vision. For the briefest of moments, I came in contact with the edge of the phone, its vibration sending a current through my arm.

Sleep was something that always evaded me this time of year for fairly obvious reasons, so I didn't complain that it came to me in shorts spurts of reprieve. I hadn't deserved the right to complain. It was my penance for living while my sister didn't.

But that didn't mean I took kindly to being interrupted by exterior forces.

Reaching my outstretched hand toward the sound, the muscle in my shoulder strained. With my eyes still squeezed shut, I made one final attempt at retrieving the phone without having to look for it, knowing it would be hours before I found sleep again once I opened them. My fingers brushed the its seam.

Just a few inches more.

With one more fortified movement, I put my all into getting the phone...and then I knocked the fucking thing to the floor. The plastic piece of shit's drop was dampened by the area rug that occupied half the room.

I wish it had broken, then at least the ringing would cease from existence and I could resume attempting to sleep again. Of course, as luck would have it, that wasn't the case, and the thing sang another high-pitched, penetrating song that saw me conceding defeat.

With my eyes open now and my blood pressure steadily rising, I reached for the phone that continued to hum a jovial reminder that someone was still trying to get my attention with half of my body still on the bed.

Lifting it to my line of vision, my frustration simmered when I read the caller ID, Penelope's name tempering the thorns of my anger.

"Hey," I greeted, the sleep heavier in my voice than even I expected, my body plunging backward until my head settled against the pillow.

"Were you already asleep?" Penelope questioned. I didn't miss the concern in her lilt, but I paid it no mind. If I gave her any indication that something was amiss in my li'l ol' head, she would end up at my apartment door toting a bottle of expensive red wine with a name I couldn't pronounce and sporting loungewear that consisted of harem pants and an over-washed Metallica hoodie, plus a raised eyebrow.

I didn't need maternal Penelope tonight, I just needed to go back to bed and be alone.

"Just a little catnap," I assured to pacify her while tucking the phone between the crook of my neck and my shoulder. I absently picked up my threadbare copy of *Valley of the Dolls*. It had been my sister's favorite book, and I always read it this time of year in memory of her.

My fingers traced all the places my sister had dog-eared the pages. I always hated that she had done that. She retorted that meant the books were well loved. I jested that she was a monster.

In the end, only one of us had been a monster, and it had never been her.

My sister and the fictional Jennifer North shared an archetype—being too giving, too kind, and in the end, too fixated on doing whatever they could to make the pain go away.

"What's up?"

Penelope was painfully reticent, despite her thoughts feeling as loud as Batty Betty's rerun of *American Idol* in the apartment upstairs.

Penelope didn't have to tell me she was worried; I could practically see her quirking brow and pinched lips, despite the seven miles and the stretch of the I-93 between us.

Finally, she cleared her throat, lifting the air of restraint with it. "O'Malley's tomorrow?"

"Sure." A yawn ripped through me.

"You okay?" she pressed, her reserve lasting all of thirty seconds—an impressive feat for someone whose favorite pastime for the past decade had been worrying about me, it seemed. "You sound off."

"I was asleep," I reminded her.

That silence returned, the one that was full of all the things she wanted to say—but wouldn't. One of my eyebrows quirked upward with suspicion, but I thought better of indulging her right now. I was tired, and she was needlessly worrying, because in typical Penelope fashion, that was just what she did.

"If you need me, you'll call, right?"

"Always."

"Okay." I heard the tight sigh escape her, the soft tuck of her golden hair behind her ear. "'Cause if you did, you know I'd be there in a heartbeat."

A smile tilted the corners of my mouth, relief I hadn't realized I needed seeping into my chest and releasing the shackles that weighed down my heart.

"I know you would."

"Raquel," she began, her voice trailing off like she wanted to say something else to me. For some reason, my body sat upright, the transient reprieve I felt only seconds ago in a sort of time suspension, the shackles dangling.

"Try to stop drinking coffee after five, you know it messes with you," she said.

The heaviness left my chest, my lungs drawing in a full breath, a laugh escaping me. "I'm starting to think you're trying to avoid riding Alaska dick in your shower right now."

Naturally, she feigned offense, a scoff on par with her pearl-clutching mother leaving her before it was replaced by an easy-natured giggle.

"Night, Kell."

"Night, Pen."

I shook my head as I ended the call, pressing my back against the black wrought iron of my headboard. I lived in a terra cotta redbrick five-story building that abutted a nearby public housing project two blocks over in Dorchester. The structure itself had been built in 1890, its age reflective on the exterior with its neoclassical structure, sash windows, various gable roofs and finial point that sat like a misplaced crown on the roof.

The interior was another story—it lacked the charm the exterior of the building possessed, and was reminiscent of an eighties sitcom. My unit was no more than four hundred square feet and consisted of all of three feet of green Formica countertops glued onto cheap yellow cabinets. My unit had the world's smallest oven and an exhausted-looking yellow fridge that was the newest appliance in this room with its 1982 purchase date (I was speculating on that salient detail, of course—it could be 1977 but a lady never shares her age.)

Like my desk at *The Advocate*, I didn't keep personal effects in my apartment, either—save for a lone framed photo of Holly Jane when she was five sporting a sundress, her hair parted into pigtails. It was my only remaining photo of her, my most prized possession. It sat proudly displayed on an antique mahogany wood secretary that was laden with gold curlicue that Penelope had given me for my twenty-fifth birthday.

I was confident that the desk cost more than any other material item I owned. It was also the last time I had allowed myself the opportunity to cry. To the average person, it might have just been a desk. To me, it was the first time someone had bought something with me exclusively in mind. Of course, she had given me plenty of things before, but the sentiment behind the desk hadn't been wasted on me.

She believed in me without apology, and yet, I had done nothing but routinely fail her.

The weight of my failure sat deep inside of the secretary drawer alongside a slew of rejection letters that would never see the light of day again.

The revered desk was nestled close to the bathroom door. The bathroom was furnished with black-and-white checkered linoleum that was lifting in the corners, an antiquated clawfoot tub that sat flush beneath the only other window in the apartment, and a pedestal sink that was littered with a tiny makeup bag, a toothbrush and a nearly empty tube of toothpaste.

My eyes bounced around the room, taking in the barrenness that was my space. An oversized, God-ugly Aztec floor rug made of red and various shades of blue fibers covered the weathered honey-oak parquet flooring that I disliked almost as much as the rug itself. In my living room/bedroom/whatever-fuckin-else main room, I had a single dark brown leather loveseat that I inherited from the apartment Penelope and I shared when we moved off campus sophomore year. That one piece of furniture served triple duty: my eating place, reading nook, and the place were I propped up my feet up when I remembered my college therapist's suggestion that I leave my bed for sleep and…well, sex.

The latter rarely, if ever, occurred. I didn't like people in my space. The idea of someone leafing through my things while I was in the bathroom or appraising me based on the location of my apartment or the mismatched furniture it contained, filled me with anxiety.

Which is perhaps what made the fact that I had done nothing but

dream about Sean Tavares for last couple of damn weeks so unbeliev-
ably humiliating. Sometimes, he would just sit all brooding on the love
seat, an ankle hooked over his knee, head tilted to the left, watching
me with his disarming dark stare until one of his infamous cavalier
smiles made their appearance. Other times, he emerged from the bathroom, the door swinging open, the steam from the shower shrouding
his features as it rushed out from the room behind him, wearing a
towel wrapped around his waist, held together by his clamped fist
because the material ran short. Droplets of water ran in a rivulet down
the plane of chest, settling into the valleys of his abs.

Abs I was merely speculating he had.

I blamed Penelope for the urgency and persistence of these...God, I
didn't want to call them fantasies. That word was so clandestine and
made me feel like I was doing wrong. It was her fault to begin with.

Machination. That's what it was. A machination formed at Penelope's behest.

Penelope, in all of her infinite well-meaning wisdom, had planted
that stupid seed of a fantasy in my mind that had sprouted into a
deep-rooted, unyielding fucking tree—and it would take a damn axe
to get it down a la Jack Torrance style in *The Shining*.

"Broaden your horizons. You liked looking at Sean."

No fucking shit. I had enjoyed his visage and lean frame with
biceps that strained against that suit jacket, so much so that I couldn't
get the son of a bitch out of my head even when I was entirely
conscious.

A dissonance erupted within me every time I thought of him, and
admittedly—to my horror—I thought of him a lot, and I liked it.

This was teetering against that dangerous line of what I considered
juvenile: an elementary school crush with the childishly scrawled
initials "R+S" encircled inside a poorly drawn heart.

Try as I may to erase the shit out of that heart and draw a jagged
fissure through its center, his stupid bedroom eyes and intoxicating
smile appeared on the back of my eyelids when I didn't want them to.
My mind was discriminatory for the number of times it would allow
itself to focus on Sean, wondering what was he doing, what did he
think about certain things, or if there was any substance inside of that

arrogant, mind of his that made him even marginally interesting? Or was he as I imagined…all muscle and cock and not a whole lot of anything else?

It felt as if the harder I fought to remove his hold on my thoughts, my brain fought back and my mind did the unthinkable: It fantasized about whether the calluses of his hands would feel as good exploring my body the way they did when my eyes drifted shut and thoughts of his lean body moving in tandem with mine filled my mind. *(Kill me, please. Someone. Just. Kill. Me.)*

The thought alone was enough to send a current of electricity that started at my toes and hit my core, inducing my knees to clamp together. My pulse quickened in my neck, breath straining in my chest as another unbidden thought slammed into me.

His greedy mouth was working against my own, demanding and taking until there was nothing left.

Stupid. I was being stupid. It was all wistful thinking, the kind that would never go anywhere, yet my roaming mind went everywhere.

This was a personal hell, my devil being six feet, two inches and two hundred pounds of rippling muscles and sex appeal.

Huffing out a languid sigh, I reached for the lamp and killed the light. The room immediately darkened with nothing but muted moonlight that teased the gossamer curtains in my room and cast subtle shadows across my body. Peeling away the top sheet, I slithered in, the cool if slightly scratchy polyester a welcome reprieve against my skin.

My lids dropped shut, and I found myself concentrating on my breathing as I did every night. Cool air filtered through my nasal cavities, my lips parted to expel the hot air out in exchange. I focused on the steady rise and fall of my chest, my lips pursing together, willing sleep to come.

Yet, it didn't.

Fuck.

I tossed to the right, working my face into the pillow. When that didn't work, I shifted to the left, my fists beating into the filling of my pillow to create clearance for the crook of my neck. Then I found myself on my back, looking at the popcorn ceiling, my eyes opened in defeat, an exasperated and pained sigh leaving me.

This was the worst part about trying to sleep at this time of year. Every thought that Sean didn't consume, my guilt from the past snatched up, ready to chase off any morsel of normality I might have felt for the briefest of moments.

Pulling the duvet over my head, I buried my face into my pillow. My inhalations felt strangled, the air hot as it filtered through my sinuses, holding a hint of lemon fresh-scented laundry detergent. My lungs expanded as I let out a muffled scream of suppressed anger and everything else that I had been toting around the last couple of weeks, the sound absorbed by the fibers of my bed linen. I screamed until my chest ached, and the unshed tears that I refused to let fall burned the back of my lids. Only when my lungs were emptied and I had nothing left to give did I stop.

When my throat ached from the frisson of rage that had left me in a state of momentary catharsis, I shifted onto my back once more, staring up at the ceiling, counting out each pebble in the popcorn pattern like sheep, waiting with bated breath for sleep to return—but even if it didn't, I felt lighter with the emotional release that had been absorbed by polyester and cotton.

Then my phone buzzed.

I reached for it out of instinct, flipping it open. My messages icon flashed. Penelope was so damn paranoid, she probably wanted to confirm I had stopped drinking coffee.

Opening the application, my heart hit the first floor of my building at the single-word text message from a number I didn't recognize.

One word.

That was all it took to speed up my heart rate, pinch together my shoulders, and tighten my core. The release I had obtained only moments earlier from my screaming session dissipated like a blown-out candle, irritation replacing it once more.

I read the text seven times, closed my phone, and placed it face down next to me, gingerly, as if it was a hand grenade and a sudden movement would cause it to detonate.

How had he gotten my number?

Hemingway.

That stupid nickname.

Was I angry at his persistence, or enthralled by his tenacity?

I fought to hold onto my indignation while reaching for the phone I'd just put down. My fingers moved furiously across the smooth edges of the keypad, returning his single-word text message with one of my own.

Asshole.

I was going to fucking *kill* Penelope. I opened up a new message and was thumbing out a haughty text to her when another appeared from the bane of my existence:

That's the best you can come up with?

My cheeks flushed as the sound of his laugh filled my mind. I sent off my disdainful message to Penelope before returning to Sean's text. My heart rate quickened, my thumbs working across the QWERTY keypad.

You're right. Dickhead sounds better.

Petty should have been my middle name. Penelope's response dinged off at the same time his came in. I read hers first.

Yes, I gave him your number. I'm not sorry about it. I meant what I said: broaden your horizons. I *know* what you're going to do with that Chuckle-head otherwise.

I mentally took back all the nice things I'd ever said about Penelope. She was a meddling pain in the ass right now, and I didn't give a shit what she thought about my yearly bed partner.

You had no right to do that!

Yes, I did. It's in the fine print of the best friend contract you signed September 1998.

As I noodled on my response to Penelope, I moved back to Sean's text, which sent my brow upward as I read his rebuttal:

You disappoint me, Hemingway.

I huffed, a strangled laugh crawling out from the back of my throat as an idea bloomed inside of me. I shot back another sarcastic remark, one that actually carried a modicum of both credence and humor:

You're not the first to be disappointed by me, Slim.

A minute passed by, as though he was considering the usage of the word at the end of the message, then an incoming message induced a small buzz from my phone:

Slim?

I couldn't contain the smarmy smile that tilted my mouth while my fingers typed out my next reply:

Yes. Slim. I've decided that's your nickname.

His response came within seconds:

Why?

My heart was a thunderous snare drum inside me, a sliver of a tremble coursing through me as I prepared to send out a response I wasn't totally convinced I believed:

Because you have a slim chance of sleeping with me.

The seconds stretched into minutes, my heartbeat tapering off into a normal rhythm. I closed the phone, wiping the sweat from my clammy palms on my duvet. I congratulated myself with a triumphant head nod, deciding that my response had been enough to set him straight.

Just like I wanted. Right?

My stomach roiled as the disappointment settled that he hadn't bothered to reply after that. Of course he wouldn't. Who would? I had done nothing but shoot him down at every attempt he had made. I would have conceded defeat, too. I didn't have the right to be dismayed by his attempts that I had thwarted.

I cannot believe you gave him my number.

Get over it, Raquel. Fuck him.

A growl burned my throat, her words boring into my mind. I hated her. I hated when she conspired to get me to do what she wanted. The screen of my phone flickered, producing a huff out of me, and my eyes watched as the backlight dimmed and then returned to a state of normality. I punched back another remark:

I'm not fucking him.

Not fucking who?

My teeth ground together as I went to type my response: *Sean!*

It made me crazy when she played coy. It was her least attractive feature. That wide blue-eyed stare didn't have the same effect through texting as it did when she was directly in front of me.

She was taking too long to reply and that just made me more incorrigible. I squeezed the phone in my fist as I looked up at the ceiling. I should have never gone to that house or done that interview. The fire department would have been happy to have their cover story, and I wouldn't be engaged in a near argument with my best friend over the violation of my trust and trying to convince a man I wanted to fuck into believing that I didn't want to fuck him.

Fuck. Had I actually thought that? No. No. No. My mind buzzed with the realization as another text message from Penelope came in.

My brows crashed downward as I read it.

Never say never. I can dream, right?

What. The. Fuck.

I shrieked in horror, kicking the bedsheets away, my heart pumping wildly in my chest. I had just done the fucking unthinkable.

My eyes lifted to the contact details, the unfamiliar 508 number staring back at me.

That wasn't Penelope's number, that was Sean's.

And I'd just said that I wasn't fucking him.

Humiliation slammed into me, my cheeks burning. How had I done that? I tried to go back to the main window of the messaging app, but the thing glitched, Sean's message staring back at me. My thumb pressed so hard on the back button of the phone that the skin on it ached. It was useless. Either the phone was frozen, or that drop had done more damage to it then I had realized.

Another message came in:

That wasn't meant for me, was it?

Well, that was a no-brainer.

No.

I moved to put the phone back onto my nightstand when another message palpitated through. I was shocked by how quick my fingers fumbled to open the phone and read his response.

Up until this point, I had survived life even when the odds had been stacked against me, but this left me certain that my cause of my impending death would be mortification.

Have you thought about it?

Heat flushed my cheeks, my jaw working at his wanton lack of care. I understood what *it* meant perfectly fine.

Absolutely not.

I don't think I've ever met anyone who has worked so hard to convince themselves that they weren't interested in sleeping with me before.

My heart set off on another drum solo, the weight of his text heavy in my heart.

Trust me, no convincing necessary.

The lies were coming to me more easily with each salacious text I composed. I hit the back button of the phone. God finally opened the sky for me, the screen skipped back, and I thumbed on Penelope's message, punching in a frantic reply to her. The darkened display sketched with each push of the keypad, my message to her revealing itself to me in short spurts.

He asked me if I thought about sleeping with him! SOS! I am going to kill you!

Have you?

I stared at the screen. *That* was all she could offer me?

Raquel? the message prompted.

I would return to lambasting her in a minute; first I needed to answer her question before she blew up my phone. My screen sputtered again. My fingers quaked as I worked out a revelation that had only just come to me definitively, and I wasn't entirely sure I wanted to admit.

Yes. Maybe. I don't know.

Well, that's a start. I can work with that. Sounds like you just need a little inspiration.

If there was a hell, I was dead smack in the middle of it, patiently waiting for a fiery chasm to split the ground in two and swallow me whole.

I had done it again.

I could feel my cheeks growing ruddy, a frisson hot enough to sweep down from the crook of my neck, burning the flesh right down to my core as another unwelcome thought infiltrated my mind, scrambling my sensibilities like eggs in a skillet. I couldn't move; my arm was suspended out in front of me, clutching the phone as if doing so would prevent it from bursting into flames at any moment, my jaw hanging open at what had just occurred.

There would be no coming back from this. I was immobilized by the horror of my actions and the reality that Sean now knew his 'feelings' (if that's what they can be called) were not only one-sided...

...they were reciprocated.

The phone vibrating elicited a gasp of surprise from me, my brain coming to after being momentarily whisked away from my rightful place in hell.

Night, Hemingway. See you in dreamland.

I was fucked. So utterly fucked.

CHAPTER TWELVE

Raquel

"I'M NOT GIVING you three hundred dollars." The idling Camry that rattled my body almost tricked me into believing that it wasn't me who was shaking as I clutched the phone in my hand, my knuckles straining. "I don't have it."

"Bullshit," my mother hissed. "Ask your little friend."

I slouched in my seat. "I am not asking Penelope for money to give to you, of all people."

"Raquel, please," she pleaded, the tone of her voice softening, as if that was supposed to alter my stance. "I'm short on rent money. I need it."

That was a fucking laugh, and we both knew it. "We both know you don't want that three hundred dollars for your rent. Half of Southie knows you're fucking your landlord and live there for free."

My heart quickened its pace, taking off in my chest as I straightened in my seat, my free hand draped in my lap, fingers sinking into my thighs to bolster myself.

The sound that came out of my mother's mouth was an animalistic and indignant war cry, followed by an insult. "You insufferable fucking little bitch."

Insufferable? A big word for my no-brains mother.

I considered that I could have kept that remark to myself, but I was tired of being fed the same bullshit sob story every month. I gave her enough money as it was; I wasn't giving her any more until the beginning of next month.

Besides, the truth hurt.

"I should have aborted you,"

"Probably," I offered noncommittally. I smoothed my hands against the stretch of the steering wheel until the shaking subsided and the trance of my fingers grazing the cool leather coaxed me into a sort of calm.

"I mean it. I wish you were never born, Raquel."

All I could manage was a snort as the thought percolated in my mind. The line wasn't particularly original, but it was one she slung at me every couple of months when she deemed I was being unreasonable.

I was sure that the exchange between Pauline—as I tended to think of my mother—and I might have given Freud himself a hard-on, but she was about as interested in therapy as she was in financially supporting herself through legal means.

"Shoulda kept your legs closed then, Pauline."

"You are an ungrateful little shit."

What was I supposed to be grateful for, exactly? Enough mommy issues to last all my days? An inferiority complex? My life?

Right. Gratitude.

"I almost did go through with aborting you, y'know," she hissed viciously, "Your good-for-nothing father wouldn't let me."

"Better luck next time."

My mother went off on another tangent that I only half listened to. If standing tall and mighty on her soapbox of superiority was something that made her feel marginally better about herself, who was I to stop her?

Ensconcing myself in the driver's seat, I moved the phone away from the shell of my ear to give my eardrum a break from the grating, high-pitched shrieking my mother was unleashing. I was convinced that even the pedestrians with whom I made eye contact as they walked past my car could hear Pauline's venomous meltdown that would have earned her an Oscar if this had been a Hollywood movie.

My free hand pinched the bridge of my nose while I drew in a tight breath.

She was giving me a fucking headache.

After twenty-eight years of this, I was nearly entirely immune to the effects of her vitriolic nature. It was as consistent as the weather, and no one balked when it rained. My mother only stopped to collect her next breath the same way the wind paused before unleashing another strong gust. I could hear the rapidness in her heavy breathing, her nicotine-filled lungs straining to keep up. She was noiseless, but her silent appraisal was deafening, as though waiting to see if her harangue had worn me down into submission.

It hadn't.

I couldn't give her what I didn't have, and there was no fucking universe in which I would ask Penelope for shit for her benefit.

"Bye, Ma."

As I moved to close the phone, I caught the tail end of her final enraged barb, "—shoulda been you in that fucking car!" I clamped the phone shut in my hand.

I sat with that thought lingering longer than I should have, considering the merit in her words.

She wasn't wrong.

I picked the pack of Pall Malls out from the cup holder and stuck one between my lips. Shaking the lighter out of habit before working the spark wheel, a small flame sprouted up that I held against the tip of the cigarette.

Slouching back against my seat, tobacco smoke filled up the car while I watched people pour in and out of O'Malley's in groups of two to five while I puffed on the cigarette. The nicotine acted like a medicated ointment on whatever superficial wounds my mother's scathing remarks might have caused that I was too numb to notice.

The red neon light of the sign flashed above the door awning, beckoning patrons inside. I kept the cigarette dangling precariously between my lips, pulled my keys from the ignition, and reached for my leather crossbody bag.

I had kept Penelope waiting long enough. Admittedly, I had been plagued by an unexplainable looming feeling that I had never had experienced before toward my friend. Somehow, I felt she was about to drop something in my lap that I was neither prepared for nor equipped to handle.

Speculating seemed like a gratuitous waste of time, so I thought better of it when I called her earlier to confirm our meeting time. She was her usual self, albeit a little more chipper than normal.

There hadn't been anything out of the ordinary in her asking to meet, but it was unlike her to call me to have drinks so far in advance, especially when she could have settled for a text message.

Ugh…text message.

My cheeks grew flush despite the frosty early November air that bit at my exposed skin when I flung open the car door, closing it with my hip before locking it.

I had spent the better half of my night yesterday rereading the text message exchange between Sean and I before I removed the battery from my phone and remedied the frozen window and any other electronic possession it might have been under. My skin still felt prickly when I recalled just how much of my private thoughts I'd shared with him. If there was a God, Sean wouldn't contact me again, and I could go through the rest of my life pretending that I'd never said anything incriminating.

Penelope owed me a beer for giving him my number, or three. When I had pressed her over the 'why' this morning, she retorted she had done it for "reasons which you are well aware of."

She was delusional, but I was too anxious about our impending meeting to press her any further about Sean Tavares. He was the last thought on my mind at this very moment—although thinking that made me realize it was completely untrue. Sean was the basis of ironic process theory. The more I tried not to think of him, the more persistent and intrusive the thoughts of him became. His constant presence in my thoughts plowed through every other contemplation or musing my brain tried to conjure in an effort to replace him. And even the mental version of him looked incredible.

It was hopeless, but I'd be damned if I didn't continue to at least try.

O'Malley's was an out-of-place local Irish pub in the North End that attracted an eclectic crew of people that varied from stockbrokers, to farmer's market workers. The one thing everyone who set foot in this dump could align with was their need to drink their troubles away before they dragged their sorry asses back home and made the same mistakes all over again. It also had the advantage of being one of the few Irish taverns ballsy enough to open up in Little Italy.

Taking another long, meditative drag on my cigarette, I paused in front of the bar door, suddenly too frozen to move. My fight-or-flight instincts were in overdrive, my breathing hitching in my chest as I stared at the door, resisting my mind's demands to go inside. It was as if my feet had been cemented to the ground and I couldn't move.

Open the door, Raquel. You've done this a hundred times before. Just do it.

"Hemingway."

I turned my head to look over my shoulder, the cigarette still pinched between my lips, a flummoxed feeling sending my eyes wide.

This really was going to be a bad night.

CHAPTER THIRTEEN

Sean

I WANTED to pluck the cigarette from her pretty lips and crush it under the heel of my boot. Its presence was the confirmation that there was, in fact, one thing about her that I couldn't stand.

Her eyes seemed to glow under the offensive red neon light of the bar, a shiver rolling through her as she appraised me with a look that was a hybrid of derision and curiosity. She stared at me like I was both the last and the only person she wanted to see. I thought I saw something that looked like a blush hit her cheeks when she looked away from me, but decided it could have been the flush of red from the signage.

"This night really is just going from bad to worse," she mumbled around the cancer stick, a plume of smoke wafting up from its lighted end.

I stepped toward her, and acting on my first impulse, pulled it from her mouth, getting caught in the fog of tobacco that left her mouth and, I suspected, she deliberately targeted in my direction.

"What the hell!" she protested, watching as I dropped what was left of the cigarette to the ground. My eyes held her gaze while I crushed it under my boot. When I was satisfied that it was out, I bent down, plucked it from the ground and tossed it into the ashtray that was parked near the bar door.

"That shit isn't good for you."

She rolled her eyes, then turned away from me to open the door. I had watched her stand deathly still in front of the bar door only moments before, a breath of wind tickling the ends of her hair, revealing the soft curve of her profile. And all it had taken was my presence in her space and she took off like I was coming for the rest of her Pall Malls.

I followed after her, catching the door that she swung back in my direction as if to slow me down. My ears were greeted by a loud cacophony, a mix of patrons talking over each other and the music of the live band that played on a small stage in the corner.

I knew I wasn't imagining Raquel's intent to lose me in the bar, as if she could—it was a neighborhood bar, not an airport terminal—but I had the advantage of the length of my legs on my side, my strides catching up to her until I was flanking her like I was her shadow.

"Don't you want to know why I'm here?" I said to her. I had considered her reaction to what was coming, though my thoughts were mostly inconclusive. Particularly after what clearly had been a technological malfunction on her part, one that made me realize I didn't really know her as well as I thought I did.

But hell if I didn't want to.

She shook her head vehemently. "That would require me to be interested, which I am not." She cast me a dismissive glare before storming through a throng of people. I was hot on her heels again, so close that I could see the highlights of her dark hair reflected from the halogen bulbs overhead.

"Wait up, Hemingway." I reached for her hand. Her skin was soft to the touch, but felt cold. Her footsteps stalled, and I took my opportunity to spin her around to face me, our palms pressed together, fingers involuntarily entwining. Raquel's eyes, shrouded by long, dark lashes, fell to where I clutched her hand in my own, as if she couldn't believe I had the audacity to touch her, confusion and awe filling her small features.

I didn't care what her smart mouth said, her stare said different. The frenetic energy that coursed through me—and her as well, I suspected—said different. The ever-present current of electricity that shot through our joint palms like a live wire threatening to ignite a fire said different as well.

It felt like time had stopped. Suddenly the tinny commotion of the bar wasn't as loud, and the people surrounding us no longer existed. It was just Raquel and I, suspended in this moment, our breathing timed and even, eyes searching each other's faces for something that had words escaping us.

Seconds passed, and then, nostrils flaring, she jerked her hand free, the warmth of her hand leaving mine, releasing time from its hold.

"Don't touch me." The control was back in her voice, her eyes tapering.

We were back to where we'd started, Raquel fighting our attraction, but I was ready. I would play whatever game she wanted until she was either too tired to continue or rendered herself exhausted by her own resolve. I leaned forward, pressing my mouth against the shell of her ear.

"That didn't sound like what you wanted yesterday," I murmured, my bottom lip against her earlobe.

She exhaled a breath it sounded like she had been holding, and I thought I saw a tremble roll through her. I felt the brief buckle of her knees when I crowded her, before she quickly straightened. The scent of her vanilla and citrus cologne mixed with tobacco intoxicated me, filling my sinus cavities and kicking my cock to life in the flex chinos I wore.

"You," she said, her voice quavering, unease bouncing in her smoldering brown-eyed stare, "don't know *what* I want."

I took a step away from her, watching as she stared me down in a daze that told me she hadn't realized she had imbibed on my presence alone. An impish simper played with my lips, my shoulders rising in a half-hearted shrug as my hands stuffed themselves inside the pockets of my peacoat. "Neither do you," I replied. Then I breezed by her, training the triumph that sang within me at the ease of my jest. I glanced back over my shoulder as I ambulated deeper into the over capacity bar. She was still standing there, rooted in her spot, eyes tracking me like I was the hunter and she was the prey.

I wasn't, though. Not really.

Unless you considered my unwavering pursuit of her an imminent threat, then I was lethal.

Raquel behaved with propriety, I would give her that. But I was committed to showing her that what was considered morally correct or proper wasn't always right. Including whatever opinion she held of me.

I easily picked Dougie and Penelope out from the back of the bar, my height giving me the advantage to see over the heads of other patrons. Whether Raquel liked it or not, she would follow after me. I was a long way from home, and I knew the writer in her wouldn't allow her to rest until she knew why I was here.

She would know soon enough.

Dougie's head was bent inward, whispering something in Penelope's ear that elicited a laugh from her and produced a shit-eating grin from him that was wide enough to nearly split his face open.

I had never seen them side-by-side like this before, looking at each other like they were the only two people who mattered on this planet. Dougie's green eyes were filled with so much deference and affection it almost nauseated me.

Almost.

He was happy with her. The pain-in-the-ass-turned-saint interior decorator who worked because she wanted to, not because she had to, who had turned her back on societal conventions and her parents' blue-blooded wishes to date a commoner, a high school graduate nobody from Fall River.

And a by-product of their love was growing inside of her.

I thought I heard the exact moment Raquel's footsteps tapered off behind me like she had forgotten how to move, like she had seen something that rendered her immobile while she was still surrounded by too many people to be noticed by the inhabitants of our soon-to-be shared table.

Penelope's gaze met mine, and she straightened in the booth, a smile sweeping across her face. Raising a hand in the air, she flitted her fingers in a wave.

"Hey!" she chirped, her expression alight with something eager, voice a notch too high-pitched. She cleared the drink menu and the pitcher of beer from the middle of the table so nothing blocked her view of my face. I settled on the edge of the banquette, waiting for Raquel to appear so she could sit on the inside.

Dougie held a hand out to me that I took in a clap.

"Thanks for coming," Penelope chirped, though her voice came out more like a stammer that produced a reddened tint to her cheeks. Her hand shook when she sipped her bubbly clear carbonated drink, which I guessed was seltzer, that made me feel a little bad for her.

Dougie smoothed her back, giving her a shy, reassuring smile as they telepathically communicated with each other. She nodded at him, though he said nothing, and I watched as her rounded shoulders dropped just a little, relaxing against the seat.

Penelope's short fingernails drummed across the table, her eyes working the room, a smile still occupying the real estate of her face like she didn't know what else to do to pass the time. And then in an instant, as if someone had come in and told her that Santa Claus wasn't real, the warmth of that smile slipped, her eyes locking. Dougie's eyes flickered in that same direction, causing my stomach to drop.

I tilted my head just enough to see Raquel shooting Penelope a look that made me think she was one breath away from hyperventilating right in the middle of the bar.

"What's she doing?" Penelope murmured, her lilt more Bostonian than Connecticut, anxiety coming to life on her blueblood face, her cheekbones as sharp as her shrewd, icy eyes.

I glanced at Hemingway again, almost feeling bad for the horror that narrowed her gaze and strained the length of her jaw. She swung her stare from Penelope to Dougie. The way her lips pursed tightly together told me everything I needed to know: She had been expecting Penelope, but not Dougie.

The surge of her anger was rolling off her in suffocating, violent waves that I felt even ten feet away from her. The fingers of the hand not wrapped around the strap of her bag were curling and uncurling into a tight fist against her thigh, her knuckles whitening from the strain, her fingernails undoubtedly leaving crescent moon shapes on her palm that I decided would have looked better against the length of my spine.

The thought was not helping my mild case of blue balls. With a slow shake of my head, I spoke through a chuckle, ready to answer Penelope's rhetorical question. "By now?" I pulled a clean glass toward me and filled it to the brim from the pitcher of beer, leaving just enough for Hemingway to start drowning her sorrows in when they unleashed their 'surprise.' "She's realizing it's not girls' night and is about to lose her shit."

"Son-of-a-bitch," Dougie bristled, cluing in. He exhaled loudly, rubbing the bridge of his busted nose, his stare directed downward.

Three.

Two.

One.

"What are they doing here?" Raquel stood in front of the booth, giving Penelope a pointed look.

"No 'hi-how-are-ya?' What's it been, like, five minutes since you two last spoke?" I coolly jabbed, the moment we shared only minutes earlier gone. I masked the smirk playing on my lips from behind my glass.

"I'm not speaking to you, *Slim*," she snarled, looking like she wanted to throttle me.

"Sit down, Kell," Penelope said, the plea in her voice not wasted on me. I took that as my cue to slide over for Raquel.

"I'm good where I am, thanks," she snapped back, leveling her stare at her best friend. I wondered how far back they went, if they had as long a history as Dougie and I.

If their friendship was as solid as it should be, it would be able to exist after something as innocuous and fortuitous as this.

It was a baby, not a terminal illness.

Penelope looked like she was on the verge of tears, and that got Dougie's hackles up. Sweat broke out across his brow as he stirred in his seat, lengthening his spine as he attempted to take control of the conversation.

"We…we wanted to…to talk to you both at the same time," he interjected with a stammer. I'd never heard the poor bastard so nervous in my life. I wondered what it was about this woman that evoked such profound and intense feelings of fear from people that they felt the need to tiptoe around her like she was a bull in a China shop.

"I wasn't talking to you, either."

"Raquel, just shut the fuck up and sit down a minute, would ya?" Penelope barked, her WASP descent leaving her for the single beat of a millisecond. Embarrassment overtook her face, her cheeks growing ruddy. She murmured out the "please," her upbringing clearly getting the better of her before tipping her chin downward and avoiding eye contact with anyone at the table.

I thought Raquel was going to bolt; her nostrils were flaring, her breaths hard and loud. Her gaze was fixed on Penelope, spine stiff and shoulders shot up to her ears, just like they had been weeks ago in my office.

Then she did something that surprised the hell out of everyone at the table.

She sat down.

Her fingers were taut on her bag that she kept in her lap, her shoulders hunched forward, a spaced-out look in her eyes, as if she was reconciling what was happening, why we were both called here at the same time, to the same place.

"Beer?" I offered, sliding the one remaining glass in front of her.

"Fuck off."

God, she had a hell of a temper on her. I barked out a short-lived laugh that faded out into nothing when a strangled sob left the back of Penelope's throat and she lifted a hand to shield her eyes.

"For fuck's sake, are you crying?" Raquel complained, throwing her head back against the banquette, looking up at the ceiling tiles.

"You're ruining our moment." Penelope sniffled, wiping under her eyes with a curled finger, her mascara smearing.

Dougie cooed beside her, and now I wanted to throw up. The chaste moment between them made me squirm in my seat while observing it unfold. I could deal with them looking loved up, but I was out once the waterworks started and the woman across from wasn't my sister or partner.

They needed to just spit this shit out so I could congratulate them and go deal with the case of blue balls that was happening in my pants. I winced, my junk screaming in protest as I adjusted myself. The proximity of Raquel and her scent wafting through my nose right now was not helping the cause by any means. My fingers strummed against the base of the glass, my hands needing to keep busy to ignore my desperation to touch her.

"Go ahead, have your moment." Raquel finally spoke, her voice unnaturally even, her whole face twisting with pained concentration. Her features were all muddled, lips flat in a tight line and eyebrows raised with the disapproval of a nun who just told you that your kilt was half an inch too short.

"We're pregnant!" Dougie cut in, saving Penelope from having another meltdown at her best friend's clear insolence and lack of social or emotional intelligence.

"You grow a uterus recently?" Raquel chuckled sardonically, a half smile lifting her mouth.

Dougie's features twisted, his jaw ticking in a way that I knew meant that everyone needed to get the hell out of his way.

He never had his chance, though, because his baby mama beat him to the punch. Her pointer finger shot at Raquel with imputation that felt unbecoming from her. "You are such a foul and nasty piece of work, Raquel."

"You knew that about me from day one," she calmly replied, picking at her nails, countenance remaining expressionless, like she couldn't be bothered with this conversation anymore.

"Well, I didn't think you would grow up to be this much of a fucking jackass."

Raquel paused, lifting her chin just enough to make eye contact with Penelope. It was impossible to figure out what was going through her mind at that point. Was she insulted? Caught off guard? Did she care what her best friend had just slung at her? Was their relationship recoverable? Dougie and I had said a lot of fucked-up shit to each other in the twenty two years we had known one another—but we always let bygones be bygones after the exchange of a couple of beers and thrown fists.

Raquel's impertinence and Penelope's need for everything to be as pristine as a sheet of unmarred printer paper didn't reassure me that they would be okay after this.

That is, until Penelope let out another one of those choked, high-pitched sobs, her hands clapping to her mouth, alarm blooming on her face at the unnatural vitriol that had left her mouth. I couldn't imagine her parents would have felt particularly happy that their daughter was slinging shit at people like someone who hadn't spent the better half of their life attending posh, private boarding schools—the kind that would have secured her admittance into an Ivy League college, had she actually given a shit about making Mr. and Mrs. Cullimore happy.

Raquel's eyebrow had risen a little less than an inch, her lips twitching like she wanted to say something. I held my breath, waiting for whatever nasty thing the spitfire was going to unleash on us next, like a barrage of errant bullets fired by a shitty marksman.

"Congrats, and good luck." That was it. That was all she managed to express, and with the stiffness of a piece of lumber.

"Kell, I'm sorry. I didn't mean it," Penelope whispered, holding out a hand that went unaccepted.

I felt bad for her in that moment. She hadn't deserved her best friend's insolence and selfishness. Penelope was worthy of a hell of a lot more than what she was getting from Raquel right now, no matter how I felt about her. Maybe Raquel didn't need to order her a mariachi band or perform an interpretive dance to express the sincerity of her happiness for the next chapter of her friend's life—but she sure as shit didn't have to make it all about her.

"You don't owe her shit, Penelope," I said, tossing my beer back. "You need people who are going to be genuinely happy for you."

"Oh, give me a fucking break," Raquel spat out, rolling her eyes. She slid out of the booth like she had finally hit her limit.

"Where are you going?" Penelope squeaked, ignoring me. Her bottom lip trembled, fear rearing its ugly little head again in her eyes.

"Home."

"Raquel, c'mon, sit down," Dougie implored, panic vibrant in the depths of his green eyes at the shitstorm we were both watching unfold.

"Shove it, Douglas," she snarled, jabbing her finger in the air at him, "Ideally somewhere that you can't impregnate her again."

I winced, knowing that would be the comment that derailed this train.

"You know what?" Dougie began, vaulting upward from the booth. His biceps strained under the short sleeves of the black t-shirt that was melded to his stocky frame, his fingertips pressing against the lip of the table to steady himself.

"What?" Raquel's eyes lit up like she was finally going to get the bloodbath she craved because there was something just a little not right with that head of hers. "What would you like to say to me?" she baited.

She was the type who lived for the rush of dancing in the middle of an open field during a thunderstorm.

She just wouldn't get struck this time.

Penelope's hand clutched Dougie's forearm, murmuring a plea for mercy while pulling him back down to his seat. His eyes continued to point laser beams at Raquel, his teeth baring like he would rip her head off clean if he was given the opportunity. Raquel gave him a derisive smile, as if she was happy he was pussy-whipped and would do anything to appease his significant other.

She thought that made him small. *I* thought that made him the bigger person.

"Typical," Raquel drawled, disappointment and boredom in her lilt. She leveled her stare with Dougie while she grabbed her handbag from the banquette and slung it over her shoulder. She disappeared through the crowd, and because she was an arrogant little shit, she didn't give us the satisfaction of looking behind her to ensure we were watching her depart into the sea of people.

She knew we were.

Fraught silence filtered between the three of us. I split the rest of the pitcher of beer between Dougie and I. Penelope sniffled some more, her head sunk as low as her shoulders, as if she was ready for the banquette to just swallow her up.

"It'll be okay," I offered. "I'm sure she'll come around." The lie felt effortless, but it was enough to garner a small nod of gratitude out of Penelope and a tiny smile.

"And congrats, you two," I added.

She preened a little in her seat, suddenly remembering that in spite of Raquel being an asshole, she was going to be a mom. Dougie threw me a look of thanks for bolstering his efforts to make her feel better… and for keeping the knowledge that I had already known to myself.

He wrapped a protective arm around Penelope's shoulders and threaded his fingers through his hair with the other. His stare was a little vacant, as if he was running through the events of the evening again, his teeth finding his lower lip, gnawing the skin.

He didn't have to say it, but I knew he hated Raquel for sure now. I knew my best friend better than Penelope knew his left testicle. He had patience for a lot of things, but blatant disrespect was not one of them. Especially when it involved his heart's desire.

I just wish I could have said the feeling was mutual, because despite her cold and callous demeanor…

…I wanted her more than ever.

CHAPTER FOURTEEN

Raquel

I WASN'T GOING to even attempt to rationalize what had come out of my mouth.

It was a new low, even for me. I had said my fair share of dumb things to Penelope over the years, and she had always taken it with a stiff upper lip and a wave of her hand, as if those manicured fingers expunged every shitty thing I had ever said or done to her.

Somehow, I didn't think that was going to apply in this situation.

I rubbed the span of my face with both palms, the heels of my palms digging into my eye sockets and the tips of my fingers pressing into my forehead to slow my racing mind. My stomach roiled with about as much contempt as my brain did, an overwhelming amount of guilt suffusing through me, settling into all the hairline cracks of my ego and heart.

The positive about not immediately fleeing the bar and racing back to Dorchester was that the emotional part of my brain was comfortably suppressed thanks to Ronan O'Malley, the owner/barkeep, and his steady flow of strong drinks. I liked him, had known the Einstein-looking old man for the better half of my life thanks to Dad, which meant that he didn't ask questions, and I didn't offer him unsolicited answers.

He just let me sit and brood while staring at the mirrored wall of liquors, wines, and spirits and pretend that the whole thing had come crashing down on me, burying me in my own glass house. Ronan hadn't even flinched when he brought me my first drink and over-heard me on the phone asking Cash for a ride.

The only person who despised Cash as much as Penelope did was Ronan. It's a long story.

The way I saw it, I was already up Shit's Creek without a paddle in Penelope's books, so I may as well make it count. What better way to do it than getting into a car drunk with the ex-boyfriend that she despised? He might make a pass at me, and I might make an early exception to our annual fuck because I was feeling particularly fucking pathetic.

I was asking for trouble. I knew it, Ronan knew it, and Penelope would have said the same. I just didn't care.

Call it loneliness, or downright stupidity. Whatever ended up happening after he came to get me, I deserved it.

Penelope would never forgive me for what I said to her. I may as well check off all the boxes on the destructive coping mechanism chart, since being a venomous bitch to her about being pregnant was the hill I had decided to die upon tonight.

Could I still call her my best friend after the way I'd reacted? How could I have done that to her? Who gets mad about their best friend's pregnancy?

Me. That's who. The insufferable.

I just hated change, and babies changed people. It was a baby today, and then...my chest squeezed in protest, not wanting to hypoth-esize what 'then' left me with.

Penelope had been a dependable constant in my life, the beacon of hope in my otherwise darkened night sky. And what had I done to that impressive structure? I lit it on fire and watched the flames become engorged from my safety in the body of water that I stood in the middle of with my airs of righteousness.

Sean had been right; she did deserve better. How much had she endured from me over the years? How much had she turned a blind eye to and tolerated because it was me? I didn't want to consider it, because somehow, I suspected it was more times than not. Maybe this was for the better.

Penelope wasn't meant to be part of my world, not forever. She was good. Honest to God good. She had never seen the difference in our social class or bank accounts as a boundary. Never frowned at me for my shoddy family legacy. She loved me, blindly.

And I, in so few words, had expressed contempt toward her and Dougie for getting pregnant. My fear had driven that conversation right off a damn cliff, and no one would be sending down a rope to save me.

I didn't deserve it, anyway. I was so far away from a redemption character arc that I couldn't even manage a laugh at the notion.

"Penny for your thoughts?" That baritone voice set my nerves on end. I tossed the drink back, knocking a fist against the bar top. Ronan cocked an eyebrow at me like he couldn't believe how quickly I was sucking them back, and didn't that make two of us.

I'm in mourning, old man. Keep 'em coming.

Ronan decided he didn't care enough to challenge me. I slid the glass away from myself, observing the bob of his head that told me he would be with me in a minute...which gave me enough time to deal with the nuisance to my right.

This was a party for one, no gate crashers welcome.

"Sean, please." My eyes squeezed together for a moment, the sound of gravel in my voice almost too much for me to bear. "If you like me even just one percent, go away."

"I like it when you beg." He chuckled, the sound resounding in his ribcage that elicited a desire to beat him with a chair until I could Ctrl+Alt+Delete him from my life—or at a minimum, lose my pants and hop up on the bar top with parted legs and a hope that he fucked as well as he spoke.

The prior was definitely the priority here.

The vacant barstool opposite me slid back against the old hardwood floor, the cushion huffing to accommodate him. I listened to the sound of his glass settling against the bar top.

To the shock and amazement of absolutely no one, Sean had not only done the opposite of what I asked, he did it while sporting a Cheshire grin that planted thoughts of strangling him while riding him at the same time in my morbid, sex-starved mind.

I should probably consider seeking professional help.

Ronan's clear blue-eyed stare narrowed at Sean as he reappeared with my drink. Misappropriated concern settled on his tired features, his focus drifting from Sean to me, the quirk in his fluffy thick brows questioning whether I needed help.

Getting Sean thrown out of O'Malley's would have been one way to guarantee I kept my pants on. But I waved a tacit hand at him. "Unfortunately, I know him," I explained, "It's not what it looks like."

Ronan's white hair was sticking out in all directions, which gave him a comical look. His throat harrumphed, and he tossed Sean an apathetic glance before his head nodded with understanding.

His Irish lilt was a whisper as he set the glass in front of me. "You let me know if that changes, *an cailín*."

I held up the glass in his direction in thanks as he left. The nice thing about Ronan was that even though he'd overheard me on the phone with Cash, his loyalty to my late father still kept him in my corner.

"What did he call you?" Sean questioned.

Sipping the liquid gold in the cup, I drew a small chip of ice into my mouth, biting down on it, the crunch of the cold chip therapeutic under my molars. "He called me 'girl'."

"Oh." His dark eyes bounced from me to the drink. "How many does that make now?"

I snorted, no longer able to keep the planes of my face smooth. "So, you don't like me smoking and you don't like me drinking, either? You've got more rules than my parents."

"You can drink. It's the smoking I hate."

"Right." I sipped at the whiskey, appreciating its burn down my throat. "Except I don't care what you think, nor do I require your permission."

I didn't have to care. I knew. I had just humiliated myself—again—in his presence, plus broken Penelope's heart, both at the same time. I was a real winner. Best friend of the century. Whether I drank like an Irish lush or smoked like a chimney wasn't going to make a damn difference in my character arc. Car over cliff, remember?

"So, what was that back there?" he asked, changing the subject.

I intercepted what I knew was a wounded feeling about to surface, managing a blank guise. "What part?"

"All if it."

"Death of a friendship, I suppose." I gave him a finite one-shoulder shrug. Penelope would never forgive me for that one. I had always been hard on her, but this time I had gone too far. I was still reeling from my conversation with my ma, then this shit with Sean that had my head spinning a mile a damn minute. I just wanted something to remain normal. Balanced. Controlled. And now that was gone, too.

I felt like I was holding onto a small fray on a thinning thread. If I received one more blow today, the rope that thread was linked to was likely to snap and take whatever remained of my headspace with it.

"Don't you think you're being a little dramatic?"

"Don't you think you should mind your own business?" I snarled.

There was my stupid heart again, joining the party unannounced, thumping so loud that I was certain he could hear its bass over the snare of the drums in the background. He was so close. Too damn close. His body was turned toward me, his right elbow leaning against the counter, chin resting on the palm of his hand, eyes boring into me like if he stared hard enough, he'd make it to my cerebrum cortex and understand all the things that made me tick.

I looked away. There was something intimate in his stare that unnerved me and left me liable to do something profoundly stupid.

Like kiss him.

I blinked the thought away just as he started to clear his throat.

"It surprised me to hear that Dougie was going to be a dad, too."

120

He stroked at the stubble that littered his jawline, giving me an earnest look that almost made my resolve falter. Almost. It was hard to accept that he could have conceptualized what was going on in my mind right now. He had someone beyond Dougie. A family. A life.

I had Penelope, and Penelope only.

And maybe that was the problem.

"It's not the same." I took another sip of the warm amber liquid.

"Why not?"

Where did he want me to start? The realization that I had placed all my self-worth into the hands of a twenty-eight-year-old blonde who I had misused as a crutch all this time?

"You wouldn't understand."

"Try me," he suggested, interrupting my thoughts in the way that only he could with his wry smile, boyish charm, and those bedroom eyes that almost tempted me into revealing the contents of my heart.

But I couldn't, I wouldn't...because if I let him in now, there was a chance that he would leave me, too. And that wasn't a risk I was willing to take.

His stare was fixed on mine until I broke it.

"I'll pass, thanks." I took a long pull on the shot of whiskey. The more I drank, the less the ache in my chest stung, and the duller the persistent litany of thoughts that percolated in my mind became.

"Y'know, I've got three sisters. I'm a surprisingly good listener."

Steadying my features, I brought my brows inward. "Fantastic," I droned, clipping my tone. I stared into the contents of what was left of my drink, "Your sisters' judgements make you sound completely impartial."

Sean's thick thighs parted, his clasped hands in his lap.

"Why?" he asked, laughing through his nose while shaking his head.

"Why what?" I questioned, wondering what I had missed.

"Why do you have to fight me every single step of the way?"

My head snapped backward, surprise slamming into me.

"Talk to me," he demanded. "If you need to get mad at someone or something, be mad at me. Give me something, anything but this well-rehearsed bullshit apathetic routine you've got going on."

121

My lids dropped, stale air coming through my nose as I pondered his words. Nothing he was going to say to me would lessen the burden of my guilt, but somehow, my mouth made the decision for me before my brain could catch up. I was going to be a mercurial liability to myself by the end of this night, and didn't that make me want to lace up my shoes and bolt for the door.

My throat worked before I spoke. "We were supposed to be spinsters together. We had this whole plan." We had talked about it at length: Penelope tossing her parents a "fuck that" when they tried to bully her into marrying some clown named Harold Huntington III with enough money to his name to fund a small country. Instead we would travel the world, see new things, explore new cultures. Maybe I'd find the will to actually write for myself again.

We discussed eventually settling down, planting roots somewhere else. California had always seemed promising, with its tepid weather during the winter months and its palm trees.

Penelope had gotten overexcited about that and started looking at houses, big, sprawling mansions that had more room than I knew what to do with. She had shown me listing after listing that had nearly identical features. Six bedrooms, a huge family room with vaulted ceilings and a skylight, a massive yard with a pool that overlooked the small town, and a nursery that was quintessential and welcoming with its neutral color palette and—

My brain hit a blip in that moment, like I was dangling on the precipice of denial. Listing upon listing ran through my memory, considering every single one she had shown me over the years. They had all felt like typical, nondescript mansions with the same list of features that had all appeared impressive to me. It was the latter detail I had missed, or perhaps ignored. The longer I sat with the thought, the worse the bleak reality of the situation became.

The nursery. Penelope had always hinted at what she wanted. I just hadn't been paying attention. She had wanted to have a baby...the guy...the life...the house. She had been telling me all along, silently, passively. *I* had been the one with the plan, and she had been patiently indulging me, waiting for me to realize that that wasn't *her* dream; it was mine. I had unknowingly burdened her by backing her into a corner surrounded by my fear of losing someone else I loved again, trapping her in my own fears and insecurities.

Sean's voice pulled me out of the depths of my thoughts. "Did you ever consider that maybe that wasn't what you were going to want forever? I mean, you're only twenty-eight."

"How do you know how old I am?" I gave him a quizzical look. When he didn't speak right away, I let out a stiff exhale, having a hard time digesting what was processing in my mind while under the spell of Sean's sheepish smiles and molten gaze.

The tilt of his lips told me he knew exactly what he was doing. "Shot in the dark. That's how old Penelope is."

"How perceptive," I muttered.

"Tell me something else, Hemingway."

There was that stare again, the one that vacuumed all the air out of my lungs and turned the insides of my mouth into the Sahara dessert. "Can we please cut the small talk?" I sputtered.

Sean's smile didn't falter, bemusement hitting the deeply-set dimples in his cheeks that I'd never noticed before. He had dimples. Fucking dimples. And wasn't that a damn turn on?

"Fine." He took a leisurely sip of his beer, looking at me over the rim of his glass, "What do you want to talk about?"

Why was I so uncomfortable every time his eyes settled on me? I felt like I was stark naked, even though I wore a leather jacket over a ribbed black turtleneck and black skinny jeans. There wasn't a single part of my body exposed save for my hands and face, but his watchful gaze nonetheless made me feel completely nude.

This had to end.

"Nothing. I don't want to talk to you about anything," I rolled my lips together, working at the granules of sand in my throat. "Your persistence is unmatched."

"Is it working?"

"No." I scowled. "It's getting kind of irritating, really. You barely know me, but you act as if you've known me your entire life, with your unsolicited advice and shitty conversational skills."

Something loosened in his gaze. It was as if the spell had been broken. His head nodded once, knuckles knocking on the bar top like he had made a judgment call. Then he slid off the barstool. I peered at him curiously as he tipped the rest of his beer down his gullet in three quick sips. He was tall enough to bend over the bar top and place the glass inside of the bin on the under bar that housed used glasses. Ronan tossed him a curious glance, as if he had never met anyone who tried to clean up after themselves before. I witnessed the moment he decided Sean was not only safe, but that he would be welcome to return. Sean offered him a half smile before he turned to glance down at me, the smile he had given Ronan vanishing.

"I'll get out of your hair, then." His hands found the pockets of his peacoat. "This conversation is going nowhere, and I'm clearly wasting my time." He paused, hesitation sweeping over the contorts of his angular face. "'Night, Hemingway."

"Where are you going?" My words tumbled out, intercepting him as he turned to leave.

He worked his fingertips back and forth across his stubbled chin. "I'm only going to run headfirst into a wall so many times, Raquel. If a door I know is there doesn't want to open, I'm not going to keep trying to push it."

Was I the door or wall in this situation? Did I double as both?

"So," I began, my straightened posture failing to mask my alarm. I could barely keep the nerves I felt out of my tone. "That's it, then? You're going to leave me alone?"

"Yep," he said flatly, then repeated, "'Night."

Sean didn't toss me so much as a wayward glance over his shoulder as he departed. He advanced back toward the horde of patrons huddled around the small stage, where the live band consisting of has-been forty-plus-year-old men played yet another cover of a Beatles song.

And without rhyme or reason, I was up on my feet chasing after him.

CHAPTER FIFTEEN

Raquel

"WAIT!" My feet pushed off the rung of the barstool, legs taking off after him. What was I doing? Why was I following him? Why was this fucker such a fast walker? I followed him through the crowd, muttering apologies for drinks I spilled when I collided with helpless bystanders. Sean dipped into the hallway that I knew housed the basement stairwell that led to the bathrooms below.

"Sean," I called, barely able to catch my breath when I rounded the corner of the empty corridor.

He glanced over his shoulder at me just as he was about to descend the stairs, a mischievous and utterly smug smile blooming on his face, as if he couldn't believe his luck.

His arms crossed over the expanse of his chest. "I thought you wanted me to leave you alone, Hemingway?"

A.L. WOODS

"I do," I stammered, my cheeks growing hot, the alcohol thickening my tongue. "I think I do. Maybe. I-I-I don't know."

His arms dropped to his side as he stepped away from the stairwell, the noisy din from the bar muted in the stretch of the narrow hallway where we stood.

"What do you want, Raquel?"

What did I want? What didn't I want? For things to be normal. To *be* normal. To take back everything I had said to Penelope. To kiss the ever-loving hell out of Sean, even though he aroused all the ire that seemed to exist inside of me. He made my insides hot and my mind hungry for his banter and unabashed attitude.

I said nothing. My chest rose and fell while we observed each other in silence. I was rooted in my spot, gaping at a man who simultaneously managed to terrify and excite me. I didn't understand what was happening, why my heart beat a little faster when he was around. Why something as innocuous as him taking my hand in his made it feel like I was coming alive for the very first time. Why the realms of space and time seemed to hold us in a time lapse, the rest of the world asleep while we remained conscious.

Why? Why him? Why me?

He must have sensed what I was thinking, because his heavy stare dropped to my mouth as I gnawed on my bottom lip in deliberation.

Sean's nostrils flared, something dark brewing in his face as he broke the distance between us in four short strides of his long legs. His hands were surprisingly gentle when they cupped my shoulders, backing me against the wood-paneled wall.

He was so tall. Why had I never noticed how tall he was before? His arms flanked the sides of my head, fingers spread wide against the wall.

"What. Do. You. Want?" he repeated, bending his head toward me, eyes daring me. If I had thought he was close before, we were practically skin-to-skin now, despite the layers that kept us apart. I could smell the cinnamon gum on his breath, the clean woody scent of his cologne. The heady combination made me feel more buzzed than the whiskey.

The acceptance of my answer slammed into me all at once, and

126

before I had time to brew another snarky remark or second guess myself, I rose on the tips of my feet, my lids dropping shut. He met me halfway, his mouth crushing against my own. It was hard to determine who groaned in relief first, him or me. Maybe it was both of us. The sound was so mellifluous, it made liquid heat pool between my legs and my head spin with a kind of euphoria I had never experienced before. My arms circled around his neck, fingers stroking the faded sides of his hair. His pelvis bit into mine, his arms dropping so his firm hands could still my bucking hips.

Sean's teeth nibbled my bottom lip, demanding I open my mouth for him. I complied. The taste of spicy cinnamon hit my taste buds as his tongue tangled with mine.

This was beyond my wildest expectations.

This was kissing a dream, and I wasn't sure that I ever wanted to wake up.

Sean

Hemingway was...frenetic, her body responsive in a way her mind had never been. Her mouth said more now, her tongue dancing with mine, than it did when it was spewing out barbs I wasn't sure she even believed. Kissing her felt like I was waking up for the first time, like I had been asleep for thirty years and never known it.

She was a voltaic cell under a chemical reaction, her body undulating beneath my roaming hands that despite keeping it PG-13, were desperate to feel all of her without a rating system.

Never before had I handled a woman more alive from a kiss alone. The intensity of her kiss sent a cordial invitation to my cock to join the party, its length tightening against the seam of my pants, straining with demand.

Not now, dickwad. You're not going to scare her off just because you're desperate to feel her hands on you instead of yours.

Some small part of me had prayed that when I finally got the chance to kiss her, the sparks I had imagined crooning into the sky would never catch flame. That there would be nothing there, just so I could get her out of my system and move on—but this woman who writhed under my greedy mouth, whose fingers entrenched themselves in my hair, whose moan was a melody in my mind, would never be out of my system. Not when kissing her suddenly became my new addiction and all it would take was the taste of her to keep me drunk forever.

Raquel's hands left my hair, palms flat against my chest. The heat of her fingers brought a welcome frisson against my body as they descended.

My cock was like a kid in the back of the class, standing upright with his hand in the air, demanding to be called upon. Her fingers tightened on my belt notch, her thumb grazing my hardened length. I jerked my body away, my mouth leaving hers in a rush of raspy breaths, my legs sending me back two steps.

Her features went muddy, her chest heaving. "What's wrong?" she panted, confusion brewing in her eyes. "Did I do something wrong?"

Wrong? my brain yelled. *No, you did something right, and that's the fucking problem.* I didn't want to fuck Raquel in a public bathroom and a grimy basement that reeked of mold and whatever else. I wanted her in my bed against clean sheets, with her hair spread out around her like a halo. I wanted her moans trapped in my pillows and the fragrance of her sweat on my skin.

Out in the bar, the crowd erupted into an off-key rendition of Neil Diamond's "Sweet Caroline," to the musical accompaniment of the cover band, the chorus kicking off just as rejection etched itself in her small features. It wasn't a look that belonged to her. I hated the ginger-looking touch of the tips of her fingers sweeping over her bottom lip.

"Hey—"

"It's okay, Sean." Her voice shook, eyes seeming apprehensive to meet mine. Why did she look so small, so innocent with that brown doe-eyed stare that looked like she was used to this happening? "Don't feel bad, okay?"

That's what she thought this was?

"I don't feel bad for anything," I ground out, pegging her with another drunken look.

Her honey irises appeared dubious, as if she was grappling with what I wasn't communicating, because I couldn't get the words out. I rubbed the edges of my mouth, the taste of her whiskey breath still dancing on my tongue. Whatever she thought she saw, she'd clearly misinterpreted again. She pushed out a tight exhale, her lips rolling together as if drinking in my unwillingness to speak.

She pushed off the wall, not sparing me a glance as her footsteps shuffled down the hall back toward the buzzing bar.

Raquel didn't make it two feet away before I was pulling her gently back by the wrist. She let out a gasp when I pivoted her around, walking her backward until her ass hit that wall again. My hips found her rib cage, my arms caging around her.

I held her stare, her eyes studying mine. "What?" she whispered. "Why won't you talk to me?"

I pressed my forehead against hers, my breaths raking out of me in a piss-poor effort to slow down my palpitating heart. "Twenty minutes ago you were complaining I talked too much."

"Well, that was twenty minutes before you kissed me. The circumstances have changed."

"Is that so?"

"Yes," she pouted, and didn't she look fucking adorable with her brows furrowed and lips drawn together.

"Do you remember what you told me when we met a few weeks ago?" I tucked a lock of her hair behind her ear, feeling the shudder roll out of her at the contact of my fingers brushing against her earlobe, my thumb dragging along the length of her smooth jawline.

Her breathing hitched under my contact, brows coming together as if she was trying to formulate a coherent response. "Not really," she finally managed, "but it was probably something nasty."

"So, you admit you have a penchant for being difficult?" My chest shook with a languorous laugh, the pad of my thumb tugging her fat bottom lip downward. She looked up at me with a gaze that made me want to bite my clenched fist.

I hated my morals, despised myself for even considering reneging on my former opinion about having sex in dodgy basement bathrooms.

"Sometimes," she said, tilting her head to the right, her hair spilling with it, exposing a small patch of creamy flesh beneath her ear from under her turtleneck. "Remind me what I said."

"You told me I wouldn't know what to do with you if I had an instruction manual."

Truthfully, I did suspect she would be more complicated to assemble than a piece of IKEA furniture that came with a detailed instruction manual the size of a tome. Dougie had warned me. Penelope had as well in so few words, yet still...I wanted Raquel like my next breath. With all of her mismatched pieces, without all the screws, nuts, and bolts that would have helped me figure out how to put her back together again, I wanted her. I wanted this erratic, short-tempered woman with her attitude, obstinance, and beauty in whatever way I could have her.

"You wouldn't," she confirmed with a soft laugh. "But I'll give you points for trying."

"Oh, yeah?" I murmured, my nose grazing hers, her whiskey breath fanning my face. "What do I get to do with these points?"

"Kiss me again and find out."

So I did. I kissed her as if my life depended on it. As if kissing was a full-time job and I was the only person who could handle it. I kissed her until her lips were swollen, until her breaths came out of her in short spurts of air.

I kissed her until I was interrupted.

CHAPTER SIXTEEN

Sean

"WELL, WELL."

At the sound of the male voice I begrudgingly left Raquel's mouth, preparing to tell off whoever the fuck was observing us: Find a different hallway. Take a leak outside. Take the keys to my car and go fuck off somewhere.

Still, the voice continued, missing my telepathic message by a long shot. "Who do we have here?"

Someone who's about to have their ass beat, that's who. I lifted my head, my eyes tracking the timbre of the voice.

Beady, nearly black eyes met mine, the low lighting from the drop lights overhead making the features of the man who looked no older than me appear as harsh as the timbre of his voice. He leaned against the wall at the end of the hallway. The relaxed set of his shoulders left me with a sick feeling that he had been standing there a lot longer than he'd let on. Delight that erred on the side of danger pulled his mouth into a lopsided smile, his leather jacket cracking as he folded his arms across his chest.

Fucking drunk voyeur.

"Beat it." I raised my bicep to shield Raquel's face. She rose on the tips of her toes to steal a look at the interloper, a curse ripping out from the back of her throat. She stiffened against me, the warmth from her body leaving her, a ghost of something flitting over her face, as if she had just met the eyes of someone she hadn't wanted to see.

Her hand found my bicep, pushing it out of her way. The guy snorted out a laugh, appraising her in a way that made my skin crawl. Her arms hung limply at her side, her back turned to me.

"Found her," he called to someone. Another guy entered the hall, shorter than the one in the leather jacket. The newcomer had his ash blond hair pulled into a bun at the base of his neck. His eyes bounced from me to Raquel and back to me again.

"We've been calling you for an hour, Cherry." Man Bun spoke, his expression hard.

"She was preoccupied," Douchebag-in-leather replied, and for a second, I thought I heard disappointment in his pitch. "We were just a few minutes too early from catching the late-night show."

"Still a prick, I see, Dominic," Raquel drawled, her head lolling to the right. I couldn't see her eyes, but I watched her spine straighten like she had to keep her wits to her now. Her whole stance and demeanor changed, shoulders squared and chin kicked forward.

I fought the urge to drag her back by the arm and use my body as the separation between her and these fucks who I was certain I'd seen on a late-night rerun of a *Cops* episode.

"Still looking like a fine piece of ass, Cherry Pie." Douchebag-in-leather, who I now knew as Dominic, snapped his jaws at her like an unmuzzled rabid dog, the sound of his molars cracking together like nails on a chalkboard to my eardrums.

I didn't like it.

"Don't talk to her that way," I snarled, stepping toward him. I wanted to break this fucker's nose. I had at least three inches on him, I could take him. My eyes flitted to the Man Bun behind him, who reminded me of a DMV clerk—bored as hell, waiting for five o'clock to arrive.

He rubbed his forehead, his expression unreadable. "Let's just go, Dom."

"Go?" Dominic crooned. "I'm just getting started." His tongue protruded from between his teeth, the tip stroking his upper lip.

"Where's Cash?" she asked, her voice so even it was unnerving. I hated the sense of familiarity when she spoke to them. It was clear to me that she had a history with these guys, the extent of which I didn't know. My mind kept wandering back to what Penelope had said: Raquel didn't have a boyfriend.

So who the fuck were these two?

"Outside," Man Bun replied, pointing his eyes toward the bar like he was telling her to wrap this up so they could get going. I had news for him: She wasn't going anywhere; not with these guys.

"You know Ronan won't let him in here," Man Bun added.

"That's his fault." She shrugged, tucking a lock of hair that had dislodged itself from behind her ear. The one that I'd tucked back only minutes ago.

"You know how he gets," Dom continued, stepping toward her, looking more like a hunter with a gun trained on an animal that didn't stand a chance. "He's never been very good about sharing."

He smirked at me, and I didn't miss the implication in his eyes, the sinister look that sent my hackles on edge.

Raquel crossed her arms over her chest. "His sister isn't a piece of property."

"That fucker had no business doing what he did to her," Dom spat out.

"Meredith was capable of taking care of herself."

Jesus Christ, there was so much going on between these three that I didn't know what they were talking about. I had become an awkward bystander in a situation that I had owned when it had simply been about her and me.

"Raquel," I cut in, drawing the attention of the two men who faced her like she was an expensive piece of artwork. She looked at me over her shoulder, the passion she had shown me for the briefest of moments gone without a trace.

"I gotta go," she said, eyes glazing over. I hated the permanence in those three words that left her pretty mouth, like we were done before we had ever really even begun.

"We don't get an introduction?" Dom complained with a sneer, moving toward me like a snake, menace twisting that mug of his into something sociopathic.

"Dom," Man Bun said with a sigh, "let's go."

"C'mon, Terry. Don't you want to know who he is?" He slithered forward, hands sliding up the sleeves of his leather jacket, revealing a fat golden band Rolex I was confident he hadn't earned by hard work and forearms marred by an intricate span of tattoos. Dom sneered at me, his glower bubbling with something I didn't trust. My brain ticked with warning, an alarm bell resounding somewhere deep in my cranium telling me I was an idiot if I pushed this, that if I did, one of us would end up in a body bag...but if this fucker wanted a fight, I was here for it.

I edged toward him until I was shoulder to shoulder with Raquel. Her eyes narrowed on my twitching fists, her eyes pleading that I didn't do what I was contemplating.

"I don't give a shit." Terry, who I decided in that moment was the more level-headed of the two if it were a competition, grabbed Dom by the shoulder, jerking him away from me. "I've got a fucking teething baby at home. Morgan's been blowing up my phone for three hours. We've got what we came for. Let's go."

Dom, his stare fixed on mine, replied, "Told you to always strap up. Now you're stuck for eighteen more years."

"I'm not interested in fucking everything that moves, so that suits me just fine." Terry pulled Dom back with enough force that the guy almost tripped over his own two feet, arms windmilling, body soaring backward. Terry set him straight toward the bar, and then with another well-placed shove, he was gone from our sight. Dom's laugh was manic-like as it faded, getting absorbed by the music and the crooning crowd.

With a curled fist and a jutted thumb, Terry indicated toward the bar while giving Raquel a domineering stare that demanded her compliance. "Move it. He's getting antsy."

"I need a minute."

"You've got thirty seconds."

"Fuck you, Terry," she hissed. He stepped toward her, a movement she mirrored, their positions reminiscent of two dogs in a fighting ring ready to tear each other to shreds.

"One minute. Don't piss me off," he conceded with a growl, as though deciding she wasn't worth the vet visit. He stepped out through the door arch, but something told me he wasn't far.

When he was gone, she turned to face me, her posture askew, like one more wrong thing would send her whole body toward the floor.

"I'm sorry," she said, running her fingers through her hair, scratching at her scalp. "I guess I lost track of time. I was hoping to be outside before he started calling, but..." her words died in her mouth.

I worked at the lump in my throat, trying to dissect what the fuck she had just dropped in my lap. "Who—"

She shook her head, her forehead creasing with deep set lines before I could get the question out. Her reticence was back from wher-ever it had gone, pissing me off further.

"I'm going to go."

"Who are they?" She owed me that much. "Where are you going? Better yet, why?"

Her weight shifted from foot to foot, hands awkwardly clenched at her sides, eyes looking down, avoiding my stare. My scoff cut through the music from the bar.

She wasn't going to fucking tell me.

"Goodnight," she paused, lifting her chin before adding, "Sean."

Under any circumstances, I could have given my right ball to hear her say my name, her inflection grouping the vowels together in a way that sounded more like the diminuendo of a song in her mouth. She was actually going to leave me standing here like an idiot, after she had pursued me, and now she was blowing me off? And worse, for some fucker named Cash who sounded more like a convict?

To say I was rightfully pissed would be an epic understatement. I felt my pulse behind my eyelids, my jaw tightening.

"So," I spat, "That's it? You kiss me and you fuck off?"

She looked slighted, brows crashing down hard over those honey browns. *"You* kissed *me,"* she corrected, mouth staying agape.

I blew out a laugh; denial wasn't a good look on her.

"You kissed me," I repeated, "And now you're leaving...with two other guys?" Saying it out loud made it sound worse, my mind hastening to draw new conclusions that twisted my insides.

As if hearing my thoughts, she frowned. "It's not like that."

I wanted to believe her, but I was struggling. "Well, I'm trying to figure out what it's like, but you're not helping, so my brain is filling in the blanks here."

"Raquel," Terry called from the hallway, knocking on the door frame. I decided he was next on my kill list after Dom.

"I gotta go; I'm sorry."

I moved after her, but she spun on her heel, steeling me with an outstretched palm. Her eyes burned with something I couldn't read. "For once, just listen to me when I ask you to do something," she said, her breathing hitched, features growing ashen. "Don't follow me. It's for your own good," she paused, drawing her bottom lip between her teeth before releasing it and adding, "and mine."

My insides were hollow, eyes tracking her as she disappeared from my view. My legs damned me to pursue her, but my pride kept me entrenched where I was. This was the brick wall again, the one I would only take a sledgehammer to if she let me, but I drew the line at self-harm...at running for that mortar-laden wall when everything she did told me not to, suspecting that the risk of injury to either my senses or heart were too great of a risk.

A group of drunken girls shrieked with laughter as they breezed by me, their crowd nearly cramming the breadth of my body against the wall as I edged out of their way, their voices carrying as they descended down the basement stairs.

Scrubbing an open palm over my face, my fingers lingered at my dropped lids, needing a moment to just catch my breath and rub my thoughts out of my mind. My head was heavy, spinning even though I'd had all of two beers. I considered for the briefest of moments how much simpler my life had been before she appeared at the door of the colonial with her smart mouth. I had been guided by simple virtues: sleep, fuck, piss, shit, eat, work, repeat. And now all of that felt terribly inconsequential, and truthfully? A little lonely, because even though I was constantly surrounded by people, they saw only what I wanted them to see. That bridled, put-together version of myself who worked twelve-hour shifts six days out of the week. The guy who took care of his ma and his sisters, who had abdicated on his own wants to provide others with theirs.

I didn't want to be that guy anymore. I didn't want to watch another thing slip through my fingers, something I had wanted just for myself. I didn't care how complicated it was. How messy it was going to be; because if the taste of Raquel alone was enough to leave me reeling; if it was enough to stoke the coals that burned the fire inside of me that now demanded I follow her outside—then I wanted to follow that inconvenient instinct.

If Raquel was inconvenient, then I didn't want simple.

CHAPTER SEVENTEEN

Raquel

WHAT WAS THAT EXPRESSION AGAIN?

You reap what you sow.

What goes around comes around.

And my personal favorite: Payback's a bitch.

I breezed through the doors of O'Malley's, the frigid air a welcome respite against my flushed and prickly skin, the traces of sweat turning the damp strands of hair on the back of my neck into cold droplets.

My rage hastened me down the sidewalk, brick pavers absorbing my footsteps. After everything I had said to Penelope tonight, I deserved this. My chest ached from the moment I had been robbed of —I had been riding a wave, a high so unlike anything I had ever experienced, only to watch that undertow claim me again and drag me under. I wasn't allowed to swim, I was only permitted to flounder.

Cash hadn't mentioned he was with Dom and Terry when I'd called, he'd just asked me where I was and said he would be there within the hour.

I'd gotten distracted, wrapped up in Sean, and now…

How could I be so careless? I'd let things go too far; I'd been caught. All it would take is for Dom to say one word about what he had seen to Cash about Sean and I and…

No, I didn't want to think about it. I'd done the right thing by telling Sean not to follow me. This was my fault, and I needed to own it. Even if being in Dominic's presence made me murderous. I tracked his yips of mirth, my breath blowing out of me in hot plumes of air. How dare he be happy, that piece of shit. My body was practically vibrating when I spotted the headlights of the car, the obtrusive light illuminating my path, my legs practically kicking up at a dead run. I felt as if someone had aborted my neural pathways, driving me further from that fine line of sanity toward the boundary of the point of no return.

It was one thing to send Terry to look for me, it was another thing entirely to send Dom in.

How could he do that to me? After everything?

Cash knew my hatred toward Dominic Espinosa went beyond his character. He was rotten to the core. If I had been the kindling for the tragedy that befell my family ten years ago, Dom had been the lighter.

Everything he touched burned, leaving nothing behind in its wake.

The anger that shook me from the inside out had breaths raking out of me faster than I could draw in oxygen. Hyperventilation threatened to consume me if I didn't get a hold on it, my lungs squeezing with a pain that made me want to throw up.

Cash was so damn smug, not a care in the world, limbs sprawled out on the hood of the car, DMX's "Party Up" reverberating through the white '98 Mercedes-Benz C 200 that had its windows open—creating a nuisance for the rest of the North End. He looked up at the starless sky above him, the hood of his sweater drawn over his head, legs crossed at the ankles, and a lit joint pinched between this fingers. I stopped at the lip of the car, my chest struggling to keep up with my hasty inhalations.

Detecting my presence, he slid down the hood of the car, feet planting on the ground with a dramatic thud. Green eyes leered at me, like he was waiting for me to step into his embrace.

His smile was shy, the kind kids give on their first day of school…a layer of innocence in that curl of his lip that we both knew was complete and utter bullshit. It was a trick that Cash had been deploying for years, only this time it wouldn't work.

He had gone too far.

"Really? You brought him?" I threw an outstretched palm in Dom's direction, who sported a smirk so sinister it left me winded. He blew me a puckered kiss. I retaliated by giving him the finger, arousing another laugh from him that was absorbed by the five-story walk-ups that lined the street.

Cash gave me an unconcerned shrug. "He was in the neighborhood, came along for the drive."

This was karmic justice being served to me. I'd let the anger, my abandonment issues, and the alcohol impair my judgement.

For the second time this evening, I was reminded how blinded I could be when I was being led by my own vindictiveness.

"You're unbelievable." I shook my head. "I'm walking home."

"You're asking to get jumped," he retorted, brows dropping.

"I'll take my chances." The only thing I had to worry about in the North End was the size of the rats. It was a little before midnight, and if I left now, I could still grab the orange line at Haymarket Station. I was in a murderous mood that would have made me a liability to any pick-pocketer or idiot dumb enough to try jump me.

"C'mon, Cherry. Don't be like that," Dom called as I set out in the direction of the bar for the ten-minute trek to the station. I ignored the sounds of bedlam behind me that tempted me to glance back. No. There wasn't a chance in hell I was getting in a car with Dom, not unless I was driving it head-first into a wall, and then into the Charles to drown the prick for good measure. My head was buzzing from the heightened effects of the alcohol and my rage, the ground feeling uneven underneath my feet as I lumbered forward.

I had just passed the door of O'Malley's when I heard it swing open. I reflexively looked. Sean's eyes met mine, a tremble rolling out of me as the heat of that imposing stare rendered me immobile. Terry slid out from behind him, the door creaking shut.

There was enough steam billowing from Sean's mouth that he looked more like a dragon, his stature casting ominous shadows that imposed on my own. 'Pissed' didn't feel like an accurate description of what was brewing from his body language. His fists were fixed into tight balls, knuckles taut against the skin. His spine was rod straight, shoulders squared, as if he was ready for anything.

I wasn't sure if I wanted to run into his arms or get mad at him too for deliberately disobeying what I had asked of him, just like he did every fucking time. As I waffled, he made the decision for me, more of that pissed-off, unadulterated energy suffusing through the sharpened angles of his face.

"What the fuck is going on?"

Behind him, Terry threw me a look that told me he was as over this night as I was, a cigarette trained between his lips. He set up post against the brick wall, his left foot perched next to his right knee, head bent while he lit his cigarette. The smell of his nicotine tickled the hunger of my own addiction.

I didn't know how to answer Sean, or where to begin even if I attempted. I was a victim to my own follies, crumbling at the behest of my own foibles. I lacked the dominion over my own mind, my mouth opening and closing but no words leaving it.

"Who's your friend, Cherry?" Dom called, breaking me from my trance, tossing a can of gasoline onto the lit match inside of me that I'd worked so hard to smother. "We never did get that introduction, since his tongue was down your throat."

That fucker. The comment hung in the air; I ignored the weight of Cash's glare in my direction.

He could spare me that shit. I didn't owe him any more than I owed Dom an introduction.

"Do you ever stop talking?" I snapped. Dom laughed, Terry watched a rat skitter by, and Cash—he watched us dead on. Nerves lodged themselves in my throat, but I swallowed the feeling away. I wasn't his anymore; I hadn't been for years.

I would deal with his attempt at possessive machismo later. In the meantime, I needed to get Sean away from all this. I couldn't control this situation if he stuck around.

I turned my attention back to Sean and found him glowering at me, brows full-on furrowed, eyes engulfed in flames, as if someone had fallen asleep with a candle on, jaw ticking as if every minute that passed without an answer put him one second closer to flipping his shit.

"Okay," he said, more to himself than to me, punctuated by a nod of his head, before his blackened eyes found mine. "I'm only going to ask you this once, Raquel." His voice was eerily smooth, sending the frozen hairs that lined the back of my neck upward. "Are you sleeping with any of those guys?"

He may as well have slapped me with an open palm. The question winded me, like someone had sucked all the oxygen out of the air.

My jaw slackened as I slammed him with my own death stare. "Are you fucking kidding me?" I snarled, leaning toward him. "I cannot believe you just asked me that."

It hadn't mattered that with enough alcohol I would have...I had thought about letting Cash...*no*, Sean had no right to ask me that.

Terry whistled, a short dropping note that sounded like he agreed that had been the wrong question to ask me.

Dom howled with laughter. "Who the fuck *is* this guy?"

"That's what I'd like to know, too," Cash said thinly, toking on the joint.

Sean didn't even so much as falter, looking at me with unadulterated stoicism, his face full of patience, as if he was waiting for confirmation on a conclusion he had already drawn.

I was such an idiot. He was just like every other guy with that territorial, dick-size contest bullshit. He fleshed out his own narrative, pieced the fragments of the story together and there he was, a full-fledged writer, too.

The longer the protracted silence stretched between us, the more upset I became.

"You know what?" I said, rocking my jaw together. "Fuck you, too." I was done with this. I turned to leave, but he caught me by the elbow, pulling me to him with a gentleness that didn't match the anger rolling off of him.

Sean searched my face, his hand warm on my bicep, thumb creating friction as it worked back and forth. Never before had any man handled me with that kind of care, and that just added fuel to an already terrible situation. "The question wasn't meant to offend you," he said, his voice dropping low enough where only he and I could hear. "I need to know what I'm working with here, Hemingway. I'm not going to rush into a burning building if you don't wanna be saved."

Saved? I blinked at him, my face collapsing. I had never needed to be rescued by anyone before; I had always been the one doing the protecting. I had warded off evil and fought the bad guys. I stuck up for myself. I didn't need a prince from Fall River sporting kingly garments to ride gallantly on his horse to try to bail me out from the shitstorm I had caused, like I was some sort of South Boston damsel in distress.

"Maybe we *should* introduce ourselves," Cash said.

Fuck, it was too late to bow out of this gracefully. If I left for the subway, they'd just set their sights on Sean...and I didn't trust them to fight fair.

This was my fault, the repercussions of *my* choices. I had to fix this, and fast.

"I don't need to be saved, Sean." My hand rose to find his, knotting our fingers together against my bicep. My frosted digits savored the heat of his warm hands, somehow knowing this would be the last time we were like this. "I'm not the princess in this situation. I'm the knight."

He flinched, his grasp softening on my arm as if the analogy was registering. I stepped out of his hold, my heart squeezing. My mind screamed at me to abort the mission as I took cautious steps backward away from him—away from the man who handled me with care, and straight into the belly of the beast.

That was what knights did.

Maybe Penelope had been right that day when she said I had a toxic dependency problem, that I did things that hurt me just to remind myself that this was all I deserved. I wouldn't get the happily ever after, the rustic castle in the country, or the prince whose aid I refused. Instead I got two sets of gleeful eyes who could barely contain their elation that I was still who I had always been at my crux: another lowly girl from Southie, too consumed by her legacy and the repetition of her bad habits to do anything about them otherwise.

The loyalty that bound me to them forever is what would keep Sean safe in the end. If they could focus on me, they would forget about him.

My shit kickers skittered across the sidewalk, carrying me toward the car. I didn't say anything to Cash or Dom, just observed as they took my cue and followed me. Sean remained rooted in his spot, his gaze trained on me while I sat in the passenger seat, hands I was sure were still balled into fists now back inside his peacoat pockets. He didn't call for me, and for the first time, he didn't follow me, either. Terry clapped him on the shoulder as he passed with a 'Better luck next time, brother' look.

The back passenger door opened, letting it in another bluster of cold late fall air that I was too numb to feel.

"Let's go."

CHAPTER EIGHTEEN

Raquel

THE CAR PULLED AWAY from the curb, performing an illegal U-turn. Sean's figure became a fuzzy silhouette in the darkened distance from the side mirror, the outline of his body disappearing as the car rolled down a hill. The headlights bounced off the glass windowpanes of shops closed for the evening, casting threatening shadows across the stretch of road, rolling to a complete stop at the bottom of the hill at a red light.

The interior of the car was chilly despite the heat being cranked, the MB-Tex imitation leather cold under the seat of my jeans. The cabin stank of roaches from joints and cigarettes. The streetlights we passed lit up the interior, revealing a layer of thick dust that lined the tortoise shell dashboard, fingerprints marring the surface. I took in the dust and stench, my foot pushing an empty Coke bottle away from my ankle. Dom's laughter at something Terry had said burned my eardrums, my mind filling with white noise that made everything seem muffled, as if my head was being held underwater.

I'd done the right thing by going with them, so why did I feel so awful?

My chin turned in Cash's direction. His fingers strummed along the perimeter of the steering wheel, his face pinched with concentration, though we both knew he didn't have a fucking care in the world other than blazing, cock blocking and epitomizing the definition of a chucklehead (damn you for reintroducing me to that term, Penelope)—and didn't that realization just send me over the edge.

Everything I had been compressing, compartmentalizing, trying to fit back inside of the tiny box that housed the rest of my bullshit came to a head. The box was finally at capacity, and I could fit nothing else in it. If there was a metaphor in there, it was wasted on me because I was suddenly driven by my need for a fight, and any one of these fuckers would do.

Cash, who looked perpetually nonchalant, nary a wrinkle between his brows. Terry, who cared about me as much as he did the empty bottle of Coke at my feet. And Dom, who had ruined my life.

My fist reared back before I slammed it into Cash's arm with all the upper body strength I could muster, abs compressing as I had plunged my waist forward. I winced as white pain flared in my hand, enough to completely sober up what was left of the buzz I had been nursing.

He shouted in response. His foot slipped from the brake, the car propelling forward through the crosswalk. A shrill shriek sounded from an unsuspecting female pedestrian with a J. Lo vibe who was sporting massive hoop earrings, and a ponytail that gave her a free facelift.

He almost hit her.

"The fuck is your problem?" she yawped, stalking toward the hood of the car with about as much finesse as a newborn doe, slamming her closed fist on the hood of the car with a *thwack* that dented it for sure. New Englanders were not afraid to express their grievances with a very prompt "Fuck you!". We were also not above physical confrontation—and no, we didn't care if you had the upper hand *and* three hundred horsepower on your side.

It was an East Coast thing.

An unconcerned look filled the soft edges of Cash's square jaw, his green eyes assessing the woman—who was questionably dressed for these frigid temperatures—that he had nearly run off the road.

A normal person would have held up a hand in apology.

Cash flipped her the bird before swinging his imposing gaze back at me like he didn't have the time to express remorse toward the woman he would have pinned under his ten-year-old car had she not jumped away in time. His stare trailed over me, his lips straining together when I didn't immediately offer him an explanation.

"Wanna tell me what that was for?" he finally asked, his tone clipped. His foot found the gas pedal, tires squealing as he depressed it. I had no idea who he was trying to impress, but the whole 'I'm-a-wannabe-drag-racer' thing died alongside the whole *The Fast and the Furious* franchise three movies ago. Him and this piece-of-shit car needed to let it go.

"Because I hate you." I looked at his response from the corner of his eye, watching his jaw tick. "And you reminded me tonight of all the reasons why."

My disdain for him was almost on par with what I felt toward myself for ending up in this predicament to begin with.

His grip tightened on the steering wheel. The comment normally would have rolled off his chest, but for some reason, that didn't appear to be the case this time.

Sadly for him, I wasn't in a remorseful mood.

I had known Tobias "Cash" Peake for a majority of my life. We grew up on the same block in South Boston, before the developers slid in with their ideas to 'improve' the gentrifying neighborhoods that surrounded us and lived up to its name over the decade to become the setting of one too many bad mob movies relating to Whitey Bulger himself. Cash's Nan, Mrs. Peake, was one of the old hags my Dad had taken care of, since Mrs. Peake's children couldn't handle the idea of living another day and—was two for two on suicidal children. That cranky witch had raised Cash and his sisters, and in the end, her hubristic piety hadn't mattered. Cash grew up to be a piece of shit, his younger half-sister had rightly fucked off, and his older sister was just waiting for their Nan to croak so she could toss her ashes into a dumpster behind a Dunkin' Donuts.

Even that sounded too kind.

Cash was by far the least put together of the siblings and had never stepped up to the plate of being the man of the house…a fact my dad had reminded him of frequently when he was still alive. Cash was lazy, and content with preserving the status quo. Dad used to smack him upside the head and tell him to get his shit together. Cash would just shrug and go smoke a joint at the end of the street because Dad didn't have patience for that shit, and he didn't want to listen to his Nan's grating Irish lilt screaming at him inside the house. She was part of the problem. Dad never told her that, but we all knew. Cash had been coddled, and I didn't entirely fault him for being a lazy scumbag— why aspire to do anything when he was on track to inherit the house from his Nan once she kicked the bucket?

No one wanted that rickety-ass thing that was a sneeze away from tumbling over except Cash. It was a damn miracle the city hadn't deemed it inhabitable with the way the foundation was cracking, the building sloped to the right, and the shingles were lifting. The lawn got cut sparingly since my dad died. Cash wouldn't know how to start a lawnmower if you gave him a thousand bucks, and every winter without fail, his Nan fell down the front steps because they hadn't seen a lick of salt in eons.

If I didn't know better, I'd think it was a plot amongst him and his sisters to try to hurry their Nan along to her grave.

Much to my father's chagrin, and Penelope's annoyance, Cash and I had dated. Dad hadn't filtered his reservations about it any better than Penelope had later on. Dad, like Penelope, wasn't the type to mince words, and while he had generally stayed out of my way, he had his own uncanny way of reminding me that the future and success of my family's legacy was riding on my back. *"Keep your head down, and your legs closed. And if you can't do that, go find yourself somethin' better than that 'igit kid. A doctor or somethin'."*

And like every other Southie hoodsie, I never listened.

For the most part, Cash had been an okay boyfriend when his ego didn't get the better of him. We had managed to make it work on and off for all of one year, two months, and three days before I found out he had been getting his dick wet in someone else the entire time we had been together.

I never did find out who she was. Suddenly, our gossip-driven neighborhood clammed up. No one said a damn word. Wouldn't even tell me the size of the bitch's hoop earrings or what color her hair was.

That had been one of the worst days of my life, but compared to what else had happened, it felt like a small scratch on my broken heart. I hadn't hesitated ending it with him. He never would confirm what he had done or with whom, but I saw it. That guilt of his betrayal etched into the planes of his face every time he stole furtive glances at me. He offered me his friendship after everything went down between us, and against Penelope's advice, I accepted.

I needed the familiar company, and at that point, didn't really give a shit if he fucked a rock or the exhaust of his Mercedes. Cash was only good for two things: drugs or sex. And I was only periodically interested in either/or.

The tips of my fingers found my lower lip, my tongue poking out just a little, the traces of Sean's kiss setting off a low tingle in my lower belly that momentarily transported me someplace other than this disgusting car.

I was torn between wanting to stay away from him and wanting to give in to my body's carnal demands, even if just for one night. If for even a moment, I could be that princess and him that knight, then maybe that would be all the saving I would ever need.

The continued chorus of laughter behind me had me twisting my body in the passenger seat, glowering at the two blundering idiots in the back with a pointed finger. "You two ruined my night."

"You better put that hand away, sweetheart, unless you want to put it to work," Dom purred, cupping himself through his jeans, a mischievous look filtering through his onyx-colored eyes. "That's one way to improve your night."

"You're disgusting, Dominic," I snarled.

Dom's smile was unruly. His lips parted when he rocked his hips, the outline of his growing erection tenting his pants. He released a low groan that made my shoulders punch up to my ears and my insides twist with discomfort.

He was crude by design, and vulgar by nature.

"He's just playing," Terry said, looking out the window. From his profile, I caught the boredom that was blooming on his face as the passing streetlights cast soft orange shadows against the curvature of his pretty boy mug. Terry's mother and Cash's father had been siblings, and the only genetic similarities they appeared to share was the family nose, slim and slightly turned up at the tip; everything else about them couldn't have been more different. Where Cash ran hot and was susceptible to emotional outbursts, Terry was calm and collected. Perhaps that was why he seemed unbothered by Dom's antics, no more than he would have been had a piece of lint landed on his pants. "Relax, Cherry."

I flustered, my face growing ruddy as I sunk back in my seat.

Cherry.

No matter how many years went by, I couldn't shed the moniker.

I hated Cash for boasting that he had popped my cherry that day. It had been the last rumor I needed circulating at the heels of my sister's death. In some sick way, I thought Cash couldn't handle not being the center of attention for once. It was deplorable, but that's Cash. Another tick inside a box of a questionnaire titled 'Is Your Ex a Bad Person?' So far, he was 8/10 for yeses.

The silence over Chamillionaire's "Ridin'" was too much for Dom, whose stare met mine in the side mirror.

"Your fuck boy seemed smitten," Dom said in what I viewed as an attempt to provoke me.

I promised myself that I wouldn't strike when I saw that smarmy smile on his face and the crazed look in his eyes, no matter what he said or did. That would only serve Dominic's twisted desires, and I had no interest in being one of his playthings or another social experiment for him to get off on.

His head lolled to the right, the shadow of his dark eyelashes soft against his bronzed skin under the tawny streetlights. If I didn't know what a sinister piece of shit he was, I would have thought he looked almost angelic.

Too bad it was the Devil himself who reigned supreme in Dominic's soul.

"Did you get down on your knees and suck him off in the bathroom?" he pressed, a twisted sycophantic smile teasing the corners of his mouth, though his eyes remained closed.

My chest squeezed as anger started to sputter in the depths of my belly. I wasn't humoring him with a response, I just needed to get home. I glanced at Cash, who shot Dom a wasted dark look from the driver's seat, but I heard his unspoken crass thoughts.

He wanted to know, too.

Cash rolled his lower lip between his teeth, stewing, even though he said nothing. I could feel it pouring off him like the suffocating waves of a tide, the violence of it threatening to pull me away from the safety of the shoreline if I let it.

Well, fuck him, too. It was none of his damn business.

I crossed my arms around my chest, tilting my head toward the window. I pegged Dom with a contemptuous stare in the mirror, my molars connecting as he feigned sleep.

I had never liked that fucker, and nothing had changed since the first time Cash had brought him around to my house, promising that he had the best Kush he'd ever smoked in his life. I regretted taking a hit. If I had declined, maybe none of this ever would have happened.

Maybe Holly Jane never would have met him.

"Ah, that's right," Dom chuckled with his eyes still closed, his voice sending the hairs on my arms upright in warning. It was as if my body knew before my mind did that whatever he said next was going to steal my breath away. "That isn't your style; you're too vanilla. Your baby sister, on the other hand...mmm...that girl was better than candy. Just as sweet, too."

The levy inside of me snapped, a rushing sound akin to water filling my ears. My heartbeat fell in time with the bass of the song, its steady pulse sounding off in my mind as my hands fought the seatbelt, struggling with the button until the buckle sprung free.

How *dare* he bring her up?

Turning in my seat, I climbed over the center console. Cash made an inhuman sound, recognizing what I was about to do. His hand caught the back of my knee, attempting to pull me back in the seat while keeping his concentration on the road. I struggled out of his grasp, my body outstretched, struggling to get to my victim.

"What the fuck!" Cash barked, the car swerving as he grappled with keeping me in place with one free arm. I heard him bite out another curse, his grip on me loosening as he fought to keep the car straight. I kicked out of his hold, my leg thrashing wildly, my right foot catching him square in the jaw.

"Fuck, Raquel!"

His sharp hiss fell on deaf ears. My lust for vengeance was too strong as my heart rate surged and my blood pumped harder, my adrenaline kicking into overdrive.

I was going to kill that sonofabitch if it was the last fucking thing I did; I didn't give a rat's ass if Cash did end up totaling the C-Class beyond recognition. At least I would go to my death satisfied that I had extracted my revenge on Dominic Espinosa.

If Dom felt even a morsel of what I had felt these last few years at his hands, I would spend the rest of my life rotting gleefully in purgatory right alongside with him.

I vaulted myself at him with full force, springing at him like an errant cat from the top branch of a tree, albeit with a little less finesse. I hated that his surprise had already worn off, that now he licked his lips as if he was about to enjoy whatever I was about to unload on him. When I got a solid right hook to his jaw, he let out a sharp and grating laugh, the pain in my hand barely registering as it competed with the rhapsody that swept over me from making contact with that stupid face of his.

My fist swung back, preparing to strike him again, but the satisfaction of my retribution was cut short. Dom strong-armed me and had my ass in his lap in a matter of seconds, his chest crushed against my back, his arms apprehending my own.

The more I struggled, the tighter he held me. I screeched out a cry of frustration, hating that he had stolen yet another thing from me.

It felt like I was playing on the losing team tonight.

His breath was hot in my ear, making, an eruption of chills break out up and down my spine. My lungs struggled for air, anxiety gripping me as he dragged his open mouth across the stretch of skin under my jaw before bringing his mouth back to my ear—the same one Sean had spoken into. He bit down hard on my earlobe, and I swallowed the blinding pain that ebbed at the surface of my sanity.

"Your precious baby sister was a good fuck," he ground out against my ear as his hand found my crotch, squeezing painfully. "And it's too bad her body burned in that car accident, 'cause I'm sure her corpse would still be a better fuck than you."

Tears sprung to my eyes, and I despised myself for letting him arouse the follies and recklessness that existed within me at all.

He wasn't worth my tears, my frustration, my irrationality. But God, did it feel good to invest all my rage into someone corporeal. Someone who wasn't a ghost. Someone who didn't deserve it.

Where Penelope offered me security, safety, and love—these three reminded me where I came from, and what I still was at my core.

Rotten, like a piece of fruit that never made it to the produce stand.

Cash was a temperamental crutch.

Terry was ambivalent, disengaged from anything outside of his own universe, coming and going as he pleased.

Dom would always be the worst of them. He liked emotionally and mentally torturing people, including my sister when she was still alive.

From time to time, he was known to give into his desire for physicality, no doubt loving the thrill of watching people crumble as much as the next sociopath.

He never drew blood, not much, anyway.

"Just enough for a little taste."

I blamed him for the lines of coke he supplied my younger sister with, the ones she confessed to snorting off his chest with a dollar bill, and for the harem of men she kept company with when he wasn't available to fill her emotional void.

I blamed him for introducing her to vices that served to only mask her pain and anger at our father's untimely death a few months before her own, instead of encouraging her to deal with it.

And I blamed him when she inevitably rolled her car on the Mass

Pike while strung out on a deadly cocktail of lorazepam and cocaine, unbeknownst to anyone three months pregnant. The coroner said she felt nothing when she died, but it was hard to say for certain if it was the heart attack that killed her or the accident.

It was inconclusive.

But just like Holly Jane's death was inconclusive, so was the extent of Dom's role in her loss.

He hadn't driven the car, Holly did—but he clearly didn't give a shit that his involvement in her life meant that Holly's blood was on his hands as much as it was on mine. The stain was an indelible mark that, although incapable of being visualized by the human eye, would always remain.

"Let her go," Cash finally gritted out, apparently no longer able to take it.

I swallowed the sob that threatened to rob my breath. Yes, it was my fault for the predicament I now found myself in, but I didn't regret hitting Dom—I only regretted that I hadn't hit him hard enough for it to amount to something that hurt him.

Dom ground his pelvis into me once, letting out a salacious laugh. I felt sick that our skirmish had left him aroused, but that was typical of him. I hated that the ridge in his pants was for me, brought on by my fear and hatred for him. Bile crept up my throat, and his hold on me finally went slack. He shoved me off his lap, propelling me into the rear of the front seat.

"You're not my type anyway, *Cherry*." He punctuated the syllables in the nickname, making me want to attempt to boot him in the face with the heel of my shoe just for good measure.

I climbed back into the front passenger seat, breaths still erratic as they raked out of me.

"You have a type?" Terry questioned, breaking up the intensity of the exchange without looking up from his phone. "I was under the impression you fucked anything with legs and a pulse."

Cash chuckled from the driver's seat, his irritation leaving while he passed a Toyota Camry, cutting back in with just a few feet to spare. The brakes screeched behind us, but Cash just kept on going. The sound drowned out the pain from the cat o'nine tails whip that had wrapped itself around my heart and squeezed.

"Big words coming from a man whose kid sister I'm banging, too. Now, there's a girl who's a real fucking spinner on my dick," Dom drawled, tucking his hands behind his head from my viewpoint of him in the side mirror.

I tore my gaze away, relief flanking me as Cash turned the car onto my street.

What sounded like the soft thump of Terry's phone dropping to the floor filled my ears, then came the exchange of knuckles landing on skin and grunts escaping from throats. The smell of sweat mixed with cheap cologne tangoed with the musty smell the car otherwise carried.

"Don't talk about my fucking sister like that," Terry snarled. Dom merely laughed.

The guy was a raging fucking sadomasochist, so I was relieved when the car finally stopped in front of a streetlight that abutted my building. Now to convince my body that felt boneless to get out, for I was exhausted.

Cash seemed unfazed by the exchange of fists occurring in the back seat of his car. That was the thing about Terry and Dom, their relationship went beyond a brotherhood, it was like they were two halves of a split soul—Terry representing what was left of the good in Dominic, and Dominic a harbinger of pain and loathing, drowning in enough agony to satiate both of them.

His mental state would have inspired a psychiatrist, if he had one, to institutionalize himself.

"You good?" Cash said to me over the strife in the back seat.

Good? Hardly. I nodded anyway, too emotionally spent to speak. He pulled the gear shift into park, just as someone was thrown against the seat in the back with an *"Oof."* I didn't want to risk checking to see who had gotten the brunt of their exchange.

"Last chance, Cherry. I'm available to keep you company," Dom said breathlessly.

I felt nothing but pity for any woman stupid enough to part their legs for him.

"One more fucking word out of you, and I'm going to kill you myself, Espinosa." Spittle sprung from Cash's mouth, his body vibrating in the driver's seat, his gaze looming. "I fucking mean it," Cash added.

"If you wanted to share, you only had to ask, Cash. Plenty of cherry pie to go around." I could hear the smile in his tone.

"Terry, I swear to God, shut him up," Cash snapped as he opened the car door and clambered out.

Terry sighed. "Shut the fuck up, will you?" he mumbled, I heard the wheel of a lighter spark as I reached for the handle of the door. "All this for a broad who doesn't want either one of you idiots."

He had that assessment correct.

The smell of marijuana burned my sinuses, its distinct skunky aroma wafting through the interior of the car just as I opened the car door to climb out, the smoke billowing out with me, getting swept up in the late fall air.

Dom's window rolled down when I turned to shut my door. He wiped his busted lip with the back of his wrist, crimson smearing on his skin. I hated the lust in his eyes, almost as much as the mouthful of blood he displayed to me with a wide smile. "Promise you'll think about me tonight, Cherry," he called, tapping the ash of the joint he accepted from Terry to the ground, the smoke masking his cold features.

Slimy piece of shit.

Slamming the door behind me, I heard the shuffle of Cash's footsteps against the asphalt behind me, my legs carrying me as far away from the car as possible.

"Hold on, Cherry." He caught up to me and slid his palm against mine. The whole thing felt awkward, his fingers tangling forcibly with my own. I felt the unspoken apology in the touch, but my body was reluctant to receive it, my hand remaining stiff in his.

"I really should have taken my chances walking," I sniffed, the cool air making my nose run.

"Not sure your Romeo would have let that happen, Juliet." His tone was clipped, but I saw the strain in his jaw as he kept his eyes directed in front of him.

He led me up the stoop steps of the building, releasing my hand so I could pull my fob and house keys out from the inside of my purse.

His comment marinated in my mind as I swiped the fob against the key reader, the door latch releasing with an audible beep. The realization that he didn't like seeing me with another guy registered, an awareness flooding me that I didn't give a flying fuck about his feelings. Cash and I had more or less been platonic since we broke up...save for the occasional fuck when I was an emotional wreck, like I would have been tonight had things not escalated with Sean. Otherwise, I had about as much sexual interest in him as I did in Penelope's pregnancy.

Ugh.

I had to fix that situation with her. Not tonight, but I owed her an apology and about ten years worth of groveling. The warmth of the old building was a pleasant respite on my flushed skin, the familiar lingering scent of my neighbors' cooking enveloping me in a kind of hug that made me feel like I was back in my own element again. Cash followed me up the two flights of stairs silently, his footsteps falling in line with mine as we came to my apartment door on the second floor.

He bowed his head, his focus trained on his shoes. "I don't know who he was, but I don't like the way he looked at you."

"What do you mean?" I asked, tilting my head with the feigned ignorance of a fifteen-year-old who had just been caught sending inappropriate MSN messages to another boy by her insecure older boyfriend.

I wondered what it would have been like to watch Sean and I side by side as a spectator. Was our sexual energy as palpable and suffocating to everyone around us? It felt all-consuming, and half the time I didn't know if I was intoxicated on the mix of whiskey and beer, or purely on the intensity of Sean's presence. He filled every crevice of my mind and aroused the fibers of my being that had been dormant all these years.

He stirred sensations in me that I wasn't sure I had ever experienced before.

Not with Cash, not with anybody.

I had been regretting most of my decisions this evening, but the biggest one—next to breaking my best friend's heart—was not going home with Sean. If I had, at least I wouldn't have had to endure Dom's bullshit for twenty minutes or face the reminder that Cash was, and always would be, a little bitch when it came to doing the right thing. He had sat there and watched the whole thing unfold and had waited until I nearly broke to speak up.

I knew children with more spine.

He finally spoke, shoving his hands in his pockets. "You know what I mean. I know I fucked up back then, and that I'm not good enough for you now." Leveling his eyes on mine, he added, "But neither is he."

"Why?" The single word dripped with venom. I quirked an impatient brow at him.

Silence.

It was for the best. I didn't need him to recite the same monologue I had listened to for ten years. We both knew the answer; he didn't need me to remind him that he was the one who had fucked our whole relationship up to shit just so he could feel as big as Dom's ego.

I didn't hate Cash anymore. I realized he hated himself enough without me having to help him.

"No one will ever be good enough for you, Raquel. Not really." He hesitated, "You're just that kind of woman, but we can all die trying." He leaned forward, brushing my cheek with his lips, his hands steady on my shoulders.

He moved away, his breath warm, the tang of the marijuana still faint on his breath while he lingered opposite me. Indecision settled on his face as he appraised me with woeful eyes. His Adam's apple bobbed in his throat, waiting for a sign that would never come.

I wasn't inviting him in.

I touched my cheek gingerly, avoiding his gaze, a gnawing void growing in my stomach. He whistled low to himself, masking the rejection for the invitation he was never going to get. My body didn't prickle with awareness when he left me the way it had when Sean had drawn away.

Cash's footsteps were soft as they ambulated away from me. "Call me if you need anything, Cherry," he called over his shoulder just before he disappeared back down the stairs. We both knew I wouldn't, because something had changed in me that night. Between Penelope's announcement—the one I had reacted so reprehensibly to—and Sean's kiss, I realized something perhaps I had known all along.

I didn't need anybody, not when I had myself.

I waited till I heard the door shut behind him before I unlocked the door of my apartment and stepped inside. With my back pressed against the door, the adrenaline from my fight-or-flight responses finally left me in a whoosh of emotional energy. The stress weakened my legs, my body giving out on me. Sliding to the floor, I ignored the throb that settled in my ass upon contact with the hard parquet.

If I didn't need anyone, why did it hurt so bad?

I pulled my knees to my chest, my arms circling around them with my forehead pressed to my thighs. Then I did something I hadn't done in what felt like forever.

I cried.

CHAPTER NINETEEN

Sean

I WOKE up in a bad fucking mood.

I had managed to get about four hours of intermittent sleep. I spent the first few restless, unsuccessful hours with eyes wide open, tracking the glow of my alarm clock on my dresser across the room, watching as the LED digits turned from two to three, three to four, and four to five. I listened to the furnace turn on and off, pushing a vortex of warm air into my bedroom that made me sweat. When I wasn't looking at the clock, I was engaged in a staring contest with my phone, willing the damn thing to vibrate, ring, implode, anything. When I fell asleep somewhere around five-fifteen, I accepted that she wasn't going to reply to my text asking her to let me know when she got home. She didn't owe me an explanation, whether I felt I deserved one or not.

I woke up to the sound of birds chirping and blinding sunlight streaming through my parted blinds.

Pathetic fallacy, my ass.

Anticipation fluttered in my chest when I reached for my phone, but it left me as quickly as it had arrived. My messages were empty, the lone sent message hanging there, unanswered and ignored. I had no idea why I was even bothering at this point to hold onto false hope. She had made her choice. I didn't know who Terry was, or that mean motherfucker Dom who looked like a criminal, or the shadowy figure looming by an old Mercedes who I assumed was "Cash," yet never dared to cross the distance between us to confront me. He had leaned there, looking aloof but chest puffed out with pride, as if he had won. And I guess in a way, he had. Raquel had left with them, not me—the guy she'd just kissed like her life had depended on it.

The urge to throw up had my throat working, my insides wrenching with warning, mind spinning with all kinds of hypotheticals that I had exhausted hours earlier. Just like that, any hope of having a good day had taken a fucking leave of absence because I was pissed again.

Kicking the sheets back, I lumbered out of bed, my bare feet working the wide plank floors of my bedroom. I dipped into the hallway and noticed Trina's door was still shut, a line of darkness beneath her door. She'd already been passed out when I got home, for which I was grateful. I wasn't up for Twenty Questions last night.

The kitchen in my house was a stark contrast from the kitchen at the colonial. Black cabinetry wrapped around the kitchen against the gray hardwood floors, white granite countertops gleaming in the sunlight that poured in from the wide window over the kitchen sink. I was damn near compelled to draw every single curtain, blind, and shutter in this house shut, but I thought better of it. I could probably afford the sobering reminder that not everything in my life was grim, and at least the sun still shone, the world still turned, and life as I knew it carried on.

That was one lesson I had taken from my father's premature death: Time doesn't stop, even if you're standing still.

Moving for the coffeemaker, I popped the lid open, stuffed a new liner inside and engaged in the necessary evil that was my caffeine fix —the intoxicating aroma of coffee hitting an indulgent part of my soul. I had strong feelings about addiction, but my love for a good cup of joe was something I would never even consider foregoing. I liked my two cups a day, three on a particularly bad one. What I consumed in coffee, I tripled in water intake. I was a solid two liters of water a day kind of guy. I took daily multivitamins and exercised regularly despite working a physical labor job. I slept a solid eight hours a night…that is, when I wasn't losing sleep over a woman who didn't so much as spare me a passing thought. I had witnessed firsthand what happened when you didn't take care of your body, what happened when you prioritized unhealthy habits and overindulgence.

I had watched addiction kill my father, who smoked a pack a day for the twenty years I'd had with him. He liked his wine in the evening, and while he never crossed that fine line of alcoholism, he had teased the perimeter of it, and that had been enough to send him to an early grave. His Stage IV lung and liver cancer diagnosis had him wither away within three months.

His death had shattered my ma, and in spite of all her typical Portuguese mother quirks and religious idiosyncrasies that were wasted on my sisters and I that she buried herself in—I don't think she ever got over it.

Who could blame her? How did you get over a man you had loved for forty years? Hell, I couldn't forget a woman I had kissed once and had all of four really fucking terrible conversations with. I couldn't fathom having to exist with a history that spanned decades, that was laden with memories, or the weight of grief on every holiday and birthday like an unshakeable shadow…their absence painfully apparent when doing simple things like grocery shopping or picking paint colors…the stupid arguments you'd never have again over socks that never made it to the hamper, or garbage that didn't make it to the curb on time. I didn't know how my ma did it day in and day out, how she managed to find her will to keep going when everything had been so grim. She never let us see her cry, though we heard her muffled, anguished sobs through her bedroom door at night when she thought we were all asleep. She hastened to get caught up in being busy, absorbing herself in make-work-projects, overextending herself to the point of exhaustion. She didn't want to think. Thinking meant she had to acknowledge her reality that my dad was never coming back.

Trina entered the room yawning, my dark reverie leaving me at her presence. She slinked to the coffee pot, rubbing the sleep out of her eyes, her pink hair sticking out in several directions from her poorly constructed topknot. "How was your night?"

"Shit." I lifted the carafe from the burner and filled my mug.

"Guess things went awesome with Raquel?"

Unable to muster a response, I dropped my ass onto a stool at the breakfast bar. My sister poured herself a cup of coffee, spooning so much sugar into the mug that I wanted to gag.

"Did she send you packing?" She blew on the steam before taking a small sip. Social cues were wasted on Trina. She didn't care about the kink in my brow, or the obvious displeasure that had me rolling my lips together.

I was susceptible to the folly of a man, so I spoke against my better judgement. "Worse." I winced as that swallow worked its way down her throat.

"Did she throw her drink at you?"

At that, I considered tossing my sister's cup of "coffee" into the sink. I blew out a breath, shaking my head with what TMI detail I was about to offer my sister that I would inevitably regret later.

"She kissed me."

My sister's enthusiasm got the better of her, the hot beverage sloshing in the mug when she jerked forward, sending rivulets down her arm. She barely flinched, her glee over my revelation too much for her to bother registering any feeling of pain.

"Wait," she said, her nose crinkling as she set the mug down on the counter, grabbing a dish towel from the handle of the oven and mopping her arm. "If she kissed you, why do you look like someone hit your dog?"

"She left with someone else." I probably should have said she left with *three* guys, except that sounded worse than I wanted it to, and I didn't want to consider that her leaving with them implied anything...

salacious. I would be lying if I hadn't thought about that, though. Actually, it had been the very source of my lack of sleep.

"Ouch," Trina said with a playful grimace.

"Tell me about it."

I took another sip from my mug, squinting at the early morning sun coming through the kitchen window.

"Now what?"

"I texted her, but she didn't reply."

"Double ouch."

I shot her a scowl. "You're not helping, Trina." My earlobes warmed as the anger I had attempted to abate started to boil again.

"Sorry. Sheesh. Someone's cranky this morning." She rolled her eyes, leaning forward on the countertop with her elbows.

Maybe I should have gone after Raquel, told her not to go with those guys who looked like they'd just broken out of a federal prison.

"Don't follow me. It's for your own good, and mine."

She was cryptic as hell about it. For all I knew, she was at the bottom of the Charles River right now in four different body bags, and that would be entirely on me.

I swept a hand over my face, scratching at the facial hair on my jaw, working the coarse hair back and forth in contemplation.

"I guess that means the kiss wasn't that great."

My ego howled with pain at my sister's low blow that had landed exactly where she wanted. Siblicide was illegal across all fifty states, I reminded myself. I made an ornery sound, glowering at the little brat who shot me a smug smile. "Y'know, you're more like Ma than you realize," I said, enjoying the way Trina gaped at me with indignation. "You both have this incredible habit of saying the wrong thing."

"Hey," she objected, "I'm just being honest. If the kiss had been better, she would have left with you instead."

"Which would have never been an option, since you live here for the foreseeable future."

"I do own noise-canceling headphones, y'know. It's not like I haven't overheard you watching porn before, with your room next to mine. And by the way," she added, her brows pinched together, "the delivery guy and lonely housewife thing is *so* nineteen ninety-five."

I didn't even want to know how my kid sister had gotten so well-versed in pornography tropes. I cradled my head in my hands, a groan of humiliation hitting me.

These were the burdens of living with your kid sister. A man had needs, and I guess that meant I needed to get friendly with the mute button.

"So, now what?" she repeated.

"What do you mean, 'now what'?" I stood up and went to the half pot of remaining coffee.

"What are you going to do now?"

"Have another cup of coffee and explore a new porn preference."

"First of all, top up my cup, too," she said, holding up her index finger, "and second of all," her middle finger joined in, making a V-shape, "you should ask Pen—"

Nope. I saw where she was going with that one, and it was a terrible idea. "Raquel is definitely the last person Penelope wants to discuss, Trina. Trust me." I could not see Penelope taking that phone call very well at all.

"Hey Penelope, I know your best friend erupted on you over the most monumental moment in your life, but I'm still trying to pursue her. What do you think?"

Uh-uh.

Trina's lips jutted forward in a contemplative pout. "Well," she sipped at the coffee I had just refilled, revulsion quirking her brow. She reached for the sugar, but I beat her to it, taking the jar and placing it on a shelf there was no way in hell she could reach without a chair. I was going to get a wrap on this girl's sweet tooth. She sent me a knowing sideways glance, a smirk tickling the corners of her mouth.

"Well, what?" I prompted, equally amused as my sister stretched on her toes in an unsuccessful attempt to reach the sugar anyhow.

"Well," she repeated, her voice straining, toes pressed into hard-wood, "You could always just…"

Sweat broke out across her forehead as I awaited the rest of her suggestion.

Which didn't come. She just continued to struggle to reach the sugar.

"Can you just try to enjoy your coffee without so much sugar?" I snapped.

"Not all of us are monsters who drink black coffee."

"That's the way you're supposed to drink it. That's the way Dad taught me."

"And you believed that?" She released a derisive snort, throwing her head back, "Please. I caught him dropping three sugar cubes into his coffee when Ma was out of the room. He gave me twenty bucks when I was ten to keep me quiet."

My jaw went slack, eyes squinting at my sister, trying to pick out the lie. Her upper lip normally quivered when she was lying, but it was completely still. Twenty bucks? She was cheap, even adjusting for inflation. I wondered what she would keep to herself if I doubled his money. Lord knew I had enough skeletons in my closet that I didn't need getting back to Ma.

"Can I have the sugar now?" Impatience made her bob her foot against the floor.

"No."

"You suck," she scolded, dumping the coffee in the sink out of spite.

What a brat.

"Got any other suggestions, genius?" I probed, rerouting her back to the forefront issue. As the youngest, Trina loved orchestrating trouble, controlling a situation, and having everyone do exactly as she wanted—and for the most part it worked. I was placing stock in her ability to help me contrive some sort of ill-put-together plan that would at least get my foot back in the door.

She blew a breath through her mouth that was hard enough to make her lips vibrate, tilting her head sideways. "Call Raquel? I'm sure there's an explanation why she went home with someone else."

I rubbed my forehead, squeezing my eyes shut. "You're terrible at this."

"I got pregnant at twenty by a guy who skipped town," she said, straightening and throwing her hands upward. "I am *not* a person to be taking relationship advice from." She forced out a laugh, but no smile appeared on her lips.

My face softened, seeing what she didn't want me to. "That has nothing to do with you, y'know." I caught the somber glint in her eyes when she chuckled softly at her own self-deprecation. "Charlie's a piece of shit." I poked her chin with my knuckles.

Trina managed another attempt at a smile, equally unsuccessful. Her brows jumped north as she moved on to the next subject. "Hey, would you mind taking me back to the house today? I need to pick up my other camera lens."

"Uh," I hedged, glancing at the time on the oven clock, trying to scrounge up an excuse. Ma's house on a Saturday was likely to be the scene of a war on dirt, dust, and grime, and I wasn't sure I wanted to be caught in the middle of the salvo.

"Ma might not throw me out if you're there." She pressed her palms together in prayer, face filled with feigned optimism.

"She wouldn't throw you out even if I wasn't."

"You weren't there in August."

"That was two days *after* you told her you were pregnant and terminating it. Too soon."

"Whatever," she said, rolling her eyes. "Will you take me or not?"

I sighed, not really wanting to go, but recognizing that there was merit to my sister's concerns. I would go and keep her out of our mother's grasp and be the decoy instead. Even if it meant being harassed for forty-five minutes over everything from the crew at the job site, my haircut, my weight, and my dating life.

Yippee.

CHAPTER TWENTY

Sean

TWENTY MINUTES LATER, I was pulling the Wrangler into the paved driveway of my childhood home. The farmhouse was tucked onto three acres of land with the nearest neighbor close enough to borrow a cup of sugar, but too far away to hear my parents' owning my ass when I got into shit as a kid. Eggshell white beaded siding made up the exterior, the gabled roof a depressing shade of gray. Rugs hung over the tailored railings of the farmer's porch, the warning that it was a Saturday morning and Ma was on her rampage.

Behind the house was an oversized barn my father had converted into a workshop. I used it as extra storage now for supplies and work tools I didn't have space for at my own house—my mother's suggestion, of course; it was the only way she could still feel like she was involved in micromanaging my life in some small way.

"You sure you can't just run in and grab the lens?"

"Turn off the Jeep, Sean."

I spat out a curse as I reached for the keys and silenced the ignition. Trina hopped out first, and I took a stiff breath before following her lead. She went to the garage door and punched in the code. The doors lifted at a tortoise's pace. Trina, ever impatient, ducked her head and stepped into the garage before the doors had cleared enough to accommodate my height, seeing as I wasn't interested in doing squats or the limbo.

"Hey," she called to me, "Maria's here."

I frowned, catching sight of my older sister's white BMW 328i parked in the garage. It was unlike Maria to just spontaneously drop in. She and Ma got on about as well as two betta fish in the same tank. All right, I was exaggerating, but they seldom saw eye to eye on anything. They were more interested in snapping their jaws at one another to assert their dominance.

Trina placed a foot onto the concrete step, her hand turning the garage door.

A distinct mouth-watering spicy aroma immediately hit me as I tucked my head inside. Trina met my eyes, and we exchanged a knowing smile. It didn't matter how sullen and stubborn Ma could be; her food was a gastronomic love affair that even her worst enemy would have partaken in. I kicked off my shoes, waiting as Trina did the same. We left our coats on the washer in the mudroom that the garage led into before stepping into the hallway to head for the kitchen.

We made it all of ten footsteps before we were stopped.

"Oh, good," a voice called with more enthusiasm than was appropriate for ten o'clock in the morning, "You're here."

I looked up to find my middle sister, Olivia, looking down at us from near the top of the stairs. I swallowed a laugh that was stuck in my chest when I caught sight of her getup. "I'll be right down."

"What...is...she..." Trina's voice trailed, looking up at our sister with mystification that mirrored mine.

Livy descended down the stairs sideways, lace-gloved hands clinging to the railing, chin looking over her shoulder, a fuzzy socked foot—the only thing from the twenty-first century—searching for every tread before she moved. Her hair was pulled back into a tidy chignon at the base of her neck, a red felt bonnet tied with a lace ribbon under her chin. The hoop frame that was obviously under the full plaid evergreen skirt she wore made it impossible for her to climb down the stairs facing the front—it made her wider than the stairs.

Trina broke first, her hyena laughter carrying through the house. She clapped a hand over her mouth, trying to suffocate the giggles, eyes welling with tears.

Livy's cognac-colored eyes tapered in Trina's direction when she cleared the last step, turning to face us head on.

"What the hell have you got on?" I said with a snort.

Livy's spine lengthened, her gloved hands knitting together, pointed chin jutting out in my direction. "For your information, I've been cast as Belle for the ETG's rendition of *A Christmas Carol*."

Livy had always been a theatre kid, but she preferred working with the Eaton Theatre Group over the companies in town—"less competition," she had explained. The truth was, my sister was good, but she had an ego that made it hard for her to fit onto a stage, so no one in Fall River wanted to cast her in shows anymore. We all knew it, but we pretended that it had been entirely her decision to work with the smaller theatre group in Eaton. She was twenty-two, and like Katrina, still had a fucking ton of growing up to do in order to check herself. On the flip side, she had acknowledged that furthering her education was a must and was starting theater classes in the new year at the New England College.

"Belle?" I asked, feigning ignorance.

Livy tsked, lips pinching together. "Belle is Ebenezer Scrooge's love interest."

"Right," Trina tittered. "So, why the costume?" She wiped tears from under her eyes that had formed from laughing so hard.

Livy elongated her neck, looking proud. "It helps me get into character." She moved in front of the mirror over the console table that served as dumping ground for car keys and mail. "Do you like it?" she asked, watching me from the mirror as a smile hit her eyes, a glint of unadulterated glee sparkling in them.

"You look like a life-sized mop," Trina remarked with ease, answering for both of us while her eyes worked over the costume.

A scowl snatched the joy from Livy's face. She turned on the ball of her foot, smacking Trina's bicep with an open palm. "You do not say that to an actress," she said, her fair features twisted into an unbecoming snarl. "And just for that, you're helping me run lines."

"I'm only here to grab my camera lens," Trina protested, waving a hand in front of her face as if to pacify Livy. "I don't have time for that."

"Shoulda thought about that before you ran your mouth." Livy pinched a nub of flesh under Trina's bicep and twisted it between her fingers, eliciting a plea of mercy from her. "My room. Now."

"Jesus," Trina snapped, yanking her arm free, her footsteps begrudging as she made her way up the stairwell as if a firing squad waited at her back, Livy marching sideways behind her.

A heavy sigh left me as I watched them disappear. So much for making this visit quick.

I followed the aromas in the air into the dated kitchen my mother refused to let me renovate for fear it would upset my father's spirit. The floor tiles in here were the original powder white, cabinets an unfortunate orange-ish oak color, with Formica countertops. The upper cabinets had glass panes, displaying clay dishes my parents had brought with them from the motherland. A signature rooster, the universal mascot for all Portuguese immigrants, preened proudly on the island.

Ma's back was turned to me, body facing the gas stove that may as well have been from the early 1800's. A checkered kerchief tied around her head kept her wavy shoulder-length hair out of her face. She caught me from the corner of her eye, a smile touching her lips.

"João."

I shook my head at the sound of my legal given name, the same as my late father's. That had been one of the first things I ditched when I started my American assimilation. João was too difficult a name for most people to pronounce properly, and it made me an easy target for the likes of Peter Filch. I adopted Sean after the wrestler Shawn

Michaels, my favourite WWE star as a kid, effectively giving birth to a whole new identity.

My mother was the only one who refused to call me that, and it wasn't worth the argument for me to try to convince her otherwise.

"*Ma a bênção.*" I placed a kiss on her outstretched cheek, the skin warm against my mouth.

"*Deus te abênçoe,*" she murmured back to me, offering me the blessing I had asked her for out of custom and habit. I looked into the pot she was working at with a wooden spoon, where collard greens swam in a thickened potato broth. I knew chouriço (not chorizo, don't get them mixed up) was at the bottom of that pot, releasing its fat content into the soup. My mouth salivated as the scent made its way through my brain, unleashing a slew of memories of my childhood. The times I had stood on a chair alongside her, looking into different pots and pans that simmered, stewed, and boiled, watching her with curious wide eyes as she transformed simple ingredients into meals that always tasted like back home.

Her cooking had been what inspired me to go into the culinary arts to begin with; I wanted to create dishes that fostered the same connection to my roots that her food had always done for me. Cooking and food had been our shared passion; I had spent countless hours here in this kitchen with her, observing and learning in silence. My eyes tracked her as she seasoned by instinct, not by the direction of a recipe card or measuring spoon. She made adjustments by taste, offering me a sample on an outstretched spoon, waiting for me to confirm what she had already known. Ma never gave away her secrets; she had made me learn the hard way.

"Look what the cat dragged in." Maria's voice was smooth as she stepped into the kitchen. Her flat-ironed dark hair was pulled into a severe-looking ponytail, and she wore a faded crimson red Harvard crew neck sweater paired with black leggings and gray knit socks that stretched over her shins—a far cry from her neutral power suits and stilettos.

"Hello to you, too."

My older sister smirked at me, traipsing over to pull me into a hug.

Maria was on the taller side at five foot nine with a sculpted face and the same dark roasted coffee eyes as me.

"What are you doing here?" I asked, leaning against the island, arms folding across the expanse of my chest. "I'm surprised you could get away from the office." *Translation: You're here out of your own volition?*

"I needed a change of scenery," she lied, her eyes flitting toward the kitchen table where her laptop was open, files carelessly scattered around it. "I have to finish a briefing." *Translation: Ma called and gave me shit about never visiting.*

A laugh shook my chest. "So you thought coming back to the loudest house in the state was the answer?" Just then, Livy screamed something indiscernible from upstairs, followed by Trina's raucous laughter, driving my point home.

Maria smiled tightly, throwing her hands in the air as if she knew as well as I did that this was all just a facade and that she had about as much interest as I did in being here.

"João, are you hungry?" Ma interrupted, speaking Portuguese. I didn't get a chance to answer, for she was already ladling soup into a bowl. She handed it to me, even though it was too early for soup. Not caring, I took it with greedy hands and carried it to the kitchen table, where I shoved my sister's papers out of my way to clear some space.

Maria settled in her own seat, her chin dipping, fingers breaking off into a steady rhythm against the keyboard.

"The *boca grande* said her son is going to have a baby." The big mouth Ma was referring to was a term of endearment for good ol' Eileen Patterson, Dougie's mother. Ma got on all right with Eileen now, but that hadn't always been the case. Ma had found her rough around the edges when I was younger, not appreciating Eileen's boisterous tendencies and animated expressions, but Eileen had redeemed herself by shuttling Ma around when I wasn't available after Dad died. Now they spoke a couple of days a week on the phone and Eileen went to church with Ma on Sundays, even though she didn't understand a word of the sermon that was spoken entirely in Portuguese.

"Yeah," I said between blowing on the soup, "he is."

Maria's typing ceased, disbelief settling in her face. "Douglas

Patterson is going to be a father?" She rubbed her right fist as if recalling a distant memory, a faraway look touching her eyes. I assumed she was recalling the time she had deviated Dougie's septum.

"Yep." My lips popped.

Maria harrumphed, shoulders slouching, fingers finding their stride once more. "What woman let him of all people impregnate her?"

I pushed the spoon around the bowl. "It was a surprise for both parties, and Penelope's all right." Never did I think there would be a day when I defended Penelope twice in forty-eight hours, but a lot had happened in a week, and at this point I might be willing to do a lot of things to ensure she remained happy.

Maria's eyes narrowed. "Penelope? The designer I referred to you?" She shifted in her seat, her fingers tugging on the collar of her sweater.

"The very one."

"I see." She cleared her throat, a hand going up to smooth her hair, even though there were no flyaways. Why was she being so weird? Maria hated Dougie. That was no secret to anyone in this house or even to Dougie himself. Before I could put her on the spot, she said, "She seems normal."

"About as normal as you." I chuckled, searching for levity. Maria darted me a look of warning, blowing out a heated breath. Whether Maria wanted to acknowledge it or not, I knew that beyond her hatred for my best friend, she had always been just a little smitten by Dougie when we were kids, even if she would take that fact to her grave. In the grand scheme of things, it would have never worked out between them. Maria was married to her work and had zero interest in anything long-term, and certainly not in reproducing. Dougie's two-can-dine-for-$6.99 coupon at McDonald's would never be enough for my sister and her desire for the finer things in life.

Her fastidious typing took off again at a blinding speed. "Speaking of normal," she began without looking up at me, brows bending inward, eyes bouncing along her screen as she continued to type with a sense of urgency, "what's this I hear about you pursuing some girl who won't give you the time of day?"

At that, I frowned. How on earth did she know that already? Trina hadn't even seen Maria yet. When would she have had the time to tell her about Raquel?

As if reading my mind, my sister filled in the blanks. "Trina told Livy and I on MSN this morning."

After she managed to convince me to bring her here, it had taken Trina all of five minutes to change out of her pajamas, brush her teeth, and supply our sisters with an update on my love life. Un-fucking-believable.

"I'm getting real close to evicting that one." I exhaled, looking up at the ceiling, Livy's projected voice carrying down the stairs as she recited her lines.

"She means well," Maria said, her eyes still transfixed on her screen, "but we're your sisters. We all want to know what's going on in the life of the enigmatic Sean Tavares."

I didn't miss the mocking undertone in her words. "Says the one who comes home only when there's a gun pressed to their temple," I retorted.

"I'm busy. I'm trying to make partner at the firm by thirty-five. I've got four years left till I'm spoiled milk." Maria was an associate attorney at McIntyre & Nesbitt LLP, one of the largest law firms in Back Bay. Her office occupied thirty percent of The Pru. Maria's primary focus was business litigation and private equity—very compelling stuff if you're into numbers with a lot of commas between them and balding fifty-something men who were the primary suspects in white collar crimes. I always thought she would go for something more cutthroat and gritty, like family law, but Maria wasn't interested in scorned lovers who had caught their partners in an illicit affair, or children who were enraptured in the maelstrom of bullshit that came with a messy divorce. She preferred to take out all her aggression on corporate bigwigs who routinely made the mistake of underestimating her by assuming she was just another pretty face.

"Right, 'partner'." I raised my brows, to which she slammed me with another glare.

"So, who's the girl?" she probed, changing the subject by shoving me into the witness box.

"You mean you don't already have a full analysis on her?" I teased, catching the briefest hint of a smile from her.

"All Trina offered us was that the girl is, like," she lifted her fingers for dramatic effect, creating air quotes, "a thunderstorm."

"More like a tempest."

Maria laughed heartily, throwing her head back. "So, she keeps you on your toes?"

That was an understatement. I felt like all I had done since I met Raquel was chase her, my shoes doing the heel to toe routine, trying to break the distance between us—but she was always a little out of reach, and that left me both enthralled and pissed off. The memory of her getting into that car slammed into me, and my molars connected, jaws rocking from side to side. Maria cocked an eyebrow at me and I immediately released the tension, straightening in my seat.

"You spaced out, where did you go?" she asked, catching the distant look that flickered in my face.

"Nowhere good," I admitted with a sigh. I was hoping Trina had managed to keep that one small detail about last night to herself. Maria would slaughter Raquel's character, not even giving her a chance if she knew how last night concluded. "What exactly did Trina tell you?"

"Not much," Maria said, glancing at notes she had made, eyes squinting to make out the eloquent scrawl of her own writing. "Just that she was a writer at the paper in Eaton and that you two are electric in a room together."

"That is…" my voice trailed off, failing to find a word for it. Relief flanked me that Trina hadn't mentioned the catastrophe from the night before. How about that? She was capable of keeping something to herself after all.

"One hell of an observation?" Maria interrupted, "Tell me about it." She both looked and sounded entertained, flipping a hand through the air. "She would be wise to put all the energy she invests into people watching into something useful, like law."

I rolled my eyes. That hadn't been quite where I was going with this. Still, Trina's observation left me with a small window of hope. If that had been her perception from her viewing post at the top of the stairwell the day of the interview, then that meant I wasn't entirely crazy…that there was something beyond logic and explanation happening between Raquel and I.

I just needed to get her to see it that way, too.

"Are you going to offer me anything else, or do I need to call in the big guns?" I narrowed my eyes at Maria, who gave me a cursory look that reminded me that she wasn't above calling in a favor or two with the right people. It was hard to know what side of the law she was on, but I knew the answer to it: she was on whatever side made her the victor.

"All right," she said, losing her patience. "She's a writer?"

"Columnist," I amended.

"Sure," she nodded, as if there was a difference between the two, taking a sip from a mug in front of her that housed coffee that had probably long since gone cold, looking unfazed. "What's she look like?"

I swallowed, blinking at my sister, who let out an exasperated sigh. "Blond? Brunette? Green, straw-like hair?"

"Brunette, shoulder length.

"Cute," she tittered, batting her lashes at me. "Eyes?"

Big, the color of burnt cinnamon, almost honey under certain lighting. Thinking about Raquel's eyes made my heart quicken and my breaths hitch in my chest.

"Brown," I replied, scratching my forehead with my thumb, as if I was expunging the rest of the details from my mind out of fear my sister would read me like a book.

"Name?"

"Raquel."

"Nice name." She clicked something on the trackpad. "Last name?"

I paused, my stare tightening on hers. She failed at doing the sweet and persuasive routine on me, her protege. "Yeah, right," I scoffed. "I'm not falling for that one." I had learned everything I knew in the art of getting what I want from Maria.

Her face split into a Cheshire grin. "You can't fault me for trying." She tapped her chin one time too many, a movement that told me she already had what she wanted, "Although there's only *one* paper in

Eaton, and you've already done the hard part by giving me her first name."

Son of a fucking bitch.

"Don't." I grumbled. It wasn't that I was embarrassed by my attraction for Raquel. It was that I didn't want my sisters getting involved. If they got involved, then it was only a matter of time before my Ma started asking questions. And then they'd flood the *Advocate's* office, grilling Raquel before I could even get her to have dinner with me. I didn't want them messing everything up before it had even had a chance to start.

"I could just look her up right now."

"Maria." My voice carried a warning, although part of me wanted to know things about Raquel beyond what she had told me. I didn't move to stop my sister, listening as her fevered fingers made their way across the keyboard, lips rolling together with anticipation.

"Here we go." She grinned, eyes alive like she had unearthed Pandora's Box. It was when that smile slid from her face that I knew something was wrong.

"What?" I questioned. Maria's silence was killing me, the tips of her finger moving quickly across the trackpad of her MacBook. Her lashes fluttered with every rapid blink of her eyes, as if taking a snapshot of what she had seen. Her eyes flitted from the screen to me.

"Raquel Flannigan?" she asked.

I confirmed with a stiff nod.

Maria's mouth rocked from side to side, her eyes roaming the room, seeking something. She leaned forward in her seat, fingers once more dancing across the keyboard of her laptop. My heart had joined the conversation now, its beat steady in my chest.

"What did you see?" I started to stand, but she held a hand up at me, warning me to not try to look at her screen. Finally, a whistle left her, and her body slouched in her chair. She shook her head and spat out a tight curse.

"Thought that name sounded familiar."

I tossed her an annoyed look just as she spun her computer around to face me. A headline screamed out at me: *Attempted Robbery Thwarted in Revere.* My stomach sank to the floor when my eyes landed on an undated mugshot the news site had opted to use. Eyes that had enchanted me in another face stared back at me, the scowl, the shade of hair the same, and, of course, that last name.

"Liam Flannigan," I said flatly.

"I'm going to wager you didn't know." Maria's fingers worked the mousepad, settling on another paragraph. "This sounds like your girl," she said, pointing out Raquel's name. Her face wore a clinical expression, devoid of even a trace of compassion.

"Why would you ever remember something like this?" I said, frowning.

My sister leaned forward, her calculated eyes on my mother's back, voice dropping to a whisper. "The guy I was sleeping with during my first year of law school was the first responder on the scene."

I was so glad my hard work to keep her in school had allotted her time to be on her back. I tapered my stare at her. "And this was your idea of pillow talk?" I grumbled, voice edged with amusement.

Maria shrugged absently, turning her computer back around to face her, "It's the nature of the field, yeah." She clicked something else, expression going ashen for a split second before that mask secured itself back in place. "She's certainly had a sad life..." her voice carried, raising an octave when my mother looked back at us with suspicion. "Looks like her sister died a couple of months later."

"What?" My brows shot up.

"Yeah," she continued, "There's another story here from ten years ago linked under related content." Her eyes moved along the screen as she read aloud. "A seventeen-year-old South Boston girl was pronounced dead at the scene of a single-car crash on the Massachusetts Turnpike on Saturday, November twenty-first. The driver and sole occupant of the vehicle was later identified as Holly Jane Flannigan, the daughter of would-be Revere robber..." Her voice trailed off, her finger working across the scroll pad. "It talks about the incident with the armored car ...and that Holly leaves behind a mother, Pauline, and sister, Raquel."

My breaths are loud when they leave my body. I had gotten more than I had bargained for in my sister's quick Google search. The information had been under my nose all along, and not once had I even considered looking it up myself, because I guess in some strange way, I had been confident that I would get to know her eventually.

Guilt unsettled me, making me feel like I had betrayed her privacy in some strange way by indulging my sister's curiosity...and my own. So much about Raquel's character and disposition made sense now, but I hadn't earned the information honestly. Dougie had told me it wasn't his story to share, and it hadn't been mine or Maria's to do a deep dive on, either.

Fuck.

Maria blew out a breath, shaking her head with what looked like disappointment. "What is it with you and the broken strays?"

"What are you talking about?" I rubbed my temple with the tips of my fingers, an impending headache looming on the horizon.

She sighed. "The girls you're attracted to all seem to be cut from the same cloth."

I goaded her on with a hand gesture.

"There was that girl when you were in high school, the blonde who purposely drove into a bank when the guy she dated before you broke up with her."

"Colleen? We dated for six weeks before she got back together with him." My lips tightened into a thin line, failing to see her point. "What made her a *stray*?"

"Uh, the twenty-five foster homes she got thrown out of isn't enough evidence?" She grimaced.

I shrugged noncommittally, urging her to continue with a kick of my bearded chin.

"Fine." Maria organized her papers into a neat pile, tapping the collection against the table so they aligned and fed into her neuroticism, "Then there was that girl a couple of years ago. The Italian one. She purposely got herself knocked up with someone else's kid because you wouldn't propose to her, and tried to pass it off as yours."

Francesca had been good, I would give her that. Almost perfect, really, if it wasn't for her being just a little fucking nuts.

"I figured her out," I lamented. That had almost been a monumental disaster, and I was glad I had taken Maria's advice about the paternity test. Francesca had all but crumbled at the suggestion and spewed the truth: I wasn't her baby's father. Last I heard, she had moved to Arizona with the kid's actual father. Good riddance.

"After you bought her an engagement ring, Sean."

Okay, the ring thing hadn't been all my doing, and I hadn't really wanted to marry her, either. That had been at the behest of the firecracker currently at the stove, who was dismally failing at being furtive. She was stealing not-so-wary looks at us while remaining taciturn. Ma, who in spite of never even having met Francesca, demanded I do the right thing. She had actually been disappointed when she learned the baby wasn't mine.

"Ma made me buy the ring," I said.

"And you listened to her," Maria spat, whipping the folder shut. I swear, she looked like she was ready to lurch over the kitchen table and bash my head with her laptop.

She wasn't wrong. Maybe I hadn't dated the best girls, but...Raquel was different. And I was on a mission to change Maria's mind about her, but first, I needed to show her that her prejudice wasn't helping. My sister was the most open-minded and liberal woman I knew, if anyone was going to see reason, it was her.

I placed an elbow on the table, resting my bearded chin on my fist. "So, what you're saying is that this one is bad news because of the actions of her deceased father?" I laid out the argument on the table. Even uttering it made me feel that shame again for giving my sister the information to investigate Raquel.

"No," Maria said, rubbing the bridge of her narrow nose, "I'm saying she's going to have a lot of baggage that I don't think you have the room to house."

"My house is fifteen hundred square feet. I think I can manage." I didn't care for her metaphors any more than she cared for mine.

Maria shook her head. "She's just another stray, Sean. And you need to concentrate on fixing yourself before you rebuild other people."

My body wrenched backward, as if she had tipped the entire bowl of soup in front of me into my lap. My skin felt aflame, my blood pressure like it was soaring, creating a pulse I could feel in my eardrums.

"What the hell is that supposed to mean?" I crossed my arms across my chest, leaning back against the wooden chair, my eyes narrowing as I waited for her explanation.

She let out a long, drawn-out exhalation, as if the mere question had exhausted her stoicism. "I mean that we both know this house flipping thing is not something you want to spend the rest of your days doing."

I dismissed the accusation with a *pfft*. I knew where she was going, and I wasn't in the mood to entertain this conversation. We had it every couple of months, when she was riding another wave of her superiority complex. I slid the chair backward, standing to my full height. My sister did the same, mirroring my stance, arms hanging by her sides, fists folding and unfolding.

"You should consider resuming your classes at the institution." She frantically shuffled her folders until she found what she was searching for. My eyes landed on the pamphlet. My insides roiled, my lower intestine tightening the way it did when you were about to erupt from deep-seated, boiling anger.

"I already called them," she continued. "They said they would honor the classes you've already taken and you can just resume where you left off. You're only a couple of credits short."

Katrina had a mild case of my mother's condition of not being able to mind her own business, but Maria? Maria was downright overbearing. She would drive your life if you let her, right down to whether you were buying two-ply rather than one-ply toilet paper, and I wasn't having any of it.

I had given up my ambition to earn a degree for good reason, and I didn't need her to go rehashing and unearthing things that were better left buried.

"Who the fuck told you to do that?" I snapped, slamming both palms on the table. Her forehead wrinkled at my outburst, and for a moment, I thought she might actually consider that her dictatorial behavior might have gone too far this time. First she was telling me who I should and shouldn't date, shaming me for who I actually *had* dated or fucked, and now she was telling me the cure to all my troubles was to resume a program I had left for *her?*

Maria recovered and tittered on as if she hadn't just violated a boundary, "You've still got all your supplies, so you'd be saving money there, too."

"I'm not going back."

"Well," she said, shaking the pamphlet in front of me, "I think you should."

I snatched it from her and tossed it with indelicate violence. It hit the table and slid to the floor. My eyes immediately went back to her, not giving a shit that she appeared affronted by my lack of decorum.

My sister's arms found her hips, standing akimbo as if she was getting ready to lawyer me into submission, but I wasn't sticking around for it. I wasn't hungry anymore, and I didn't care to indulge any more of my sister's ascendancy lectures. She could save the shit for a fucking jury or the pathetic motherfuckers in their skinny ties that she charged two-hundred-and-fifty dollars an hour.

"If I wanted your opinion, I would ask for it, Maria." I pushed the chair back in place, taking my soup bowl and placing the remnants on the counter, before stalking toward Ma, who looked less than impressed. Her English was good at best if people communicated slowly, but she didn't have to be fluent to discern that my sister and I were less than enthused with each other, based on our rising voices.

Ma tsk-tsked at my sister for upsetting me, lips compressing together.

"Don't listen to her, *meu rico filhe*." There was the *my rich son* bullshit I loved so much.

"Stop filling his head up with bullshit just because you're afraid of forgetting Dad's memory."

That had been a low blow, even by Maria's standards. She was in full-on attorney attack mode, pleading her case, her countenance pained. "You cannot spend the rest of your life being a substitute for Dad for her," she said to me, holding out a hand in our mother's direction. "That is not what he would have wanted from you. He wanted you to go after your dreams, he wanted your name on a resta—"

Ma slapped a palm on the counter, the ricochet deafening the entire house. Maria and I both jolted at the suddenness of the sound, and my sisters upstairs even stopped their squabbling. Ma's whole body shook when she spun on her heel, face quivering with something indefinable.

183

"*Cala a boca*, Maria." She shot my sister a stare that God himself would fear, sending a shiver rolling through us both. It was a rare event for Ma to be volatile like that, especially against Maria. Pushy? Definitely. But this...this was a new side of her; I couldn't remember a time she had ever told any of us to just shut up like that. The room thickened with silence, save for the food that bubbled in a stockpot on the stove.

I thought my sister would say more, but Maria merely blew through her nose and shook her head at me. She collected her belongings and stalked toward me, discomfort etched into the planes of her face.

"You're better than this," she scolded, not looking at me as she left the room. My jaw set, my breathing strained as the thought settled into the recesses of my mind.

What was her angle? Why did she care so much what I did with my life? It was because of me that she had gone to fucking Harvard. *Me.* And she wanted to what? Lengthen her neck and look down at me over that fucking nose job we all knew she got two years ago but no one talked about. Give me a fucking break.

I scrubbed my face with my palms, my fingers rubbing into my eye sockets.

"You want food to take home?" Ma asked, her voice cheery, as if my sister and I hadn't just been arguing. Like Ma herself hadn't just interceded with her own emotional explosion. My stomach churned again at the thought of food, but I found myself nodding out of habit—because my sister was right. I had always done what she said anyway, hadn't I?

Ma sighed with contentment, like everything had gone back to normal. "You're a good boy, João." She patted my cheek.

Any other day, that remark would have lessened the knot in my chest.

Today, it only made it worse.

CHAPTER TWENTY ONE

Sean

THEY SAY things happen in threes. It had been almost a week since the bar incident, six days since my falling out with my sister, and three days since the house had sold to some unlikely buyers—for over the asking price. I was dumbstruck, mouth opening and closing as I tried to collect my thoughts when the listing agent of the house called to inform me. After months of struggling to get that thing off my hands, the bouncing checks, and an unlikely couple forging within these four walls—the house was sold, and no longer a source of contention for me.

I'd had the bulk of the furniture cleared out as soon as the ink was dry on the contract. Trina had wrapped the smaller decorative pieces herself, neatly tucking them back into a box. Penelope was out of commission due to a bad bout of morning sickness that left her needing to be within five feet of a toilet at all times. The one time she had come in this week, she'd puked on the front steps. I sent her packing. I didn't trust that the hardwood wouldn't stain if she didn't make it the bathroom in time. She was a liability I didn't need.

I had been pissed for a solid seven days and had vested all that pent-up rage toward both Raquel and Maria into being busy. My mind craved the consistency of a task, needing the steady rhythm of being concentrated on just about anything to console my thoughts and nurse my bruised ego. I cycled between being furious with Raquel, to feeling so damn sorry for her that I was ashamed of myself.

Being preoccupied had been a welcome respite, and now with the house officially out of my hair, I had to find something else to bury myself in. I hadn't wasted time once the deal had closed and applied any last-minute touches when I wasn't clearing the staging furniture out. The buyers had asked for a short closing of two weeks, and I wanted to use what was left of that time to pack up and figure out what the hell was next. I had my eye on another house three blocks over that had potential and wasn't nearly as worse for wear as the colonial had been. Parts of me had wanted a break, but this oppressive niggling voice in the back of my head dragged up Maria's words from our argument—and that made me want to do the exact opposite.

"You're better than this."

I wasn't sure who I was pissed off with more right now, Raquel for getting into the car with those guys, or my sister for running her mouth. Then, when I popped a lid onto a box and moved it from the table onto the floor next to the rest of the stack, I suddenly decided I was infinitely more upset with Maria and her superiority complex and pretension.

There was nothing wrong with what I did for a living. I had provided for my family for years, and no one batted an eye. Now, for whatever reason, Maria had plenty to say about my job. Suddenly, it wasn't good enough for her. She didn't need my money anymore, so of course she could afford to provide me unsolicited feedback, preach to me about how I was fulfilling someone else's legacy. It had nothing to do with that...it was a *job*. We all made choices when Dad had died, and this had been mine. My decisions kept the lights on in Ma's house, money in my bank account, kept my two kid sisters' bellies full, and apparently gave Maria the very platform which she stood upon now, all high and mighty. I knew we would eventually come to an impasse, as we did in the majority of our arguments, but this entire thing had left a piss-poor taste in my mouth.

I was better than what, exactly? Plenty of people gave up their initial ambitions, countless people before me had gone to college with their eyes set on some incredible career that gained them notoriety, fame, an eclectic menu that acquired them a reputation that preceded them, only to have it fall apart once they graduated. How many would-be chefs did I know right now who were just like me, working a job they needed, forgetting about the career they had wanted? At least I had bowed out before I could even really work in my knives. That was life—sometimes you didn't get what you wanted.

I thrusted another stack of folders into a nearly full box with more aggression than necessary, not really thinking about what was going where. I would figure it out when I got the keys to the next project and started the unpacking process again in a makeshift office space. For now, this would all get shoved into the workshop behind Ma's house until things were more concrete and my plan was solidified. The potential project house I had put an offer on was a three-bedroom, two bath, First Period colonial, with a gambrel roof and three front-facing dormers that looked like they were a sneeze away from falling down. There was a lot of original chamfer that with a little tender finessing could be restored to its former glory.

As I pulled a book off the shelf, the sound of gravel kicking up in the driveway drew my attention to the window overlooking the front yard. The sun was already setting for the day, the sky a brilliant blend of pink and orange as it descended amongst the barren treetops and houses in the distance. I leaned forward, my breath catching in my chest at the sight of a familiar battered-looking black Toyota Camry rolling into the driveway.

Of all the places, and all the people—what was Raquel doing here?

My throat worked at the lump, eyes tracking the car that came to a stop next to my Jeep, which was opposite the silver Range Rover Penelope had left here two days ago when Dougie had to take her home sick. From my concealed vantage point in the darkened office, I watched her sit there, like she was trying to find her metaphorical balls before she could convince herself to get out of the car. It was five more minutes before the rattling engine that caused an ungodly amount of noise pollution finally stopped.

The car door swung open, an ear-grating creak resounding through the driveway. One lean leg, foot clad in her black Doc Martens, found the ground with overzealous caution, as if she was finally committing to getting out of the car. The other leg followed. She emulated a newborn doe with the way she clambered out, the car door squeaking in protest when she closed it with one arm. Her chin kicked upward, looking up at the house with the expression one might have if the building was on fire and they had left their dog inside.

For a split second, I thought she would turn back, worry etching into her delicate bone structure as though if she continued her approach, the flames would claim her, too. She debated a moment more before her face stiffened and her shoulders dropped. Plucking her gumption from places unknown, her legs worked across the even gravel, strides long and purposeful. I listened to her boots on the steps of the porch, the soles heavy against the wood, and then there was silence, save for the faint sound of the bare tree branches rustling in the early evening wind.

A war of listlessness and anticipation set my equilibrium off kilter as the seconds stretched on, my heart a steady thumping in my chest. Turning away from the window, I walked back to the bookshelf, struggling to stabilize my shallow breaths as they left my parted lips. My eyes bounced from the bookshelf to the front door I knew she stood on the other side of. I considered for a moment that there was still a good chance she would change her mind and book it back to her car, but then the front door opened. I chose to not put on an air of covert surprise, instead taking on a deliberate look of indifference as she stepped into the house.

"Hello?" she called out, shutting the door behind her. "Penelope?"

Her head was tilted toward the living room. Her eyes took in the vast emptiness of the space: the mirrorless walls, the lack of furniture. Her shoulders drooped. My heart fluttered over the near proximity, the realization that she was a mere ten feet away from me. The late fall breeze she had let in with the door carried her scent over to me, and my sinuses drew it in with deep breaths that triggered the hippocampus of my brain, a flurry of memories flying at me that almost made me want to reconsider how pissed I was at her.

Clearing my throat loud enough to draw her attention, she whipped her head in my direction, eyes wide when they met mine, something in her countenance softening upon recognizing me. Her warm appraisal left me unnerved the longer she stared. Why the hell did she have to look at me like I was the best damn thing she'd seen in days when she hadn't even bothered to acknowledge my text message? Images of her getting into that car had my blood pressure heading north, a stiff breath leaving me as I considered for the briefest moment to tell her to fuck off and get out, simply because I fucking deserved better than whatever table scraps she tossed my way when it suited her.

"Sean."

And there was the sound of my name on her tongue, and I was done. That was all it took to officially abate my anger. One syllable, four letters, and that Southie drawl, and my balls were already holding up the white flag of surrender, ready to propose a truce.

We stared at each other as if we had forgotten what the other looked like, drinking in the other's presence until our respective minds were abuzz with something hazy. I broke eye contact first, needing some semblance of self-control, or else I was going to stalk over to her, and there would go what was left of my dignity and self-respect again.

"You're the last person I expected to see here, Hemingway," I sniffed, mustering up artificial annoyance while turning my back to her. I removed another book from the shelf, tossing it carelessly to the desk.

"You sold the house," she marveled, voice spilling into the space of the office, ignoring my remark. The glass paneled doors opened wider on a whisper; I listened as her hand found the doorknob. "I saw the sign out front. That's great! You must be relieved."

Glancing at her over my shoulder, I took in the small details that wouldn't have mattered to anyone else, but they made me feel off-put. Her tight fingers clung to the doorknob as if it was the only thing keeping her upright, the bags under her eyes that had been poorly covered by makeup, the way her full brows were drawn inward, the weak smile that didn't reach eyes bloodshot from crying—though I suspected that if I asked her, she would deny it.

A curse rang out through my mind, eyes focusing on the calendar pinned to the wall, gaze honing in on the date. The tears that had resulted in her red-rimmed eyes weren't for Penelope, though I'm sure the newfound loneliness didn't help—the anniversary of her sister's death was tomorrow.

My molars clenched together tightly, a pain shooting to my temple with each squeeze. It was a clandestine detail I had no business being aware of, but my own sister's inquisitive and intrusive lawyer instincts had planted the seed of the idea in my mind. As soon as I found myself alone, I scraped the internet for whatever else I could find on Raquel. I read every news report available about her family, cataloging the smallest, most inconsequential details. I devoured the archived columns she had published at *The Daily Free Press* when she was a student at BU a few years ago, falling in love with the spirit of her words from her days as a student, determined to be heard, fighting for her chance to be seen. The pieces were entirely different from what she now wrote for *The Advocate*. Her current columns were toned down, sugary and formulaic, as if someone had reined her in and taken her spirit with them. Her stuff from ten years ago had been raw, gritty... beautiful. It made me think that somewhere along the way, she hadn't just lost her father and her sister, but her passion, too.

I could certainly empathize with that. I knew what it was like to fall out of love with something that had always been your crutch, the essence of your existence. I knew what it was like to experience something so life-altering that it was a struggle to look at what you had once loved with every essence of your being through the same lens.

Raquel shifted her weight from foot to foot, her right hand clinging onto the elbow of her left arm, appearing guarded and small. Tomorrow would be another day for anyone else in the world. They would get up, go to work, perhaps go home to their two-point-five kids, loveless marriage, and yappy lap dog, the sun would set in the evening and rise in the morning just like it always had, and life would go on. For Raquel, though, every breath would feel laborious. Every attempted smile would require the strength of a two-ton truck. Every effort would be on borrowed energy for the following day. And when she was finally alone, she would crack. She would succumb to her emotions, the tears would fall freely, and she would silently scream to a higher power, *"Why?"*

I hated that our grief was a mirror of one another. It was as interchangeable as our loss of ambition.

My heart squeezed, but I resisted the urge to round the desk and take her into my arms. Instead, I cleared my throat, not bothering to spare her a look, concentrating on the front door where just a few weeks ago, touching her for the first time had set my whole world aflame.

"I am," I managed with a curt nod, turning away from her again.

"Is, um," she began, her feet shuffling across the floor as she rounded the desk. I looked down and had to swallow a smile; she had taken off her shoes. Black socks stark against the hardwood, her toes curling against the planks of the floors.

"Penelope's not here, no."

She blew out a breath. Lifting a thumb to her mouth, she bit her nail, her unusually golden eyes pensive.

"Okay," she said, nodding her head. Her eyes flitted to the nearly emptied bookshelf, hesitation filling those tired features. "I saw her car out front, so I thought…" The words sounded like they were dying in her mouth.

"She's got a bad spell of morning sickness and has been off the last couple of days."

Guilt filled her face, as though realizing this was another detail of her friend's life she had missed out on in her absence.

"Oh." She released her hold on her elbow, both arms now dangling loosely at her side. Raquel's eyes roamed the room, gaze bouncing between the half-packed box and the emptied bookshelf. "Do you want some help?"

The out-of-character offer of assistance nearly put me on my ass. I glanced at her, seeing a flash of something indiscernible in her eyes. Was this her attempt at an olive branch?

The part of me that was still bitter with her about last week wanted to tell her to get the fuck out. The weaker part of me—the one whose teenage wet dream was standing in front of him again, whose heart was thundering at the smell of her shampoo, at the faint trace of cigarettes that were tangled into the fold and had scrambled my logic—nodded in silence.

I was almost pissed at myself for agreeing until that weak, cold smile of hers grew just a little tepid. I resisted the urge to puff out my chest, as if I had done something worthy. It was a smile, for heaven's sake, not a cure for cancer. She moved to my side, accepting the books I handed her, stowing them into boxes. We worked in tandem, the room thick with our silence, though neither of us made an effort to speak. She frowned when she peered into one of the other banker's boxes into which I had carelessly tossed books and files.

"Can I reorganize these?"

"Why?" I asked, my tone plain.

Her eyes met mine, discomfort testing her composure, slender fingers leafing through my things. "You'll just never find anything this way."

"It's fine."

"I promise, if you just let me reorganize this, you'll thank me," she reassured. I wasn't used to this uncertain side of her. Even her voice had become timorous, no sign of that even cadence I had grown fond of with her vitriol and sarcasm.

"I've managed before you just fine," I pointed out. She stilled, arms dropping to her sides, looking downtrodden.

"Okay." She bit her lower lip, the same one I had nibbled a few weeks ago. "I know you're pissed at me, but it really..." she trailed off, eyes looking at some unknown object above her in a crude attempt to avoid my gaze.

"It 'really' what?"

A tense breath left her, her lissome shoulders squaring. She found her balls, because she met my eyes dead on. "It wouldn't have worked between us long term, y'know?"

"Wow." I laughed through my nose, shaking my head as she continued to look at me confidently, as if it had been totally within reason for her to up and leave with the shittiest people I'd encountered in a long time.

"I'm complicated," she continued. "We had a bit of fun at the bar, but let's be honest, there was no future between you and I."

My jaw rocked back and forth. She couldn't just relax and just see where things went? Couldn't she just give me a fair shot at getting to know her first before she ruled me out? What did those scumbags have over me? If she wanted a rap sheet, I could start off with beating all three of those guys within an inch of their lives—would battery and assault charges score me some more of those points she'd spoken of last week when her body had been practically undulating beneath mine?

Contemplation turned my jaw to granite, the vein in my neck ticking as my temper surged.

"Are you done?" I said with a sigh of irritation, cocking an eyebrow at her.

"Excuse me?" she deadpanned, eyes narrowing. "Done what?"

"Feeding yourself that heaping pile of bullshit." Damn, it felt good to say that. "'Cause I don't know about you, but it stinks in here."

"You know what?" she huffed, a lick of something familiar and dark flickering in her eyes that had my stomach lurching with hunger for something that was more like her. "Forget I said anything." She spun around and walked toward the door of the office.

A bitter laugh escaped me, watching the unintentional sashay of her hips as she approached the office door.

"That's right, Raquel. Run away," I taunted, slamming her with a look of derision when she whipped around to give me an evil eye. "I'm figuring out that's what you do best."

"You don't know anything about me," she snapped.

My mouth curled into a snide smile. "I don't have to, Hemingway." I casually rounded the desk, approaching her lithe frame, my blood pumping hard in my veins, my teeth grinding together. "I've got you all figured out." My body crowded her space, but the little shit wouldn't move. She was rooted in that spot, shooting me a look that was determined to call my bluff. That got my body hot, the predator in me wanting to force her into submission.

She wanted a fight? I would give her one she would never forget.

"You don't want to keep anyone around because you're terrified of what it means to need someone, anyone." My eyes searched hers, and if it wasn't for the tiny twitch in her right nostril, I would have almost thought she was indifferent to my accusation.

Raquel wasn't a hardened bitch or a harpy like Dougie believed; she was a battered and bruised animal. She behaved so squirrelly because getting comfortable with the consistency of someone's presence had gotten her hurt in the past. How did you trust anyone after that much loss? Her father's crime had dragged her family's name through the mud, and just when the fog had started to clear, her sister died, too. I couldn't fault her for wanting to avoid creating an emotional dependency on anyone, but that didn't mean I would allow her to bow down to that fear. Whether she and I had a future was irrelevant if she didn't believe she was deserving of one.

Life was a careful balancing act of give and take, of fostering emotional connections with people and trusting them to do right by you. That came at a cost, specifically vulnerability, and that was frightening. It had the capacity to be rewarding as well—but Raquel needed to realize that the reward negated the risk.

"I don't need anyone." Her eyes burned a hole in me. I checked the pride I felt at the sight of her derision. Good, this was a start.

"Then why are you still here?"

Her head snapped back, mouth popping open as though she hadn't foreseen that. My Raquel, who was calculated, cunning, and sharp-tongued, hadn't predicted my statement. She drew in a sharp breath, but it was too late. I had her where I wanted her, and I was about to drive my point home.

"You say don't need anyone, but you're here looking for Penelope because you fucked up. You stayed, even after learning she's not here, because you like me, and that fucking terrifies you."

Her breathing went ragged, as if each pull of oxygen physically pained her, a petrified look in her eyes.

"I don't like you," she denied, her lips pinching together, as if she didn't like the way those words tasted in her mouth anymore than I had liked hearing them.

"So, you're a coward *and* a liar?" I edged closer to her, a cocky smile lifting my lips. "Good to know."

"You—"

"Don't know anything about you?" I finished. I took another step toward her, catching the glimmer of panic that sparked in her face, as if she'd just realized that she was about to lose the war within her that she had been fighting. Raquel jerked away when my near proximity became too much for her to bear, her body ripping itself free from the floorboards, taking backward steps into the office.

I tracked after her, my body looming close to hers. Her ass the hit edge of my desk with a soft thud, her fingers curling around the lip of the cherry wood as she sat on the desk, her breaths heavy. The alluring rise and fall of her chest mesmerized me into an exhilarating trance.

"I never lie," she whispered.

"I think you lie all the time." Standing opposite her now, my hands came down around either side of her hips, my palms pressing into the top of the desk, bending at the waist so I could glare into her frightened eyes. "I think you lie because reality scares you too much. You like the way the lie feels, and you accept that as your truth instead."

"I never lie," she repeated, her pitch higher this time, that little chin of hers jutting out, her defiance a massive unintentional turn-on that I was about to school.

"You know what the sad thing is, Hemingway?" I murmured, watching as my hand took on a mind of its own, reaching up to touch her face, the pads of my fingers hungry for contact. The soft skin of her jawline sent a current through my body that left me reeling, but it was the drop of her eyelids that made me realize this conversation was all but over.

"What's that?" she finally managed to say, her eyes remaining lidded, lips parting.

My mouth hovered over hers, my words fanning her face. "You don't believe your lies, either."

She leaned forward and found my mouth. Her kiss was urgent, a sound of release leaving her on a hiss that made my heart kick in my chest. Raquel's legs parted—I didn't know if it was involuntary or subconsciously—and her fists bunched the hemline of my gray fitted Henley, drawing me closer to her until her hot core was grinding against my cock, which was delighted to be invited to this impromptu tea party. Her body was like a magnet, pulling me forward whether I wanted it to or not. Her kiss scorched my mouth like fucking whiskey, a slow burn that ached all the way down, inciting an inextinguishable blaze in my body.

There was no threat of someone else coming into the house, no one to take her away from me. Right now, she was entirely mine.

Her hands felt cold when they slid under my shirt, her fingertips a languorous assault that warmed themselves as they worked over the planes of my abs. A moan of approval freed itself from the back of her throat that had my cock straining against my jeans, demanding to be released from the restraints. When her hands started a slow descent, I intercepted, grabbing her wrists with both hands, pinning them to either side of her, using the opportunity to deepen the kiss. My tongue teased her bottom lip, demanding access that she readily gave me. Her tongue circled mine in a slow dance that made my head spin, every nerve in my body tingling with anticipation. I let go of my hold on her wrists, cupping her cheeks with my palms, dipping her head back, my greedy mouth working against hers. Her tongue met each stroke of mine.

Her freed hands found my belt loops and pulled me against her. The responsive freneticism of her hips as her core worked against mine nearly sent me over the edge, the loss of control imminent. I released my hold on her cheeks, dropping my hands to her waist to drag her closer against me. I had a decision to make here, one that I had had to consider a week ago. A decision that carried consequences, for if not handled delicately it could have lasting ramifications with a ripple effect felt for years to come. Raquel wasn't just the girl you hit it and quit it with, in spite of the skewed lens through which she viewed herself. She was the one you fought for, the one you spent most of your life searching for.

I wanted to do differently by her, but first she had to learn. Fortunately for her, I was a great teacher.

"Can I touch you?" I cautiously asked, voice heavy with gravel.

Her eyes widened, like she had never been asked that question before. Her nod was brief if enthusiastic, and of course her kiss had already told me everything I needed to know.

She was all in.

I picked her up by the waist with ease, she was an easy hundred and fifteen pounds soaking wet. I had lifted bags of cement heavier than her. Her long legs raised to circle my waist, arms wrapping around my neck as her fingers found my hair. Throughout it all, her mouth never left mine. There was a desperation in the way she kissed me, as if she was trying to smother whatever pain was stoking the fire that raged inside of her. I walked us over to the chair behind the desk and dropped my ass into it, our combined weight sending the chair back into the nearly emptied bookshelf with a rattle. Before she could settle in my lap, I guided her back to her feet, keeping her steady by her hips.

She surveyed me through lids that were half open, my thumb and pointer finger popping the button of her jeans open. My heartbeat pounded as loud as a snare drum in my ears as I pulled down the zipper, exposing lace-trimmed her black panties contrasting against her alabaster skin. She stabilized herself by resting her hand on my shoulder as I leaned forward, blowing out a breath to mask the pain of my aching balls while I shimmied the dark denim of her jeans over her toned thighs, bunching them at her knees.

Weeks. I had wanted this for fucking *weeks*.

Leaning back in the chair, I rubbed my fingers across my mouth, taking her in. The slight jut of her diminutive hips and the thin strip of lace from her thong that kept her concealed from me had me yearning in a way I never had before. I had wanted this from the first moment I saw her, and now I had her. I guided her to me, turning her so her ass settled across my hard-on. She settled her nose under the scruff of my jawline, tilting her head back to lean against my hard pecs. The faint heady scent of her arousal labored my breathing, my hand sliding down her long torso. Her hips rose to greet my hand that cupped the damp heat of her core.

Every pull of oxygen she took seemed to come to her urgently, as if her lungs couldn't keep up. I nuzzled her with my nose, my eyes taking in the beauty etched with need in her face. Her teeth sank into her plump lower lip as my finger teased the edge of her underwear, wanting to savor every moment.

She released her bite on her lower lip when my mouth crashed against hers. Her arm reached up to curl around the back of my neck, pulling me closer.

"Hemingway," I murmured breathlessly, my middle finger coaxing that hot seam of hers that I desperately wanted to bury myself in, "admit that you're a liar."

"If I do," her voice sounded strained, "will you touch me properly?"

Fuck. Her request almost made me lose my resolve and abandon my game plan entirely. No. I had to see this through. I had been raised with the belief that some lessons couldn't be taught, they had to be experienced.

And this was an experience Raquel would feel for days to come.

"Admit that you're a liar and we'll see," I coaxed, teasing her through her panties.

"I'm a liar." The mewl she let out sent the hair on my arms upright.

"Good girl." I kissed her jawline, her head leaning to rest on my chest, revealing a better view of what was going on between her legs. My big palm was over her heat, her jeans bunched at her knees. Her hips bucked against my hand, but I stilled her.

I swallowed the tight lodge in my throat, my next request forming in my head, her heart beating so hard that I could feel it reverberating through her ribcage against my chest.

"Now tell me you like me."

Her heartbeat quickened, whether from anticipatory anxiety, her arousal, or the threat of the impending truth materializing inside of her, I didn't know, but I could practically feel the ache coming from her core.

"No," she hissed, eyes shrewd and daring. She seemed to have figured out my game and was denying me the simple pleasure I would have derived from the admission. Whether she liked it or not, I would coax the truth out of her.

A cocky smirk teased the edges of my mouth. With a laggard touch, I pushed her thong aside, a trimmed smattering of pubic hair greeting me as I dragged my index finger against the slippery slit, her guise of resilience slipping at the skin-on-skin contact. Her body shuddered, but her profile masked her thoughts, her eyes trained on me. This girl was good, but I was better. Her arousal coated the finger that I slipped into her tight entrance, and she was all but putty in my hands. The sound that came out of her nearly made me lose my load inside my own pants, like a teenage boy touching a girl for the first time.

My thumb found her clit, working her with just the right amount of pressure. I released my hold on her hips, watching as she fucked herself against my hand to the hilt, nearly making me forget what I was trying to do in the first place until my mind jerked me back into reality.

"Tell me the truth, or I'll stop."

"No," she pleaded breathlessly, but it was impossible to discern what part of my statement she was objecting to. Deciding there was only one way to figure that out, I pulled my hand away. Raquel immediately jerked in my lap, I all but shoved her off me. With a yelp of surprise, she stumbled toward the desk, giving me full view of that plump, supple ass, making me want to bend her over the desk right now and undo my pants.

No. I had a mission here, and a point to drive home, and whether that ended with her spread open for me or with me kicking her out, we were going to settle this here and now, once and for all. I got up and bent her over the desk, her ass in the air.

"Are you going to fuck me now, Slim?" she challenged. Her palms spread out on the desk, bracing herself for what she probably thought was going to be the fucking of her lifetime.

I wanted to oblige, desperately. I wanted to fuck Hemingway more than I wanted to see the Pats win the Super Bowl every year. I had imagined the beauty of her cunt for weeks on end, and now it was here for my taking, dripping with her need for *me*.

But I wasn't going to fuck her.

What I was going to do to her would be worse.

Much worse.

And whether Raquel wanted to acknowledge it or not, she wouldn't just admit she liked me.

She would beg for me.

It would be painful for her, but not as much as it would pain me.

I sat up from the chair, my lips rolling together as I dragged her jeans off of her legs. I stood to my full height, my body draping over hers like a heavy blanket, my hands pushing her shirt and bra up until I felt the small swells of her breasts.

"Oh, I'm not going to fuck you, Hemingway," I ground out against her ear, palming her left breast with one hand. I bunched her thin panties around my fist, and with a quick wrench of my wrist, the material tore, the sound tangling with the tortured moan from the back of her throat. I dropped the panties in her line of vision on the desk, and if she had looked high before, the expression on her face now was nearly an out-of-body experience.

I backed my body away just enough to give myself room so I could slide my hand down the small of her back, my fingers feather light against the flesh of her ass, another impatient cry escaping her lips.

Her profile appeared strained from my torment. "Please," she panted, pressing her chest into my palm, her hips rocking against the desktop.

"I like you, okay?" Her voice was breathless. "I like you a lot."

My chest almost exploded with pride, but it didn't change anything.

She was going to learn the hard way.

I teased her pussy with the side of my hand, and she all but screamed from the anguish of the buildup.

"Say it again."

Venom sprang to life in her darkening eyes. "Fuck you," she bit out, wrestling underneath me, backing her ass into my hard-on. Raquel ground herself against me in an effort to take control of the situation,

as if I would be feeble-minded enough to abdicate my plan to domi-
nate her over something as innocuous as that ass of hers grinding
against me.

"Not this time, Hemingway." My laugh salacious, I sent her back
into the desk with a forward thrust of my hips "But someday." I slid
two fingers into her, spinning them inside of her until I set off into a
steady rhythm of pumps, loving the feel of her and wishing like hell
that I didn't have a point to prove.

"I like you, I like you…oh God, I fucking like you," she cried out,
her body meeting each thrust of my furious fingers.

"That's my girl." Whether she liked it or not, she was mine.

I sank to my knees, my fingers sliding out of her. I brought my
mouth to her dripping heat.

"Wait, what—" her shock died in her mouth when my tongue met
her clit. She was sweeter than I expected for someone so damn bitter. I
expected a tang of salt to her arousal, but what I got was a sugary
syrup that challenged my willpower. I flattened my tongue against her,
flicking at her clit until moans raked out of her mouth as I pushed her
toward the edge.

"Tell me you're sorry for being such an asshole," I demanded
against her pulsating pussy, my taut tongue taunting her entrance.

"I'm sorry," she sputtered. She was so high on the thrill, chasing
her impending orgasm, that I believed she was willing to do or say just
about anything.

My tongue worked back and forth, flicking at the nub until I felt
her thighs trembling. Her juices dribbled over my mouth, running
down to my chin.

Raquel thought she was going to come, but she was wrong.

She had shown up here looking for Penelope, to make amends for
her wrong. But what she was about to get was a whole lot worse.

I'd leave her dangling on that painful precipice, the brink of an
orgasm that wasn't going to come–not by my hands, anyway.

Maybe next time she would think twice about leaving with
someone else, maybe she would finally be able to give up the story
she'd built up in her head and accepted as her truth. Maybe she would
finally abandon the comfort of her own lies.

Reaching for her jeans, I climbed to my feet, my ears registering the indignant sound of frustration she made.

"What the fuck, Sean?" Raquel hissed, her pitch sharp. She pushed herself up just as I tossed her jeans on the desk. A wounded look settled onto her ruddy face, sweat matting her hair to her forehead as her eyes bounced between her pants and me, as if she was piecing together my ploy all along.

Her dry laugh filled the office. "You son of a bitch."

"Hurts, doesn't it?" I asked, stroking my chin, unable to suppress my smarmy smile. "To watch what you want escape you."

Fight for yourself, Raquel. Fight for me. Fight for what I know could be an us.

Her nostrils flared as she placed the last puzzle piece into its rightful home: My calculation, my careful machination to make her vulnerable, to build her up, only to tear her back down. I didn't want this version of Raquel, her bullshit, her misplaced anger. I hated her resistance to her own vulnerability, the innate weakness she fought to conceal. I wanted her truths, not her lies. I wanted her to look within that mirror of herself and acknowledge all the parts that made her Raquel.

The cracks that marred her surface didn't make her any less beautiful to me.

But in order to rebuild her, I would first need to destroy her, to slay the demons that rendered her still. Even if it took every tool in my tool belt to accomplish.

I suspected the ache of the female equivalent of blue balls was settling in. Did she have a pained tight churning settling into her flesh? Was she experiencing the ache of a blood rush in her clit that made her want to climb out of her prickling skin?

She ripped her jeans from the desk, thrusting one leg through a pant leg, followed by the other, and pulled them over her hips, fixing her gaze on me as she zipped her fly and snapped the button closed. "Oh, it hurts," she snarled, bounding toward the foyer like she couldn't get away from me fast enough, her body practically vibrating with anger while she shoved her feet back into her shoes. "But guess what? I know guys who, unlike you, finish what they start."

A veil of red dropped over my eyes that nearly sent me after her when the front door whipped open and closed with a bang.

Hemingway always did need to get the last word in, didn't she? The trouble for her was, she wasn't the only writer on this book anymore. I was writing in it, too. And in our story…

She would fall in love with me.

Even if she needed to hate me first.

CHAPTER TWENTY TWO

Raquel

THAT FUCKING PRICK.

I all but floored it out of the driveway, tires screeching as I peeled onto the quiet suburban street, my blood pressure kicking my adrenaline into overdrive.

He had toyed with me, made a fool out of me. And what was worse? I had let him. I should have left as soon as I realized Penelope wasn't there, but I had been so...desperate when I saw him that I put myself into that situation. Sean got under my skin in the best and worst ways possible. He pissed me off, but in the same breath could make me feel like I was buoyant.

My breaths came fast and furious as I sped for the freeway, nearly blasting through every stop sign. I was grateful that Eaton wasn't laden with cops who had a point to prove, because I was not in the damn mood. Frankly, I was likely to proposition sex just as much to get that fucking asshole out of my system as to get myself out of a stupid speeding ticket.

The resounding thought percolating in my mind as I clocked 80 mph on the freeway was that I didn't like him, I hated him. I hated his arrogance, his rugged charm, hated the way my heart beat a little faster whenever he was around, how each touch from him felt like an over-flowing stream of pleasure that I never wanted to stop.

Fuck him. He could rot. I hoped his damn dick fell off. I hoped every single one of his dexterous fingers spontaneously snapped off. I hoped he never smiled again. And most of all, I hoped like hell he would call me and finish what he fucking started.

My foot found the brake just as an Audi changed lanes in front of me, a flurry of curses leaving my mouth that would have given a priest a nervous breakdown.

I was on edge, my temper reaching a level I hadn't experienced in years, but it was the constant throbbing in my bare pussy that had tears springing to my eyes. No matter how much I rocked myself against the driver's seat, nothing would soothe that burn. All I could think about was that this was fucking Penelope's fault. I would have never gone to that house to make amends if she had just returned one damn phone call, humored me with a one-word text message, or at a minimum, indulged me with one of those stupid chain emails she loved so much.

I got nothing but radio fucking silence for a damn week.

I was done being patient. I had just had my ego torn to shreds by a guy who had something to prove and a dick that could have turned a lesbian straight.

Maybe.

I didn't actually know about the latter, but I was too fucking horny to think straight, so I was pulling out all the stops here.

A drive that normally took me almost an hour on a good day, took me forty-five minutes and four cigarettes before I arrived in Beacon Hill and was parallel parking in front of Penelope's Federal style row house that had been converted into a series of apartments. I ripped the seatbelt out of its holster, climbed out of the car and slammed the door behind me. Moonlight lit up the cobblestone I walked across, my body vibrating when I pounded up the stone steps. I caught the door of the row house just as one of her neighbors stepped out, my thunderous expression apparently making the woman too nervous to challenge whether I had any business in the building.

The rush of warm air from the HVAC system made me break out into a sweat that had the fibers of my shirt sticking to my back when I took the stairwell two steps at a time, my anger absorbing the brunt of my weight when I cleared the final step on the third floor landing.

I let myself into her darkened apartment with the key she had given me years ago, the distinct smell of the black cherry merlot candles she liked so much hitting me as I shrugged out of my jacket and hung it on the coat rack opposite the door. I bent over to undo the laces of my boots just as the light turned on. I caught sight of a pair of men's sock-laden feet. I didn't bother turning on the polite formalities when I saw Dougie standing at the other end of the hall, arms akimbo as he looked at me with murder in his eyes.

"You've got some fucking nerve just letting yourself in, Raquel," he growled, teeth bared like the rabid dog we both knew he was. I didn't have the patience to cull his ass today; he needed to stay clear of me.

"I'm not in the fucking mood." I tossed him an apathetic look while I straightened my spine, kicking my chin at him. His mouth opened as if he wanted to say something, but I cut him off. "Get out of my way."

I shoved past the breadth of his stocky frame. Penelope's lofty thousand-square-foot condo with its ten-foot ceilings, delicate crown moulding, and antique wood-burning fireplace belonged in a lifestyle magazine.

"She doesn't want to see you," he called out, stalking after me as I cut through the pristine galley kitchen equipped with stainless steel Wolf appliances and white cabinetry against gray marble floors, the stark cream-colored quartz countertops spotless. I ignored the sting of his remark, playing it off as his attempt at foiling my mission. That bitch was going to hear me loud and clear and then I was going home to masturbate until I passed the fuck out.

"She doesn't need you doing her thinking for her, trust me," I snarled.

"That's what you think this is?" he shouted back at me, tracking me down the dim hallway that led toward Penelope's master and two other spacious bedrooms. One of the extra rooms was used as an office, laden with decorative pieces she used for staging. The other room had been converted into an over-glorified walk in closet that housed clothes and shoes with labels I had never even heard of.

"You're a real fucking asshole, Raquel," Dougie declared.

My footsteps tapered off as my hand found the doorknob of Penelope's bedroom door, a simpering smile tilting my lips as I glanced at him over the curve of my shoulder.

"That the best you got, Douglas?"

His fingers curled into his palms, thumb extending to rub over the valley of his knuckles, as if trying on the idea of beating my ass, arousing a sly snigger from me that made him shoot a scowl in my direction.

"There's a lot of fucking things I want to say to you, but won't."

"Oh?" I said, releasing my hold on the knob to glare at him. My hand propped itself on my hip. "Indulge me."

I watched the steady rise and fall of his chest, his mind as loud as a freight train, steam practically coming out of his ears. "You're self-absorbed. Everything is about you, you don't give a shit about Penelope or anyone else."

My laugh came out as a patronizing titter that set my own nerves on edge. "Right, coming from the guy who treated her like a piece of ass for the first three months. Tell. Me. More," I punctuated sarcastically.

He vaulted himself in my direction, not stopping until he was close enough where I could see the granite of his jaw, the vein in his forehead pulsating, and smell the faint traces of beer on his breath.

"Her terms, not mine." His eyes burned as he spoke. "She was never a piece of ass for me. Ever."

My spine steeled at that, my mouth popping open.

Dougie's nostrils flared, fists tight against his thick thighs. My head snapped back at his admission, vignettes from the bar indolently flipping through my mind as the pieces of the puzzle settled themselves into place.

Penelope *had* wanted to have fun with him, but she *hadn't* antici-pated…oh, God.

The baby and the guy.

The vehemence left his face as reality registered in my own, my features slackening as he considered the gravity of what he'd said.

Just like it had last week, the truth was staring me dead in the face, if I was only willing to look.

He was…Dougie was…fuck. I couldn't even get the words out of my brain, the idea moving around like an uninhibited pinball I couldn't get control of.

The writer in me demanded I ask the question that crawled painfully out from the back of my throat with talons that scratched the closer they inched toward my tongue.

"Are you…" the words got stuck in my throat. I took an uneven breath and managed to complete my sentence. "Are you in love with her?"

"Yes." He didn't hesitate. Nothing in his visage so much as twitched or indicated even an iota of misgiving. My jaw rocked together as I processed his proclamation. I had thought—no, I had *believed* so wholeheartedly that Dougie was to blame for the rift between Penelope and me…that he and his seed had played a central role in my downfall, that his presence was at fault—right up until this moment. Just like his being in love with my best friend was true, it was also true that *I* had been at the crux of our falling out, not him.

Me, in all my infinite, entitled, self-serving wisdom.

Dougie was simply providing Penelope with the life she had always been trying to tell me she wanted.

We stood there, looking at each other like two dejected morons, shuffling our weight on the balls of our feet inside a property that cost more than either of us would ever earn in five years, now owned by a woman who would happily forego it all if it meant the two of us could figure out how to get along.

I didn't even know where the hell to start. I broke eye contact first, looking down at my black socks for something to do, noting that the fibers around my big toe were thinning.

"Look." The breathlessness of his voice summoned my attention.

Dougie's face was rankled, his fingers threading through his unkempt dark hair. "Contrary to whatever narrative you've convinced yourself is true, I'm not trying to come between you two."

"Feels that way," I muttered.

His expression softened, his shoulders dropping in defeat. "I'm not trying to replace you, Raquel. I know my place in the hierarchy of Penelope's heart."

I cocked an eyebrow at him, waiting.

He used his fingers to list them, starting with his thumb. "This baby, you, Louboutins, and then me." Then his pinky finger jutted forward unexpectedly. "Unless there's a sale at Restoration Hardware, then I am rightfully demoted to number five."

Laughter I hadn't realized I desperately needed erupted from my belly, filling the narrow hallway. Dougie smiled sheepishly at me, relief settling into the tired lines under his eyes. "Can we please try to get along, for her sake? I could really use an ally right now."

The heat of my anger waned as I evaluated his offer. Whether I liked it or not, he was the one Penelope had chosen, and if I loved her as much as I felt I did, I had to accept it.

Making a quick decision, I held out my hand gingerly in his direction, fingers flitting impatiently with my armistice. His face softened, his own gruff hand taking mine, giving it a squeeze. I thought that sealed the deal, but then he surprised me by jerking me forward, my mind not even having time to react before he pulled me into an impromptu hug. His arms crushed around me, and it took everything I had to temper the unexpected sob that crawled up my throat.

I hadn't realized until now how desperately I needed to be hugged.

We stood there, the moment no longer feeling awkward with Dougie's massive biceps circling me and my arms wrapped around the width of his waist. He was sturdy, like a tree trunk, a warmth to him that made me feel safe, as if I was in the care of an older brother I'd never had. I let myself relax in his hold, concentrating on the first pulls of oxygen into my lungs that hadn't felt forced.

We continued to stand in silence, holding onto each other, until he uttered the most unanticipated statement. "Sean likes you, y'know," he murmured into my hair.

My body stiffened in his hold as his words settled over me like the season's first snowfall, soft flakes kissing the frozen surface that beckoned winter anew. The sentiment held a startling beauty that left me unnerved, the yearning I had momentarily forgotten brewing beneath my belly button once more.

I swallowed the blades in my throat, mustering a muffled reply against his chest. "I know." Logic be damned, I liked that smug shithead, too.

"Give him a chance, Raquel," he quietly implored. "He won't hurt you."

Easy for Dougie to say; they were friends. Cash had promised me the very same thing a long time ago.

Aloud I said, "He might." Despite how things had ended between Sean and I that afternoon, some small part of me recognized the point he had been trying to make, now that I had calmed down and could examine it logically. It just didn't change the overwhelming trepidation I felt every time I was in his presence. Sean and Cash weren't even in the same stratosphere, but the shadows of my past lingered in the areas of my life that the sun would never touch.

"He won't," Dougie repeated, his arms tightening, as if to crush the mountain of doubt out of me.

I pushed out of his embrace, looking up to meet his stare. "You don't know that." Sean was a real-life threat to the safety of the walls I had built around myself. He wanted me to drop the shield that I had kept close to me for so many years to protect myself. If I let him in, if I allowed myself to fall...I didn't trust myself to survive when it all inevitably blew up in my face again—because it would.

I wasn't the woman who got the fairy tale ending; I was the one who got the war.

"You're right, I can't know that for sure," he agreed with a sigh, "but I know him. That has to count for something."

His resolve was unfaltering as he surveyed me over his twisted nose, a reassuring glint in his forest green eyes that beckoned me to trust him.

Dougie moved a rogue lock of hair out of my line in vision, shucking it under my chin in a brotherly kind of way.

"Now, go make peace with our girl while I go order a pizza."

"No mushrooms," I called over my shoulder, watching him disappear down the hall.

I took in a breath, staring at the handle of Penelope's bedroom.

It was time to bury this hatchet.

CHAPTER TWENTY THREE

Raquel

THE BLACKOUT CURTAINS were drawn together tightly. They served their purpose, for Penelope's bedroom was dark, save for the oppressive blue-tinged light coming from the TV on her dresser. She was propped up in bed, a mountain of pillows behind her, her golden hair looking uncharacteristically greasy and piled high on the crown of her head. She met my eyes, her expression impassive as she schooled her surprise, her lips a flat line. She looked away, her gaze going to the TV screen as the audience of the show she was watching erupted into laughter.

I stepped inside and shut the door behind me. Penelope's face grew sullen when I turned to face her, her under-eye bags deep enough to contend with my own as her shrewd blue eyes assessed me.

I shoved my hands into my back pocket, glancing at the TV. It looked like she was watching a rerun of *How I Met Your Mother*. It was one of her favorite shows next to *Friends*. No one appreciated sitcoms the way Penelope did. *Friends* was a welcome background noise for her in college when she was studying, was her default when she was in a bad mood, or just when she wanted to laugh. She learned everything she knew about fashion from Jennifer Aniston's Rachel Green, and in a lot of ways, they were similar in the sense that they both came from well-to-do families in pursuit of something simpler. Something of their own.

Penelope had tried to get me into *How I Met Your Mother*, assuring me that the tone was similar to that of her beloved *Friends*...but I hadn't understood the appeal. That was, until last week, when I was desperate to participate in anything that reminded me of her.

"I watched this episode a few days ago," I tentatively said, just as the characters of Ted and Stella began to argue over the invitation of Cobie Smulders's character, Robin, to their spontaneous wedding.

A caustic grunt left her. "You hate this show," Penelope reminded me, not meeting my eyes.

"I don't hate it." I lifted a hand to scratch my cheek. "I guess I just didn't really give it a chance."

"Like you don't with most things," she retorted hotly.

I didn't miss the backhanded nature of her remark and its relevance to nearly every facet of my life.

"You don't like giving anything that you don't understand right away a chance," she continued.

"That's not entirely true." I forced myself to modulate my annoyance at her rapier-like remarks. Her brow arched at me as though to say, "Isn't it?" and I found myself rendered mute.

All right, so there was *some* truth to it.

She had every right to be mad at me, but that didn't mean she needed to make this harder than necessary, did it? My confidence wavered as my hands freed themselves from the safety of my pockets, arms swinging back and forth as I skittered toward the bed, fearing she might dismiss me before I met my destination. I dropped my weight onto the edge of the king-sized mattress, recognizing its bedspread as the one she had bought at Nordstrom—the one I'd hated but she'd been crazy about. The sheet felt warm under my resting palm; I figured Dougie had been lying beside her just before I showed up. As I shimmied into his spot, I considered how many times before him that Penelope and I had holed up in this very bedroom, eating Indian takeout and watching terrible B-rated horror movies after a crappy night out until one of us passed out and tucked the other in.

Settling against Dougie's firm pillow—the only one Penelope hadn't taken over—my nose caught traces of his body wash in the cotton. I watched her out of the corner of my eye. Her profile failed to give away her disposition: lips a thin line, eyes blinking every few seconds, the TV casting harsh shadows against her sallow-appearing skin.

"How have you been feeling?" I coaxed.

Penelope pursed her lips like she wanted to say something nasty, but apparently thought better of it. "I'm swell." She adjusted the duvet, settling it at her hips. "This is the first time in a week that I've gone twenty-five minutes without throwing up. I can barely keep saltines and water down, I haven't washed my hair in five days, and my best friend resents me for being pregnant."

A grimace settled on my features. "I don't resent you," I amended with a shake of my head.

"Don't you?" She didn't look at me as she expressed the doubt.

My stomach twisted. It felt like someone had wedged a hot serrated blade in my gut. "Penelope—"

"Someone you claim to care about tells you that they're pregnant, and you make it into a *you* problem." She scowled at me, her eyes icy pools oddly fringed with tears. "I needed you."

I sucked my quivering bottom lip between my teeth under Penelope's surveying stare. Guilt slammed into me like a jackknifing semi, sucking the air out of my lungs until I felt like I was bartering for my next breath.

"I needed you, and you weren't there," she repeated, her voice cracking, breaking my resolve.

Tears stung my eyes, and tried as I may to blink them back, they spilled over in hot rivulets down the stretch of my cheeks. It felt like all I had done the past week was cycle between crying and being pissed off, but there was something strangely cathartic about crying in front of Penelope.

I didn't want her to feel isolated. I hated that she felt I'd abandoned her, that I had been the source of her hurt…I had been a terrible friend.

A sob choked in the back of my throat. I grabbed her hand in my own, knitting our fingers together, hating how stiff they felt in my grasp. "I'm sorry, Pen. I never wanted to hurt you."

"I've always supported you," she whispered.

My tears blurred my vision as I tilted my chin down listening to her continue.

"I never made you feel inferior. I've never ostracized you for doing things I knew were bad for you. I respected your decisions and loved you for them."

"I know." I nodded stiffly, sniffling. "You didn't deserve any of that." I swallowed the painful lump in my throat. "You've been trying to tell me for a long time that…this was the life you wanted. I just…I wasn't hearing it."

Penelope's inhalation shook through her as my observation lingered between us. A beat of a second passed, her thumb working across my knuckles before she spoke.

"I love him, Raquel," she said, the apology in her pitch making my chest constrict with contrition, "but I can't happily have this baby without knowing that you support us, too."

My lids squeezed shut, my head working up and down with a nod. I got it now. "I do support you. I really am sorry, Penelope. I was a dick."

When I opened my eyes, she parted her arms, beckoning me to her. I leaned forward, hugging her as if the future of our friendship depended on it. Penelope had always been my safety net, but now it was time for me to be hers, too. I didn't know what the future had in store for either one of us. All I knew was that no matter what happened, we would do it together.

She kissed the top of my head, smoothing my hair, a hum vibrating through her chest that melted away all the anxiety and stress of the day.

She was going to be a fantastic mother.

By the time I settled back on my haunches, something devilish was blooming in Penelope's face, her mouth tilting with mischief. "I accept your apology." Then she tapped her chin. "Although, I have to say, that might be the worst one I've ever received in my life."

My mind spun as I tried to come up with a logical response until I caught her chewing her bottom lip, as if she was trying to conceal a smile at her injection of levity.

"I would like you to redact that apology and try again. With more feeling this time, preferably."

I don't know if it had been her intention to make me smile, but I did just that. "Sorry. They didn't teach apology etiquette at public school."

"Oh, you bitch." She laughed, flinging a small pillow at me. "You really piss me off sometimes, Raquel. You're stubborn, and an asshole." She grabbed my hand again, squeezing it painfully. "But there is no one I would rather call my best friend than you."

"I really am so sorry. You deserve so much better from me. It won't happen again, I swear."

Warmth filled Penelope's eyes, her grip on my hand loosening. "That attempt was a little better. I'd suggest you dial up the histrionics, though. I want a performance that makes DiCaprio lose his Oscar again."

Her laugh at her own joke sounded mellifluous to my ears and made me think for just the briefest of moments that everything would be okay.

I embraced her once more, ignoring the fact that she smelled nothing like her usual Chanel No. 5. "I'll work at being more understanding."

"I need you to be a hell of a lot more understanding," she said, tucking my hair behind my ears. "This kid is going to need a godmother to rely on so they don't lose their shit every time something scary occurs. And let me tell you, kids are fucking horrifying."

My fingers seized her shoulders, squeezing the bone as my eyes searched hers. "Godmother? Me?"

Penelope gave me a "No shit, Sherlock" look, that brow of hers shooting north. "Who else would I pick?"

I hadn't considered that.

Me. A godmother.

To a baby.

The weight of the responsibility should have made my insides roil like churning cement, but what bloomed amongst the mounds of mud made my heart sing a tiny song that spoke to my soul.

"I need to tell you one more thing, and I would rather you didn't have another stage five meltdown, because I am not pacifying your ass anymore on this subject."

"Jesus, Penelope."

Her perfunctory look told me I deserved whatever barb she tossed my way and that she expected me to eat it like it was a delicious bull-shit sandwich.

"Dougie and I are moving to Eaton."

Somebody give me some sub sauce, 'cause that BS sandwich was dry as hell. A lump formed in my throat as I considered what she had just said to me.

"More specifically," she casually continued, twisting at her waist to primp the stack of pillows behind her, "we bought the colonial from Sean."

The darkened room spun out before me, and I wasn't sure if it was because my only lifeline was leaving me or because she was moving into a house that had been the start of something I wasn't sure I could dig my way out of.

"Now would be a good time to say 'congratulations'," Penelope prompted.

My mouth quirked with effort, but no sound came out.

Penelope let out an exasperated sigh, but her eyes were forgiving. "I'll still see you all the time. The house isn't far from *The Advocate*. And it'll be a lot easier for us to shuttle back and forth to Fall River to see his mother from there. The bulk of the design work I do is there, anyway."

My hands folded in my lap, my shoulders shrinking. I blinked at her, wondering when she had stopped being my mosh pit, whiskey-loving best friend into a full-fledged adult with her whole life figured the fuck out. Somehow along the way, she had kept growing, while I had stood still, drowning in my guilt about the responsibility I had for my sister's demise.

"Are you having a panic attack?" She leaned forward, eyes wide with curiosity. "'Cause if you are, I have some lorazepam under the bathroom sink."

My head felt stiff as I shook it. I needed something a little stronger than a sedative. I drew in a sharp breath, holding it tightly in my lungs for several seconds before I released it.

She didn't need my permission, or my judgment—she just needed my support.

And I needed to take a leap of faith, too.

"Congratulations, Pen. I'm happy for you guys."

Her shoulders rounded, a sigh of relief leaving her lips.

"Thank you."

I rolled onto my ass, settling against the pillows, reaching for the remote of the TV to turn up the volume. "Pen?" I said tentatively.

"Hmm?"

"Since we're doing the whole healthy communication thing, is it okay if I practice on you some more?" My voice edged on the saccharine.

Penelope's eyes immediately grew suspicious. "Of course," she said with a dry laugh, looking uneasy.

My face split into a shit-eating grin. "'I'm *so sorry* to tell you this, but you smell like absolute shit.'"

Penelope's snort was an unattractive albeit welcomed reprieve, her scowl ornery as she pushed her bedsheets back and clambered to her feet. "Y'know, I think Dougie wanted to say the same thing, but didn't," she said as she staggered toward the bathroom. "He's been at the edge of the bed all afternoon. When he heard your keys in the door, he all but sprinted out of here."

"Communication is key!" I called out to her.

She responded by shooting me an eye roll over her shoulder. "I'm hitting the shower. Don't leave."

"Your man ordered pizza. I'm not going anywhere."

CHAPTER TWENTY FOUR

Raquel

TWENTY-FIVE MINUTES LATER, we sat in bed hip-to-hip, a half-empty box of pizza settled on the floor while discussing the events of the last week. I let her lead. Penelope was diligent about not skipping any details, right down to gleefully describing her newfound anxiety surrounding placental abruption—a situation she was still at least sixteen weeks from even needing to consider as a possibility.

For someone who had been bedridden with morning sickness for the majority of the week, she had no issues getting the pizza down her gullet—in fact, she had eaten the rest of the third slice I hadn't been able to get through, reminding me that she was "literally growing another human inside of her." She even ate the crust, and I had *never* seen Penelope eat pizza crust.

"I think that's everything on my end," she said with a contented sigh, settling against the pillows, hand smoothing over the barely-there arch of her stomach.

"No venereal or other incurable diseases you're dying of?"

"Not yet," she assured, "but just you wait, soon it'll be the edema in my ankles." I didn't know what that was, nor did I want to. The name alone made my stomach heave.

"I'll call the priest," I quipped.

"Please do." She feigned a sniffle, dabbing under her eyes with a curled finger. "I fear I won't make it through my first trimester."

"Drama queen."

She threw her head back with a laugh, her smile turning coy. "Speaking of drama," she neatly maneuvered, her hands knitted together and settling demurely between her thighs. "How goes Operation Upgrade?"

I lifted my eyes skyward, as though the answers to my evasion laid hidden amongst the hardened clusters of friable material that made up the popcorn ceiling.

"I mean Sean," she offered, as if the insinuation had gone over my head.

I pegged her with a disapproving look. "I know who you mean."

I allowed the conversation to steer toward dangerous territory in which I caught her up to speed on my possessed cellphone fiasco, the text messages with Sean (at which time she demanded I give her my phone, because "your narration sucks"), and my less than stellar phone call with my mother before our argument.

"So *that's* why your panties were in such a bunch that night."

I blanched at her choice of words, recalling that at this very moment in time, my torn panties lay on a desk inside her new house.

Harrumphing, I kept my eyes on the TV, glad that the bedroom was darkened and that the blush flooding my cheeks couldn't easily be identified.

"Has anything else happened since?" she probed, suspicion lacing the question while she appraised my reaction.

My heart kicked up a shitstorm. From the corner of my eye, I could feel her scanning my face, her quizzical brow quirking the longer I remained silent.

I considered not telling her, but I didn't trust Sean not to tell Dougie, who would inevitably tell Penelope, and then I suspected I would end up groveling again, and I was sort of over having to do that.

"Define 'happened'." My body went rigid at the real threat of having to reveal what I had done...or had done to me.

"Raquel." Penelope's mascara-free lashes blinked at me the same way they did when she was about to drop an atomic bomb in my lap. "You're sitting next to me in my bed, and every time you've hugged me this evening, I get a whiff of cologne that is too expensive to be Cash's, too woody to be Dougie's, but smells a lot like *Sean's*."

God, even the sound of his name made my body radiate with a drunken heat that imbibed my senses. I told myself to keep my expression vacuous, but I could feel the damn rupture tearing my resolve into two warring entities, the dissonance a deafening buzz in my head.

My exhale was short, recognizing it was now or never. "I want to preface by saying I went to the house before I came here." My countenance twisted at that. "Your *new* house," I amended, the words feeling strange as I said them.

"Okay?"

"I went there with the intention of apologizing to you." My breath hitched as I started the story over. Unbidden thoughts kicked off the tightening in my core again, an intoxicating pang nestling itself with the same all-consuming feeling you get when you have a hangnail that keeps getting caught on everything that finally drives you to just rip it off.

"And...?" she probed, eyes greedy for information, her upper lip twitching with dwindling patience.

"You obviously weren't there, but," the words caught in my throat as my reverie sent me back hours into the past. When I heard the sound of his throat clearing and my eyes found his, I felt as if all the anxiety I felt up until that point had melted away. My wrath had tapered off, the disquiet in my soul dispelling the longer he looked at me with that mesmerizing stare of his that saw all the things I didn't like about myself. The cracks in my armor, the parts of me that were better off broken.

221

He confused me. One minute, I hated how vulnerable and insecure he made me feel. The next, all I wanted was for him to see me, all of me—and help me glue those parts back together again.

When he tore his gaze away from mine, the only thing I could concentrate on was getting his attention back. I craved the warmth of his banter…the wry smiles…the boyish charm. He was indifferent and cold, confirming that he was mad at me for what occurred a week earlier. I could see that judgment in his face every time his reluctant stare landed on me, the discomfort straining his jaw whenever his unwilling eyes bounced to mine.

I imagined he had drawn his own conclusions about what had gone on with me leaving with Cash that night—all of which were wrong. But he had never asked me about it.

He had simply punished me for it instead.

"Okay, honey, I know you're a writer," Penelope prompted, waving a hand in my face, "but you kinda need to become an orator right now and use your words here."

I blinked at her, catching her waning patience. Right. Words. Full sentences. There was no way for me to sugar-coat this one, so I went with the crassest analogy I could come up with while valiantly trying not to die of humiliation inside of Penelope's palatial condo.

"He ate me out," I said with a single perfunctory nod.

The silence swallowed me whole in that moment. Penelope's baby blues blinked once, twice, three times.

"Sorry." She let out a nervous titter, making a gesture like she was clearing out a blockade of wax from her ear. "I must not have heard you correctly."

"You did." I gulped, my throat desperately working at freeing the lump that had built its residence along the length.

Penelope was rarely dumbstruck, but this was one of those times. Her mouth hung open, her expression shell-shocked. "Well, shit," she declared, sitting upright, her hands steepling together in front of her mouth to block the animation of what I knew was bubbling excitement. "How was it? Did you see stars?"

I appreciated that she hadn't cared to ask just how I found myself bent over naked from the waist down on the desk she had eaten lunch off of more times than she could count...nor did I volunteer that information. She wanted the good part; the rest were just minor details.

Truthfully, I did see stars—hot, brilliant specks of light—briefly, anyway. It had the potential of being catastrophically good, like an eruption that overtook my senses. For a minute there, I didn't think I could have recalled my own middle name. My vision had been on the fritz, the room darkening as if someone had dropped a veil over my eyes the more he worked at me. I had been amenable, pliant, and willing to agree to his every whim on the condition that he didn't stop. My body had spasmed in the throes of mounting pleasure that had me forgetting how to breathe. For those few minutes, I had felt alive.

"Raquel," Penelope snapped, clapping her hands together. "Words. Use them."

I chewed the inside of my cheek, contemplation making me dizzy. "It had the potential to be amazing if..."

"If...?" she pressed.

I blew out a breath. "If he hadn't turned it into some sort of punishment."

"Ooh, kinky." She grinned, that salacious smile faltering at the sight of my expression. "But you weren't down with that?"

"No," I sputtered, shaking my head. "I don't need be *punished* by him for shit that doesn't concern him." And there I went putting my foot in my mouth, and of course she didn't miss it.

"Like what?" Penelope's eyes narrowed, giving me the distinct impression that she knew what was about to come out of my mouth was going to seriously piss her off.

I had skirted around one small detail when recounting what had occurred because I knew she wouldn't like it. I almost considered playing it off because of how well the evening had been going, but we were on a new trajectory where we told the truth...no lies.

"I stupidly had Cash pick me up the night of the bar fiasco, and it was a whole damn thing." I hesitated, pausing to find my footing before I could get the rest of it out. "And he brought Terry and Dom with him."

Penelope's face was tight, but not as tight as the unsympathetic hand she perched on my shoulder, the tips of her fingers curling into curve of my skin like the talons of a falcon. "I'm not going to say I told you so about Cash or his band of goons for the thousandth time, but..."

"Yeah, I know. I get it," I said with a sigh, shrugging out of her abrasive hold, a pulse forming where she had gripped me as blood rushed back to the surface.

"You know there's only one way to fix this," she said as she relaxed against the pillows again, head tilting, looking owlish. "You let Sean fuck you, and then you start over on a fresh slate."

I resented the ease and simplicity of her sage advice. My heart thundered in my chest at the very idea that this situation could be remedied with the dropping of undergarments and joining of genitals. "No, absolutely not."

"Should have thought about that before you dropped your panties."

"He tore them off!" I corrected.

A suggestive smile sprouted on her smug mouth while my cheeks flushed, heat creeping up my neck and settling through every strand of hair on my fucking head.

I dropped my voice, suddenly aware of Dougie's presence in the apartment, hearing his footsteps in the hall through the closed bedroom door and then the bathroom door creaking shut. "I'm not sleeping with him. Things would get too complicated."

"For whom?"

"All of us." Dougie might have been honest with me when he said Sean wouldn't hurt me, but that didn't change the fact that there was a massive risk associated with this whole... "thing" if it didn't work out. "Not when you and Dougie are now–"

"Oh, no you don't." She wagged a corrective finger at me. "You don't get to use Dougie and I as your cop-out at your opportunity for happiness, Raquel Marie."

Her use of my middle name and the serious undertone of her admonishment made me breathlessly guffaw. "Are you practicing your mean mommy voice?" I arched an eyebrow at her, watching as she practically preened under my observation.

"I sounded like a badass, huh?" I managed a weak half-smile. Sure, she sounded as badass as a broad from Connecticut could get. She was more Stepford Wife than South Boston mom screaming for her kids when the streetlights came on, but it was a start. I didn't have the heart to knock her down a peg.

"You need a little more grit when you drop the middle name. You want to inflict fear," I suggested, tapping my chin with thought.

"I'll work on it," she agreed with a giggle, tilting her head at me, a look of mischief forming on her face. "And you'll work on getting fucked, right?"

"Penelope," I pleaded, becoming more laconic the longer this went on. "Just drop it."

"You'll feel better when you get over your bruised ego," she assured. "C'mon, think about it." She glided her hand across the air in front of her face as though it were a paintbrush on canvas. "Coffee dates, long walks through the Public Garden, dinner at Faneuil Hall, Christmas at the in-laws, a beach proposal—"

"You said fuck, not dating," I interrupted, my skin flushing as the pictures she painted assaulted my mind. I resented the butterflies that swirled inside of me. "Or an engagement."

She flitted her fingers at me with indifference. "Semantics. The order of preference is your choice."

"None of the above."

"Ah, ah. That wasn't one of the options on the menu."

"I don't like your menu."

"Tough shit," she declared with a noncommittal shrug, "Your vegetables are good for you, you need a healthy balance of protein on that plate, and sex is a good enough dessert for anyone who wants to burn a few hundred calories."

"Someone obviously has their appetite back." I shook my head.

I wanted to pretend I was only marginally affected by Sean, by the sweeping possession he held over my body for those few stolen moments of time, or how he consumed my every thought.

"Pen?"

"Hmm?"

My salivary glands had seemingly gone on vacation, leaving my mouth parched as my admission came to me. "I do like him." I focused my eyes on the TV, watching a commercial for a local used car dealership. "But I'm terrified of the idea of getting that close to anyone again."

Penelope's hand found mine, her skin soft as velvet against my palm.

"I know you are, but..." My lids dropped, the familiar burn settling in them, the tears I told myself I would never shed threatening to fall. "...not everyone you meet in life is going to hurt you or leave you, Raquel."

It was hard for me to reconcile what she was saying when it felt like I had spent the better half of my life feeling isolated despite being surrounded by people. My father's death had been the fulcrum of everything that had happened, setting events off like a domino effect.

Holly Jane had died shortly after.

I'd forced Cash away.

Why would Sean be any different?

"Life is a lot like a car, Kell," Penelope continued. "Some of us choose to drive and be in control, others resolve ourselves to life in the passenger seat, where we waste our days away wondering why we never got to our destination."

I sat up, looking at her with wistful eyes. This woman was no longer just my best friend. Some day in the not-too-distant future, she would become a mother. Some day, she would be doling out advice to her child, mending his or her broken heart.

"Get in the driver's seat of your life, Raquel. You might be surprised to see where your journey takes you."

Her sentiment hung between us as I settled back against the pillows, feeling a little lightheaded from the weight of what she had said to me. Had I been sitting in the passenger seat this entire time? I had been so sure I had been driving that metaphorical car by keeping people out that I never even considered that maybe the car had been on autopilot the whole time. As I sat there in silence, Penelope's hand reached for mine again.

"Tomorrow is going to mark ten years. You've survived an entire decade when you thought you wouldn't."

Her words served as an emblematic intro that drew a shaky,

uneven breath from my lips. The tears that had been stinging the back of my eye lids pooled once more, and this time, I allowed them to fall.

Penelope hesitated, her hold on my hand tightening. "I want you to promise me that you'll try to start living instead of looking in your rear view mirror. Nothing good is waiting for you back there."

Whether I wanted to or not, my head moved in a steady nod, the tears streaming freely as she took me into her arms and held me like she could smother the pain out of me. Her palm was flat against my back, moving in consoling circles as the sobs freely emerged from the back of my throat. I had never realized it before, but I wanted to live. Maybe I had always wanted to live, but felt I would never be able to extricate myself from who I was supposed to be. I had always felt that I owed it to Holly Jane to serve my lifelong contrition by starving myself of basic human needs. I ate out of sustenance, not from desire. I drank to suppress my pain. I lashed out at those who usually didn't deserve it. And I was starving myself from the opportunity to experience some-thing that could change my life as I knew it forever.

I pulled back, sniffling as Penelope's glossy eyes appraised mine, her warm hands cupping my cheeks.

"I want you to live," she murmured, crystallizing a significant starting point in the next chapter of my life. "Live, Raquel. That's what *she* would have wanted."

Any other time, I would have told her she was wrong. This time, though, I didn't just believe Penelope's words.

I wanted to live by them.

CHAPTER TWENTY FIVE

Sean

TRUTH TO BE TOLD, I knew this was edging on the cusp of brazen, even for me. After she had rightly fled the house yesterday, I staggered back to the desk in a befuddled mess, rocking the world's largest hard-on. My dick could have penetrated steel, never mind the massive paperweights that were my balls. I wasn't embarrassed to admit that I undid my pants just enough to pull my dick out and stroke it out to the image of her writhing against my mouth and the sound of her pleasured moans, now forever burned into my mind.

I lost my load before she was even officially out of the driveway—she was that hot.

I would spare Dougie and Penelope the FYI on that one—they didn't need to know that I had christened their house before they did.

Still, I wasn't happy with the way things left off between Raquel and me. I had had a point to make and a lesson to teach her, but even I knew when to take my foot off the gas.

Especially today. Today's lesson was going to take a different approach, and I ideally needed to keep my hands to myself. My mouth might be a different question, though.

I parked the Jeep in the nearly empty parking lot of *The Advocate*, my eyes finding the dash, where the reading of 4:55PM glowed proudly at me like a beacon against the darkened skies as the day drew to a close. Metallica's "Seek and Destroy" drifted out of the sound system of the car, the steady beat of my heart falling in time with the song's melancholic bass line.

Lifting my gaze to the rear view mirror, I met the familiarity of my dark stare. I had indulged myself and managed a quick trim of my beard this morning, cleaning up the uneven and overgrown lines. I looked presentable in the make-a-good-impression-on-Mom-and-Dad kind of way, but somehow, I suspected my efforts would be entirely wasted on her. Given the way we had left off, this was going to go down one way only: She was going to be really fucking pissed to see me.

Silencing the ignition, I popped the car door free, my feet finding the pavement with ease. *The Advocate* offices were in a distinguished, two-story redbrick heritage edifice that was tucked in the heart of town. The late fall air grew bitter as I drifted toward the refurbished nineteenth century-looking black door. The door squeaked when I pushed it in, the heavy stench of printer ink and aging paper immediately hitting my nose.

The reception area was nothing more than a small sitting room with four dark blue upholstered Bergère chairs and a circular coffee table laden with past issues of the paper. Behind an oversized wraparound receptionist desk sat a mousy looking woman with corkscrew flaxen curls who gawked at me through round eyes.

"May I help you?" Her voice sounded like a bird's chirp, her smile a little shy, but warm enough as her eyes worked over the length of my frame. I caught the small albeit nervous bob of her throat, a flint of appreciation flooding her too-far-apart hazel eyes the longer she swept her roving gaze over me.

My eyes dipped to read the brass-trimmed nameplate on her desk.

Sheryl Jones

The name fit her like a leather glove.

She straightened in her seat, hands grasping a pen tightly between her plump fingers.

"Is Raquel Flannigan here?"

Sheryl's eyes practically distended when she heard Raquel's name come out of my mouth.

"Do you have an appointment?" Her eyes narrowed slightly, and it would be hard to miss the hint of mistrust in both the question and on her face. I considered for a moment that maybe I wasn't the first man who had shown up here looking for Raquel—but I didn't want any trouble, I just wanted to make it right.

It was time to turn on the charm. I leaned forward, dropping my elbows on the lip of the desk.

"Ms. Jones," I said, my mouth slipping into a wry smile, the one that had gotten me out of detention in my youth, earned me loan extensions, and entrenched me deep inside of Raquel's thoughts in the first place, "I know this is completely unorthodox, but my appearance is a bit of a surprise."

That sent her overplucked brows north, her thin lips shifting from side to side as though she was working at the idea, as if she was trying Brussel sprouts for the first time and couldn't decide whether she liked them.

"Raquel doesn't..." She pulled her lip between her teeth, eyes flitting across her desk at the quandary she'd seemingly found herself in. "She doesn't like having visitors."

The guilt I was becoming well versed in sank my heart like a tarnished anvil that was losing the war to an unruly, choppy sea. She deserved better, and suddenly I felt stupid for not bringing her flowers or some shit.

Although, knowing her, she would have beat me over the head with a bouquet, ensuring that the thorns drew blood and petals were scattered everywhere. It was probably better to not give her anything she could turn into a weapon.

I didn't know her well enough to even know what she liked, other than her clit being sucked, but you couldn't exactly fit that into a gilded gift box, could you?

Before I could even launch into reassurance, I was waylaid by a shadow in my peripheral vision.

"And who do we have here?"

My spine steeled at the sound of a female voice that had me turning on my heel, my face slipping into an inadvertent scowl.

This must have been the pain in the ass that had been Raquel's trigger on the phone a few weeks back.

The tall, thirty-something redhead appraised me greedily, her shrewd jackal eyes trailing over me like she was going to commit me to memory, and let me tell you, that was not a place I wanted to be.

"I know you," she said, my stomach churning at the confidence in her pitch.

Before I could question how she knew who I was, she moved to the coffee table, picking up the paper from a few weeks back.

"You're Sean Tavares." She held the paper up in my direction.

Sure enough, there was my grim as shit face on the front page. Right, that was how this whole thing started.

My hands slid themselves into my coat pockets, my chin dipping downwards, eyes trained on hers as I attempted my best interpretation of Raquel's 'I don't give a fuck' and hoping like hell it was just as effective.

"I am," I confirmed.

The jackal's eyes looked delighted, and that's when I became acutely aware that the only reason that stare worked for Raquel so well was because she sported it like a damn accessory.

The redhead appeared entirely unfazed by my indifference. Instead, she examined me like she was about to be awarded a Pulitzer, her Mary Jane version of a shit-eating grin a languorous bloom on a face that lacked any interesting dimension.

Placing the paper back on the table, she stepped toward me. "I'm

Karen Chalmers," she said, holding out her hand. I winced at her approach, the sickening floral perfume she wore entrapping its scent in the hairs of my nose. I could barely contain my repulsion at her extended hand, wishing there was a way to avoid having to make skin-to-skin contact with this woman. I took in a shallow breath, steeling my nerves. If I wanted a chance in hell at penetrating the inner sanctum of *The Advocate*, I had to play nice—and somehow, I suspected that the only way I was going to breach enemy territory was at this woman's ordinance.

Karen Chalmers's hand was clammy and damp with recently applied moisturizer as it enveloped mine. I had hoped the calluses of my palm would unnerve her, but that broad just held on, as if I was doing her bareback and she wanted me to lose my load inside of her so she could tie me down for eighteen years. She struck me as being that type. I wrenched my hand free at first opportunity, watching as she dropped her hand as if nothing had been amiss. My fingers jerked with the desire to wipe my palm on the outside of my jeans just to get that greasy shit and her DNA off me.

"What can I do for you, Mr. Tavares?" Someone needed to let her know that her fixed crazed stare and arched brow was not screaming sexy, it was shouting mental hospital.

Before I had a chance to speak, Sheryl piped up, suddenly appearing very confident. "He's here for Raquel."

Karen's jackal eyes flared like an inferno had engulfed the very building we stood in.

"Is that so?" she clipped, shoulders squaring, her nose tilting skyward. "And what is the nature of your visit?"

"I'm not sure that's any of your business." Raquel's Southie drawl struck like a hot blade on a boulder of ice.

My eyes left Karen's to look at her. I had been right; her ire manifested as a slight tick in her set jaw. The rest of her face was impassive, an implacable gleam in her cinnamon eyes that looked like dark pools under the offensive halogen lighting of the office.

I blew out a breath, sweeping my stare over her. High-waisted denim jeans clung to the curve of her hips, and a black long-sleeved shirt with a scoop neckline that exposed her clavicle was tucked into her waistline, making her appear waif-like and dangerously fuckable. Her hair was swept back into a low-set messy bun at the nape of her neck, a few loose strands framing her heart-shaped face.

I glanced at her jeans, considering for one stupid moment how difficult it would be to get her out of them. Hell, I could manage if I got them to her knees. Heat hit me, my heart rate all but spiking to dangerous levels until I lifted my eyes to hers and she obliterated what was left of my ego with a single stare.

Oh yeah, she was really fucking pissed to see me.

"You have a private audience with one of your sources?" Karen squeaked, interrupting the silence.

Raquel's expression was still, nary so much a crinkle on her forehead at the question. Instead she released a bored sigh, indifference burning in her cinnamon gaze that made me feel as though they had done this song and dance countless times before.

"You're conflating, Karen. Unless one of us is going to pen an expose story on the origins of screws and nuts," her mouth went lopsided with the jut of a smile, "there's nothing further he can assist *The Advocate* with as a *source.*"

Karen's grating voice rose an octave, growing shrill. "So, you admit that the nature of your relationship would infringe upon our in-house ethics manual?"

"Karen." Alarm bells rang out in the way Raquel said her name, caution lacing the two syllables. Raquel's stare made goosebumps erupt on my arms. When the volume of her voice dropped to a whisper, my skin crawled with a threat of danger. "Do you really want to speak to me about in-house ethics?"

At that, Karen all but slammed her pointed heel into the ground like a petulant child, the threat of a tantrum hanging over her, a storm brewing on her face. She was clearly unnerved by Raquel's veiled threat, which meant little to me, but Sheryl, who was on her feet watching the two spar, clapped a chubby hand over her mouth.

"I don't know what you're talking about, Raquel," Karen said defensively, "but it's my duty to inform Earl of this."

That was when I knew that Raquel had backed her into a corner.

"Go for it. There's nothing to inform him of. Sean is a friend. That doesn't break any rules."

Did she just friend-zone me? With Karen's back to me, I threw Raquel a wounded look, but her stare landed like shrapnel and my grim expression cleared as easily as shaking an Etch-a-Sketch.

Maybe, I thought, I should be happy that she had referred to me as a friend. That at least meant we were getting somewhere, and maybe I'd get to keep my head—the one in my pants—for one more day after all.

Karen stalked toward the doorway where Raquel stood, and just as she moved to pass her, I watched Raquel lean towards Karen and murmur something too soft to reach my ears. The jackal's eyes went wide, pure pandemonium burning behind them.

"You wouldn't," she hissed, spittle flying from her mouth.

"Try. Me," Raquel punctuated, looking perfectly capable of doing whatever the fuck she had just threatened to do.

Karen stood in front of her for some time, the two of them filling the threshold, eyes boring into each other like fire fighting ice. There had to be twenty years between them, a clash of youth and seniority pitted against each other in competition. Karen straightened, hitching her handbag higher on her shoulder. Her neck craned with her attempt to appear regal, but she just ended up looking more like the village idiot in a floral print dress and tan trench coat.

"I believe there's been a bit of a misunderstanding, Mr. Tavares," she deigned, her smile deep and pained. "Ladies, goodnight." And like that, she was gone, the entrance door slamming behind her telling us how she really felt.

Sheryl's eyes flitted from me to Raquel, as if she didn't know what to do with herself next. "I guess, I'll, uh…" she trailed off, that irksome squeak returning to her, eyes wide as dinner plates.

"'Night, Sheryl. I'll grab the lights on my way out." Raquel dismissed her with a wave of her hand. She turned on her heel, glancing at me over her shoulder, silently demanding I follow.

And I did, like a lost puppy desperate to do anything to stay in this woman's presence. *The Advocate's* office was small, cubicles tucked close together like teeth in an overcrowded jaw. A boardroom with frosted windows was off to the left, and after two turns, we entered a cubicle that, if not for her coat hanging up in a corner and her handbag draped over the back of the chair, I would have assumed was vacant.

"Is this where you sit?" Stupid question, but I needed to cull the silence.

"Yes."

My eyes searched for photos, but there were none. No gifts from ex-boyfriends or printouts of motivational quotes to get her through the lull of the afternoon. Her computer wallpaper was the default Mac OS X. To the left of the screen was a black wire framed cupholder that held exactly one pen and one highlighter. I had hoped that by infiltrating her space, that I would at least get another layer of complexity to her, but her desk was as inhibited as she was.

"Didn't feel like personalizing it?" I asked with a laugh that died in my throat, her head tilting ever so slightly to the left, stare working over me like she couldn't place something.

"Why are you here, Sean?"

Could I kiss her? Was that allowed? I felt like the kiss would be a better answer than anything I could have articulated, and frankly, it might spur a better reaction. My tongue stroked my bottom lip in hypothetical preparation, and while her face staved me off, it was the dilation of her pupils that told me the small act had gotten her attention.

"Because I wanted to see you."

She responded with a snort. "Well, I gathered that much," she said, arms crossed over her chest. "Why?"

I blew out a breath, still debating kissing her. The protracted silence between us was masked by the hum of the building's HVAC system.

"I like you, Raquel." There it was. No bullshit. No games. No filter. No beating around the bush or letting my tongue or mouth do my talking for me. "I like you a lot." I stuffed my hands inside of my coat pockets in wait.

Her eyes shot to mine, a wistful look filtering over her features. Not until then did I notice that under the offensive halogen lighting that she appeared enervated, as if she had struggled unsuccessfully to get a good night's sleep the night before.

"Sean," she began, shifting her weight, eyes locking on mine. I knew she was standing on some sort of precipice that left her fear-stricken, as though if she got too close to the edge, the cliff would fissure. I waited with bated breath, watching as she lifted her nose toward the ceiling, her teeth dragging over her bottom lip with indecision.

Then she lowered her face, her eyes finding mine. I almost didn't want her to finish that sentence. If it would result in her dismissing me in some way, I didn't want to hear it.

"Raquel," I stopped at her surprised look.

A smile curled the corners of her mouth. "I think that's the second time you've said my name."

"Would you prefer Hemingway?" I jested, watching as those folded arms of hers lowered to her midsection.

"Raquel just sounds so serious now," she confessed with a shrug.

"It's the most appropriate, given the circumstances," I replied, stepping closer to her. Her arms dropped to her sides, eyes tracking me as I closed the distance between us. I lifted a nervous hand to her cheek, the heart shape fitting perfectly into my palm. Her skin felt warm under my cold touch, and her lids dropped, concealing her thoughts from me.

I hated the idea that she had been mostly alone all these years with only Penelope by her side. I didn't need to meet her mother to know she wasn't a good person, I had enough deductive reasoning on my side to look at her photos and read the comments she'd given to the media about her family to know that that woman was out strictly for herself.

My thumb worked back and forth across the arch of Raquel's cheekbone, my eyes taking in every soft feature of her face that should have appeared harsh under this lighting. Her lashes were long and dark, coated with mascara. Her skin felt like velvet under my rough palm, lips plump in a relaxed pout. This was the first time her full brows weren't drawn tightly together in my presence. She was relaxed.

"You weren't supposed to happen," she muttered, her chest rising and falling.

I swallowed, considering the gravity of her statement against my confession. "Is that a good thing or a bad thing?"

"I haven't decided yet." My chuckle was a muted sound in my chest.

She blindly found either fold of my parted jacket, fingers fisting the two halves, her balance shifting as if she was trying to keep herself upright. "Dougie said I should give you a chance."

I was grateful her eyes were closed, or she would see the bewilderment that I knew had taken over my face. I hadn't spoken to that fucker in two days—which wasn't entirely unusual since he met Penelope—but something had obviously changed in forty-eight hours. Two days ago he hated Hemingway.

Now she was standing here, telling me that he'd told her to give me a chance. I almost didn't want to believe it.

"And will you?" I pressed, leaning forward until my mouth was inches from hers. There had only been three cars left in the parking lot, two of which I assumed belonged to Sheryl and Karen, and the other I knew belonged to Raquel.

It was safe to assume we were alone, but I selfishly didn't really care if we weren't, either.

She deserved to be worshipped and kissed for the rest of her life, and if that was a problem—throw the damn book at me.

Raquel's gingerly rose to rest on my chest, fingertips sinking into my pectoral muscle. That touch alone was enough to set off my heart into a steady thrumming that reverberated in my ears.

"That depends," she whispered, her height shifting as she stretched on the tips of her toes to graze my nose.

"On?" All it would take was an inch of movement and those lips of hers would be on mine. I almost wanted to suffocate the answer out of her before she could say it, but my curiosity got the better of me.

Her lids fluttered open, revealing her beautiful unearthly golden-brown eyes with wisps of mischief flickering through them. Then in almost a mere whisper, she blew me away with an answer that would stay with me for a lifetime. "Whether or not you intend to deprive me of proper orgasms in the future, 'cause that shit wasn't cool."

I erupted into laughter, stepping back from her, grabbing my knees as the deep howl split my sides. I had not foreseen that.

But I hadn't seen her coming, either.

"Also," she continued, leaning her ass against the edge of the built-in workstation, ankles hooking over one another, arms back across her chest. "If you're going to make a habit of tearing off my underwear, you're going to need to start replacing 'em, too."

"You got it, Hemingway." My smile went smug as I straightened, moving next to her to drop my weight on the workstation, too. I just hoped it could support us.

"Are you agreeing to both terms?" she pressed, looking sheepish.

"I'm agreeing to replace your torn underwear," I said with a chuckle, matching her stance. "But I make no promises about your deprival. Your orgasms are reliant on your behavior."

Her face crumpled with mortification, cheeks flushing rouge.

"Wanna get out of here?" I stood up, hands slipping into my pockets, watching her as her thoughts of guilt no doubt assailed her mind. Her stare found the small calendar on her desk, that doubt disturbing the clarity of her eyes before she settled on the time. I crossed my arms over my chest, tilting my head to the left. Hesitation spurred me to speak, "Do you have to be somewhere at the stroke of midnight, Cinderella?"

"What?" She turned her head in my direction, pulling her bottom lip between her teeth.

"You looked at the calendar, and then the time, so I was wondering if maybe you were nervous about the coach outside turning into a pumpkin." I dropped my gaze to her Doc Martens. "I think your glass slippers will take you till after 12:01, though."

She released her lip, hands hatching together in front of her. "I always considered myself more of a Belle," she amended, a smile smothering the flames of worry that had been lingering on her features.

Of course she was a Belle; books and her beast.

"You can be whoever you want, Hemingway." I grinned, tossing her coat at her, which she caught with ease. She slid into it, staring at my hand that I held out. For a split second, I thought she was oscillating between accepting it and declining. Reluctance or some sort of small miracle gave her the courage to accept my proffered hand.

Her palm felt warm in mine, and it took everything in me not to puff out my chest over something as innocuous as our fingers being scissored together as we headed out the doors of *The Advocate*.

Because with Raquel, even the small moments felt like a wish only my heart could make.

CHAPTER TWENTY SIX

Raquel

I WASN'T GOING to accept his invitation. I had been honest with Penelope that morning when she called to do a welfare check about my desire to be alone—but one look at him standing in the lobby of *The Advocate* and my equilibrium had been shaken and my only wanton desire on a day that was always so painfully bleak was to be near him. The thought that resounded in my head was as loud as the roar of a jet flying overhead to the point that I considered declining out of necessity to temporize the situation for just a little while longer while I sorted my headspace and this unusual somatic response when I was in his presence.

But the heart wanted what it wanted...and right now, my mourning spirit wanted to be around Sean. When I was with him, I felt like he saw me differently than anyone else, as though the veil everyone else saw me through had lifted for him. Penelope knew me, but there were always going to be darkened parts of myself that I kept boarded up and safely stowed away someplace where she could never find them. Cash knew the ugly, but he didn't lessen the burden of its existence. And with Sean, I had wanted to show him everything: Every scar, every mark, every sliver of ugly.

A poker player would call me foolish, but whether I wanted it or not, I felt myself going all in.

"You can be whoever you want, Hemingway."

Sean's smile had been sly when he had said it, as if he'd been joking, but somehow, the words felt heavy with a significance I'd never before experienced from a man.

I knew he meant them, and that's what made the crumbling walls that made up my facade give way at the foundation. I didn't hesitate when he held the passenger door of his Jeep open for me, pegging me with a wry smirk as he bent at the waist with a deep bow, one arm tucked to his chest, the other outstretched to the door.

"M'lady."

I swatted playfully at him, but he grabbed me by the hips, pulling me against him till his chest was flush with my back. He cupped my chin and raised it until my mouth was slanted against his, a feat that would have been impossible if he wasn't eight inches taller than me. My mind buzzed with lustful abandon that had my fingers sinking into his thighs until he released me, guiding me into the car. He grinned as he slammed the passenger door and rounded the hood of the car, rubbing the corners of his as if he couldn't believe this any more than I could.

This was a date. Our first real date, and maybe, just maybe, one of many. Whether I had wanted to readily admit it or not, when I was with Sean, I forgot who I was. I wasn't Liam Flannigan's daughter, or Holly Jane's surviving sister. I hadn't had a lifetime of hurt, or enough baggage to fill a mega-mansion. I wasn't the writer who had dreamed of being prolific only to watch those dreams die, too.

I was simply Raquel.

And Raquel liked Sean.

"Where are we going?" I probed when he started the Jeep. The interior of the Wrangler smelled like him—all leather and cinnamon. I found myself drawing laconic breaths as the smell imbibed my senses and curbed whatever lingering anxieties I had about my impetuous decision making.

"Why?" he asked, something heady and dark washing over his features.

"I need to know if I'm ever going to see the inside of this building again, or if my death will be the story that acts as a launch pad for Karen's career."

Sean shook his head, a laugh reverberating in his chest. "What's with you two anyway? She looked like she wanted to kill you."

I worked my teeth back and forth across my bottom lip. "I caught her and the mayor fucking."

"Jesus Christ." His head snapped in my direction. "Are you serious?"

I blinked at him, boredom coating my expression. "So, then? Where are we going?"

He shook his head, bemusement teasing his expression. "Nowhere that ends up with you in the river." He pulled the gear shift into reverse, the dash casting bright lights against his visage as he twisted in his seat, edging the car out of the vacant parking spot like a condemned man buying himself time.

"Good," I sighed, feigning relief, "I'm not a very good swimmer."

"That's what you would be worried about?" He chuckled as he shifted the Wrangler into drive. He turned right onto Ward Street, and then left onto Main Street, taking us in the direction of the town square.

"You don't worry about death when you've seen so much of it," I said evenly.

His nostrils flared, a heavy silence immediately settling over us.

Fuck.

I rolled my lips together, recognizing my social gaffe. I had always been flippant about death; it was my weird way of coping with the reality that my sister and father had died just a few years apart. Penelope's mother thought that made me a sociopath, and from the way

Sean looked like he had just seen a ghost, I was beginning to think that the pearl-clutching witch had been right.

Flattening my spine against the cold leather, I felt the heat of my embarrassment rushing up the length of my neck, settling itself on my cheeks. My eyes bounced to the temperature dial, resenting that the heat wasn't even on. Distress radiated from me, a desperation for the car I had been so eager to jump into only moments ago to swallow me whole.

I should have declined. The cogs of my mind raced to come up with an excuse that would buy us both an out.

Sean cleared his throat, his concentration trained on the street ahead of us as the tree-lined, picturesque streetscape of the square came into our line of vision.

"Who died?"

I felt that a better question would have been who *hadn't* died, because it sure as shit felt like it was fucking everyone.

I fixed my focus on the lining of the Jeep's ceiling. This was great first date material. This was for sure in the prologue of that dating book Penelope had kept on her bookshelf when we were in college, right under the part that said, "Don't put out to the first stable guy who gives you a morsel of attention."

I didn't have to read the entirety of that dating handbook to know I was terrible at this. We hadn't even made it to wherever we were going.

"Raquel?" he probed, stealing a glance at me that melted my insides. Concern tipped his brows inward, his eyes bouncing from me to the parking spot he was now pulling into.

I was fucking this up, royally. As soon as the car was parked, I was going to walk back to *The Advocate* and pretend this whole thing hadn't happened. This was idiotic. I was emotionally fragile because of the significance of today—that had to be the reason for my blatant stupidity.

This was wrong. *I* was wrong. I was out of my element, and the way I had already gone and fucked this to shit before we made it all of two streets from *The Advocate* was perfect evidence of that. I knew when I had breached enemy territory. I was raised to know when the fuck to raise that white flag and retreat. No one survived my pocket of Southie without knowing when they needed to cut their losses and make a fucking run for it.

Sean put the gear stick into park, killing the engine. He rubbed the scruff on his chin, lids dropping for the briefest of moments, as though he was collecting himself. I looked to see where we had parked. We were in front of Four Corners, a nondescript twenty-four-hour diner in town that appealed to the bedroom community that seemed to always be coming or going.

He shifted in his seat to look at me. I could feel the vacancy settling on my face the longer the silence stretched on between us while I hatched my grand getaway plan: door open, body out, legs running. Then a thought sank my stomach: I had left my cigarettes in my car, and didn't that just heighten my anxiety to the nth degree. My frantic gaze searched the rest of the well-lit street looking for a Cumby's.

Okay, new plan: door open, body out, legs swiftly carrying me to Cumby's so I can chain smoke myself into a stupor.

"Hey," he summoned. My body responded before I could process it, my chin jerking in his direction, eyes growing wide with terror that felt all too familiar to me the longer I sat here.

"I'm not going to pressure you, okay?" he murmured, his hand settling on my knee, thumb working back and forth. "You don't want to talk about it, we won't talk about it."

My eyes found his, the warmth in those darkened pools ensnaring my anxiety in its place. I forced out another deep breath, the familiar tightness releasing its hold on my chest. His eyes searched mine, and I watched the concern evaporate and something impish slide into place.

"Waffles?" he asked, pulling the keys from the ignition. I blinked at him, struggling to process what he meant.

"Oh," he said when I didn't immediately respond, looking startled. He folded his arms across the breadth of his chest. "You're a French toast girl?"

When I didn't reply, his countenance took on something akin to being told I had a tail, an extra toe, and a penis he didn't know about. His voice came out grave as he spoke. "Do not say you prefer pancakes. That will be an actual dealbreaker for me."

I wasn't sure if I wanted to laugh or cry at the ludicrous inquest. A pensive smile formed on my face, the shame that had peppered my skin like droplets of rain evaporating the longer I stared at this man who knew how to push my every button and then just as gracefully, melt all my worries away.

"I've never given it much thought before." My voice came out meek. We had seldom gone out as a family when my father was alive, and even on my own, I had never indulged in anything of that ilk. Breakfast foods beyond eggs and bacon always seemed too sweet and frivolous, especially when you lived life like you could barely taste any food. When food was an inconvenient necessity, you rarely spent time on sustenance that would make a glutton palpitate.

Still, I didn't like the gobsmacked expression Sean sported. He looked like I had reeled my fist back and punched him square in the jaw. His dark eyes rounded, mouth popping open, thick brows shooting north.

He was a man who had a hundred questions, and instead of throwing them all at me like I knew he was dying to do, he tossed me another one of those infamous boyish smiles that sent my heart aflutter and had my thighs clenching together.

"Have breakfast with me, Raquel."

CHAPTER TWENTY SEVEN

Sean

RAQUEL and I were tucked into a booth against a window near the middle of the quiet diner. Save for a few other patrons, the place was as dead as a funeral home at midnight. She clutched the white mug that housed her coffee like it was her only saving grace, her profile turned toward the window, the soft strands of her hair curling around her chin, lips strained with concentration.

"Do you know what you want to eat?" I asked, eyeballing her from over the two-page menu.

She regarded me from the corner of her eye, her head shake just barely perceptible. While we had left the car on even ground, by the time we were seated, she'd become reticent once more.

"I'm probably good with just the coffee," she said.

"I asked you out for breakfast, Hemingway—not coffee. Do you want something else?"

Her cheeks flushed, a satisfied smile curling the corners of my mouth at her response. An idea struck me, inspired by her obstinance.

Straightening in my seat, I broke eye contact with her to flash a thumbs-up at our waitress, Rhonda, who was leaning against the bar top of the counter, gossiping with an older woman. Both sported the signature sugarplum pink carhop uniform and off-white apron that were speckled with unidentifiable stains.

Rhonda's once-white Keds squeaked against the checkered floors as she skittered over to us. Fishing her notepad and pen from her apron pocket, she held the pen flush against the notepad ready to collect our order.

"What's it gonna be, Seany?" she wheezed, her lungs screaming at her to lay off the Camels.

For theatrical purposes, my eyes skimmed over the menu once more, Raquel's chin tipping toward me with silent curiosity at what I would order. I made a sound of contentment that aroused Raquel's attention, her eyes growing wary, like she knew what I was going to say before I said it.

Four Corners was practically known in the county for their breakfast fare, and if she wouldn't specify *what* she wanted, I'd take the decision-making work out of it.

"We'll take everything on the breakfast menu." I punctuated the sentiment by flipping the menu closed.

Rhonda's head jerked back, as if she hadn't heard me correctly.

"Are you insane?" Raquel hissed at me on both her and Rhonda's behalf, glancing at the closed menu in front of her. "There's easily a dozen different items on that menu."

"Cool," I said with a noncommittal shrug, reaching for the untouched vinyl laminated menu in front of her and handing both hers and mine to Rhonda. "We'll be here for a while, then."

"Uh," Rhonda hedged. "Do you...want it all at once?"

"Let's prioritize with the waffles, French toast and pancakes, Ronnie. Eggs can be cooked any way, and hold the toast. We're probably good on the carbs."

"O-okay," Rhonda stammered in response, nodding her head and turning on the soles of her sneakers, retreating to the kitchen.

"You're out of your mind," Raquel hissed.

She didn't know the fucking half of it.

I sent a salacious smirk in her direction. "Next time when I ask you what you want to eat, give me an answer."

"With that kind of attitude, there won't *be* a next time, *Slim.*" she spat, narrowing her rapier-like eyes at me.

I pretended to be affronted, clutching the center of my chest like she had just stabbed me before a snicker escaped me that broke her fleeting frosty facade, the blush I liked so much hitting her cheeks. She settled against the banquette, lower teeth grazing against her upper lip like she wanted to say something, but was doubting herself.

"How was your day?" I asked, fiddling with the packets of sugar I wouldn't use.

She looked up at me under her long lashes, curiosity setting her golden irises a glow at my ice breaker. I didn't know why that was the question I chose to lead with, or what kind of response I was expecting in return. Her shrug was short, barely touching the midpoint of her neck.

"Before or after you showed up?" she quipped, though I heard the hint of humor in her sarcasm. "It was okay." She paused, as if she wanted to say more but changed her mind, "how was yours?"

"Well," I began, tapping my fingers against the blemished wood of the diner table, training my stare on her. "I spent the majority of my day working up the courage to go talk to this woman I like. She hasn't really been interested in giving me the time of day."

"Why's that?" she asked, her voice steady, head lolling to the right.

"I got her to confirm she liked me a few days ago, but," his tongue edged his lip, "I've got a theory that she might like me even more than she's willing to let on."

"What gives you that impression?" Nerves laced the question, the tremble evident.

I folded my hands together, bracing myself against the wave of heat radiating off her body, beckoning me toward her like the opposite end of a magnet. "When I kiss her, it feels like she's coming alive for the first time." I watched as her lips parted and her eyes grew hooded. "And when I touch her, she moves like she's never been touched that way before."

Her lids dropped for a moment, as she appeared to contemplate her next move.

With her eyes still shut, she spoke with a new set of conviction. "Does that really mean she likes you, though? Or does that mean she just likes the way you make her body feel?"

I reached for her hand, and her eyes shot open at the contact, her eyes tracking my moving thumb against the span of her slim knuckles.

"Aren't they one and the same, Raquel?"

She shook her head, shrugging her shoulders again. "I don't know," she confessed, "I've never really done this before."

My left brow cocked upward, a sigh leaving her at my reaction. "Done what?"

"Dated outside of my circle." She bit her lower lip, another labored breath leaving her. "I've had one boyfriend in my life. And before yesterday," she paused to look at the ceiling tiles, "I had only been with one other guy...*that* way."

My head snapped back at her confession, awe setting off a buzz in my head. How had that happened? Why? I dragged an open palm over my face, suddenly feeling stupid for all the hypothetical theories I had spent time creating in my mind when she left with those guys. I swallowed the knot in my throat, my hand still on hers.

I didn't want to rehash it, but the question left me before I knew what I was really doing. "So then, when you left with those guys..."

"One of them was my ex boyfriend, yes," she confirmed, darting me a pointed look. "But we're not together that way anymore."

"But you still hang out?" I wasn't sure if it was relief that flanked me at the knowledge I wasn't competing with anyone else, or confusion as to why he wasn't out of the picture entirely, either.

"It's complicated." One slender shoulder rose and fell as her eyes searched my face.

"Want to try to uncomplicate it for me?" I kept my voice gentle. Her unease had her rubbing her forehead with her free hand. As the silence stretched on, I thought she was going to refuse my request, but then her cheeks puffed with another long exhale, her shoulders dropping an inch.

"I grew up in a really rough part of South Boston that hasn't been gentrified yet. Cash was my neighbor and one of the few people not absolutely petrified of my dad," she explained with a laugh that sounded pained, a ghost of wistfulness passing over her. "Reliable friends are surprisingly hard to come by when your dad is a known convict with a penchant for assault. So even though our relationship didn't work, Cash has always been around in some capacity when I've needed him."

I didn't like the way "some capacity" sounded any more than the realization that some of this information wasn't new to me, but I kept my face relaxed, refusing to give anything away.

Raquel tilted her head slightly toward the window, giving me her profile once more. "It was in my junior year of high school when Cash started coming around. He's a couple of years older than me, so it was strange when he started waiting for me out front of my school. I was so confused by his sudden interest in me, but no matter how many threats my dad sent in his direction, he just kept showing up." She blinked, as if she was watching a movie of her life play in the reflection of the window. "I spent my formative years preferring the solace of books and my younger sister Holly Jane's company."

My stomach sank, the acidity of my own coffee roiling at her mention of her sister.

"My sister and I were close," Raquel continued, "but I had always taken on a maternal role with her. Which meant a lot of the time, I felt invisible...and with Cash, suddenly I felt noticed. My needs and wants were important for the first time. I felt a kind of warmth enveloping me that I had never experienced before." She turned her head to glance at me, her eyes wide. "Cash made me feel like I mattered."

A shiver shuddered through her before she continued speaking. "My father was in and out of Walpole a lot. He struggled to hold down a job after he was forced to retire from his boxing career a few years after I was born. Too many punches to the head; he was a liability." She swallowed visibly. "My parents had gotten pregnant really young. My dad was an Irish expat who had been raised in a traditional Catholic family, so the right thing to do was to marry my ma, who had about as much interest in raising a family as most people do in paying their taxes."

My jaw rocked together, hating that every word she said was laced with something poignant that made my insides ache.

"When you spend most of your life feeling like you don't matter, and someone walks into your life and makes you feel…worthy…" she shook her head "…it was life-changing." She licked her lips, wilting in her seat. "But it came at a cost."

That vacancy from earlier was back in her expression. "As Cash and I got closer, my sister and I drifted further apart. My parents used to argue until dawn most nights, and Holly Jane would come and sleep with me, but when Cash and I started dating, she stopped."

She squinted, her face tightening, likely fighting off the demons I knew were plaguing her. "I never questioned it, y'know?" She rolled her lips together. "I just figured this was normal. She was growing up, and I was focused on trying to study for the SATs, that it was easy for me to slip into this alternate universe where all that mattered was Cash and me, and that meant I ignored a lot of the signs that were right in front of me."

"Like what?"

She lifted her eyes to me. "My sister was…" She paused before trying again. "She was getting mixed up with the wrong people. People she didn't have any business being around. I was so angry for spending so many years of my life not feeling important that I didn't care about anything once I got to college. I wanted to focus on myself, I didn't want to worry about what kind of trouble my kid sister was getting into. That was for my ma and dad. I thought if I pulled back, that they would feel obligated to parent their child." She looked at me, eyes haunted by what I knew was coming next. "Financially, things were always hard for my parents, and about ten years ago in a moment of pure desperation and stupidity, my father attempted to rob an armored truck in Revere…he was shot to death." She swiped a quick hand under her eye, blinking hard.

A cold sweat broke out across my chest that I was grateful she couldn't see. It was one thing to know what she was going to say and an entirely different thing to hear her say it. The headline of the first article came to life in my mind: *"Attempted Robbery Thwarted in Revere."*

I knew he had died, but it was an entirely different thing to hear her say it.

Rhonda appeared with a plate at that moment and Raquel withdrew her hand, a coldness settling between us. Steam rose from the hot plate of Belgian waffles in front of us.

I wasn't hungry anymore.

"The only thing I kept thinking about after he died was how angry I was that he had left us with *her*." The last word was punctuated by venom toward her mother. "People don't really care when a convict dies. They don't bring you a tuna casserole or send you condolences. I spent that summer at Cash's nan's house, sneaking in and out and trying to make myself scarce until I got to move into my dorm." She blinked, pulling herself out of her own mental detachment. "Cash and I had been together for a while by the time I started my freshman year at BU, but I had held out on sleeping with him. I didn't want to be another notch on his belt until I was certain."

My insides bristled at the idea that he had been the first man to touch her. It was stupid and primitive, but even with the knowledge that I was the only other man she had been with since, I hated that she had been with him in any capacity at all. That fucker wasn't deserving of her. He didn't even have the courtesy to fucking meet her at the bar door, even if he was barred from entering. He sent in that sociopath and his shadow to retrieve her like she was a piece of property. The memory had me gritting my teeth.

Raquel picked up her fork, using the flattened edge to cut off a corner of the waffle. She speared the waffle but didn't put it in her mouth. "Holly Jane called me the day I was set to lose my virginity. She said she needed to talk and wanted to come see me." She set the fork down, resting it against the plate. "And I, of course, told her no. I'd spent all morning cleaning up my dorm room. Clean sheets, a scented candle, a box of condoms. The plan was foolproof."

Her eyes lidded, and I tracked the slow rise and fall of her chest, her breaths soft and shallow. "So, there I was, eighteen years old, the first one in my family to go to college, about to lose my virginity to my older boyfriend, and I'm completely oblivious—no, I'm *ignorant* to the fact that there is a crisis going on in my sister's life." She shook her head, a strained laugh that lacked any warmth leaving her. "About three hours later, Cash and I were in bed, half asleep, when the room was filled with bright red and blue lights pouring in from the window.

"Then someone knocked on the door. I was immobile." She looked at me, tears settling in the corners of her eyes, her bottom lip trembled. "I couldn't even get up. It was like I knew what they were going to tell me was going to change everything." She squeezed her eyes together, the tears that had been puddling now coasting down her cheeks. My hand itched to wipe them away, but I remained in my seat and instead slid my hand across the table.

"Hey," I said softly. She sniffled, her lids flipping open, her irises amber from her tears. She glanced at my outstretched hand and shook her head, as though she felt undeserving of human contact.

She was depriving herself of the one thing I realized she wanted more than anything.

Love.

"Give me your hand," I demanded. Our eyes warred with each other, but she broke first. My hand crushed around hers, stilling the rattle in her apprehensive touch.

"Fuck," she gasped, leaning forward against the table, resting her elbow on the edge, shielding her eyes from me with her other hand. I squeezed her palm tightly. I knew what came next in her story, but I wanted to give her the opportunity to collect herself.

She appeared to be fighting for her next breath.

"It's okay," I whispered. "If you can't finish the story, you don't have to."

"I want to." She exhaled audibly and clarified, "I need to. If you and I stand any chance in hell of making whatever this is between us work, you need to understand what kind of person I am. What I did. Who my family is." She swiped under her eyes with her free hand. "Because we're not good people, Sean."

My chest tightened with resistance at her observation. "I don't think that's true, Raquel."

"It is, though." She crushed her lips together, torment swimming in

253

her eyes. "Ten years ago today, they couldn't find my mother to tell her that her daughter had rolled her car on the Mass Pike. My mother was on a bender with our landlord at O'Malley's, so they had to tell me because I was the only other immediate family member they could find." She brushed the knuckles of her free hand under her eyes. "I had to confront that my sister was dead, and she was dead because of me."

"No," I objected, catching the jolt of dismay that flickered in her face as she met my eyes. "I'm so sorry about what happened to her, but you're not responsible."

Raquel flinched. "How can you say that? Did you even listen to what I said?"

"Every last word, Hemingway. That doesn't change what I see."

"It's my fault that I wasn't there for her," she insisted. "If I had been, I wouldn't have had to learn she was almost three months pregnant through an autopsy report."

I was assailed by that detail, which hadn't been reported. Somehow, that had been left out, probably for privacy reasons. Was that why Raquel felt responsible for what had happened to Holly Jane?

Raquel looked so small in that banquette, her eyes somber and distant as they locked with mine. Shame shattered the vitreous pane of her hardened exterior that had struggled to be vulnerable and real. What she projected to the world was a far cry from who and what she really was on the inside.

My voice was a whisper over the clang of plates being cleared from a nearby table. "You're shouldering the blame for something you didn't do, Raquel. If you don't forgive yourself, you're going to carry the guilt of what happened with you forever."

Brief cognizance flickered in her face, but it was gone before it could even fully register, like a candle wick that wouldn't catch a flame. "I wasn't there to protect her from herself. I didn't intervene when I learned who she was hanging out with..." She squeezed her lids together, unable to finish the sentence. "I wasn't there when I knew what the consequences of leaving her in my mother's care meant. I don't even know for sure whose baby she was having." She slammed a fist into her chest as though to drive the message home, her facial expression grim. "That *is* my fault." Her impassioned speech would have brooked no argument with any other person, but I wasn't any other person.

"Can I ask you something?" I hedged, my mouth slipping into a frown. Her puzzled eyes ran over me, lips taut with tension, and I plunged ahead. "Do you think your mother blames herself?"

A fracture of a laugh came out of her, followed by another head shake. "That would require my mother to have a conscience."

"So why is this your responsibility?"

"You don't get it," she huffed, pulling her hand away from me. I held on, refusing to let her go. Crazed bewilderment erupted on her face, her concentration fixed on where I kept her small hand trapped in my own.

She wasn't going to punish herself on my watch for something she didn't do, something she couldn't control.

This was another lesson she was going to learn.

"I get it perfectly. You're making yourself accountable for parenting your kid sister when you were a kid yourself. You're punishing your-self for what happened to her when you could have never prevented it, unless you now want to confess to moonlighting as a clairvoyant and taking that night off."

"You don't need to be—"

"Condescending? A smug prick? An asshole? Yeah, I do, because you won't listen otherwise. You're sitting here being angry and self-deprecating for something that was entirely out of your control. Some-thing you could have never prevented."

She blanched at that, her head snapping back, nostrils flaring, telling me I'd struck a chord that reverberated within her. "Yeah, sure, okay—let's hypothesize that you were more involved in monitoring your sister's life, maybe you deferred college for a year...but do you know what that would have looked like long-term, Hemingway? You guys would have fucking hated each other because you put so much energy into trying to save her from herself." I saw a shift in her equilib-rium, sensed my statements were planting consideration in places where guilt had always bloomed. The instability that had previously been present had slipped into the void of the night, dissipating in darkened eddies around her until there was nothing. A flush of calmness was taking residence in her disposition, her eyes returning to their honeyed color as she digested what I had said. Her tongue peeked out to outline her bottom lip as she prepared her next question.

"Do you know this from experience?" she murmured, looking up at me with red-rimmed eyes under long lashes.

I never wanted to see her cry again. I knew that request was unrealistic, it was a declaration of intent at best—but something told me she had spent most of her life crying, and at most...I never wanted to be the reason for her to shed another tear.

"I already told you." My thumb scraped against the fine lines in her upturned palm. "I've got three sisters." I gave her a sideways smile, tossing my chin at her. "You'd better start eating that waffle. Rhonda looks like she's one order up away from a nervous breakdown."

CHAPTER TWENTY EIGHT

Raquel

THIS HAD NOT BEEN part of the plan. I had come in here with the intention of being as normal as humanly possible, but then I overheard a patron at a table talking to someone on the phone about their Thanksgiving plans through a mouthful of food and I just…I struggled to keep it together. I felt that restrained hesitation filling my body with each minute that passed. I had hoped that by sticking to coffee, the night would be over sooner.

Sean was never going to let that one slide, though.

I yo-yoed with my desire to be as close to him as physically possible, hip to hip, flesh against flesh. Yet, I was simultaneously overwhelmed by the fear that urged me to deign to its commands and keep as far away from him as our zip codes would permit.

I thought I'd get away with tucking myself against the banquette until he tired of my antics and silent routine.

He had read me like a book, and I surprised myself by wanting to talk about it. About Cash. About Dad. About Holly Jane. About her pregnancy.

I had supervised every single expression he made as I recounted my story to him over a waffle that had sat untouched for some time. I held my breath, waiting for the moment where something would finally register within him that I wasn't worth the effort. That pursuing this thing with me would be an epic mistake. That there was too much risk and not enough to gain.

But he just held onto my hand like he never had any intention of letting me go, and that made dropping my walls just a little easier. One by one, my internal bricklayers removed another layer into a crumbling pile by my feet, exposing more of me to him in a way that made me feel vulnerable enough to want to throw my hands over my chest and protect my exposed heart.

Because being around Sean made everything easier, and if I allowed myself...

I might fall.

"That is way too much syrup," Sean chuckled, invading my reverie. His eyes were trained on the dispenser in my hand and the free flow of syrup that flowed from the tilted end.

"There are no rules to breakfast foods."

"You're an expert now?" He snorted, shaking his head at me. "Your teeth are going to hurt."

"Good," I chirped, setting the dispenser down and arming myself with my fork. "I'll make my dentist work for his paycheck this time."

We had fallen into a steady flow of conversation after Rhonda had appeared with the pancakes and French toast shortly after depositing the waffles, a vein in her forehead straining as though she had been waiting for the most opportune moment to reappear at our table. I felt a shadow of doubt hovering over me, worry nipping at my heels that I had said too much, had volunteered prematurely and given him information that went beyond the scope of first date territory.

Oh, who the fuck was I kidding? His tongue had been three inches deep in my vagina less than forty-eight hours ago. We were probably past the point of no return. The scope of rules surrounding a first date did not apply to us.

We had never fit inside the conventional confines of norms.

Still, this was now the second time I had unloaded on him in a public place. At least I was sober for this one; the first time had just been at the behest of Samuel Adams and Jack Daniels.

"So," I began, cutting off the edge of the French toast, deciding this really was the better of the three options currently on the table...not that I would ever confess that to him. "Now that you gotten my life story, let's hear yours."

Sean's demeanor turned serious as his jaw worked at the forkful of French toast I had saturated. "That wasn't your life story, Hemingway. That was just a few chapters."

My expression softened, his eyes boring into mine as though rewriting the synapses and schematic responses in my brain. I didn't feel overwhelmed by his focus. Perhaps, if anything, I wanted to reveal parts of myself to him that I hadn't shown to anyone before.

The feeling should have left me unsettled, but the longer I sat there waiting for that chasm to crack the stable ground I stood upon, the more evident it became that the ground would not combust into fissures.

That I would be able to remain upright and unscathed.

"What do you want to know?" he asked, rearranging the plates on the table, consolidating them when he could, just as Rhonda reappeared to deposit a skillet laden with a mountain of home fries, grilled peppers and onions, and a poached egg. She set it next to a bowl of granola, yogurt with fresh fruit she had brought a few minutes ago and took the cleared plates with her when she left.

"Everything."

"Bold statement, Hemingway." His laugh softening the edges of my stupid heart from whatever residual anxiety still lingered there. "You gave me the Cole's Notes version of your chapter, and you want my life story?"

"I'm a columnist," I said, giving him a perfunctory look. "It's in my nature."

"I'll bet you use that line on all the boys." He snorted.

"Nah, just the ones I like."

"So you admit it, then." His lips fell into a lopsided grin, a carnal look heating his eyes. "You like me."

That tingle I'd had earlier in his Jeep returned, settling itself between my legs, my core tightening. "I plead the fifth," I croaked out, not even convincing myself that I believed my own bullshit. I had already admitted I liked him under the slow, tantalizing assault of his fingers and mouth yesterday—I wasn't going to give him the satisfaction of hearing it again.

"I could get you to talk." Sean's stare fell to where I had folded the corners of my napkin like a nervous tick. "And give you something else to do with your hands."

Why did he have to be so easy on the eyes? Why did every sweep of his gaze feel sensual? I crumpled the napkin and laid it next to my plate. My throat could barely coax the lump that had forged along my trachea. I shook my head briskly, disentangling the salacious thoughts he had filled my head with. "You're deflecting," I pointed out, narrowing my eyes at him.

"Is it working?"

"Absolutely not."

I didn't like the confidence he radiated as his arms crossed over his chest, his eyes slanting with interest that set off every alarm system in my brain, telling me I was approaching full-on nuclear warfare.

"So, if I followed you to the ladies' room right now and slid my hands into your panties, you wouldn't be wet for me?"

Too late. The nuclear plant that was my heart was in full meltdown, and so was my throbbing pussy, to the point where I was tempted to run to the ladies' room just for the thrill of it all.

"Stop!" My voice shook, my breaths hitching. "Answer my question."

"Would you prefer that?" he asked seriously, his tongue peeking out to run along his bottom lip, his stare dark and unyielding as he appraised me.

Nod your head, Raquel. To my surprise, I mustered something that must have been a semblance of a nod, barely aware of my body sagging into the booth that I was practically creaming all over to begin with.

Damn him.

He sighed in defeat. "My family emigrated here when I was eight. I'm the second child of four, but the only son."

"Four?" I deadpanned. I knew he had mentioned close to a half dozen times that he had three sisters, but some part of me thought that had been a running joke, not reality. My mother would have offed herself. "Your parents were busy."

He picked at a rogue piece of bacon. "My big fat Portuguese family."

"Why did they decide to come to the States?"

Sean popped a piece of bacon into his mouth, moving onto the bowl of granola and yogurt that he busied himself deconstructing. "I think they were hoping life would be easier here, and in some ways, it was," he said as he paved a path in the middle of the yogurt bowl, revealing a stark line white line. "But things were also hard, and not speaking a lick of English back then didn't help."

I could imagine some of what he described. My family had struggled, and aside from the depths of Dad's Irish accent, my family's struggles had never been due to a language barrier. I couldn't imagine what that kind of move would be like for someone who didn't speak English.

"What do your sisters do?"

"I gotta be honest," he said with a sigh. "I preferred this the other way around."

"Of course you did. No one likes feeling like they're in the hot seat, but," I waved my fork in his direction, "I'm the one conducting this interview now."

Sean threw his head back, another laugh ripping through his chest. "Is that what this is?"

"Didn't you know? I'm getting my do-over."

"Your do-over," he repeated, his head tilted laconically. "I just thought I was on a date with a beautiful girl."

That flustered me. Heat hit the back of my neck as it made its ascent toward my cheeks. I didn't know what to do with this kind of attention that didn't dilute. I had expected that by now, the interest would have waned even just a little from either one of us, but he just gripped me. I wanted to know everything about him, learn what made him tick, etch every detail into smooth stone.

"Why do I get the impression you don't hear that much?" he asked, reaching for his mug and lifting it to sip his coffee.

"Hear what?"

"That you're beautiful."

I lifted my gaze to meet his. I did feel beautiful under his arresting gaze that ceased my heart, seated across from him in this forgettable diner that I had never stepped inside of in all the years I had worked in Eaton.

"I guess I never really have," I said with a half shrug. "Cash might have said it here and there, but I suspect it was deployed to get out of trouble."

He opened his mouth to speak but I held out a hand, silencing him. "You're deflecting. You got more than a chapter of my life, and now I want something from yours."

Sean's frown was so brief, I thought it maybe I'd imagined it until his focus concentrated on my lips. "I'd rather deflect in other ways."

I cocked an eyebrow in his direction. "Should have thought about that before you ordered the entire breakfast menu."

"Think it's too late to cancel?"

"I'm pretty sure someone ran out to grab eggs to fulfill this order, so yes."

"Fuck," he grumbled. "Okay, okay. I'm ready, your honor."

I rolled my eyes. He wasn't on trial, and I had been forthcoming with him—so what was he avoiding? For someone who had been so gung-ho about talking about feelings and pushing all the boundaries, he clammed up tighter than a chastity belt now that he was on the receiving end of the questions.

"What are you avoiding telling me?"

"Nothing." He was emphatic.

My eyes narrowed at him.

"I was like this with you the first time we met, too, I'll remind you."

He wasn't wrong, but I had assumed he would be a little more open now that...I had been beyond open with him. Literally, I didn't think my legs could have parted any farther apart the day before, and I had had a bad case of verbal diarrhea not that long ago.

"Go on," he coaxed. "Ask your questions."

"I've met Trina, but what are your other sister's names?"

"Maria and Olivia."

"What do they all do?"

"My older sister Maria is a lawyer."

I didn't miss the morose way he said her name and wondered why.

"Livy wants to be the next Emma Watson, and Trina is living in my guest bedroom and helping me with odd jobs."

"I didn't realize Trina lived with you." It made me think of all the times I had fantasized about Holly Jane and I living together on our own. I felt a small tug on my heartstrings.

Sean looked uncomfortable, pushing the home fries around on one of the plates. "Yeah." His brows crashed down hard on his surly face.

"Yeah," I repeated. "I think it's nice that you guys live together."

He snorted.

"What?"

"Nothing." He shook his head. "Next question."

I didn't like the grim mask of disapproval that he had slid on. Was he actually uncomfortable with all of this?

Reaching for my mug, I pondered my next question before I asked it. "Why did you really take over your father's business?"

Sean's jaw rocked from side to side. Time came to an impasse, the seconds stretching to a full minute before he uttered a terse, "Pass."

"You don't get to pass!" I exclaimed, unable to contain my incredulity. "Are you kidding me?"

His glower was unrelenting. "I don't want to answer. I pass."

"Answer the question or I'm outta here." It was a petty move on my part, but I had been nothing but an unequivocal open book this evening, and dammit, he was going to do the same. He was the reason we were both here to begin with. I wasn't playing this game with him where he got to be selectively dismissive—not after I had just shared my demons with him.

"Are *you* kidding *me*?" he echoed, his darkening eyes daring me.

Without a word, I grabbed my jacket from beside me and slid out of the banquette.

"Raquel, c'mon," he called as I moved for the door. I heard him voice a slurry of curses as the door chimed and the cold air hit me, my nipples puckering under the cups of my bra as I wrestled into my leather jacket.

The door chime signaled his approach. His footsteps were heavy behind me, his advancement growing closer and closer until his hand hooked my elbow, spinning me around to face him. All six feet, two inches of him scowled at me, like he couldn't believe I had had the audacity to up and leave.

"Did you just walk out on me?"

I shifted my gaze to the tree opposite us, then back at the diner before my stare landed back on his face and the jaw that ticked with annoyance. "It would appear that way, yes," I said caustically.

"Why?" His expression said he was taxed, but his eyes screamed rejection. That softened my frostiness by only a degree or two.

My spine lengthening, I replied, "Because it's not fair that I'm willing to be forthright and you're going to withhold information from me because they clearly make you uncomfortable. Do you think it was easy for me?"

The lids of his eyes flickered, processing what I had tossed at him. His stare tightened on me, lips pinching together like he was trying to suffocate whatever was brewing inside of him. "I need time."

"What do you mean, you need time?" As far as I was concerned, his time ran out when he walked into my place of employment seeking me out. He should have thought about that before he pushed me at the bar. Before he pursued me the day I met him. Before he ever kissed me.

I squared my shoulders, fixing my stare at him. "I just told you that today is the anniversary of my sister's death, and my father was shot and killed. Don't talk to me about needing time."

His expression grew pained, his hold on the crook of my elbow slackening. He remained mute. I wasn't sure if there was a deeper meaning in the loss of his touch, but at this moment in time, it didn't matter to me.

My body staved off the tremble from the cold gust of wind that pushed my hair from my face. "You have been relentless since I met you. You've barely given me time to figure anything out before you're back for more."

"Shit," he bristled, rubbing his face, his hand lingering to scratch at the stubble on his chin. "I knew I was coming on too strong."

"That's not it, Sean." I sighed, wrapping my arms around myself. "I'm just asking you to reciprocate. It's a give and take."

With each quiet second that passed, I considered that this really might be our last date.

This was not where I had foreseen us ending up—not that I had ever had any indication that we would ever be at this point at all.

My initial plan had been to avoid him at all costs, but he had been there at any opportunity he could find. And I had wanted him to be there, without rhyme or reason, I had wanted his attention. I had basked in the warmth of his presence, I had grown enamored with his laugh, his smell, his touch.

I liked him.

I really liked him.

I would be the first to admit that I had been standoffish in the beginning—but I had just jumped over monumental emotional hurdles that had felt nearly insurmountable, that had been tantamount to extracting what was left of my frayed soul for him.

But it didn't look like he was going to be able to do the same, and I was past the point of compromising myself for people who couldn't reciprocate—regardless of how he had flipped everything I had ever known upside down.

Sean looked up at the inky sky above us, puffs of hot air leaving his mouth in stiff, short clouds that evaporated into the atmosphere.

"Can we go back inside at least?" he huffed, bouncing on the heels of his shoes, hands burying themselves in his pockets. "My balls are going to turn into ice cubes if we stay out here."

I rolled my lips together to smother the laugh that crawled up my throat, swallowing it back down. I didn't trust him to not seek an out again if I gave him an inch, and something told me he would perceive that laugh as acquiescing, but I meant every word I said.

"Will you tell me about your father if I do?"

"I'll tell you whatever the fuck you want to know, just get your ass back inside."

I considered the order a minute longer than he would have liked. Sean's presence filled my space as he stepped toward me, placing his hands on the brick wall on either side of my head. Our faces were barely an inch apart, the tip of his nose chilled as he grazed it against my own.

"You can walk back in there out of your own volition, or I can sling you over my shoulder," he said. "Your choice, but either way, the night isn't over and you're not leaving until you help me eat at least twenty percent of the clusterfuck that is our table right now."

I considered testing his patience just for the sake of curiosity—science, if you will. But I could feel Rhonda's eyes burning a hole through the glass of the window, her mouth ajar while she watched the scene unfold.

Indoors it was.

CHAPTER TWENTY NINE

Sean

I KNEW Raquel's question didn't warrant this kind of reaction from me, but I was hot off the heels of having my sister badger me days ago about my choices spanning the past decade, and I wasn't entirely interested in revisiting the subject.

Raquel was literally dangling her continued presence in my life like a carrot in front of my nose, and regardless of how mulish I could be, I knew when to fucking walk when I needed to avoid getting my ass whipped.

Which was the only reason why she was sitting across from me, staring at me over her made-up lashes, looking thoroughly unimpressed. Rhonda topped off our coffees and I bought myself more time by downing the cup, scalding my tongue in the process.

Fucking peachy.

Raquel sighed, glancing at the wall clock over the cash register. "I'd like to be back in Boston before midnight, ideally."

"Thanks for that pep talk, Hemingway." I glared at her, and she just fucking blinked at me like I was wasting her time. I retraced my steps, wondering how I had found myself in this predicament where I now owed this woman my life story. It wasn't even a bad life story. My life probably looked like a trip to Disney compared to hers. My parents had been happily married for two decades. They loved each other right up until the day my father died. I had three sisters who were brilliant and talented in their own right—and life breathed through all of them.

I hadn't had to live through any of my sister's deaths, and I self-ishly prayed to God that I never did. Unlike Raquel, I wasn't a fighter.

But I *had* given up in some way when my father had died. I had conceded to the unspoken expectation and done what I thought was right.

It was just hard for me to admit that Maria had nailed it and I had not only stopped living, I had spent the last decade focused entirely on surviving.

"I wanted…" the word was already stuck in my throat. It was as if tiny granules of sand were filling my larynx, making it nearly impossible to speak. She tilted her head down, brows furrowing together over her unearthly eyes that burned like an inferno, forging a clearance for me like a guide in a darkened forest. They were the only light in my life at the moment, and it was the only thing that helped me get the words out.

"To be a chef," I concluded. I ran my tongue over the roof of my mouth. "That had always been my plan. I loved cooking more than I loved anything else. Food makes people feel good. It cures every malady, every heartache. Food brings people together."

My heart set off in a gallop, my pulse throbbing in my throat as I focused on slowing my breathing. This wasn't anything to hyperventi-late over, but shit, it was damn hard to talk about.

"My parents were generally supportive about my ambitions, and as soon as they were financially able, they did whatever they could to make our every hope and dream possible." I felt myself shrinking in my seat, hating how pathetic I must have appeared. Poor little Sean

Tavares. His parents did everything possible to fulfill his and his sisters' every want and whim.

Raquel's face was impossible to read, her eyes impassive in a way that made me break out into a cold sweat with fear she was judging me.

She remained quiet, that brevity of speech Penelope had warned me about weeks ago finally making its appearance. I dragged a tight inhale through my nose, filtering the oxygen out through my parted lips to slow my racing heart before I continued.

"My dad never wanted me to be like him. Didn't want me to take over the business, although there was nothing wrong with my doing so, it just had never been the plan. He dreamed of more for us." Raquel was staring at me with rapt attention. She leaned forward, placing an elbow on the table, cupping her chin with the palm of her hand.

"When Maria got into Harvard, it was the happiest day of his life. It was the first time I ever saw my father cry. He was a man of few words, but that day he hooted and hollered loud enough for the entire town to hear him." I was mired in my own discomfort as I approached the impending climax of the story.

"But there was a lot going on in the background that I wasn't aware of."

Her eyes searched mine, as if she could excavate the latent answer outta me that way. When I didn't go on, she prompted me to continue. "Like what?"

I scratched at my jawline, trying to collect my befuddled thoughts.

"Things weren't going as well with the business as we thought," I said, swallowing hard. "We were north of half a million dollars in debt. The contracts we thought my dad was procuring weren't going through, but he just kept carrying on like everything was fine. He had taken another mortgage out on the house to pay for Maria's Harvard tuition without my ma's knowledge. I think he thought it was just a blip, that things would get better and he'd be able to pay it all back." The words became trapped in my throat, and it took every ounce of strength I had in me to get them out. "But then he got sick."

Raquel's face grew ashen, that sternness evaporating from the angles of her face as she uncoiled herself in her spot, correcting her posture.

"He was never honest with us about what was going on. I think he thought he would get better, y'know?" The laugh that left me was hollow, that empty feeling that had suffused me on and off for years swimming over me. "He died, and we didn't have a damn clue about our financial situation until we went to buy him a casket and there was nothing in the account."

"Sean."

"Do not say you're sorry, please," I implored her, my voice gruff. "You're the last person who should be commiserating with me. You went through so much worse."

"That's subjective," she said evenly, tearing at the edges of a napkin she had pulled from the dispenser. "You can't compare apples to oranges."

"Your dad and your pregnant teenage sister died. Your entire life was laden with disappointment and heartache. My life was fine up until I was twenty. When was your life ever fine?" I had possessed no scruples about saying that to her right up until the moment the words were out of my mouth. I watched with bated breath as they landed in a place that I could tell left her wounded from the stricken look on her face.

Fuck, fucking, fuck.

Contrition yanked at my insides as Raquel turned her head for the briefest of moments, her breath pushing out through her parted lips, the transient drop of her lids nearly wrenching my heart from its place behind my ribcage. Then those eyes of hers opened again, and she shifted her attention back in my direction.

"You're allowed to mourn and be sad about what you were deprived of regardless of the circumstances, Sean." She cleared her throat, pulling her upper lip between her teeth only to set it free. "It's not a competition."

"That's not what I meant."

"I know it's not," she offered with a sad nod of her head, "but I don't want you to feel like you have to hide those things from me. It's true that my life hasn't been conventional up until this point, but," she paused, "I'd like to try conventional with you, and that means talking about all the ugly bits that make us a little uncomfortable."

My back slammed against the banquette, my eyes wide as the hand that had been propping her chin up slid across the table, skirting past our mountain of half-eaten food.

Had I heard her correctly? My stare flitted from her eyes, the sincerity in them overwhelming, to the tips of her fingers that grazed against mine. Ten minutes ago, she had fled this diner like I wasn't worth another minute of her time.

Now, she was giving me the chance I had always asked of her.

I swallowed the ache in my throat, my tongue sweeping my lips for moisture. "What does that mean?"

"I don't know. I've never done this before, remember?" she said.

What had happened between her and Cash that had made her apprehensive about dating years later? What had he done to make her feel so special back then that she had been willing to give so much of herself to him? She hadn't struck me as the naive type, and yet somehow she had found herself wrapped up with him like he was a cancer sucking the very life from her.

"What does the average couple do when they're getting to know each other?"

"So, we're a couple now?" I liked the way that sounded. Her cheeks blistered the color of a tomato, her shoulders shooting toward her ears as if she was trying to recede into herself.

"Sorry, that's an antiquated term, isn't it?" She was too damn adorable right now as she visibly shifted in her seat.

"Nah," I said, sweeping my thumb across her knuckles as my insides swirled. "I like it."

"Can I ask you something else?" she asked, her eyes falling to the table.

"Shoot." The worst of it was out; everything else was inferior compared to having to relive my father's unintended deception. She could ask me whatever she wanted.

"Did you," she paused, appearing reluctant to finish the sentence. "Did you get to be a chef, ever?"

Thinking about the loss of that dream hurt like hell. She must have detected the shift in my mood, as recollection cascaded through me. I could still recall the feel the weight of the chef's knife in my hand, the frenetic energy that came to life inside of me when I was in a kitchen, creating. I could feel the fibers of the chef's jacket that clung to my frame, the warmth of sweat that broke across my brow as I worked in tandem with my classmates, who were all fighting for the same dream as me.

The dream I'd never see come to fruition.

My jaw rocked from side to side. "No."

Raquel's mouth opened, then closed, as if she was about to say something but then thought better of it. I was glad. I didn't want to hear it. Not tonight. We had had our fill of heavy conversations for one day. I wanted something easy now. I wanted her in my lap, and her mouth on mine, and my fingers in her hair. I wanted her moans in my ears, and my name on her tongue. I wanted to drag her against me, to feel the thump of her heart as it beat in sync with mine.

I could lose myself in this woman. I *was* losing myself in this woman.

"Wanna get outta here?"

"Not yet." She picked at the pancake, popping a piece into her mouth. She dropped her lids, lips pursing with satisfaction, a making a moan that tightened my balls.

"I think the pancakes might be my favorite."

I shook my head as she teased the edge of what I had warned her was my dealbreaker.

The pancakes could be her favorite—because lucky for both of us, Raquel was mine.

Dealbreakers be damned.

CHAPTER THIRTY

Raquel

IT FELT like we had gone everywhere and nowhere at the same time. After leaving the diner, we climbed back inside the Wrangler and drove laps around Eaton, rolling through the winding roads that led to sleepy neighborhoods, then into the small industrial section of town and back through the historic downtown strip.

"What's your favorite song?" Sean asked me, stealing a glance in my direction as he drove us to our next destination. The road in front of us was dark and ambling as he followed its curves, the moon guiding our way. I stretched in the passenger seat, deliberating as my mind ran through the discography that lived in my mind. We had embarked on a game of twenty-one questions, although by now, we were well into the fifty-plus territory.

"New or old?"

"Doesn't matter."

"Well, that's hard," I said with a laugh.

"Okay." He drummed his fingers against the steering wheel. "What song can you listen to over and over again without getting sick of it?"

I mulled over the question a minute longer before I finally settled on the song. "'You are the Moon' by The Hush Sound."

"Never heard of it. What do you like about it?"

A sad smile touched my lips. "When Holly and I were kids, in moments of worry or anxiety, I used to tell her to look for the moon. For a split second, we'd get lost under its spell. Your problems suddenly seem small in comparison to something so big. Its existence eclipses everything else."

"Spoken like a true writer." He shot me a quick smile.

I swallowed the lump in my throat, the pace of my heart quickening. I felt as though he was undressing me with his eyes and revealing my inner thoughts. I managed a small shrug of my shoulders for the sake of doing something, all while remaining eerily indecipherable under his gaze.

"I'll have to check it out, then." As though detecting the shift in my spirit, Sean reached for my hand across the console, giving it a gentle squeeze.

"Where have you traveled to?" he asked next, the car slowing as he turned left onto a street where I'd never before ventured.

"Nowhere. I've never left Massachusetts."

"Never?" His brow rose an inch.

"I mean, I saw the border of New Hampshire one time. Does that count?" I chortled.

He gave me a feigned look of pity before erupting into laughter.

"What's your favourite song?" I asked, rerouting the conversation and reclaiming the game.

"Easy," Sean said, breaking out into an ebullient grin that surprised me. "'Cry Little Sister'."

I scrunched up my nose with interest. "That's the song from *The Lost Boys*, right?"

"Best movie ever," he proclaimed with a decisive nod of his head, another laugh leaving him that shot arrows from Cupid's bow directly into my heart.

I wasn't sure if I hated or despised the way my insides twirled and spun like the innards of a kaleidoscope every time his laughter filled the Jeep or he looked at me the way he was doing right now. It was as if time came to an impasse and nothing else mattered in those moments except him and me. His stare on mine was deliberate this time, like everything I had thought had been said out loud. I cleared my throat, breaking our eye contact to glance back out the window to finally figure out where we were going.

There was nothing cookie cutter to be found here. Stately century houses spilled into my peripheral vision as we came into a part of Eaton that I'd never been to before, but knew of. The well-fenestrated houses here were made up of rich redbrick with slate gabled roofs and porches that protruded from the frame of the house.

"You brought me to Heritage Park?" It was a few blocks north of Penelope and Dougie's new place. People here were cut from the same Mulberry silk cloth as the Cullimores: Affluent WASPs with a closet full of polo shirts, and a side piece that did all the kinky shit their spouses weren't into.

Mayor Murphy included.

"Yeah. I wanna show you something," Sean said. He pulled the Wrangler into a circular driveway of a darkened house that stood out like a sore thumb amongst the pristine collection of otherwise impressive homes. The dilapidated First Period English American colonial not only looked entirely out of place amongst the opulence—it was plain fucking ugly. And I'm not talking about ugly duckling turned swan princess, I'm talking no chance in hell unless you took a wrecking ball to the thing and started over.

"Where are we?" I asked with unease as the Jeep came to a stop in the circular driveway.

"Come and find out." Sean shot me a toothy grin that at any other time would have been an absolute panty melter. Right now, in front of what was on par with 1428 Elm Street, I wasn't convinced my death wouldn't be imminent.

"You want me to go in *there?*" I wavered, swallowing hard. I leaned forward in my seat, the seat belt wheezing in protest while I peered up at the ominous, darkened house.

He couldn't be serious.

"Are you scared?" He chuckled.

I whipped my head in his direction, my face twisting with bewilderment. Scared? Had he not seen *Nightmare on Elm Street*? People like us died in houses like these. That stupid nursery rhyme rang off like a litany in my mind that put my hackles on end and my mind on high alert.

Sean reached out and cupped my chin, the coarse pads of his digits igniting an eruption of goosebumps across my skin and subdued my nerves, killing the parodied song in my brain.

That drunken heat slammed into me again. I released the breath I was holding, the warmth of my arousal settling into my skin and making my whole body hum in a way that yearned for him to touch me. As though reading my thoughts, he undid his seatbelt and leaned over the center console, his thumb finding the ejection on my belt.

"Hemingway, Hemingway, Hemingway." His voice strained, reaching forward to pull me into his lap. There was a duality in this moment. My fear of the house and him. They both felt like imposing figures that commanded all my attention with the enormity of their presence. And where they both consumed my thoughts, they were the unequivocal cause of the steady beat of my heart that thrummed in a way it never had before. A fear of what could be lost paired with the first taste of real life at the same time was like a treat that was both savory and sweet.

I worried my lip with my teeth, as his hands settled on my hips, his fingers locking around my belt loops to pull me closer, and my body went willingly. His dark eyes were roguish as they assessed me, his crooked smile slipping into something sly.

"I can hear your heartbeat," he murmured, releasing his hold on my belt loop to settle his palm over the urgent thumping of my heart. "What are you afraid of?"

Dying and missing out on more moments like these.

My eyebrows shot north as that unspoken realization settled over me, filling my pores and the empty crevices of my mind. I had spent a decade before this moment not caring when or if it was my time, drinking myself into stupors without worry about the ramifications, smoking until plumes filled my apartment or the inside of my car. Indulging on what was bad for me. Starving myself of what was good.

Right up until him.

He had flipped my whole world upside down, undid everything I had ever known, all while reminding me that even after death, the world keeps turning.

I wanted to see what life had in store for me. I wanted to see what was next. I wanted to feel it.

With him.

I watched as that playful look left his face, his expression growing dire as he straightened in his seat.

"Hey, wh—"

I cut him off, slanting my mouth over his, sinking my newfound awareness into the intensity of that kiss. The house wasn't so scary now. The burden of my worries lifted from my shoulders as his body relaxed under my kiss. Sean's fingers threaded into my hair, tightening at the base of my neck to hold me still, his teeth grazing my bottom lip, demanding access that I readily gave him. His tongue circled mine, the sweet notes of maple syrup and coffee lingering there that elicited a moan out of me.

He broke our kiss, his breaths coming hard and fast. "You make the sexiest little sounds." Sean settled against the seat, his hooded eyes tracing over me like he couldn't believe any more than I could that I was here with him, in his lap, parked in front of a house that looked like it belonged on the set of a horror movie.

My hips shifted in his lap, my core grinding against him in the most tantalizing kind of way that extracted a groan of approval from him. I worked across him in languorous figure eight motions, the friction against my clit sending every hair on my body upright. I could feel my heartbeat in the tips of my fingers as they sank into the stretch of his firm shoulders, my body swiveling atop of his as that mounting pleasure created a pulse in my pussy that was making it hard to think.

I wanted him, and I didn't care about the consequences.

I met his eyes, drowning in the smoldering heat of his drunken stare, watching as the tip of his tongue smoothed across a small, dried crack in his lip, his massive hands leaving my hair to settle on my jiving hips, holding me still.

"Are you going to fuck me, or what?" I said with a smirk.

The color vanished from his face for a split second. Without warning, the driver's seat slid back roughly as far as it could go. He rolled us over until my back was against the seat, his weight pinned against me. Sean's knee parted my thighs as his body settled against me.

The pressure of his erection against my core made me writhe beneath him, desperate for more. I had never been this emboldened, this needy, this hungry.

"Is that a 'yes'?" I croaked.

"No," he ground out, rolling himself against me. "I'm not."

Rejection and disappointment sizzled across my skin the dismissal settling in my expression. I was easy. I was here for the taking, and still he wouldn't act on it.

"Why not?" I demanded.

He met my gaze, his expression an arresting combination of anguish and eroticism.

"Because you deserve better than being fucked in a bar bathroom, on a desk, or in my car."

"That's not what your cock says," I grinned, wrapping my legs around his waist, connecting our groins.

"Of course not." His breath was shaky, as though he was reconsidering the offer for a moment. Through clenched teeth he added, "But I'm choosing to think with the right head. Let me do right by you, Raquel."

My insides coiled as his words swept over me. I didn't know what that meant.

"Stop overthinking it and trust me," he whispered, his mouth hovering over mine. "You gotta trust me."

I blew out the breath I'd been holding, lifting my eyes to meet his. "I'm willing and you won't fuck me." My cheeks burned, the heat stretching to the tips of my ears as I withered under his stare and my own embarrassment, "So, while I trust you, I can't help but think you don't want me."

"I *will* fuck you." He grabbed my hand, his thumb finding the pulse in my palm, giving it a squeeze. "And I *do* want you." He settled my other hand against him, and out of instinct, I cupped the thickened outline of his erection. He grunted a curse that ripped from the back of his throat, his eyes burning, jaw steeling.

"I want you bad enough that I'm willing to give myself blue balls just to do things the right way, the way you deserve," he said. "Do you understand?"

I had never been a woman who had been done right by to begin with, so that concept was as foreign to me as it was new. Whether or not I wanted to, I managed a nod that felt feeble. His smile was a fleeting, whimsical thing that was lost when he pressed his mouth against mine once more. I accepted the kiss, erupting into laughter as he moved from my mouth and peppered the rest of my face with kisses until I was giggling breathlessly.

Me, *giggling*.

"Okay, okay. Stop," I protested.

"Not until you tell me you understand." He nipped my skin.

"I understand!" I shrieked, choking on my laughter as I turned my head frantically while he left a trail of kisses across my jawline, his coarse beard tickling my skin, sending my body ablaze.

"Not convinced that you do."

It was impossible to reconcile that this was the same man who weeks ago had behaved like he hadn't even wanted to be on my radar while I probed him for answers to questions that he skirted around, masking himself like an enigma. It hadn't been until he pressed me back that I felt myself loosening my hold on what I had always held near and dear to me: control.

Sean made me want to relinquish the hold on the reigns that I had always wrapped tight around my fists. I had wielded it like a shield, sported it like a facade. Control had been all I was left with after everything that had happened.

I couldn't control people, nor could I control what happened.

But I could control me, and that had always felt like a small respite in some way.

Now, that control felt like a burden that I didn't want anymore. I had been suffocating under the restraint; the reins I had once cherished and revered had become like shackles at my wrists and neck that threatened to deprive me of the life I never realized I had wanted up until this very night.

Sean made me feel again. After years of feeling nothing, I felt everything.

And for the first time, I wanted to fight for it. For that freedom. For the life. For that possibility at a chance at...well, I didn't want to say it. It was presumptive. He could be terrible in bed, and then maybe that would be the thing that drove us away.

"You ready to go in?" he asked, his lips on the tip of my chin, dark eyes looking up at me with playful debauchery that made my whole body hum and my heartbeat quicken.

Who the fuck was I kidding? There was no chance in hell he didn't know what he was doing with his cock. He had me panting with a single titillating look. A look that stopped my heart, that slowed my breathing, that tilted my earth on its axis. Even if he was awful...as long as he continued to look at me like I was the best thing he had ever seen, to hell with the rest.

I settled my hands on either side of his cheeks, urging him to my lips. "If I die in there—"

"No one's dying; enough dead people talk." He chuckled, the sound vibrating his chest while he placed a light kiss on the tip of my nose that made my body shudder as though it was awakening from a deep state of sleep, my limbs undulating into a stretch.

"Besides," he said after he had gotten out and opened the passenger door for me, "I own the house." Smug confidence was etched all over his angular face as he held out a hand to me in offering.

The cold November air enveloped me through the open car door. He *owned* that thing?

"You paid money for that?" I asked with a grimace. "You might want to ask for a refund."

"Get your ass out of the car, Hemingway." He laughed, his arresting stare sending a current right into my core that had me nearly tempting him to get back into the Jeep. I could think of a hundred other things I'd rather be doing than walking around that scary-looking house, and he was number one. To my misfortune, he wasn't budging, he just continued to stand there with expectancy.

All right, I wasn't getting out of this one.

My eyes flitted from the gloomy house back to the crucifix that hung around his rear view mirror. I reached out and unlatched it.

"What are you doing?" Bemusement sent his mouth into a lopsided smirk.

"Just for good measure," I muttered, wrapping the beads around my fist twice. I was not a God-fearing woman, and I hadn't set foot inside of a church since Holly Jane died. But Dad had believed in this shit, so that by extension had to count for something. And the crucifix to Freddy Krueger was like garlic to a vampire...right?

"Jesus isn't going to save you, y'know."

I rolled my eyes at him. "Shut up, Slim," I said, accepting his hand, allowing him to pull me out of the Jeep.

He kept my hand trapped in his, his fingers looping around mine, his hip checking the door shut. Then he led me to the door, rolling off into a steady stream of consciousness. He pointed out the things he wanted to improve on the exterior. New windows, restore the door, add on a porch, a whole new garden bed.

The stench inside the house was a pungent combination of stale and musky air and...well, dead things. Still, I loved the animation in his face, the scintillating rumination that lit up his eyes as he used a flashlight he had pulled from the vehicle like a laser pointer.

"What would you do in here?" I asked when we stopped in what I could only assume had once been a kitchen. Cabinet doors hung from their hinges, no appliances were present, the linoleum under my feet worn. Motes of dust danced in the moonlight that gleamed through the windows in brilliant whitened beams that acted as our only source of illumination save for Sean's flashlight.

"There's definitely hardwood under there," he said, kicking at a loose edge of linoleum. "We'll pull this up and then see what we can salvage. I let Penelope come up with the plans for the last kitchen," he confessed with a nervous laugh. "I hate being in here."

"Why? You love cooking."

"Exactly," he said with a shrug, regret lining his face. "Every kitchen I enter is another reminder of what I never did."

My expression crumpled at that. "But most people are in a kitchen every day."

"Yeah, it's kind of a fucked-up position to be in." His admission left him appearing sheepish. "I guess I'm a bit of a masochist."

"Or just human," I said with a shrug. I could understand his stance. The conversation made my thoughts turn to the desk in my apartment, the one that buried my secret.

"I wrote a book once," I offered.

He turned, looking at me seriously. "Oh, yeah?"

I nodded, rolling my lips together as I considered the consequences of my confession.

"What did you do with it?"

"Collected rejection letters like Penelope collects designer handbags."

His face fell, and I could tell that hadn't been what he had wanted to hear. "I'm sure those fuckers will regret that some day."

I doubted it, but it was a nice thought.

Sean jerked me forward, I collided into his hard chest, my arms going around his waist. On instinct, I inhaled his scent, loving the burn as it settled in my sinuses, taking the edge off my busy mind that went everywhere it wasn't supposed to.

I didn't like thinking about my failures.

"C'mon, let me show you the rest of the house."

"Told you that nothing would happen to you in there." Sean said thirty minutes later as we were climbing back into the Jeep.

"You had to pick a spider as wide as an ice cream cone off of me," I reminded him, dislodging the thought of the spider that had crept up my pant leg until it grazed the tips of my fingers, making me flip my shit. Arachnid incident aside, the rest of the tour had been uneventful.

"You didn't tell me you were afraid of spiders."

"You didn't tell *me* we were coming here. And I wasn't afraid. Just surprised."

"Right, except no one flails their arms like that when they've got a spider on them unless they're afraid." A smirk edged the corner of his mouth. That was my favorite smile, the ones he tried to fight, the ones that never quite materialized. I knew those near-smiles were just for me.

His hand stretched out and settled on my knee, his other hand loose on the steering wheel of the Jeep as we drove in silence back toward *The Advocate*. Today had been such a strange day. I hadn't known what to expect or feel after ten years without my sister, but my mind kept considering that maybe Sean's presence in my realm of reality was Holly's divine intervention...a gift from beyond the grave. A sign that it was okay for me to experience what she hadn't.

And that she was okay with me moving on with my life, too.

I relaxed against the seat, my eyes growing lidded as a calm I couldn't recall ever having experienced before swept over me. I wasn't sure how I was going to make the drive back to Boston, and I considered taking a catnap in my car before I attempted it. This night had lessened nearly every ounce of strain that had been settled in the vertebrae of my back, knotted my shoulders, and made my chest constrict. Part of me didn't want it to end.

I would never forget my sister; I would love and miss her forever— but it didn't feel like her death had to be the epicenter of my identity anymore, either.

"Shit," Sean muttered as the car came to a standstill. I wasn't sure how long I'd had my eyes closed, or if I had inadvertently dozed off.

I stirred in my seat, but his hand tightened around my knee, stilling me. I didn't like the unspoken message in the tension of his grip. My eyes flew open, and I felt my body grow leaden.

We were back in *The Advocate's* parking lot.

And we weren't alone.

AUTHOR'S NOTE

Dear readers,

Before you send the calvary and pull out your pitchforks to come after me for that cliff-hanger ending, hear me out...

I never intended for Mirrors to be a trilogy.

When I went into writing this novel, I had a very clear and concise understanding of how the beginning, middle, and end would work. What I did not expect was that the background characters would begin speaking to me as I was writing–that their voices would become just as loud, as just as urgent as Sean and Raquel's. I didn't foresee that this universe connected with other ideas I had brewing in my mind, that events in Mirrors would impact these other future storylines, too.

Try as I may to ignore them, they weren't having it. In retaliation for trying to drown their voices out, Sean and Raquel stopped communicating, too. Now, I know this sounds a tad ridiculous, because surely how can fictional characters try to derail your outline... but let me tell you, when you try to control your art, your art gives you a big ol' fuck you. My characters are real to me, I feel their presence in every facet of my life. It was within their right to tell me to shove it up my ass until I was ready to give them what they demanded.

So, I did what the little voices in my head wanted me to do–I let go of the reins and let them lead me on their journey. In hindsight, I'm sure I could have written you a condensed version of Mirrors that encapsulated the beginning, middle and end just as I intended–but to do so would have meant to be cheating these characters, and you, the reader, out of what you and they deserve.

Writing this novel and the subsequent novels in this trilogy has been an arduous labor of love. I adore these characters and this world more than I ever could have imagined, and I want nothing more than to remain as authentic as possible. (Also, my editor strongly discouraged me from trying to ship a two-hundred-and-sixty-eight-thousand book to the printer, so we can give her a head nod in thanks for that.)

So, what's next? Shattered is book two in the Reflections trilogy and I am tentatively shooting for a December 31st, 2020 publication date. The last novel, Awake, I am hoping to have released for early 2021.

I hope this note will encourage you to lower your pitchforks and call off the cavalcade. In the meantime, I invite you to hang out with me on social media or sign up for my newsletter–I'm sure you'll get glimpses of Shattered before release day. (Also, I have an adorable dog, and she is the genuine star of my accounts–no bullshit.)

Thank you so much for giving me your time, I hope I'll catch you in the next book, too.

ACKNOWLEDGMENTS

It will come as a surprise to no one that writing a book is hard. It is a brutal and intense labor of love filled with sacrifices, an uptick of caffeine consumption, and many early, sleep-deprived mornings.

But it is my passion. It is the beat in my heart, the pulse in my bloodstream, and the song in my soul that keeps me going even when I wanted to give up.

I've been grappling with Sean and Raquel for much longer than I care to admit–seven years to be exact. Seven years of plot ideas, of character development, and world building.

Sean and Raquel are not the first characters to populate in my mind. They are, however, the ones who taught me the most about writing, about trusting the inner voice, and to never–and I mean never–try to tell your characters what to do. They've got teeth and aren't afraid to use them.

While this is book one in a trilogy, please know that each book carries a sliver of me within its pages and it was all made possible because of these individuals who deserve to be recognized.

First and foremost, you, the reader–thank you for taking a chance on another indie author trying to make her mark on the world. Thank you for giving me your time, a place on your bookshelf, and the real estate on your eReader. I do not take this honor lightly.

MAR–I cannot thank you enough for letting me keep you up till the wee hours of the morning so I could run ideas by you–many of which never came to fruition. Your respect of my time, my need to create, and understanding that I have more conversations in my head with fictional characters in a day than I do with you is a level of unwavering support that I never thought capable. Thank you for keeping the Nibs flowing and for helping me realize that this was meant to be a trilogy! (LOL, there I admitted it. You have your proof in writing–are you happy?!)

My brother, JP–whose admiration I am utterly undeserving of. Thank you for being my first cheerleader, for believing in me when they wouldn't. I am who I am today because of you.

ABC–Pãozinha, minha amiga, your creativity and talent are unmatched. Your willingness to go above and beyond, to capture every single detail and nuance and applying it in the creative assets of this project has left me overwhelmed and emotional. Your gift to see the big picture and inject color into things fills me with so much joy.

HF–where would I be without you, Ham? You've read a lot of my earliest work–most of which was offensively bad–but you never complained and encouraged me to keep going. Thank you for giving me the confidence to stand out amongst the crowd in my formative years, for pushing me to always be the best version of myself.

LCR–I can say with confidence that you are the leader of the A.L. Woods fan club. Thank you for teaching me the true meaning of what being a Nakama is, for your endless support, and for understanding when I need good cop and bad cop.

My editor, BLU–without you, this book would still be one long-winded mess laden with Canadian spelling and comma abuse. Thank you for your keen eye and guidance to get me to the crux of what I'm trying to convey.

KN–who allowed me to bounce ideas off of her brain while I was in the early stages of the rewrite of this book and borrow her last name for Maria's law firm.

SD–without your help, I'd still be mulling over a single line in my book blurb. Thank you for empathizing with me over Snapchat for an entire year.

KJN–for correcting me when I referred to myself as an "aspiring writer." You saw what I couldn't back then.

To the friends, family and acquaintances that I may have missed– know that your words, your cheering, and your support has meant so much to me over the years.

To the aspiring authors, the writers who want to hit publish–Do it. There is no better moment than this one to chase your dreams and make them a reality. I believe in you!

ABOUT THE AUTHOR

A.L. Woods is an author of roller coaster romances, caffeine aficionado, and collector of Sailor Moon paraphernalia.

She lives 40 minutes west of Toronto, Ontario with her partner, Michael, and their 8lb larger-than-life miniature dachshund, Maia–whom they lovingly refer to as their 'doghter.'

Woods can be found holed away in her office writing her next novel with a bowl of Nibs within arm's reach. When she's not writing, she's likely belting out an ad-libbed song, emotionally investing in a fictional bad boy with a strong jawline and fluency in sarcasm or inventing fresh ways to procrastinate.

She believes that burritos should be in their own food group, loves the fall, winged liner, and listening to metalcore at an offensive level.

For photographic evidence of her shenanigans, or cute photos of Maia, follow her on social media.

Website: amandawrites.ca

Be sure to subscribe to her newsletter on her website so you don't miss out on exclusive content!

twitter.com/AmandaWrites_

instagram.com/amandalwrites

pinterest.com/ALWoodsBooks

Made in the USA
Monee, IL
29 October 2020